In Her Name: Empire

By
Michael R. Hicks

This is a work of fiction. All of the characters and events portrayed in this novel are products of the author's imagination or are used fictitiously.

Copyright © 2012 by Imperial Guard Publishing, LLC
ISBN: 9780984673049
IN HER NAME: EMPIRE

All rights reserved, including the right to reproduce this book, or portions thereof, in any form.

For Jan.
Your love saved me.

What Readers Are Saying

"This book is EXACTLY what I expect of a good sci-fi book. Between the depth of the characters and the extent of the backstory, I quickly lost myself in this wonderful novel. The only downer for me was turning the last page, and there not being any more pages!"

"Michael Hicks has shown great mastery of his subject. This is the Harry Potter of SciFi."

"What many people forget is that at the heart of the In Her Name Omnibus there is a love story that makes Romeo and Juliet look tame. Readers will find themselves experiencing both the joys as well as the despair of the main characters, and I for one, sometimes had to wipe away the tears before I could continue reading, though this is by no means a sad story."

"I took a chance on the first volume of this series and couldn't stop reading until I had finished it all. Although military science fiction is not usually my first choice, an engrossing plot line, a fully developed alien culture and thoughtful characters held my attention and left me wanting more."

"The *In Her Name* series is great. When an author can tell a story of humanity's interactions with an alien race, and make you feel like you know alien people and their culture, I feel like a wonderful job of "universe building" has been done. Also great military storytelling. Great job, Michael!"

“Thank you Michael R. Hicks for deciding to write. I now own everything you've published to Kindle and am anxiously waiting for the final book of the In Her Name series!! HURRY UP!”

“I do not have much to say other than this series was amazing.”

“This is the most I have enjoyed a series since C.J. Cherryh's compact space series, and goes miles beyond anything I have read in the last decade. If you want a good read, and a fantastic universe to bury yourself in... this one is high on the mark.”

“I found myself reading until 2-3 AM. Lots of action and good character development. Highly recommend this series.”

“This series is well worth the money. I buy books all the time, and some are the same cookie-cutter formula as the next; I didn't get that feeling from this collection of books. This may be the first author I can rank next to Heinlein and Asimov on my bookshelf in a very long time.”

“The last time I was so hung-up on a book it was Pillars of the Earth. I read fast because I couldn't wait to find out what happened next and then slowed down because I didn't want it to end. I just couldn't slow down on these books.”

“Michael Hicks apparently channels the blood of Heinlein and Asimov in his veins. I read all three of these books in 3 days. As a SF fan from the 1950's and 1960's, I grew up with the "greats" of SF and the "trekies". However, in recent years SF has failed to ignite that sense of wonder and I had stopped reading anything new. This series, In Her Name, is absolutely amazing.”

“Be warned that once you start reading this book, it would be very hard to put it down. Requirements: 1. alarm clock - to remind you that you have to go to work today. 2. Another alarm clock to remind you of meal times. 3. A very understanding wife.”

Discover Other Books By Michael R. Hicks

The *In Her Name* Series

First Contact
Legend Of The Sword
Dead Soul
Empire
Confederation
Final Battle
From Chaos Born

"Boxed Set" Collections

In Her Name (Omnibus)
In Her Name: The Last War

Thrillers

Season Of The Harvest

Visit *AuthorMichaelHicks.com* for the latest updates!

ONE

The blast caught Solon Gard, an exhausted captain of New Constantinople's beleaguered Territorial Army, completely by surprise. He had not known that the enemy had sited a heavy gun to the north of his decimated unit's last redoubt, a thick-walled house of a style made popular in recent years. Like most other houses in the planet's capitol city, this one was now little more than a gutted wreck.

But the Kreelan gun's introductory salvo was also its last: a human heavy weapons team destroyed it with a lucky shot before the Territorial Army soldiers were silenced by a barrage of inhumanly accurate plasma rifle fire.

The battle had become a vicious stalemate.

A woman's voice suddenly cut through the fog in Solon's head as he fought his way out from under the smoking rubble left by the cannon hit. He found himself looking up at the helmeted face of his wife, Camilla. Her eyes were hidden behind the mirrored faceplate of the battered combat helmet she wore.

"Solon, are you hurt?"

"No," he groaned, shaking his head, "I'm all right."

She helped him up, her petite form struggling with her husband's greater bulk: two armored mannequins embracing in an awkward dance.

Solon glanced around. "Where's Armand?"

"Dead," she said in a brittle voice. She wiped the dust from her husband's helmet, wishing she could touch his hair, his face, instead of the cold, scarred metal. She gestured to the pile of debris that Solon had been buried in. The wall had exploded inward a few feet from where he and Armand had been. The muddy light of day, flickering blood-red from the smoke that hung over the city, revealed an armored glove that jutted from under a plastisteel girder. Armand. He had been a friend of their family for many years and was the godfather of their only son. Now... now he was simply gone, like so many others.

Solon reached down and gently touched the armored hand of his best friend. "Silly fool," he whispered hoarsely. "You should have gone to the shelter with the others, like I told you. You could never fight, even when we were children." Armand had never had any military training, but after his wife and daughter were killed in the abattoir their city had become, he had come looking for Solon, to fight and die by his side. And so he had.

"It's only the two of us," Camilla told him wearily, "and Enrique and Snowden." Behind her was a pile of bodies in a dark corner, looking like a monstrous spider in the long shadows that flickered over them. The survivors had not had the time or strength to array them properly. Their goal had simply been to get them out of the way. Honor to the dead came a distant second to the desperation to stay among the living. "I think Jennings's squad across the street may be gone, too."

"Lord of All," Solon murmured, still trying to get his bearings and come to grips with the extent of their disaster. With only the four of them left, particularly if Jennings's squad had been wiped out, the Kreelans had but to breathe hard and the last human defensive line would be broken.

"It can always get worse," a different female voice told him drily.

Solon turned to see Snowden raise her hand unenthusiastically. Platinum hair was plastered to her skull in a greasy matte of sweat and blood, a legacy of the flying glass that had peeled away half her scalp during an earlier attack. She looked at him with eyes too exhausted for sleep, and did not make any move to get up from where she was sitting. Her left leg was broken above the knee, the protruding bone covered by a field dressing and hasty splint that Camilla had put together.

Enrique peered at them from the corner where he and Camilla had set up their only remaining heavy weapon, a pulse gun that took two to operate. Its snout poked through a convenient hole in the wall. From there, Enrique could see over most of their platoon's assigned sector of responsibility, or what was left of it. In the dreary orange light that made ghosts of the swirling smoke over the dying city, Enrique watched the dark figures of the enemy come closer, threading their way through the piles of shattered rubble that had once been New Constantinople's premier shopkeeper's district. He watched as their sandaled feet trod over the crumpled spires of the Izmir All-Faith Temple, the most beautiful building on the planet until a couple of weeks ago. Since the Kreelans arrived, nearly twenty million people and thirty Navy ships had died, and nothing made by human hands had gone untouched.

But beyond the searching muzzle of Enrique's gun, the advancing Kreelans passed many of their sisters who had died as the battle here had ebbed and flowed. Their burned and twisted bodies were stacked like cordwood at the approaches to the humans' crumbling defense perimeter, often enmeshed with the humans who had killed them. Enemies in life, they were bound together in death with bayonets and claws in passionate, if gruesome, embraces.

Still, they came. They always came.

Solon caught himself trying to rub his forehead through his battered helmet. *Lord, am I tired*, he thought. Their company was part of the battalion that had been among the last of the reserves to be activated for the city's final stand, and the Territorial Army commander had brought them into action three days before. Three days. It had been a lifetime.

"One-hundred and sixty-two people, dead," he whispered to himself, thinking of the soldiers he had lost in the last few days. But they had lasted longer than most. Nearly every company of the first defensive ring had been wiped out to the last man and woman in less than twenty-four hours. Solon and his company were part of the fourth and final ring around the last of the defense shelters in this sector of the city. If the Kreelans got through...

"Hey, boss," Enrique called quietly. "I hate to interrupt, but they're getting a bit close over here. You want me to light 'em up?"

"I'll do the honors," Camilla told Solon, patting him on the helmet. "You need to get yourself back together."

"No arguments here," he answered wearily, propping himself against the remains of the wall. "I'll keep on eye on this side."

Camilla quickly took her place next to the gunner. "I'm glad you didn't wait much longer to let us know we had company, Enrique," she chided after carefully peering out at the enemy. "They're so close I can see their fangs." She checked the charge on the pulse gun's power pack. A fresh one would last for about thirty seconds of continuous firing, an appetite that made having both a gunner and a loader to service the hungry weapon a necessity.

"Yeah," Enrique smiled, his lips curling around the remains of an unlit cigarette butt he held clenched between his dirt-covered lips. He had tossed his helmet away the first thing, preferring to wear only a black bandanna around his forehead. His grime stained hands tightened on the gun's controls and his eyes sighted on the line of advancing Kreelans. "Looks like they think we're all finished, since we haven't shot back at 'em for a while." He snickered, then snugged his shoulder in tight to the shoulder stock of the gun. "Surprise..."

Solon was hunched down next to a blown-out window, looking for signs of the Kreelans trying to flank them, when he noticed the shattered portrait of a man and woman on the floor next to him. He picked up the crushed holo image of the young man and his bride and wondered who they might have been. Saying a silent prayer for their souls, he carefully set the picture out of his way. Somehow, the image seemed sacred, a tiny reminder of the precariousness of human existence, of good times past, and perhaps, hopes for the future. These two, who undoubtedly lay dead somewhere in this wasteland, would never know that their own lives were more fragile and finite than the plastic that still struggled to protect their images.

He turned as he heard the coughing roar of Enrique's pulse gun as it tore into the alien skirmish line. He listened as the gunner moderated his bursts, conserving the weapon's power while choosing his targets. Solon was glad Enrique had lived this long. He was as good a soldier as could be found in the Territorial Army. They had all been good soldiers, and would make the Kreelans pay dearly for taking the last four lives that Solon had left to offer as an interest payment toward humanity's survival.

As he looked through the dust and smoke, the thermal imager in Solon's visor gave him an enhanced view of the devastation around him, the computer turning the sunset into a scene of a scarlet Hell. He prayed that his seven-year-old son, Reza, remained safe in the nearby bunker. He had lost count of the number of times he had prayed for his boy, but it did not matter. He prayed again, and would go on praying, because it was the only thing he could do. Reza and the other children of their defense district had been taken to the local shelter, a deep underground bunker that could withstand all but a direct orbital bombardment, or so they hoped. Solon only wished that he had been able to see his little boy again before he died. "I love you, son," he whispered to the burning night.

Behind him, Camilla hurriedly stripped off the expended power pack from the pulse gun and clipped on another. She had come to do it so well that Enrique barely missed a beat in his firing.

Solon saw movement in a nearby building that was occupied by one of the other platoons: a hand waving at him from a darkened doorway. He raised his own hand in a quick salute, not daring to risk his head or arm for a more dashing salutation.

He made one more careful sweep of the street with his enhanced vision. Although he had spent his life in service to the Confederation as a shipbuilder, not as a hardened Marine or sailor, Solon knew that he needed to be extra careful in everything he did now. His body was past its physical limit, and the need for sleep was dragging all of them toward mistakes that could lead them to their deaths. Vigilance was survival.

As he finished his visual check, he relaxed slightly. All was as he had seen it before. Nothing moved. Nothing changed but the direction of the smoke's drift, and the smell of burning wood and flesh that went with it. He felt more than heard the hits the other side of his little fortress was taking from Kreelan light guns, and was relieved to hear Enrique's pulse gun yammer back at them like an enraged dog.

He glanced back toward the building occupied by the other platoon just as a massive barrage of Kreelan weapons fire erupted on the far side. He watched in horror as the structure began to crumble under the onslaught. The human defenders, sensing the futility of holding on, came boiling out into the street, heading for Solon's position, only to be cut down in a brutal crossfire from further down the lane.

The firing tapered off, and Solon saw shadows rapidly flowing toward the other platoon's survivors: Kreelan warriors silently advancing, swords drawn. They killed with energy weapons when they had to, but preferred more personal means of combat.

"Oh my God," Solon whispered, knowing that his own final stand would soon be upon him: they were surrounded now, cut off. His throat constricted and his stomach threatened to heave up the handful of tasteless ration cake he had eaten earlier in the day. He flipped up the visor for a moment to look at the scene with his own eyes, then flipped it back down to penetrate the smoky darkness.

Suddenly, a lone figure darted across the street, plunging suicidally into the raging battle. Under the figure's arm swung what could have been an oversized doll, but Solon knew that it was not. The little arms clung to the neck of the madly running soldier and the rag doll's little legs kicked at empty air. With a sinking sensation, Solon realized who it was.

"Reza!" he shouted, his heart hammering with fear and joy, wondering how in the Lord's name the boy had gotten here.

With a crack of thunder, the soldier's luck ran out as a crimson lance struck him, spinning him around like a top. He collapsed into the rubble, shielding the boy's body with his own.

Solon roared in the protective fury only a parent can know, his voice thundering above the clamoring of the guns. Camilla turned just in time to see him leap through the blasted wall into the carnage raging beyond.

"Solon!" she screamed, struggling up from her position next to the hammering pulse gun.

"No!" Enrique yelled at her, grabbing for her arm. He was too late to stop her as she bolted from the pit. "Dammit!" he hissed, struggling to change the empty and useless magazine himself. He pried the heavy canister off the gun's breech section with blind, groping hands while his bloodshot eyes tracked the rapidly approaching shadows of the enemy.

Solon suddenly staggered back over the shattered wall. His breath came in long heaves as if he had just finished running a marathon, and his armor was pitted and smoking from half a dozen glancing hits. In his arms was a small bundle of rags. Camilla nearly fainted at the sight of Reza's face, his skin black with soot and streaked with tears of fright.

"Mama," the boy cried, reaching for her.

"Oh, baby," she said softly, taking him in her arms and rocking him. "What are you doing here?" Camilla asked.

Solon collapsed next to her, wrapping his arms around his wife and child.

"What happened to the bunker?" Snowden shouted in between bursts from her rifle as she tried to kill the Kreelans who escaped Enrique's non-stop firing.

"The same thing that's going to happen to us if you guys don't start shooting!" Enrique screamed hoarsely, finally slamming a new – and the last – magazine into his pulse gun. "The Blues are all over the place out here!"

Reluctantly letting go of his wife and son, Solon grabbed up his rifle and thrust its muzzle through a hole in the wall. Gritting his teeth in rage and a newfound determination to survive, to protect his wife and son, he opened fire on the wraiths that moved through the darkness.

Camilla, after a last hug, set Reza down next to Snowden. "Take care of him," she begged before taking up her station next to Enrique.

Snowden nodded and held Reza tightly as the thunder of gunfire surrounded them.

* * *

The sky was black as pitch, black as death, as the priestess walked alone over the arena this world had become. Her sandaled feet touched the ground but left no sound, no footprint. She looked up toward where the stars should be, yearning for the great moon that shone over the Homeworld. But the only sight to be had was the glowing red smears of the fires that were reflected by the wafting smoke and dust.

As she made her way across the field of carnage, she touched the bodies of the fallen children to honor them as they had honored their Empress. They had sacrificed their lives to show their love for Her. She grieved for them all, that they had died this day, never again to feel the flame that drove them to battle, the thrill of sword and claw, never again to serve the Empress through their flesh. Now they basked in the quiet sunset of the Afterlife, someday perhaps to join the ranks of the Ancient Ones, the warriors of the spirit.

She moved on toward her destination. It had once been a human dwelling, but now was a mound of ashen rubble. It squatted impetuously in the wasteland created by weapons the Kreela disdained to use. The humans had never realized that the destruction of their worlds was caused by their own predilection for such weaponry, to which the Kreela sometimes had to respond in kind. The warriors of the Empress sought battles of the mind, body, and spirit, of sword and claw, and not of brute destruction.

Watching the battles rage here for several cycles of the sun across the sky, she had become increasingly curious about these particular humans who fought so well, and at last had decided that perhaps they were worthy of her personal attention. She bade the young warriors to rest, to wait for her return, before setting out on her own journey of discovery.

She paused when she reached the back of the crumbled structure that hid the humans she sought. She listened for their heartbeats, smelled their pungent body odor, and felt for their strange alien spirit with her mind. After a moment she had an image of them, of where they sat and stood within.

Silent as the dead around her, she moved to a chosen point along the wall. Her breathing and heart stilled, she concealed everything about herself that made her presence real. Unless one of the humans looked directly at her, she would be utterly invisible.

Then she stepped through the wall, her flesh and armor melding with the essence of the barrier as she passed through without so much as a whisper.

* * *

"Is that all you remember, honey?" Camilla asked Reza softly, brushing his unruly hair back with her hand, which was temporarily freed from the armored skin she had been wearing for the past several days.

"Yes, Mama," he replied. The fear had mostly left him, now that he was with them again, and that they thought he had done the right thing. "All I remember was lots of smoke. Then someone started to scream. People ran, hurting each other, because they were afraid. Someone, Madame Barnault, I think, led me out, but I lost her after we got outside. I remembered where Papa said you would be, so I came here to find you. I almost made it, except the Kreelans were everywhere. That's when Kerry–"

"That's enough, son," Solon said gently, not wanting to force the boy to describe the death of the soldier, who had been another friend of their family. "It's all right, now. You're here and safe, and that's all that counts." He exchanged a quick glance with Camilla. *Safe* was hardly the word to use, he knew, even though the Kreelans had apparently given up for the day. Reza would now have to suffer whatever fate was in store for the rest of them. Solon could not justify risking someone else's life for the boy's benefit. One had already died for him.

"Reza," Camilla told him, "I want you to stay with Snowden and help her find more ammunition for us." She leaned close to his ear and whispered, "And I want you to watch out for her and protect her. She's hurt and needs a big boy like you to care for her."

Reza nodded vigorously, glancing in Snowden's direction, the horrors of the past few hours fading. He had a mission now, some responsibility that helped to displace his fear. "I will, Mama," he said quietly so that Snowden would not hear.

Later, as his father and mother rested under Enrique's watchful eyes, Snowden kept an eye on Reza as he busied himself with hunting for the things she had told him to look for.

Peering through the darkness, his father having told him that they could not use a light for fear of bringing the Kreelans, Reza spied what Snowden had told him would be a great prize in the game they were playing. A bright metal clip protruded from under a stairway crawlspace, its surface reflecting the occasional flash of artillery fire that showed through the mangled roof. He saw that it was attached to a big, gray cylinder: a pulse gun magazine. Grinning with excitement, he scampered forward to retrieve it. He had heard Enrique say that they didn't have any more of the magazines, and the big gun wouldn't work.

He reached down to pick it up, but found that it was much heavier than he had imagined. He pulled and heaved, but the magazine would not move. He started sweeping the dirt away from around it, to try and dig it out. His hand brushed against something, something smooth and warm, totally different from the rubbery pocked coating of the magazine that was supposed to make it less slippery.

Curious, he reached out to feel what it was. He did not need a light to tell him that he was touching someone's leg, and they had their foot resting on the magazine. Looking up into the darkness above him, he could see only a shadow.

"Who are you?" he asked quietly, curious as to how and why someone would have come into the house without letting his father know about it. "Are you one of Papa's soldiers?"

Silence.

A flare burst far down the street, slowly settling toward the ground. In its flickering glow, Reza saw clearly the monstrous shape above him, saw the eyes that glared down from the dark-skinned face and the glistening ivory fangs that emerged from the mouth in a silent snarl.

Reza stumbled back, screaming at the nightmarish shape, all thoughts of the precious magazine vanished from his mind. He scrambled backward on all fours like a terrified crab, screaming. "Mama! Papa!"

"Reza, what is it?" Solon asked, picking the boy up from the debris-strewn floor as he burst from the hallway. "What's wrong?"

"One of them's in here! By the stairs! There, Papa!" Reza pointed, but the monster had disappeared. "It was right there!" he cried, stabbing at the air with his trembling finger.

Solon peered through the darkness, but could see nothing. "Reza, there's no way anyone could be back there. That's the one place where they can't get in, because it's a solid wall, no doors or windows, no holes."

"Papa, one of them's in here!" Reza wailed, his terrified eyes still fixed on where he knew the monster had been.

Solon hesitated. He knew how tired and confused Reza must be, how much they all were, and he knew he had to humor the boy.

"I'll take a look," Snowden volunteered. In the time since the last wave of Kreelans had attacked, Camilla had finally had time to splint her leg properly and block the nerves. Walking on it would probably do permanent damage, but Snowden had figured that it was better to be alive and mostly functional than just plain dead. She snatched up her helmet and put it on. The shattered interior of the house, enhanced into precise detail by the visor, came into focus. "He's probably just wired over what happened at the bunker," she said. Camilla nodded, but Snowden could tell that she was nervous. "Don't worry, Camilla," Snowden reassured her, hefting her rifle. "I'll take care of him." Then, turning to the boy, she said, "Can you show me, Reza?"

Reza did not want to go anywhere near the stairs or the back rooms again. But everyone was looking at him, and he would not act like a baby in front of them. After all, he was seven years old now. "All right," he said, his voice shaking.

Solon set him down, and then looked at Snowden. "Just be careful, okay?"

"No problem, boss," she replied easily. Her outward confidence wasn't foolish arrogance: even as exhausted as she was, she was still the best sharpshooter in the entire company. "C'mon, Reza." Taking the boy's hand, her other arm cradling the rifle, she led him down the dark hallway toward the back of the house.

Once into the hallway, she became increasingly edgy with every crunch of plaster under her boots, only one of which she could feel, the other having been deadened to stifle the pain. The hairs on the back of her neck were standing at stiff attention, but she could not figure out why. *There's nothing here,* she told herself firmly.

She finally decided that it must be because Reza's grip had tightened with every step. It was a gauge of the little boy's fear. But her own senses registered nothing at all.

Reza moved forward, about half a step ahead of her, one hand clinging to hers, the other probing ahead of him through the murk. He knew he had seen the alien warrior. But as his fear grew, so did his self-doubt. *Maybe I was wrong,* he thought.

Behind them came a scraping sound like a knife against a sharpening stone. Snowden whirled around, pushing Reza to the ground behind her with one hand while the other brought the rifle to bear.

"Hell!" she hissed. A fiber optic connector that had been part of the house's control system dangled from the ceiling, the cable scraping against the wall. She shook her head, blowing out her breath. *Don't be so tense,* she told herself. *Take it easy.* "Reza," she said, turning around, "I think we better head back to the others. There's nothing–"

She stopped in mid-sentence as she saw a clawed fist emerge from the wall in front of her, the alien flesh and sinew momentarily merging with stone and steel in a pulsating mass of swirling colors. The hand closed around Snowden's neck with a chilling *snick.* The alien warrior's hand was so large that her talons overlapped Snowden's spine. Gasping in horror, Snowden was forced backward as the Kreelan made her way through the wall and into the dark hallway.

Snowden's mouth gaped open, but no words came. There was only a muted stuttering that was building toward an uncontrollable ululation of terror. She dropped her rifle, the tiny gap between her body and the alien making it as useless as a medieval pike in a dense thicket. Desperately, she groped for the pistol strapped to her lower thigh, her other hand vainly trying to break the Kreelan's grip on her neck.

His mind reeling from the horror in front of him, Reza backpedaled away, his mouth open in a scream for help that he would never remember making. He watched helplessly as the warrior's sword, free from the wall's impossible embrace, pierced Snowden's breastplate. It burst from her back with a thin metallic screech and a jet of blood. Snowden's body twitched like a grotesque marionette, her legs dancing in the confusion of signals coursing through her severed spine, her arms battering weakly at the enemy's face. The pistol had fallen to the floor, its safety still on.

Satisfied that the human was beaten, the Kreelan let go of Snowden's neck. As the young woman's body fell to the floor, the alien warrior pulled the sword free, the blade dragging at Snowden's insides with its serrated upper edge. She was dead before her helmeted head hit the floor.

Reza bolted for the main room, his scream of terror reverberating from the walls and battered ceiling.

"Reza!" Solon cried as his son burst into the room to fall at his father's feet. "Where's Snowden?"

"Solon," Camilla whispered, slowly rising to her feet as she saw the dark shape silently move from the hallway. A burst from down the street lit the thing's face with a hellish glow, leaving no doubt as to its origin.

The Kreelan stopped just beyond the hallway. Watching. Waiting.

Enrique reacted first. Instinctively he brought up his rifle, aiming it at the alien's chest.

"Bitch!" he cried, his finger convulsing on the trigger.

Solon saw her arm move like a scythe in the eerie display of his helmet visor. The movement was accompanied by a strange whistling noise, like a storm wind howling against a windowpane.

Enrique suddenly grunted. Solon saw the gunner's eyes register disbelief, then nothing at all as they rolled up into his head. His body sagged backward and the gun discharged once into the ceiling before clattering to the floor at his side. Solon saw a huge wet horizontal gash in Enrique's chest armor that was wide enough to put both fists in, as if someone had split him open with an ax.

Camilla reached for her rifle, propped against the wall behind her.

"No," Solon said softly. "Don't move."

She stopped.

Reza lay face down on the floor, his body pointing like an arrow toward where his father now stood frozen. He blinked away the tears in his eyes, his entire body trembling with fear. He felt something sharp under his right hand, and without thinking he closed his fingers around it: a knife. He clung to it desperately, for he had no weapon of his own. A brief glance told him that it was his father's. He knew that his father always carried two, but must have somehow lost this one in the rubble during the fighting. Reza held it tightly to his chest.

"Why doesn't she attack?" Camilla whispered, terribly tempted to reach for her pistol or rifle. The sight of Enrique's gutted body stayed her hand. And then there was Snowden. Undoubtedly, she lay dead somewhere deeper in the house.

"I don't know, but..." Solon hesitated. He suddenly had an idea. "I'm going to try something."

Before Camilla could say a word, he drew the long-bladed knife he carried in his web gear. It was an inferior weapon to the Kreelan's sword, but it was all he had, and he didn't know where his regular combat knife had disappeared to. Then he slowly moved his free hand to the clasps that held his web gear to his armor. With two quick yanks, the webbing that held his grenades, pistol and extra weapon power packs clattered to the floor.

"So far, so good," he muttered. Sweat poured from his brow down the inside of his helmet. "Now you do it," he ordered his wife. "Draw your knife and drop the rest of your gear."

"What about Reza?" she asked, her eyes fixed on the alien as she repeated what Solon had done, her own equipment rattling to the floor around her feet a moment later. "Solon, we've got to get him out of here."

Crouching down slowly under the Kreelan's watchful, almost benevolent gaze, Solon reached down to where his son lay.

"Reza," he whispered, the external helmet speaker making his voice sound tinny, far away, "stand up, very slowly, and look at me."

Reza did as he was told, his body shaking with fright.

"Listen carefully, son," he said, tearing his eyes away from the Kreelan to look at his son for what he knew would be the last time. He fought against the tears that welled up in his eyes. "You must do exactly what I tell you, without question, without being too afraid. You're a young man, now, and your mother and I need you to help us."

"Yes, Papa," Reza whispered shakily as he stared into his father's dirty helmet visor. But instead of his father's face, Reza saw only the dull reflection of the apparition standing behind him, only a few paces away.

Holding his son by both quivering shoulders, Solon went on, "Not far from here, there used to be a really big schoolhouse, the university. Do you remember?"

Reza nodded. His father had taken him there many times to show him the great library there. It had always been one of his favorite places.

"Our people have built a big, strong fortress there," Solon continued. "That's where I need you to go. Tell them your mother and I need help, and they'll send soldiers for us." He pulled Reza to him. "We love you, son," he whispered. Then he let him go. "Go on, son. Get out of here and don't look back."

"But Papa..." Reza started to object, crying now.

"Go on!" Camilla said softly, but with unmistakable firmness. Her own body shook in silent anguish that she could not even hold her son one last time. Fate had held that last card from her hand, an alien Queen of Spades standing between her and her child. "Go on," she urged again, somehow sensing the Kreelan's growing impatience, "before it's too late."

"I love you," Reza whispered as stumbled toward a hole in the wall, a doorway to the Hell that lay beyond.

"I love you, too, baby," Camilla choked.

As her only son crawled through the hole to the street beyond, Camilla turned her attention back to the waiting Kreelan. "All right, you bitch," she sneered, her upper lip curled like a wolf's, exposing the teeth that had once illuminated a smile that had been a young man's enchantment, the man who later became her husband. But there was no trace of that smile now. "It's time for you to die." The blade of her knife glinted in the fiery glow that lit the horizon of the burning city.

Together, husband and wife moved toward their enemy.

* * *

Reza stumbled and fell to the ground when the blast lit up the night behind him. The knoll of debris that had been his parents' stronghold vanished in a fiery ball of flame and splinters, with smoke mushrooming up into the night sky like the glowing pillar of a funeral pyre.

"Mama!" he screamed. "Papa!"

But only the flames answered, crackling as they consumed the building's remains with a boundless hunger.

Reza lay there, watching his world burn away to ashes. A final tear coursed its way down his face in a lonely journey, its wet track reflecting the brilliant flames. Alone now, fearful of the terrors that stalked the night, he curled up beneath a tangle of timbers and bricks, watching the flames dance to music only the fire itself could hear.

"Goodbye, Mama and Papa," he whispered before succumbing to the wracking sobs that had been standing by like friends in mourning.

* * *

Not far away, another lone figure stood watching those same flames through alien eyes. The priestess's heart raced with the energy that surged through her body, her blood singing the chorus of battle that had been the heart and spirit of her people for countless generations.

The two humans had fought well, she granted, feeling a twinge of what might have been sorrow at their deaths. It was so rare that she found opponents worthy of her mettle. The humans would never know it, but they had come closer to killing her than any others had come in many cycles. Had she not heard the *click* made by the grenade, set off by the mortally stricken male while the female held her attention, she might have joined them in the fire that now devoured their frail bodies. Some of her hair, her precious raven hair, had been scorched by the blast as she leaped through the wall to safety.

What a pity, she thought, *that animals with such instincts did not possess souls*. Such creatures could certainly be taught how to make themselves more than moving targets for her to toy with, but her heart ached to give something more to her Empress.

Standing there, nauseated by the acrid stench of the burning plasticrete around her, she heaved a mournful sigh before turning back toward where the young ones lay resting. Her time here was terribly short, but a single moon cycle of the Homeworld, and she had yet much to see, much on which she would report to the Empress.

She had just started back when she heard a peculiar sound, an unsteady pulse under the current of the winds that carried the embers of the fire. It came at once from one direction, then from another as the fickle winds sought new paths over the dying city. She closed her eyes and reached out with her mind, her spirit flowing from her body to become one with the scorched earth and smoldering sky, using senses that went well beyond any her body could provide.

The child.

She hesitated, tempted simply to let it go, to die on its own while she returned to the young warriors who awaited her. But she found herself overcome with curiosity, for she had only seen their children in death. Never had she seen a live one. She debated for a moment what she should do, but in the end her curiosity demanded satisfaction. To blunt the pup's whimpering misery with death would be an indulgent, if unchallenging, act.

* * *

Reza blinked. Had he fallen asleep? He rubbed his eyes with grimy fists. His cheeks were caked with a mortar of tears and masonry dust. He glanced around, unable to see much in the dim glow that filtered into his hideout. Not really wanting to, but unable to help himself, he looked toward where his parents had died.

He sucked in his breath in surprise. A shadow blocked the entrance to his tiny hideaway. With arms and legs that felt weak as stalks of thin grass, he crawled forward a bit to see better.

"Mama?" he whispered cautiously, his young mind hoping that perhaps all had not been lost. "Papa?" he said a little louder, his voice barely rising above the wind that had begun to howl outside.

The figure stood immobile, but for one thing. Extending one arm, the fingers slowly, rhythmically curled back one by one in a gesture he had long been taught meant *come, come to me*.

His teeth chattering with fear and anticipation, he gripped his father's knife, his fingers barely long enough to close around the handle. He crawled forward toward the gesturing apparition, still unsure if it was a man or woman, or perhaps something else. He was terrified, but he had to know.

Coming to the last barrier of fallen timbers that formed the doorway to his hideaway, Reza gathered his courage. He fixed his eyes on the shadow hand that continued to call him, mesmerizing him with the thought that help had arrived and that his parents might yet be saved. Placing his empty hand on the bottom-most timber, the other clutching the knife by his side, he poked his head out the hole.

The shape seemed to shimmer and change in the light. It moved with such speed that Reza's eyes only registered a dark streak before an iron hand clamped around his neck and plucked him from the hole with a force that nearly snapped his spine. He cried out in pain and fear, never noticing the warm flood that coursed down his legs as his bladder emptied.

His cries and struggling ended when he found the cat-like eyes of the Kreelan warrior a mere hand's breadth from his own. Her lips parted to reveal the ivory fangs that adorned the upper and lower jaws.

For a moment, the two simply stared at one other, Reza's feet dangling nearly a meter from the ground as the Kreelan held him. Her grip, strong enough to pop his head like a grape with a gentle squeeze, was restrained to a force that barely allowed him to breathe. His pulse hammered in his ears as his heart fought to push blood through the constricted carotid arteries to his brain. Spots began to appear in his vision, as if he were looking at the Kreelan through a curtain of shimmering stars.

Then the alien closed her mouth, hiding away the terrible fangs. Her lips formed a proud, forceful line on her face, and Reza felt the hand around his tiny neck begin to contract with a strength that seemed to him as powerful as anything in the Universe.

As his lungs strained for their last breath through his constricted windpipe, a voice in his brain began to shout something. The words were repeated again and again, like a maniacal litany, the rhythm surging through his darkening brain. As his body's oxygen reserves dwindled and his vision dimmed, he finally understood.

The knife!

With a strength born of desperation, he thrust the knife straight at the Kreelan's face.

Suddenly she released him, and he fell to the ground. His feet crashed into the brick rubble over which he had been suspended, his legs crumpling like flimsy paper rods. Stunned, he fought to get air back into his lungs, his chest heaving rapidly. His vision returned at an agonizingly slow pace through the fireworks dancing on his retinas. He groped about, desperately trying to get away from the alien warrior.

His hand smacked into something, and he knew instantly what it was. He had felt it before. It was the Kreelan's leg. He looked up in time to see her kneel next to him, her mountainous form overshadowing the world in his frightened eyes. He tried to push himself away, to roll down into the flat part of the street where he might be able to run, but a massive clawed hand grasped him by the shoulder, the tips of her talons just pricking his skin.

His pounding fear giving way to resignation, he turned to face her. He did not want to watch as she killed him, but he had to see her. Whether out of curiosity or to face down the shame of being a coward, he did not know. Reluctantly, his eyes sought hers.

The knife, he saw, even in his tiny hand, had done its work. A vertical gash ran from a point halfway up the brow above the Kreelan's left eye down to the point of her graceful cheekbone. The blade had somehow missed the eye itself, although it was awash in the blood that oozed from the wound. The weapon had fallen from Reza's hand after doing its damage, and he held out little hope of recovering it. Besides, he thought as he waited for the final blow, what was the point?

He sat still as she reached toward him with her other hand. He flinched as one of the talons touched the skin of his forehead, just above his eye. But he did not look away, nor did he cry out. He had faced enough fear during this one night to last a lifetime, and when death came, he thought he might welcome it.

Slowly, she drew a thin line of blood that mimicked the wound he had given her. Her talon cut deep, right to the bone, as it glided down his face. Just missing his left eye, it lingered at last on his cheek.

He blinked, trying to clear the blood away as it dribbled over his eyebrow and into his eye. The flesh around the wound throbbed with the beating of his heart, but that was all. He was sure she was going to skin him alive, and he knew that her claws were as sharp as carving knives.

Instead, the Kreelan's hand drew back, and her other hand released his shoulder. She looked at him pensively, lightly tapping the talon smeared with his blood against her dark lips, her eyes narrowed slightly in thought.

His heart skipped a beat as she abruptly reached forward toward his hair. He felt a small pull on his scalp and instinctively reached to where he had felt the tug, expecting to feel the wet stickiness of more blood. But there was none. He looked up in surprise as the Kreelan held out a lock of his normally golden brown hair, now a filthy black from the dirt and smoke.

With obvious care, she put it into a small pouch that was affixed to the black belt at her waist.

A prize, Reza thought, his mouth dropping open in wonder, a faint spark of hope sizzling in his breast. Was she about to let him live?

In answer to his unvoiced question, the huge warrior stood up. She made no sound, not even a tiny whisper, as her body uncoiled to its towering height. She glanced down to the ground at her feet and, leaning down, scooped up his father's knife. Turning the blade over in her hand, she made a low *humph* and put it in her belt. She looked at Reza one last time, acting as if the bleeding wound on her face was nothing, and bowed her head to him.

He blinked.

And she was gone.

Two

Five Years Later, On The Planet Hallmark

A plume of dust rising into the dry air warned of the approaching vehicle, a bulbous van that could hold over a dozen passengers. Like a fat beetle on some unfathomable insectoid quest, it crept across the arid land, threading its way through the pyramids of rocks strewn across the landscape that marked the labor and toil of tens of thousands of young hands. The vehicle's paint, reassuringly bright at a distance, faded to a chipped, diseased gray as it drew closer. The rattling cough and billowing blue smoke from its poorly maintained engine announced the unwelcome noontime visit to those who hadn't already been watching its approach.

The vehicle wheezed to a stop, its four oversized wheels sending skyward a last cloud of bitter dust. On the side of the van, in letters that had once been a bright cheery blue, was stenciled "House 48."

A side door slid open with a tired shriek of metal, and eight frightened children stepped out into the harsh sunlight. Aged from five to fourteen, the newcomers – war orphans all – looked with disbelieving eyes at the bleak and arid plain that was to be their home until the day they left the orphanage. These were the fields of the planet Hallmark, the home of nearly a hundred Confederation Emergency Orphanages, and here the children would begin their service to the state that now provided for them. Each of the orphanage complexes housed a thousand or more children who had lost their families. And each and every child would spend his or her youth pulling rocks from the soil to help make more room for grain to grow, grain that fed Confederation troops and helped the planet's corrupt administrators grow rich on illegal trading and price fixing.

The van suddenly groaned and shuddered as the driver's door was thrown open, and a tree stump of a leg probed downward until it found the firmness of the ground. As the man – at least his chromosome structure made him a man – put his full weight on the resilient earth, the vehicle's springs gave an audible sigh of relief. On the florid face, shaded by a gaudy aqua baseball cap, was a humorless smile exposing teeth that were as rotten as the soul within. His name was Francis Early Muldoon, and he was the overseer of House 48's field labor teams.

He wasted no time, barking harsh orders to the children and gesturing with his arms. Sausage-like fingers pointed out the various labor teams. In singles and twos they began to trudge toward their assigned groups, staying close together like longtime friends, though they were yet strangers to one another.

All had been assigned but a pretty teenage girl, the oldest of the group at fourteen years, who was left to stand alone. She watched, uncertain, as the giant thing that masqueraded as a man turned his attention to her, his smile transforming into a leer.

* * *

Some meters away, a group of tired, sweat- and dirt-stained children, having paused from their labor of wrenching the sharp-edged rocks from the unyielding soil, watched the newcomers with grim interest. Standing at the front was a lean, brown-haired boy now twelve years old, holding the work-smoothed wooden handle of a pickax in his callused right hand. His jade green eyes had been following the van since it had appeared on the horizon, and now he felt his grip involuntarily tighten around the pick's handle as Muldoon turned his attention to the girl.

"Is he going to hurt her, Reza?" a young girl beside him asked in a hushed voice, her wide eyes fixed on the overseer and his latest object of interest.

"No," Reza growled as he watched Muldoon step closer to the new girl. Reza could not hear what was being said between the two, but he could well imagine. In exchange for food and protection from some of the older children who were as dangerous as rabid wolves, Muldoon usually got whatever piece of flesh – male and female alike – that his diseased cravings called for. Reza could remember many days when the van was parked near one of the little stone pyramids, rocking chaotically from the hideous sexual ballet playing within, and he well knew that participation was not strictly voluntary. But trying to tell the orphanage administration, whose bureaucratic heart had no room for the mindless prattling of youngsters with over-active imaginations, had led to more than one untimely death under "mysterious circumstances." The children had gotten the message: they were on their own against Muldoon.

But this girl, new to Muldoon's little operation, resolutely refused him. She met his groping advances with scratching nails and a hail of curses in a language Reza did not understand.

"You little bitch!" Reza heard Muldoon shout as she raked the nails of one hand across his face, drawing several streaks of blood. Reza's heart turned cold as the overseer struck the girl in the face with a meaty fist, knocking her to the ground. The man reached down for her, grabbed her blouse and pulled her toward him, ripping the vibrant yellow fabric that had struck Reza as being so pretty, so out of place here. Muldoon's hands grabbed for her budding breasts, now showing through the torn blouse. She tried to roll away, but he pinned her with his bulk, crushing her beneath him as his hands worked greedily at her clothing.

Reza had seen enough. He hefted his pickax and ran to where the girl lay writhing under Muldoon's gelatinous body. The other members of his work team followed him instantly, without question. Reza was their guardian, the only one who had cared about any of them, and their loyalty to him was absolute.

* * *

Muldoon was enjoying himself. He had wrapped his arms around the girl's chest, and now his hands were firmly clamped to her breasts as she struggled beneath him. Her face was pressed into the hard ground, the breath crushed from her by his one hundred and fifty kilos. He brutally squeezed her tender flesh, his fingertips pressing against her ribs just as his throbbing penis bulged against her buttocks. Only once before had he taken one of the children in the open, outside the van; he was normally very conscientious about that kind of thing. He firmly believed that sex was a private matter. But there were exceptions to every rule.

And this one was definitely an exception, he thought as his hands groped downward and began to work on unfastening her pants, his untrimmed fingernails cutting into her smooth skin.

The ground beside his face suddenly exploded, with dirt flying into his face. Crying out in surprise and pain, he struggled to free a hand to wipe at his stinging eyes. His vision cleared enough for him to see the gleaming metal sprouting from the earth not five centimeters from his sweating nose. As he watched, the metal spike levered itself out of the ground and rose above his head. He followed its trail until his eyes were drawn to the silhouetted form standing over him.

"Let her go, Muldoon," Reza ordered quietly. He held the pickax easily in his hands, hands that were stronger than those of most adults after the years of hard field work he had endured. Its splintered metal end was poised directly above Muldoon's head. "God knows, I should split your skull open just on principle, but the stench would probably be more than I could bear."

"Mind your own business, you little bastard," Muldoon hissed, his face twisting into the one that he saved for scaring the little children when they did something that really pissed him off. His hands bit even further into the girl's chest and belly, eliciting a groan of pain.

"This is your last warning, Muldoon," Reza said, raising the pickax to strike. He figured that he would almost certainly go to juvenile prison for killing this beast that almost looked like a man, but how much worse could prison be over this place? Besides, for all the suffering this bastard had caused, it would be worth it.

"You'd never get away with it, you little fuck," Muldoon warned. "You've got too many witnesses. You'd spend the rest of your worthless life in prison, if they didn't just fry your ass first."

Reza laughed. "Look around you, Muldoon. Do you think anybody here is going to be sorry if I ram this thing into your rat brain? And arranging an 'accident' would be pretty easy, you know. You don't drive so well sometimes. It would be a real shame if you hit one of the rock piles and flipped over or something. Maybe even the fuel tank would light off." Reza smiled a death's head smile. "Let her go," he said one last time, his voice hard as the stones they pulled from the ground.

"Kill him, Reza," one child said fiercely. Muldoon had been the monster of his nightmares until Reza had taken him in. "Kill him. Please."

Several others joined in until it was a chant. Reza knew that in a moment he wouldn't need the pickaxe to take care of Muldoon: the children would work themselves into such a frenzy that they would fall on him like hyenas and rip him to pieces with their bare hands. *And maybe that wouldn't be such a bad thing*, he thought.

But Muldoon saw it, too. He was many things, but he was no fool. He had heard stories of children murdering their overseers, and he had no intention of letting it happen to him. It was one of the reasons he sought to keep them terrorized, so he could keep them under rigid control.

With a grunt of effort, Muldoon rolled himself off of the girl. Eyeing Reza with unconcealed contempt, he got to his feet. The girl lay motionless between them like a beautiful garden that had been trampled, corrupted.

For a moment, the only sound above the dry breeze that constantly swept this arid land was the wheezing of Muldoon's overtaxed lungs as they fought to support a body that was at least three times Reza's own weight.

Muldoon's eyes flitted from Reza to the girl, then to the others who stood watching him, silent now. Muldoon considered his options, and decided that he would have to yield. This time.

"Listen, boy," he growled, his voice barely audible as he leaned toward Reza, "I'm going to get you one of these days. Maybe not today. Maybe not tomorrow. But I'll get you." He nodded to the girl, curled now into a fetal position on the ground. "And then I'll get your little slut, here, too." He hawked and spat on her, a gesture of defiance, of promise.

He turned away and headed back toward the van, conscious of the two dozen sets of eyes boring into his back. Once safe inside the vehicle, having slammed the driver's door shut, he leaned his head out the window. "You'd better have this section of the field cleared by sundown, boy, or your ass is gonna be in a sling with the headmaster!" As if noticing the other children for the first time, he bellowed, "What are you gawking at, you little shits? Get back to work!" Then he started up the van, gunned the engine, and drove off in a swirl of dust and choking exhaust.

"Go on, guys," Reza urged the others. "Get back to work. We don't need him back again today."

Heads down, the group began to break up as the children reluctantly made their way back to their work groups.

Reza was about to turn his attention to the girl Muldoon had been mauling when he suddenly found himself facing a child whose drawn face could have been mistaken for hundreds, thousands of others throughout the orphanage houses that dotted Hallmark.

"You should have killed him," she said quietly. Then she was gone, trailing after her two teammates as they trudged back to their designated spot. Like lifeless rag dolls, they collapsed onto their hands and knees and got back to work.

Reza turned his attention to the girl, who still lay on the ground, weeping. Three of the biggest boys from his own team stood around her like guards, waiting for his orders.

"It's all right," he told them. "You guys get back to work, but keep your eyes open. I'll take care of her." Kneeling next to the girl, Reza said softly, "How bad are you hurt?"

Almost unwillingly, she turned over, and Reza helped her to sit up. His face flushed with anger at the sight of the scratches and bruises that were already rising against her porcelain skin. She said nothing, but shook her head. Since hardly anything was left of her pretty blouse, Reza took off his shirt and offered it to her, careful not to touch her. She had already been touched enough for one day.

"Here," he said gently, "put this on."

She looked at him with her dark eyes, brown like a doe's, but with the spirit of a leopard's. There were tears there, but Reza saw no weakness.

"*Merci*," she said, wincing in pain as she reached for the shirt. He caught a quick glimpse of her exposed breasts and quickly averted his gaze, blushing with embarrassment at seeing that part of her body and anger at the mottled bruises he saw there. He turned his back to her as she stripped off the torn blouse and put on his shirt.

"Sorry it's so dirty," he said about the shirt, suddenly ashamed that he did not have something clean to offer her. "It probably doesn't smell too good, either."

"It is fine," she said, her voice quivering only slightly. "Thank you. You're very kind." He felt a light touch on his shoulder. "You may turn around, now."

He found himself looking at a girl whose skin was a flawless ivory that he knew from long experience would have a hard time under Hallmark's brutal sun. Her aristocratic face was framed by auburn hair that fell well below her shoulders, untrimmed bangs blowing across her eyes. Reza felt his throat tighten for no reason he could explain, other than that he thought she was the most beautiful girl he had ever seen.

"I'm Reza," he said, fighting through the sudden rasp that had invaded his voice, "Reza Gard." He held out his hand to her.

Smiling tentatively, she took it, and Reza was relieved to note that her grip was strong. This one, he could tell from long experience, was tough. A survivor.

"I am Nicole," she said, her voice carrying a thick accent that Reza had never heard before, "Nicole Carré."

* * *

Wearing a blouse loaned from a sympathetic girl, Nicole sat next to Reza that evening at the mess table that Reza and his group had staked out as their own. Many of the boys and girls here, Nicole noted with disbelief, had formed alliances to protect one individual or group from another, almost like a system of fiefdoms, replete with feudal lords. Those who did not belong to one of the gangs sat alone or in very small groups at the fringe tables, their eyes alert for intruders. Sadly, from what Nicole had seen today, she thought that the loners would not stand a chance without mutual protection. Truly, she thought, there was safety in numbers.

What she found even more surprising was that the groups were not necessarily led by the oldest or strongest. Reza clearly led the group she now found herself in, although there were at least four others here – not including herself – who were older or stronger.

"Everybody," Reza said to the dozen or so sitting at their table, "I want to introduce Nicole Carré, the latest addition to House 48 and the one who put those neat scratches on Muldoon's ugly face." Reza had found out through the grapevine about the questioning Muldoon had been put through by the chief administrator about the scratches, scratches that would leave scars, Reza had noted with glee. But, as usual, Muldoon had explained it all away. Not all the administrators were bad and not all of them were idiots, Reza knew; it just seemed like the ones who were in positions to influence things were. It was just tragic fate that the children had to pay the price.

A little cheer went up from the group at the thought that someone had struck a real blow against Muldoon and lived to tell about it, and it was accompanied by a chorus of spoons banging on the metal table in celebration.

"Story time! Story time!" called out a young girl, maybe six, with lanky blond hair and a large purple birthmark across her chin. The others joined in, chanting "Story time! Story time!" while looking expectantly at Nicole.

"What is this?" she asked Reza, unsure of what was happening. She wanted to trust this boy and his friends, but her once bright and loving world had become dark and dangerous with the coming of the Kreelans, and had not improved with her arrival on Hallmark.

"It's just a little tradition we have," he said easily, gesturing for the others to quiet down. "Whenever someone new comes, we like to have them tell us how they came to be here, what rotten luck landed them on Hallmark." He noted her discomfort and shook his head. "It's totally up to you. It's just... it helps people sometimes to talk about it. But if you don't want to, it's okay."

She looked at him a moment, unable to believe that a boy his age could have such bearing and strength. The children around him were tired and unhappy about their fate, yes, but they were hopeful, even proud, and obviously stuck together because they cared for one another. It was a sharp contrast to many of the other faces she saw about her: frightened, angry or hateful, dead. She had not realized before how lucky she had been to fall into this group.

"There is not much to it, really," she said at last, embarrassed at the rapt attention the others were giving her and saddened at having to recount her recent past, "but I will tell it to you, if that is what you wish."

She paused for a moment, her mind caught on the realization that she had never really related to anyone what had happened. No one had ever asked or seemed to care, outside of establishing the simple fact that her parents were dead. The adults saw Nicole as just one more burden to be tended by the state until she was old enough to take care of herself or serve in the government or the military. The looks and rote lines of compassion she had received from the endless bureaucratic chain had once been sincere, she thought. But after hearing the same stories and seeing the same young faces thousands of times over, the orphans had become a commodity of war, and the compassion the administrators might once have felt had long since given way to weariness.

Yet here, in this group of children, total strangers with only tragedy to bind them together, she found an audience for her grief, and it was almost too much to bear.

"I come from La Seyne," she began, her eyes fixed on the table before her, "one of the provincial capitals of Ariane. It is a pretty place," she said, briefly glancing up at the others and giving them a quick, shy smile, as if they would hold the claim of her homeworld's beauty against her. But their attention was rapt, their minds already far away from Hallmark, imagining to themselves what such a place might be like, a place that to them was equivalent to the paradise of the gods. "The Kreelans have never successfully attacked it, though they have tried several times.

"Papa is..." she bit her lip, "...*was* a master shipfitter, and he decided that we should have a vacation away from home this year, to get away from the yards for a while. He told Mama that we should go to Earth. He wanted us to see Paris, a place he always talked about – he had grown up there – but we had never seen it, Mama and I having been born on La Seyne. He never stopped talking about the wonderful tower, *La Tour Eiffel* that had been built before the days of artificial gravity and load lifters. He spoke of the lights at night, of the buildings that dated back to the times of great kings and queens. And so we boarded a starliner for Earth. There were three other ships in our little convoy, two merchantmen and a light cruiser."

Reza saw her eyes mist over, her gaze somewhere far away. God, he thought, how many times have I had to see this? And how many more times before I can leave this godforsaken place? Under the table, he sought out one of her hands and took it in his. She held it tightly.

She nodded as her mind sifted through the images of times she wished she could forget. "We were only two days out from La Seyne when the convoy was attacked. I do not know how many enemy ships there were, or exactly what happened. I suppose it does not matter. Our ship, the *Il de France*, was badly hit soon after the alarms sounded, and Papa went aft to the engineering spaces to try and help them." Her lower lip trembled as a tear streaked down her face. "We never saw him after that."

She paused a moment, her eyes closed as she remembered her father's parting hug to her and her mother before he ran down the companionway with the frightened young petty officer. "The ship kept getting hit like it was being pounded with a great hammer. Either the bridge was destroyed, or perhaps the speaker system was damaged, because the order to abandon ship never came, even though we knew for sure that the hull had been breached in many places. Mama, who herself had never been on a ship before, did not seem scared at all, like she had been through it all many times in her head as she worked in the kitchen at home, making Papa's supper. When the normal lights went out and the emergency lights came on, she said only, 'We are leaving,' and took me by the hand to where one of the lifeboats was still docked." A sob caught her breath, but she forced herself to get on with it. "But the boat was already filled, except for one seat. But the aisle down the middle was clear. 'Look, Mama,' I told her, 'there is plenty of room for us.'

"But I did not know that these boats had no artificial gravity, and that anyone not in a seat might be killed during the launch. I did not hear the warning the boat was giving in Standard. There was so much noise coming from our dying ship, and Mama spoke only French. She made me take the seat and she knelt in the aisle, praying, when the door closed. I... I blacked out after that. And when I woke up, she... she..."

Nicole collapsed in wracking sobs, the guilt and loss that had been eating away at her heart finally exposed. But a part – be it ever so tiny – of the burden had been lifted from her shoulders. She felt the comforting touch of caring hands as the others extended their sympathy, and Reza wrapped his arm around her shoulder, drawing her to him.

"It's all right," he said softly. "It wasn't your fault–"

"But the warning," she gasped angrily. "I knew Standard! I should have listened! I could have saved her!"

"And where would that have left your mom?" asked Tamil, an acne-scarred girl with hair cropped close to her skull. "Back on the ship to get spaced when the hull gave way?"

"I would have stayed with her!" Nicole shouted defiantly. "At least we all would have been together."

Tamil shook her head. "She wouldn't have let you, girl, and you know it." While she was not very old when her own mother had died, Tamil remembered her mother well, and how she had saved her daughter's life at the cost of her own. "She would have knocked you over the head and strapped you into that last seat to save you, if it came down to it. She loved you. She wouldn't have let you die."

That remark was met with nods and murmurs of agreement from the others.

Nicole suddenly understood that a consensus had been reached, and the look of sympathy in their eyes was joined by something akin to forgiveness. It was a tacit understanding that Fate was to blame. There was nothing she could have done to avert the tragedy that had taken her family away. More than that, they had accepted her. She was one of them now, if she wanted to be. Thinking back to what Muldoon had done, she gave thanks to God for her good fortune.

"Listen," Reza told her, "the pain... never really goes away. But you learn to deal with it." His voice was nearly lost in the background banter and clatter of nearly a thousand spoons scraping the remnants of the evening meal from the trays of House 48, her new home. "You have to, if you want to get out of this lousy place in one piece. If you don't, people like Muldoon and some of the kids here will use you and throw you away like a toilet wipe. And you've got friends now to help."

"Besides," said a short, stocky red-haired girl two seats down from Reza, "you're a short timer. What are you, fourteen, or so?" Nicole nodded. "Jesus, Nicole, you've got less than a year here until you're fifteen and you can apply for one of the academies. You look like you're pretty sharp and in good shape. They'll probably take you. If you don't," she shrugged, "you'll just have to wait it out until you're seventeen."

"Fifteen," she lamented. "It is forever." The thought of spending the next six months here until her fifteenth birthday was appalling, but having to wait until she was seventeen was simply unbearable. Strangely, applying to one of the academies was a thought that had never occurred to her in her former life. La Seyne was very traditional, clinging to many of the ancient Western traditions brought by its early settlers. Most of the women born there spent their lives caring for their husbands and raising their children, any thoughts of becoming a "professional" being scorned as sacrilegiously self-serving. But, to get out of here in six months instead of two and a half years, she was more than willing to abandon tradition.

"It's a lot less than I've had to spend on this rock," Reza said darkly, his pre-pubescent voice carrying the resignation of the damned. His eyes blazed so fiercely that they burned her with shame for thinking that the paltry time she would have to spend here was unendurable. Reza had been here for some time before she had arrived, and would still be here after she had gone.

"Please," she choked, suddenly flushing with empathy for him, for all of them, "forgive me. I did not mean it that way." She reached out and gently stroked his cheek with her hand. "*Mon Dieu*," she whispered, "how horrible."

Reza shrugged, his face dropping its melancholy veil. "It could be worse," he said. "At least it's not like for some of the really little kids who came here without even remembering or knowing their parents, like little

Darrow over there." A tiny black boy a few seats down nodded heartily and gave her an enchanting smile. "At least we knew our parents and can remember them."

Nicole nodded thoughtfully as Reza turned his attention back to the others.

"Does anybody else have anything?" He looked around the table like a chairman of the board or councilman, his eyes intense pools of jade. "Okay, that's it, then, except to remind you that we're on alert for Muldoon and his slugs. Nobody goes anywhere alone, so stay with your blockmates. Jam your doors when you go to sleep and don't open them again until your team leader – Thad, Henson, or Charles – comes to pick you up in the morning. Little kids, if you hear the fire alarm, don't leave your room unless you recognize one of our voices outside and we give you the right signal on the door. Muldoon pulled that trick last year and nailed a girl from Screamer's bunch. He's going to be gunning for us for a while this time, and there won't be another load of newbies for him to go after for another two weeks, so watch out and stick together."

With a murmur of acknowledgments, the children quickly got up from the table. Moving in formation with almost military precision, they dumped their trays in the waiting bins and followed their team leaders to the bunkhouse, leaving only Reza and Nicole behind.

"Should we not go with them?" she asked, wondering if the two of them would be safe, alone.

"No," he told her, gesturing for her to follow as he got up from the table and headed toward the tray bin. "We're not going back with them tonight. They'll be all right, but I think it's too dangerous for us to go back to the bunkhouse until tomorrow, at least."

"But," Nicole stammered, "where will we sleep?"

"Trust me," Reza told her. "I have a place Muldoon can't get into very easily."

He led her outside, following a path that led them through the various buildings that made up the House 48 complex. It comprised the bunkhouse itself, which was really a collection of dormitories; the school, which was only occupied during the winter, when even Muldoon could not bear to herd the children into the fields; the tiny medical clinic; and the administration building. The last, ironically, was also the largest, as it also housed House 48's shelter, visible from the outside by the universal red and black striped blast portal that was kept lit at all times. The exact same buildings could be found at any of the other Houses dotting Hallmark's surface. All of them were pre-fabricated, tough, cheap and easy to build and maintain. They were true modern architectural wonders, and all ugly as sin.

Up ahead, Nicole could make out a squat structure at the end of the path, the last of House 48's buildings that didn't seem to fit in with the others. Light showed through the slender windows, evenly distributed around the circumference of the octagonal building, reaching from about waist-high nearly to the roof over the second story.

"My home away from home," Reza announced, gesturing toward the revolving door. It looked almost like an airlock, and was intended to keep the dust of the fields out of the building.

"What is it?" Nicole asked as Reza ushered her through the door, the cylinder swishing closed behind them.

"It's the House 48 Library," he answered.

Nicole was about to laugh until she realized that Reza was completely serious. As they emerged through the door and into the light of the interior, she saw the look of unabashed wonder on his face. Her smile slipped as she thought of how many times he must have come through that door, and yet his expression was as if this was the very first.

"Reza," she asked, following after him into what must have been the lobby, "what is so important here?" She looked around at the meager collection of holo displays and the disk racks. "These devices are very nearly antique!"

Reza favored her with a quizzical look, as if her question had revealed a stratum of incredible, if easily forgivable, ignorance. "This," he said disdainfully, pointing to the disk racks and study carrels arrayed around the lobby, "is junk: old periodicals, some of the new literature, and other stuff. I stopped bothering with that a long time ago." He led her around the front desk as if he owned the place, which she suspected he might, in a way. Then he punched in an access code to a locked door. She noted that there appeared to be no one else here, a thought that was not entirely comforting. "This," he explained quietly, "is why this place is important."

Pushing open the door, they found themselves in a darkened room, but there was still enough light for Nicole to see angular shapes that radiated away into the darkness. Reza closed and locked the door behind them. Only then did he switch on a light.

"Oh," Nicole gasped. In the gentle light that flooded the room, she saw row after row of books, real books, with pages and bindings. Some were made of the micro plastic that had found its way into favor over the years, but most were made of genuine paper, the exposed edges yellowed with age, their covers and bindings carefully protected with a glistening epoxy sealant.

"Besides being real antiques," Reza told her, "and having some monetary value for anyone who can waste the transport mass charge to haul them around, they can be a real brain saver in this place." He picked up a volume, seemingly at random – although he knew by heart the place of every book in the room – and held it up for her to see. *Hamlet*, the book's binding said, followed by some strange symbols and then the author's name: Shakespeare.

She took the book from him, careful not to drop it. It was terribly old, and one of the few such books she had ever seen. Every major publisher had long since done away with physical books. Electronic media were so much cheaper and more efficient.

But it was not the same, as her own father, a devoted book reader himself, had often told her. Watching the action on a holo screen left too little to the imagination, he had said once, holding one of his own precious volumes up as if it were on an imaginary pedestal. The screen fed the mind, but its calories were empty ones, bereft of the stuff on which thought depended. She had thought him quite comical at the time, her own young life having evolved around the holo images that invaded their home daily. But perhaps, as was most often the case, his words had more than just a kernel of truth in them.

"You asked why this place is so important to me," Reza said, watching as she turned the pages, his ears thrilling to the sound. "I'll tell you why. When you come in from the fields, you eat, you sleep, and then you get up to go to the fields again. Over and over, for as long as you have until you can leave here.

"And every day that you let yourself do just that, just the stuff you have to do to get by, even when you're so tired you can't see straight, you die just a little bit. Not much, not so much that you notice that day, or even the next, but just a little. Your mind starts eroding, and you start forgetting about anything that you used to think was interesting or important, whether anyone else thought it was or not. Pretty soon, all the useless crap that we do here becomes more and more important to you, as if it really had some meaning." He spat out the last few words, disgust evident on his face and in his voice. "After a while, you start finding yourself in conversations about how many kilos of rocks people dug up. There's even an official contest. Did you know that? People talk about how many blisters so-and-so got, and who had sex with whom, what kind of stunt Muldoon pulled today, on and on and on. Remember the porridge you liked so much?" Nicole grimaced, the tasteless paste still coagulating in her stomach. "That's what your brain starts turning into around here. Mush.

"And the worst part is that they start not to care about anything or anyone, even themselves. Why should they, when the most important thing they did today is clear a few more meters for some farming combine that doesn't even give us a percentage of the grain they grow?"

Nicole's mouth fell open at that.

"That's right," Reza told her, his eyes burning with anger. "All of our food is imported from Peraclion, because the grain there has a higher bulk than stuff grown here, for whatever reason, and so it's more expensive to ship long distances. So all our stuff goes out-system, and Peraclion feeds us... after a few kickbacks get paid off to some of the admins here.

"So," he shrugged, "here we all sit, droning our lives away until we're old enough to either enlist directly or apply for an academy assignment. We're slave labor for the farming combines that need the land cleared but are too cheap to send machines to do it."

His expression turned grim. "But the worst part for most of the kids here is that, regardless of how bright they were when they came, they fail the entrance exams because they haven't gotten the right schooling, or can't even figure out what *abstract* means, let alone come up with an abstract thought." His face twisted in an ironic smile. "No fighter jocks coming out of that group."

Reza had no way of knowing at the time, but his last remark struck Nicole to the core. She loved the thought of flying, and had always secretly dreamed of piloting one of the tiny, darting fighter ships she saw in the movies. And in that instant, she knew what she wanted to do with her life, now that the old one was gone, washed away.

"And what of you, Reza?" she asked, her thoughts returning from her own hoped-for future. "Your mind has not turned to mush, I take it?"

"No," he told her, his expression softening as he lovingly ran his fingers along the spine of a book, "not yet, anyway. Thanks to this place."

"I still do not understand, *mon ami*." She still could not see what Reza was driving at.

"When you come in here and pick up one of these," he gestured at *Hamlet*, "or even watch one of the crappy holos out in the main room, you're not just an orphaned kid marooned on a dustbowl planet anymore, with no more rights than any slave might have. It's a way out of here. You're a hero, or a villain, or anything else you could imagine, and a lot of things you probably can't. Every time you turn a page you can go somewhere, even someplace that's never been. But anywhere you go is somewhere far away from here. And the best part about it, the part that keeps me alive and sane, is that the words in the books leave a lot of blanks that your mind has to fill in. It makes your mind work without you forcing it to, and you get better and better at it without killing yourself like you have to sometimes in the fields."

Nicole considered his words for a moment, her mind conjuring up images of some of the children she had seen around her since arriving at House 48. So many of them, it now seemed to her, had just been blank, without expression, without animation. Had they not been breathing, one might have thought them dead. And, perhaps, in a way they were.

"But Reza," she asked, suddenly finding a hole in his escape theory, "how do you find the time? Or the energy?"

"I make it," he said grimly. "I come here every night after dinner, no matter how tired I am, no matter if there's mud from the rain or snow in the winter. And on the one day off we have after our six workdays, I spend all day here." He shrugged. "What else am I going to do? I'd like to just spend that time sleeping like most of the others. I hate being tired all the time, but it's too important. I'm not going to let myself turn into a vegetable in this place. When I'm fifteen," he vowed, "I'm going to pass the academy entrance exams. I'm going to make it into OCS and be a Marine."

"And then," Nicole said, finishing the thought, "you will seek revenge." He nodded, but turned his eyes away from her. He did not want her to see the hate that burned so fiercely there for the enemy that had stolen his parents, his life, from him to leave him marooned here.

"Reza?" a voice called from the desk area. "Are you in there?"

Nicole was surprised at the immediate change in Reza's expression as a smile lit up his face like a beacon.

"Hi, Wiley!" he called, quickly unlocking the door and letting it swing open. "Hey, I've got someone I want you to meet."

A face poked through the door, and for a moment Nicole was sure it was an enormous apple, left too long to dry, its sun-worn skin crinkled into innumerable peaks and valleys as it aged. The wrinkled face was topped by an unruly mop of gray hair that must have been cut with scissors by the man himself. Peering out from the apple-face was a pair of ice blue eyes that once might have been the object of interest and desire for many a woman, but now were clouded with an expression that left some degree of doubt as to the owner's intelligence.

Those eyes swept from Reza to Nicole, and a mischievous smile crept across the man's face. "You got yourself a lady-friend," he exclaimed, his voice one of neutral innocence, rather than with the lecherous undertones that Reza would have expected from almost anyone else. "Showing her your collection, are you?"

"Yeah, Wiley," Reza nodded, turning to Nicole. "This is Nicole Carré, one of the newbies who came in this morning, and the newest member of our group. Nicole," he gestured toward the old man, "meet William Hickock, Colonel, Confederation Marine Corps, Retired. He's been my mentor and protector since I came to Hallmark," Reza explained. "And in case you were wondering, these are all his books. He brought them with him when he first came here."

Nicole's eyes widened. A collection like this must be worth a fortune.

The old man stuck out his hand, nodding his head toward Reza. "Nice to meet you!" he said with a disarming grin. "All my friends just call me Wiley."

Nicole could not help but smile as she took the man's hand, noting the restrained strength of his grip. "*Enchanté, monsieur*," she said, bowing her head slightly.

As she looked back up at Wiley, she knew that something was not quite right, but she was not sure what it might be. There was something in his voice, or the way he carried himself, slouching slightly as if in acquiescence, that seemed out of character for a former Marine colonel.

Then she noticed the scar that crept away from the man's forehead and into his scalp like a lumpy, pink centipede, and she realized that his last battle – for that surely was where the scar was from – must have very nearly killed him. As it was, it left him less a man than he used to be, with some tiny part of his brain destroyed. She immediately pitied him, but she did not let it show on her face.

But Wiley, slightly brain damaged though he was, was nonetheless quite astute. "Yeah, missy," he told her, his voice wistful as he traced his finger along the scar as it wandered halfway across his skull, "I lost a few marbles, I guess. Lost this, too," he said, rapping on his right leg, the metal prosthesis echoing hollowly.

"But hey, that there's old news," he said, brightening suddenly as if someone had just turned an invisible toy wind-up crank on his back. "What are you all up to?"

"We're watching out for Muldoon again," Reza told him seriously, his voice reflecting as much concern as if a Kreelan attack had been underway. "He really took a fancy to Nicole."

Wiley's face changed for just a moment, so quickly that Nicole might have missed it had she not been looking right at him. A glow of anger flared in his eyes, the kind of chilled anger that came from living a life where death was always just a moment away, a life that was far too short for sorting out the complexities of human evil. She was sure that, had Muldoon been within arm's reach of the old man, he would have killed him in that blink of an eye.

Then it was gone.

"Well isn't that the damnedest thing," Wiley whispered, shaking his head. "I just wish he'd leave you kids alone."

"That's the main reason we're here, Wiley," Reza said, looking sadly at Nicole. Reza had read – memorized, more like it – the biography of Colonel Hickock, and he knew that the tragedy of the man's intellectual demise was little short of monumental. "I was wondering if we might be able to stay with you for a couple days or so."

"Why, sure, Reza!" the old man exclaimed, delighted. "You know you're always welcome. I like company, you know." He gestured with his still-strong hands for them to come with him. "Come on, come on, let's get you settled in downstairs."

They followed him out the door, Reza locking it behind them. They went through the lobby and down some stairs into the building's basement, the bare plasticrete walls echoing their footsteps.

Opening a door that had MAINTENANCE stenciled on it in neat block letters, Wiley showed them into the room beyond. "It ain't much," he said, ushering them in, "but it's home."

Nicole found herself in what looked like an apartment, replete with a tiny kitchen, a separate bedroom, bathroom, and a fluffy, comfortable-looking sofa that took up nearly half of the living room. On the walls, themselves painted a light pastel blue, were holos of ships and people in uniform, even a few actual photographs, all presented in what Nicole guessed were expensive frames. While various other knickknacks could be found throughout the room, everything was neat and orderly, every visible surface clean of dust or the slightest trace of dirt. It was immaculate, but homey, without any of the fastidiousness that was nearly pathological with some people.

Looking at the sofa, she suddenly realized how tired she was. She had forgotten how long she had been awake, and was trying hard not to think of the ordeal she had faced earlier in the day with Muldoon.

"C'mon, honey," Wiley said gently, taking her by the arm. Even with his damaged brain, he could see when someone was exhausted. "Let's get you to bed."

Reza unfolded the sofa into a bed that nearly took up the whole room, quickly spreading out the sheets and blanket wrapped within. Nicole could see that it was an operation he had gone through many times before, and was glad for his quick handling of the matter.

She fell more than lay down on the old mattress, the clean, crisp smell of the sheets penetrating her brain, the downy blanket soft in her hands. Burying her face in the pillow, she closed her eyes.

Reza watched her fall away into sleep, and hoped that her dreams would not be troubled by the events of the day or the trials he was sure would yet come. He found that he liked this girl very much, and vowed to never let her come to harm, regardless of the cost.

THREE

Hallmark's hot summer gave way to fall without any noticeable change. The fall was still warm – hot, on many days – with rain that fell regularly and predictably across huge sections of the planet's three continents. It was an ideal location to grow grain, but offered little else of any strategic value.

And so it was no surprise that Hallmark had turned into a major grain producer, supplying nearly twenty percent of the quota for the sector, enough to feed forty combat regiments and all the ships and logistical support necessary to keep them in action. Much of the initial clearing had been done by machines. But the rock clearers were taken elsewhere after someone had come up with the idea of putting orphans there to build on the initial clearing efforts. Hallmark was safe from attack, they had said, since it had no military installations that might appeal to the Kreelans, who seemed to be far more interested in contesting well-defended worlds.

On the other hand, Reza had often thought, that philosophy had left Hallmark utterly defenseless. But that's the way things had been for the last twenty or more years, and clearing the rocks from the land had become the traditional – and enforced – role of the orphans there.

"Busy hands are happy hands," Reza grunted as he heaved at a rock that must have weighed nearly fifty kilos, trying to pry it from the clutches of the hard earth beneath the loose topsoil. The rains had made the ground a bit less reluctant to give up its rocky treasures, but it was still backbreaking work that had to be done. For only after the rocks were removed and the tilling machines came through, adding nutrients as they did their normal work, would the field resemble something akin to arable land. Now there was only the indigenous steppe grass that blew in the wind, its razor-thin edges a constant hazard to exposed skin.

"What?" Nicole managed through her clenched teeth as she pushed against the rock's other side. She seemed to be doing little more than digging a hole in the ground with her feet as she pushed against the unyielding stone. But at last it started to give way.

"Nothing," Reza sighed as the rock finally came out like a pulled tooth, flopping over onto the ground with a solid thump. "Just philosophizing."

"About what?"

"*Je ne sais pas.*" He smiled at her reaction to his intentionally atrocious accent.

His talent with French had surprised even Nicole, who carried a trace of the linguistic chauvinism that had characterized her forebears. In the months the two had spent together, however, Nicole knew that he spoke it well enough to almost be mistaken for a native. *Well*, she thought to herself with an inner smile, *almost*. She was terribly proud of him.

She grimaced theatrically, wiping her forehead clean of sweat with her bandanna in a sweeping gesture. "You need beaten, *mon ami*," she chided, using a colloquialism she had picked up from Wiley. She sat down against the rock to take a break. "Your instructor has not been so deficient as to allow the language of kings to be so horribly mutilated."

Reza favored her with an impish grin as he looked around at the nearby groups of laboring children, then at the sun. "I think it's time to have lunch," he announced, clapping his hands and rubbing them together as if a truly tasty meal awaited them. He stood up, cupping his hands to his mouth, and shouted, "BREAK!" to several figures off to their right. He repeated it to the left, and the other eleven members of his field team gratefully sat down for their noon meal break. It was the only one they were allowed during their twelve to sixteen hour workday.

Nicole got out the meatloaf sandwiches she made for them that morning. The meatloaf was a spread from a can. Reza had observed drily that it had probably not come from any sort of animal, so probably was not any sort of meat, nor had it ever been part of any kind of loaf. But that was their feast for today. She set the sandwiches out on a white embroidered cloth she always brought with her for the occasion. It was something she had managed to make in her free time, virtually all of which she spent in the library with Reza and Wiley. Making their lunch had been her idea, and the extra work it took made her feel good, and it had since become a kind of tradition. It was a tiny thing that bound them a bit more closely together, staving off a little of the ugliness that filled their lives. Again reaching into her pack, she pulled out two battered metal cups and poured water for the two of them. Then she settled down to wait as Reza went about his noontime ritual.

She watched as he walked toward one pair of his team. He talked with them for a moment as they ate, making sure they were all right, then moved on to the next. He had always made it a point to take care of his people first, something he once told her he had learned from Wiley. On days when there were problems – and there were plenty of those, even on a job as mundane as this – he often did not get to rest or eat at all. The librarian, Mary Acherlein, whom Nicole had instantly liked, once told her that Reza had been a team leader for over a year before Nicole had arrived, despite his young age and Muldoon's best efforts to the contrary. Of course, Muldoon did not try overly hard to get in Reza's way: his team consistently outperformed the others in House 48's field clearing totals, and that made Muldoon look good.

If that was possible, she thought sourly, thankful that the ponderous bulk of a man had left her alone, aside from an occasional visual appraisal that left her skin crawling with the memory of that loathsome first day when she had been trapped under his throbbing mass. She shuddered, pushing away the memory.

Watching as Reza started back toward her, most of his own eating time gone, she could not help but wonder if someday they might not become something more than friends. It was a pleasant thought, a dream that she kept quietly to herself. But for now, she treated him much like a brother who just happened to be very mature for a boy so young. He was still prone to mischief and the other emotional conundrums that plagued children his age, perhaps even more so now that he had someone to express them to, but there was no denying that he was already a young man, and she found herself very attracted to him. *Someday*, she thought.

"Well?" she prompted, handing him a sandwich.

He peered between the thick slabs of bread – one thing they had plenty of – and made a face. "Gross," he said, a grin touching his lips. Nicole batted him in the shoulder. "Everybody's okay. No more than the usual, except for Minkman. Said he had a broken finger on his left hand."

"What did you do?"

Reza laughed. "I told him to use his right hand and not to worry about it." Nicole frowned, sometimes not quite sure if he was joking or not. "Okay, okay. I splinted it for him, too. If he wants more than that before he can get to the infirmary tonight, he has to go to Muldoon, which he did not want to do. I can't imagine why."

"*Bon*," she said. "Now, sit down and eat."

"*Oui, madame*," he said, this time with a perfect La Seyne accent. He plopped down across from her, somehow not getting dirt all over the picnic cloth. Taking a long swallow of water from his cup, he began to devour the first of three sandwiches and an anemic apple that served as dessert. The first day Nicole had offered to pack his lunch for him she had only made one sandwich, and Reza had been more anxious than usual to get back from the fields, this time to the dining hall instead of the library. He had never said a word about it, but she had felt awful when she saw how hungry he was that evening. She had not repeated that mistake since.

She stole a glance at him as he was looking off into the distance at something, the left side of his face turned toward her. Despite the scar that marred his skin, the keepsake left by the Kreelan warrior who had killed his parents, he was a handsome boy. He wasn't gorgeous or glamorous as some children promised to be upon their entry into puberty, but his face and his body radiated his inner strength and spirit. His skin was a golden color, not all of it from the tan from his years of work in the fields. Nor was it quite the olive color often associated with descendants of Terran Mediterranean races, nor was it European. He was all of those, yet none of them. The same was true of his hair. Almost chocolate brown, bleached somewhat by the sun, it was thick and lush, almost oriental in its texture. Haphazardly cut close to his skull when she had first met him, she had taken it upon herself to give him a proper haircut. Now it tapered evenly in the back to his neckline, with his ears and forehead neatly exposed in what she jokingly referred to as House 48's *haute couture* hairstyle.

"You'll be leaving soon," he said quietly.

"What?" she asked, unsure if she had heard him correctly.

"Wiley got your acceptance papers this morning from Lakenheath Training Center," he told her, his eyes focused on the ground. "You maxed out on almost all those tests you took a few months ago. Made you look like kind of a hot shot, I guess. There'll be a ship coming to pick you up on your birthday next week." He smiled, still not looking at her. "You've reached 'free fifteen.'" He finally looked up. His eyes were a confused mixture of relief that she had been accepted and sorrow that she would be leaving him, probably forever. "I... I wanted to tell you as soon as I found out this morning, but..." He trailed off. "I couldn't," he finally whispered. "I didn't want to say it, that you're really going to be leaving. But I couldn't put it off any longer." He offered her a sad smile. "Congratulations, trainee fighter pilot Carré."

Nicole was speechless for a moment, her mouth working, but no words came out. The time had passed so quickly, her brain sputtered. It was too soon. It was impossible.

"Reza..." she managed. And then, like a dam bursting, she began to cry. She wrapped her arms around Reza and held him tight, overcome with joy that her future was not completely bleak, that she had something to look forward to. "Oh, Reza," she exclaimed, her French accent nearly obliterating the Standard words, "this is so wonderful! We can leave this rotten place! And in only a few days! We..."

"I can't leave, remember?" Reza reminded her softly, fighting to hold back tears of his own as he held her. He had lost so many friends to time and circumstance that he thought he would be hardened to this, ready for it when it came, when it was time for her to leave. But he wasn't. He could never be ready for the things he felt now, inside himself. He knew she had to go, knew that it was the only thing for her. But it hurt so much to think of what things were going to be like without her.

In that moment he knew the truth about his feelings. He loved her. He knew he was only a barely pubescent boy with emerging hormones, but he knew in his heart that it was true.

Her voice faded away as the realization forced itself upon her like Muldoon's groping hands.

"*Mon cher,*" she whispered, the joyful tears suddenly becoming bitter and empty. "Oh, Reza, what will you do?"

He tried to smile, failed. "The same as I always do," he choked, shrugging. "I'll make do somehow. I'm just happy that you made it, Nicole," he told her. "As much as it's going to hurt to see you go, I'm so glad for you."

They held each other for a while longer, trying to forestall the bittersweet future that vowed to separate them, brother and sister in a family bound together not by blood, but by trust and love.

Finally, without saying another word, they rose unsteadily to their feet and got back to work.

* * *

Muldoon let the field glasses he had been holding to his eyes slap against his chest, the once bright finish of the instrument long since corroded by hours of being held in his sweaty palms.

He spent a goodly portion of his day watching Gard and his crew from an unobtrusive distance. He especially enjoyed watching the French girl. *Yes,* he thought, licking the sticky sweat from his lips, *especially her.* After the confrontation that very first day, Muldoon had been forced by Reza's tactics to leave them more or less alone. He had taken out his frustrations on his usual victims, although he had never thought of them as such. To Muldoon they were only young children who should have liked him, but did not for some inexplicable reason. But the lust in him for the little wench from La Seyne refused to die. If anything, it grew the more he tried to satisfy his urgings in other ways.

Muldoon had received word through his grapevine that Nicole would be leaving soon, and the diabolical device that served as his brain was churning through possibilities, looking for options, an opening.

Yeah, he thought to himself, feeling his crotch begin to throb, *I'd like to explore an opening, right between the little bitch's legs*. And he would not mind sticking it to her little boy benefactor, either, he thought as his teeth ground together in frustration. Just before he choked the life out of the little bastard.

He turned to get back in the van, his mind still churning, looking for a scenario that would work. He was not worried about the house administrators, or even the Navy ship coming to get the girl. It was the kids themselves, plus the joker that was the old man. Muldoon had always thought him a senile idiot, at least until he had tried to push the old Marine around, threatening him after Wiley had witnessed one of Muldoon's little indiscretions. The ground had never hit Muldoon that hard or fast. When he came to, the old man was sweeping the floor nearby as if nothing had happened. He was a wild card, and one thing Muldoon despised was unpredictability.

His mind began to bubble with frustration. He was usually so good at making plans quickly, and he kicked one broken-arched foot at the steppe grass, watching the dust trail away like smoke.

Like smoke.

And then it came to him. "Oh, that's just rich," he told himself, chuckling softly as he swung his bulk into the driver's seat. "Brother Muldoon," he said, "you certainly do have a way."

He started the engine and drove off, heading for the compound to make the arrangements for the French girl's coming of age.

* * *

Reza frowned. "That Muldoon," he muttered under his breath. "What an idiot."

It was the day before Nicole was to leave. The two of them, plus four others from Reza's team, had been assigned a ridiculously small quadrangle to clear. But it was not the area's size or shape that puzzled Reza, but the location: on all four sides there were quads of wheat that were almost ready to be harvested. Genetically modified over decades from original Earth stock, Hallmark's grain grew taller than Reza could reach with his arms extended over his head and produced four times as much grain per hectare. Normally that didn't matter to him. But now, standing inside this quad, it was impossible to see anything past the wall of gently waving stalks, and it made Reza nervous.

"What difference does it make, *mon ami*?" Nicole asked, reluctantly putting her gloves on. "Rocks are rocks, *non*?"

"Sure," he replied, "but you don't normally bother clearing little patches like this just before the harvest. It's easier to wait until the wheat's been taken out so you can get the rocks through to the road." He remembered how Muldoon had come to pick them up that morning in one of the huge combines, a first in Reza's time on-planet. Neither the large buses that were their normal transport when working far from the house, nor Muldoon's van could penetrate the wheat to get them to the barren quad where they now stood. They had to walk in from the road. And it wasn't his full team, just the six of them.

She touched his shoulder. "Perhaps we should get to work, Reza," she told him quietly, a tentative smile on her lips. "I think perhaps you have other things on your mind that make a little thing seem very big."

Reza looked at her. "Yeah, you're probably right," he sighed. Her leaving was indeed a big thing on his mind, and it did seem to make everything else – the bad things – worse. But a part of his mind still wondered why Muldoon had put them here. It was different, out of his normal routine, and that made Reza worry.

* * *

The morning passed without incident. Reza was working hard on digging out a particularly recalcitrant rock, simultaneously considering the feasibility of a lunch break, when he heard Nicole call to him from where she was digging a meter or so away.

"Reza," she asked, pointing to the north, "what is that?"

He looked up, and his heart tripped in his chest. There was smoke. Lots of it. And close.

"Oh, damn," he hissed, tossing down his pickaxe. His eyes swept the horizon around them, his stomach sinking like a lead weight over a deep ocean trench. Smoke billowed out of all the adjoining quads, as if nearly a combined hectare's worth of wheat had simply decided to ignite.

And he knew that was simply not possible.

"Goddammit!" he cursed. "Drop everything and get over here, now!" he ordered the others, his eyes judging the flames while the touch of the air against his skin helped him gauge the wind. He knew that wheat that was ready for harvest would not normally catch fire too easily, but once it really caught – especially if there was a wind to drive it – it would burn as well as kerosene.

The others joined him and Nicole at a full run. Their eyes were wide with fear. Every child who had worked in the fields for very long knew the danger of fire. Whipped along by the winds, it killed or maimed hundreds of orphans across the planet every year. Those who died were generally the lucky ones, for the house clinics were ill-prepared to deal with major burns, and off-planet medical transport for orphans was hardly considered a priority by the bureaucracies that controlled the planet's operation. The fires, a constant hazard throughout the year, were started by everything from lighting strikes to spontaneous combustion; any of a dozen causes. Not least of which was arson.

Reza called up an image in his mind of the field they were in, a process made difficult because he had not worked this area for nearly two years. Since then, it had been bursting with wheat, and the orphans had nothing to do with that; that was the Hallmark Farm Combine's business.

"There should be a road about a klick south of here," he remembered, the image of the arrow-straight track coming to him from a map of the area he had studied with Wiley a long time back. He looked in the direction he thought the road should be, and was relieved to see that smoke had not yet begun to boil toward the sky.

"We're going to have to move fast," he said, "or the wind'll help the fire kill us. Come on!"

He led them in the direction of the road at a restrained jog so the younger kids could keep up. Moving through the tall wheat was tricky as it was, the stalks grasping at clothes and skin, fouling their legs when it was stepped on. The others followed Reza without complaint or argument, with Nicole bringing up the rear. Reza pushed the pace as fast as he dared, his biggest fear hearing the crackling of a blazing fire but not being able to see where it was coming from. Should they lose their sense of direction, they could find themselves trapped in the middle of an inferno with no escape.

Nicole, last in the line of fleeing refugees, kept looking behind them. Her eyes reflected the licking tongues of the flames now just visible over the tops of the wheat stalks, coming closer under the driving influence of the wind.

The child in front of her – a new girl, Nicole did not know her name – stumbled and fell to her hands and knees. Nicole helped her struggle to her feet, urging her onward. "*Allez! Allez!*" she cried, pushing the girl forward.

"We're almost there!" Reza called from the front. He had spent enough time in and around the fields to have learned how to navigate with a sort of dead reckoning, using the sun's position and his pace count to keep him on track. "Only about fifty meters left!"

A few moments later, he breathed a sigh of relief as he saw the regular outline of the road through the last layers of wheat. He stood to one side and passed the others of his team on through first, giving Nicole a quick hug as she emerged from the trampled trail behind them.

The road would not necessarily protect them from the fire, Reza knew. But at least they could move in a direction opposite to the one that the fire was taking, keeping out of its way.

"Oh," Nicole gasped, her chest heaving with adrenaline and the effort of running what had seemed like such a long way, "*Zut alors*. I did not think–"

"Reza!" someone shrieked. "Look ou–"

The voice was suddenly cut off with a sound Reza knew all too well: the *smack* of a powerful hand striking a child's face.

Darting through the wheat to the road's edge, Reza just had time to see the other children fleeing down the road past Muldoon's van. The field master and three of his goons, his teenage hatchet men, stood in two-man cordons off to either side of where Reza stood, blocking the road. They had let the other children pass, even the one who had tried to warn Reza, because they were not of interest.

For that, at least, Reza was thankful. Without wasting another second, he disappeared back into the wheat, grabbing Nicole's hand.

"Follow me!" he hissed, dragging her along behind him.

"What is it?" she gasped.

"Muldoon," Reza replied, his breath a controlled heaving of his chest as he fought a new path through the wheat. He was desperate to avoid their pursuers, whose footsteps he could hear somewhere behind them, crashing through the stalks. "He brought some friends with him this time."

Nicole quickened her pace.

Muldoon watched as the two older boys, whom the other kids called Scurvy and Dodger, chased Reza and Nicole through the field. Climbing atop a specially fortified portion of the van's roof, Muldoon was high enough that he could see the bending and weaving of the stalks as his remote hunters closed on their quarry. The older boys were able to make better time through the wheat, especially with the trail the Gard kid left behind him. A smile of certainty crept across Muldoon's face. Gard wasn't going to get away this time, and neither was the girl. It had been easy to track their progress to the road. Now he would track them as his human hounds chased them down.

He glanced down at the other boy waiting below, whom he had dubbed Big John in honor of a certain very important part of the boy's anatomy. Muldoon had given him his own special touch over ten years ago, and the boy had been unflinchingly loyal ever since.

Big John mutely smiled back.

Reza wove through the wheat in an intricate pattern that he had learned from other kids when playing in the fields. That was in the days before Wiley had convinced him to spend that time in the library, earning himself a ticket off of Hallmark that few of the other kids would ever receive.

While it appeared to Muldoon that Scurvy and Dodger were gaining, Reza was keeping them at about the same distance, but at a cost. He and Nicole, already flushed from fleeing the fire – which still boomed and crackled around them – were getting tired. The weaving that confused their pursuers also meant that Reza and Nicole had to take at two or three steps to Scurvy and Dodger's one or two, the time being made up by the older boys hunting around for their path after missing one of Reza's sharp turns. Worse, Reza now had no idea where they were.

"Reza," Nicole gasped behind him, "we cannot run forever!"

"Don't stop!" he ordered grimly. His legs and lungs were burning as hot as the flames that consumed the wheat around them. Some of the smoke was now settling toward the ground, causing him to gag. "Keep going!"

Without warning they burst into an open quad. Reza, his legs accustomed to trampling through the wheat stalks, lost his footing and fell to the ground, skinning his palms and knees.

"Damn!" he cursed, grabbing Nicole's hands as she helped him up.

They were only thirty meters or so across the quad – less than a quarter of the way – when their pursuers appeared behind them.

"Give it up, maggot!" Scurvy cried. His acne scarred face was flushed with the exertion of running. "Game's over."

"Save it, Gard," Dodger chimed in. His lopsided eyes, one placed nearly two centimeters higher than the other, were bright with anticipation, and his brutishly large hands flexed at his sides. "You're good in the wheat, man, but you're dead meat in the open." He smiled, showing perfect vid-star teeth that were completely out of place in his lumpy face.

Reza slowed at the boy's words, then stopped.

"Reza!" Nicole cried, "What are you doing?"

"He's right," Reza told her as he caught his breath. "Those two bastards are quick. They'll catch us before we get to the wheat on the other side."

"Then what do we do?" Nicole whispered. Her eyes were fixed on the two approaching boys who now merely sauntered, apparently sure that she and Reza could not get away.

Reza smiled thinly, the fear in his eyes overshadowed by determination. "I'll have to use my secret weapon," he replied cryptically.

She watched as he reached into the little cloth bag that he always kept at his belt. Knowing what was in it – a few polished stones that she thought were pretty, some scraps of paper with names of books written on them, and a strip of leather that Reza sometimes did a parody of jumping rope with – did not make her feel any better. But her trust in him, especially now, was implicit.

Unhurriedly, he withdrew the leather strip and one of the stones, a spherical piece of quartz that he had meticulously ground and polished with the tools in Wiley's little handyman shop in the admin building's basement.

"Stand behind me," he said quietly, and Nicole gladly moved herself a few paces back, putting Reza between herself and the two advancing boys, who were now about twenty meters away.

"What's that supposed to be?" Scurvy demanded mockingly. "A wimp-sized whip?"

"Maybe he's gonna hang himself," Dodger said, laughing. "Too bad there's no tree, or we could give him a hand."

Reza paid them no attention as he placed the stone carefully in the center of the leather strap, which Nicole now saw formed a perfect pouch for the sparkling rock. He let it dangle to his side, his right wrist beginning to flex, judging the weight and response of the sling and its ammunition.

He looked up to see Scurvy and Dodger still approaching at a leisurely pace, confident in their victory. Reza's mouth was compressed in a thin line of concentration, his eye calculating the distance and speed with the accuracy of a computerized laser range finder.

"Reza," Nicole said quietly.

"Shhh," he responded softly, his mind now focused on Scurvy. In precisely measured movements, he began to rock the sling. As it built up momentum, he brought it up into an orbit above his head, the sling now a brown blur as it whirled around like a propeller blade.

Reza had become an expert in the sling's use under Wiley's tutelage, and sometimes used it to focus himself when his mind seemed listless, or just to have fun. He and the old man would have contests, setting up old food cans at various distances and then trying to see who could knock the most down the fastest. Wiley won most of the time, but Reza never pushed too hard just to win. To him, it was the camaraderie that counted, the togetherness, not who bested whom. Wiley was, in fact if not in blood, his father, and had been since the first day Reza came to this world. It was Wiley who met him at the spaceport, Muldoon having fallen ill that day, and the old man had taken the boy under his wing as if Reza was his only begotten son. It was one of the few twists of fate that had gone in Reza's favor, and he had given thanks for Wiley's patronage every day since then.

But it was now, here in a vacant quad in the middle of a burning wheat field, that the games of the past were about to show their dividends.

Scurvy and Dodger had taken notice of the whirling leather, but they had no idea what it was or what it could do. Wiley had never shown his little toy to any of the other children, and Reza had carried on the tradition.

Until now.

"Maybe he thinks he's just gonna take off," Dodger joked.

Scurvy smiled as his hand reached into the rear left pocket of his jumper, extracting a knife that Reza easily recognized, even at this distance. Illegal on most worlds because of the harder-than-diamond metallurgy that made them the galaxy's best edged weapons, the Kreelan blade now in Scurvy's hands was undoubtedly a gift bestowed on him by Muldoon. The boy's arrogant smile grew larger as he turned the knife in his hand, the blade winking with the reflected light of the sun.

With a last mental calculation, one end of the sling slipped from Reza's fingers, releasing the stone in a straight line tangent to the whirling circle over Reza's head. The buzzing of the sling sighed to a stop as it fell, empty, to Reza's side.

Scurvy had time to blink once before the stone, about the size of a large marble but much heavier, hit him precisely between the eyes. The impact staved in his forehead and drove a splinter of bone into his brain. His sightless eyes fluttered upward as his body collapsed to the ground, twitched once, and then lay still.

There was utter, complete silence in the quad. Even the crackling of the fire seemed muted.

"Son of a bitch," Dodger whispered, looking at his fallen companion. He looked at the little white rock that now lay on the ground near Scurvy's head, partly covered with his blood.

The humming of the sling began again as Reza readied his next salvo.

But Dodger was not as dull-witted as Reza had hoped. Fortunately forgetting the knife still clutched in Scurvy's dead hand, he burst into an all-out charge at Reza, his legs eating up the distance between them as Reza readied for another shot.

"Run, Nicole!" he cried.

"But, Reza–"

"Run, dammit!" he shouted as he loosed his second shot at less than ten meters range.

Nicole watched as Dodger earned his nickname, his torso performing an uncanny twist as Reza released the sling. Had Reza not aimed at the boy's center of mass rather than his head, the rock would have missed completely. As it was, it hit Dodger in the left shoulder with a hearty thump. It was enough to splinter the bone in his shoulder joint, making him stagger with pain, but it only slowed him down for a moment.

Nicole turned and fled.

Reza did not waste time trying to finesse another shot with the sling. He reached down and picked up the nearest rock and hurled it at Dodger, hitting him in the stomach and doing no damage other than making the boy even angrier. Then he turned to follow Nicole across the quad and into the wheat.

"You're dead, you little bastard!" Dodger shrieked as he held his injured shoulder, the bone splinter grinding painfully as he raced after his quarry.

* * *

Nicole was terrified. She had lost Reza, and now was lost herself. Running blindly through the wheat, her nose clotted with the smoke that swirled through the fields, she had no idea which way to go. She just ran.

Stopping for a moment to catch her breath, she wondered if she should call out to Reza. But no, she decided angrily, that would alert Dodger to her presence, and Reza might even be dead.

"I never should have left you," she cursed herself, angrily wiping away the tears of guilt that sprang to her eyes. Memories of her mother, dead because Nicole had not thought to warn her of a lethal danger, rose unbidden. Perhaps, she thought miserably, she and Reza could have beaten Dodger. She knew she should have stayed with him...

"*Merde!*" she cried quietly, pulling at her hair in self-recrimination. She had to find a way out of this, she had to find Reza. Looking at the sun, now past its zenith, she tried to guess which way to go. Picking a direction, hoping it was the right way, she headed toward where she thought the road to the orphanage might be.

Such was her surprise when, after only a few tens of meters, she burst from the wheat onto the road that led to the orphanage. Falling to her knees, she sobbed in relief, at the same time wondering what had happened to Reza, knowing that she had to find help.

"Well, I'll be," she heard a familiar voice coo from nearby. "Look what we have here."

She looked up just in time to see Muldoon's obesity blot out the sun, his shadow falling across her face like a burial shroud.

* * *

Reza's time was almost up. His legs were ready to give out, and he could hear Dodger's labored breathing close behind him. No number of maze tricks was going to save him now.

"Got you, you little freak!" Dodger cried as he latched onto the collar of Reza's shirt.

Reza tried to struggle out of it, but it was too late. He collapsed to the ground, quickly rolling onto his back to free his hands for his last great act of defiance.

Dodger straddled him, pinning him to the ground. Balling up his good fist, he said, "You're gonna pay, you little fuck," before he slammed it into Reza's face.

Reza did his best to ward off the piston-blows that rained down with unerring precision, but no war was ever won through defense alone. Leaving his face completely open to attack, Reza shot his own fist upward while Dodger was cocking his arm for another blow, managing to land a glancing hit to the older boy's injured shoulder.

Dodger let out a cry of agony, and Reza bucked his body upward and to the side like a wrestler fighting a pin, squirming from between Dodger's legs. Reza plunged away into a curtain of smoke as Dodger tried to get back on his feet.

Through the slits left him by the swelling around his battered eyes, Reza suddenly became aware that he had led himself into a trap. Flames danced all around him and his skin prickled with the heat. His nose, accustomed now to the acrid smell of smoke, could no longer screen it from his lungs, and he began to gag and cough.

"Where are you, you little son of a bitch?" he heard Dodger call from somewhere off to his left. "Come on out!"

He can't see me, Reza told himself. The smoke was a much better screen than was the wheat itself. *Now, if only I can get myself out of here*, he worried. Carefully avoiding the ravenous flames and Dodger's angry searching, Reza managed to work his way out of the fiery trap.

Behind him, lost in the smoke, he heard Dodger's voice calling, calling...

* * *

Nicole lay spread-eagled on her back inside the closed van. Muldoon's silent assistant had stuffed a rag in her mouth and bound her hands and feet to the cargo tie-downs with heavy tape. She quivered in fear, her eyes locked on the rolls of blubber emerging from Muldoon's uniform as he fought with the overstressed velcro down its front. The van was filled with the mingled scent of his body odor and the breath mints he always chewed before taking one of his pleasure rides. The smell alone made her want to gag.

The boy who had taped her to the floor had only smiled at her, no matter how much she had struggled. He had not hit her or threatened her, but treated her like she was amiss for not wanting to participate willingly, as if sure that she would chastise herself later for being so silly. He kneeled in the back of the vehicle, near her head, his eyes gleaming knowingly, as if she were about to learn a very important secret, a very special one.

"Ah," Muldoon gasped as the uniform suddenly flew open down to his crotch, releasing his manhood from its fleshy confines. "I've been waiting for you for a long time, honey," he said in quick gasps as he waddled forward on his knees, taking up station between her legs. His hands groped under her blouse, and he sighed as he squeezed her breasts. "They've grown since last time," he said over the muffled screaming that made its way through the sock stuffed in her mouth. "Did you know that?"

His hands, shaking from the adrenaline rushing through his system, worked their way down, down over her belly, then grabbed roughly between her legs, his fingers probing through her panties.

Nicole closed her eyes and fought against the wave of nausea that would kill her with the gag in her mouth. But she knew that suffocating on her own vomit would be better than succumbing to what this man had in mind. She squirmed as his fingers grabbed the elastic waistband of the flimsy panties the orphanage issued, his dirty, untrimmed fingernails scraping her tender pubis as he began to pull them down, to tear them off.

"You'll like it," he soothed. "I know I wi–"

The last word was cut off by the sudden grating of the van's cargo door as it slammed open, letting the bright glare of the sun shine into the darkened interior and momentarily blinding its occupants.

"What the hell?" Muldoon roared, whirling around like a rutting walrus facing off against a competitor, his erect penis pointing like an accusing finger toward the man who stood in the doorway.

It was Wiley. But in Muldoon's state of hormonal confusion, he did not notice the eyes that burned from under the knitted brow or the expression that had once belonged to a fierce warrior, a man who had killed – and, in a way, died – for God and country. He wasn't looking at Wiley. He was staring into the face of a colonel of the Confederation Marine Corps.

"Close that door and get out of here, you senile old fart!" Muldoon screamed, his face turning a beet red as he reached for the door. His hand faltered when he caught a glimpse of something metallic in the old Marine's hand.

Without saying a word, Colonel Hickock pumped two rounds from the pistol into Muldoon's skull. The tiny flechettes minced the big man's brain as they ricocheted within the bony structure, lacking enough velocity to make a clean exit out the back.

A third red eye gracing his forehead – the only evidence of injury and proof of the colonel's marksmanship – Muldoon somersaulted out of the van like an obscene high diver, his twitching body flopping to the dirt like a two hundred kilo bag of fertilizer.

"Come on out, son," Hickock said in a low growl that Nicole would not have recognized without seeing the man's lips move in time to the words.

Big John, his face sad now, crawled out of the van as he was told, neither his face nor his body reflecting any sign of defiance or resistance. And when the colonel turned away toward Nicole, sure that the boy was not a threat, Big John walked into the wheat field toward where the hungry fires burned. With his lover and benefactor dead, his own twisted and defiled soul had no more desire to live. Unseen and unheard, he cast himself into the flames.

"Wiley!"

The old man turned to see Reza huffing up the road from where he had emerged from the blazing fields, his face mottled with bruises and caked with blood.

"Where's Nicole?" he gasped, running up to the van, "Muldoon, he–" Then he caught sight of the mound of flesh lying motionless on the ground and the gun in Wiley's hand. "Oh, Jesus."

"Better help your girl, son," the old man said slowly, shaking his head as if something was in his ear. "And take this," he handed Reza the gun. "I won't be able to keep track of it much longer. The other kids," he went on groggily, "they came and told me what happened, and..."

The man who was Colonel Hickock never finished what he set out to say.

Taking the gun, Reza watched with soul-deep sorrow as the man's eyes suddenly transformed to reflect the good-natured innocence of Wiley the janitor. All traces of Colonel Hickock that had been there just a moment before disappeared like mist under a hot sun.

"Where's Nicole?" Wiley asked, cocking his head and looking around as if he had just come on the scene.

"Oh, God," Reza gasped, leaping into the van, terrified of what he might find. "Nicole!"

Relieved to find that she still had most of her clothes on, Reza carefully pried away the tape that covered her mouth, pulling the roll of gauze bandage out of her throat. Then he freed her hands and feet.

"Reza," she choked, hugging him so hard he heard one of his ribs crack. "Reza, I was afraid...I thought you had died."

He kissed her, and then held her even tighter, rocking her back and forth. He never wanted to let her go.

"You know what they say about bad pennies," he whispered, not willing to let on just how close he had come to losing it out there, how close he had come to losing her. "They just keep turning up."

"If Wiley had not shown up," she shuddered, "Muldoon would have–"

"Shh," Reza whispered in her ear. "Don't think about that." He looked down at Muldoon's bloated corpse. "It's over now. For good."

"Come on, kids," Wiley said quietly, his child-like eyes watching the smoke as the wind shifted back toward them, the dark curls billowing into the sky. Even in his senile state, he was no fool. There were no firefighters on Hallmark. The fires would be left to burn themselves out, and anyone caught in them would be dead or horribly maimed. "I think we'd better be getting back."

Reza helped Nicole out of the van, careful to keep her clear of Muldoon's stiffening body. She paused to give it a single look, just to make sure he was really and truly dead. Satisfied, she let Reza lead her away.

Arms around each other's waists, the three of them made their way back to Wiley's battered utility truck. They were a tiny family with no home, but with enough love to make life worth living on any world.

Four

Mon cher Reza,

Things are going so fast here. I have been here only ten months, and already I have begun the real flight training, my head now filled with tactics and maneuvers that we will only now begin to apply. I made my first flight yesterday – with an instructor, of course – and might be able to solo in another twenty flight hours.

I cannot tell you how exciting it is to fly! To be so free, strapped to such a powerful machine (*oui*, even the tiny trainers they use here!) is like nothing I have ever imagined. I have spent many hours in the simulators, but they do not do justice to the real thing. My only regret is that you are not here to share in my happiness. I know you would love it.

As you suspected, I have many 'suitors,' as you call them, but I have not the time for them. To study and learn to fly and fight is all I allow myself to be interested in, for I am determined to be the best pilot in my class. Perhaps later I will consider such things, but we have gone through too much getting me here, *non*? I will not throw that away for anything, ever.

I must go now, my brother. The Officer of the Deck is shouting for lights out, and I am so very tired. The days sometimes are so long here that it reminds me of working the fields! I will write again as soon as I can, probably next week after a class exercise that is coming up.

Please, Reza, take care of yourself and give my love to Wiley. I have leave coming up for next month and hope to find a transport to Hallmark so I may visit. I will let you know. Please – write when you can. Sometimes it is all that keeps me going.

All my love,
Nicole

Reza read the letter several times, as he always did, before he folded the paper and put it in his breast pocket. Mary, the librarian, was hardly liberal when it came to printing out hard copies of personal mail (paper – even synthetic – was very expensive), but she made an exception for Reza. He did not even bother to read Nicole's letters on the vid-screen when they first arrived, but printed them out straight away. Holding the paper in his hand when he read her words made her seem a bit closer, more real. They had agreed to write this way, rather than send personal vids. Most of the other kids thought he was crazy and ridiculously old-fashioned, but somehow it made Nicole seem more real to him. His hand strayed to the small silver crucifix around his neck, his most prized possession that he never let out of his sight. It was her gift to him on the tear-filled day when she left for Lakenheath, nearly a year ago now.

He looked out the window to watch the kids file by on the way to their noonday meal, and he wondered if Nicole would even recognize this place when she came to visit on her first leave. *When she came home*, he told himself. For that is what he had finally decided Hallmark was: home.

Muldoon's death had sparked a high-level Confederation investigation of the orphanage system and the Hallmark Farming Combine, and had resulted in nothing short of a miraculous change in the lives of the orphans. The field work, a back-breaking tradition for more than twenty years, was abolished as cruel child labor. The chief administrators of the orphanage system – not just at House 48, but all across the planet – were interviewed, cross-examined, and dismissed if they could not answer the commission's questions satisfactorily. Many of them now found themselves in prison at the sort of hard labor that the children had endured.

The farm combine itself received a tremendous fine for its part in the exploitation of the children, and more than a few of its senior managers also wound up in Confederation prisons.

All this was no surprise to Reza after he had first seen the makeup of the commission: thirty-five Navy and Marine Corps officers, with a handful of civilians from the General Counsel. Though he had been retired for quite some time, the name of Colonel William Hickock still carried a lot of weight. The Marine Corps took care of its own.

Now the orphans enjoyed three solid meals a day (although the food wasn't much better than it used to be, Reza lamented), went to school full time, and did not have to go to the fields anymore except to play baseball.

Reza had to shake his head at that, remembering how Wiley had taught them how to play the ancient Earth game in one of the open, dusty quads. The children, their minds focused on futile toil for so long, ate up what Wiley showed them. Soon there were baseball games going on all over the complex every day after school using bats, balls, and mitts that the older kids put together in the machine shops that were part of the physical plant and power generator station.

The game had spread like wildfire, and kids had been sent from almost every other house to see how it was played. There was even talk of forming a league with equipment donated by the Marine Corps. Reza was terrible when he came up to bat, but he could pitch better than anyone else in his house, and was looking forward to meeting the kids from other houses.

It would be a first for all of them.

Yes, Reza thought, *things certainly have changed.* He now spent time in the library not only because he wanted to, but because Mary had appointed him chief assistant librarian. He attended school, alternating half days and full days, depending on the courses that were being taught by the new instructors who had been brought in. He spent the rest of his time before dinner working the desk and helping the other kids who had begun to mob the little building, so much so that the administration was thinking about expanding it. Preparing school papers, reading tutorials, or just for fun, Reza had never seen so many kids here before. They had never had time under the old regime, and Reza often wondered why the combine had financed the library in the first place, it had been so little used.

Fate certainly could be fickle, he told himself wonderingly as he watched the animation on the faces of the other children, where before one could only see exhausted eyes and blank expressions.

"We're human again," he said quietly to himself, unconsciously patting Nicole's letter in his pocket

Getting up from his desk in Mary's office, Reza headed out to answer the bell at the front desk, thinking that his remaining time on Hallmark wasn't going to be so bad after all.

* * *

Thirty million kilometers away, deep in the blackness beyond the orbit of Hallmark around its yellow star, a gravity well appeared at a point without a name or special significance, warping the void around it into a vortex of space and time. As the well deepened toward infinity, it created a fleeting, transient event horizon, and matter was instantaneously injected through the tiny rift in the fabric of the universe.

A solitary Kreelan warship, an enormous battlecruiser that dwarfed any vessel ever built by Man, emerged from hyperspace. Her sublight drive activated, and she turned her raked prow onto a trajectory toward the nearby planet. Her sensors reached out before her like ethereal hounds sniffing out their quarry, searching for the planetary defense network orbiting the human world.

On what humans would have called the ship's bridge, a warrior priestess sat in the throne-like chair from which she commanded the great vessel and its crew. She tapped her ebony talons in a gesture of anticipation that had been one of her trademarks for many cycles of the Empress Moon, the sharp rapier tips eroding even the resilient metal of the chair's arm. She had left her mark in many ships of the Fleet in the hundred and more cycles of service she had rendered unto her Empress. But this ship, the *Tarikh-Da*, had always been her favorite. It was the greatest warship the Empire had ever built.

She had been greatly honored when the Empress had chosen her for this mission, for it was the first of its kind in the war against the humans. For all the cycles since the Empire had made contact with them, the ships of the Empress had come to the enemy's planets to do battle. They came to destroy these lesser beings in feats of combat to honor their ruler and expunge the plague of yet another species not worthy of Her spirit.

But this was to be different. There would be killing, yes, but only the older ones. The pups, the young, these were to be spared. They were to be taken back to the Empire.

She glanced at the tactical display, noting with satisfaction that hers was the only ship within parsecs of this *human enclave*. Not that it would have mattered, she thought. The Empire's flagship could annihilate a fleet of lesser vessels, but had never been unleashed upon the humans; it would have offered the Children of the Empress no challenge, no honor.

"Their defenses have activated," the weapons officer reported. "Orbital batteries are reorienting toward our approach vector." A pause as she studied her instruments. "There are no planetary emplacements."

Which they already knew, the priestess thought to herself. She nodded toward her subordinate, pleased with her diligence. Prudence required that they be sure. Humans would never have made such good opponents had they been perfectly predictable.

"Very well," she replied. "You may deal with them at your leisure, Mar'ya-Nagil." She did not have to add that the ship's main batteries were to remain silent; the huge guns would not only destroy any satellite defenses, but the planet's surface below, as well. "Report to me when the defenses are destroyed."

"Yes, Tesh-Dar," the young warrior replied, proud that the priestess was again in command of her vessel, the ship on which she had spent most of her own life. She turned to her task as if the Empress herself had given the command.

Tesh-Dar, high priestess of the Desh-Ka, watched the golden planet grow larger in the huge three-dimensional display before her. One hand softly drummed on the command chair, while the other reflectively probed the scar that stretched down across her left eye.

* * *

Reza was putting books back on the shelves when the raid sirens began to wail. He looked up, wondering at the sound. Drill sirens erupted frequently enough, their goat-like bleating the butt of many jokes among adults and children alike.

But this was no drill. The low, mournful growl of the raid siren boomed from a rickety tower atop the main admin building, then rose to a screeching pitch that set the windows shuddering before dropping back again.

A chill slithered its way up Reza's spine and froze him in place for a moment. His gaze met with several others nearby, all of them welded to their seats or the floor where they stood as the siren began to climb toward a deafening crescendo once again.

Then pandemonium erupted. Children and adults broke free of their momentary paralysis and began to flee. They poured from the library stacks like forest animals driven before a blazing fire, tossing about whatever they were holding like plastic confetti.

"Reza!"

He heard his name called above the commotion as people pushed through the exits and into the street beyond. The children headed for the shelter while the adults ran for the Territorial Army armory to draw their weapons.

"Reza! Where are you?"

He looked stupidly at the armload of books he was still carrying, suddenly realizing that picking up *Canton's Sonnets: A Jubilee Collection* probably was not terribly important at the moment, if for no other reason than the collection was filled with uniquely ghastly verse.

"Here, Mary!" he called, carefully putting the books down on a shelf before running to the banister that overlooked the first floor atrium.

"Reza, make sure there isn't anyone left up there, will you?" she asked, her face flushed with excitement and anxiety. "Hurry, dear, we've got to get to the shelter!" The younger children were gathered around her like ducklings to their mother, their faces registering the fear of the adults who were now running headlong to their defense posts.

Reza called back, "Go ahead and get started. I'll meet you there!"

Mary looked toward the door, then back at Reza, indecision checking her. Reza was mature for his age, but she was not sure if she should leave a boy not quite fourteen years old to his own devices in an emergency like this.

"Go on, Mary," he called quickly, deciding the matter for her. "I'll be all right."

Mary finally nodded and began herding the preschoolers and the dozen or so numbed teens out of the lobby and into the street, forming them into a line that she aimed at the huge shelter blast door a block away. A stream of bodies was already pouring into it.

"Be careful!" she cautioned him.

He waved, then turned to begin his task. Starting at the end of the second floor that was bounded by a wall and no adjoining rooms, he worked his way through the stacks, noting with amazement the number of books, disks, and other things that had wound up on the floor. It was as if an army of gremlins had declared war on his tiny domain, flinging to the floor everything they could get their tiny invisible hands on.

"God, what a mess," he murmured to himself as he continued to weave up and down the aisles, his eyes darting all around him to make sure there wasn't anyone hiding behind a cart or under a desk.

Having finished clearing the upstairs, he paused a moment to take a quick look at the sky through the windows. Everything looked normal to him: the same pale blue sky, a few scudding clouds, and the ever present fiery ball that was Hallmark's sun.

He turned away just in time to avoid being blinded by a flash that erupted from sunward and threw his shadow deep into the library's atrium.

Reacting instinctively, he dove for the nearest cover he could find, a study carrel next to the teen non-fiction section, and waited for a blast wave to come rolling across the fields from whatever had caused the explosion. A dozen seconds later came but a single thunderclap, then several more explosions that sounded like huge fireworks.

"Orbital bombardment," he muttered, daring to open one eye to peek toward the window. But nothing was visible on this side of the building.

He got up and quickly continued his sweep of the library, finishing up in the basement.

"Wiley?" he called, opening the door to his surrogate father's apartment. "Wiley? Are you here?" Quickly checking all the rooms, Reza satisfied himself that the old Marine was not there.

"Probably in the shelter," he told himself as he headed back out into the hall and bounded up the stairs into the lobby. His own feelings about the shelter were clear: while they had undoubtedly saved many lives, he still had nightmares about the one he was in on New Constantinople that had been breached. It had been a death trap, and he did not think he would be able to willingly lock himself into such a giant sarcophagus again.

As he came around the last row of books and past the desk, he caught sight through one of the tall thin windows of a black cloud rising in the direction of the spaceport. He skidded to a stop. Leaning forward, his quickened breath fogged the glass as he looked outside.

That's what the flash and explosions were, he thought grimly. A single salvo from the attacking force had obliterated the spaceport and any interceptors it could have launched, had there been any. The two defenseless grain transports there had been reduced to molten heaps of slag. Their internal explosions had sent debris, including thousands of tons of wheat from their holds, into the air to fall onto the parched fields, which were now burning out of control.

He turned his attention to House 48 itself. The complex looked dead. Nothing outside moved except the Confederation flag, which fluttered in the light breeze with all the vigor of an unenthused geriatric. The street and walkways were deserted, people having hastened somewhere else before the inevitable landing began.

Perhaps the drills will pay off, Reza thought hopefully as he watched the sky. Maybe everyone managed to get to their posts and could protect this rock from whatever the Kreelans had to throw against them, at least until the Navy could bring in some real Marines to help.

But then white streaks appeared in the sky, trailing behind tiny pinpoints that bobbed erratically as they descended: the condensation trails of incoming assault boats. Reza hissed a curse at them, wishing them to fall from the sky like rocks and crush themselves against the unyielding soil of the fields, spattering their death-dealing passengers into lifeless jelly.

He stood there, counting them as they wound their way down, some arcing far away over the horizon toward the other houses and the few actual settlements Hallmark could boast. His hopes withered as he counted more and more, finally dying out completely as he reached fifty. And still more trails swarmed from the sky.

"Oh, God," he moaned. Hallmark's tiny Territorial Army – more than half of them untrained teenage orphans – could field a little over two thousand soldiers across the entire planet. But even if they had all reached their positions, and Reza doubted they had, it would not be enough. Not nearly enough.

The crackle of light weapon fire startled him. He looked to his right just in time to see a group of six camouflaged human figures diving for cover behind one of the thick stone fences in the House 48 complex.

A line of enemy warriors suddenly appeared out of the waving stalks of wheat at the end of town, coming in behind the humans crouched by the wall. Not being professional soldiers or killers from birth as were their opponents, the squad of defenders did not realize that they were being flanked. For the Kreelans, they were nothing more than a target of opportunity.

"No!" Reza shouted, banging his fists on the glass in a futile attempt to warn the defenders as the Kreelans filtered through an old gap in the wall that had never been repaired, their ebony armor glinting with Death's promise. "Look behind you!" He watched helplessly as the encirclement began to close like a hangman's noose, and he wished desperately for some way to warn them.

But it was too late. The Kreelans swept down upon the unsuspecting amateur soldiers like vultures converging on a dying man, too weak and confused to defend himself from their frenzied slashing and tearing. Reza watched the gleam of the blades as they hacked and pierced their victims, the Kreelans disdaining the use of energy weapons in any fight at close quarters.

He thought he saw a soldier reach out a bloody arm toward him, his face contorted in a plea for help, for mercy. In that instant, he was sure that the face was his father's.

Reza closed his eyes as the blade fell.

* * *

Wiley was lying on his back under the old truck, tinkering with one of the servos that acted as a brake motor on the left rear wheel when he heard the thunder of the attack on the spaceport.

"What the devil?" he cried, banging his head hard on the old hauler's frame as he tried to sit up. Gasping in pain, he flopped back down on the dolly, his hands clutching his temples as his head threatened to burst with pain. "Lord of the Universe," he muttered, blinking his eyes.

But the eyes were no longer those of Wiley the janitor. They were hard and commanding, as the body and mind once had been. When the sound of the two grounded transports blowing apart reached his ears a moment later, he reacted as if a different man had inherited the old body. Without hesitation, he pulled himself completely under the truck in case the ceiling of the garage collapsed.

When it was clear that he was in no immediate danger, he moved out from under the truck with a grace and speed extraordinary for a man his age, moving his artificial leg with the finesse of a dancer. After hitting the switch that opened the garage's rust-streaked articulated door, he jumped into the truck's cab and started backing out through the still-opening door into the blinding sunlight beyond.

He raced down the rough track that connected the garage complex with House 48's main buildings a few kilometers away, keeping his eyes on the sky. He ground his teeth when he saw the telltale streaks appear that heralded a landing with boats only, no decoys. He muttered a curse, knowing that the Kreelans must have been completely confident of an easy victory to leave such targets open to anti-air defenses, had any existed.

But this was Hallmark, not Ballantyne, or Sevastopol', or Earth. The keen military mind that had temporarily retaken its proper place in the battered skull knew that Hallmark was about as easy a target as an invader could wish for. The Kreelans always preferred more heavily defended planets, but it was no excuse for leaving a world like this one so lightly defended. With the orbital satellites gone, there was nothing standing between the invaders and the children but Hallmark's joke of a Territorial Army. They didn't stand a chance.

With a white-knuckled grip on the steering wheel, Colonel William Hickock raced toward House 48 as the first exchanges of ground fire began.

* * *

"Mary, the door has to be closed!" the man said, his voice flushed with fear as his finger hovered over the oversized red button. It was the emergency control for the massive vault's blast doors and glowed like a flickering coal.

"But Reza hasn't come back from the library!" she protested hotly, prepared to come to blows with the man if his finger moved any closer to the door controls.

"Look behind you, woman," the man demanded, pointing over Mary's shoulder with his other hand. "There's nearly a thousand people in here, the Blues are popping rounds off out there, and you want me to keep this damned thing open?"

"What's going on?" a steely voice suddenly demanded.

They turned back to the doorway to see Wiley striding across the hash-marked frame of the meter-thick blast door.

"Why isn't this door closed, Parsons?" he growled. Wiley leaned past the open-mouthed Parsons to hit the button himself. The enormous door immediately began to cycle closed.

"But Wiley," Mary blurted, suddenly realizing that the man before her wasn't the one who normally wore this body, "Reza's still out there!"

The old colonel's eyes narrowed. "Where?"

"In the library," she said. "I asked him to make sure everyone else got out. He said he–"

Wiley did not wait for her to finish. In one smooth motion he snatched the flechette rifle from Parsons and disappeared back out the door as it closed.

"Hey!" Parsons shouted indignantly after him. "That's mine!"

But he did not try to pursue the old man as the door thrummed into its lock, the huge bolts driving home to seal them in, and the enemy out.

They hoped.

* * *

Reza found himself frozen at the window, watching the enemy's advance. The landing boats had set down in a rough circle around the house complex, and the warriors they had been carrying were now emerging from out of the wheat like black-clad wraiths, their armor bristling with weapons. He couldn't hear any more firing, and figured that the last of the defenders had been mopped up. It had been a massacre.

That was why Reza had decided not to make a run for the shelter. There was no point. Assuming he was not cut down on the way there, he would certainly be trapped in a tomb that the Kreelans could open without too much difficulty. The shelter's vault should hold them off for a while, but not nearly long enough for human reinforcements to arrive.

Only one thing really puzzled him: why hadn't the Kreelans used their ships' guns to blast the vault like they did the freighters at the spaceport? Why go to the trouble of making a landing at all?

He was startled by the sound of small arms fire from right outside the library, followed by someone crashing through the front door, knocking the smoothly turning cylinder off its bearings.

Dropping without a sound to the floor under the heavy desk he had dragged near the upstairs windows, he waited for the inevitable.

"Reza!" he heard a voice unexpectedly shout from below. "Are you here, boy?"

Reza thought the voice sounded vaguely familiar, but he could not quite place it. Not knowing that the Kreelans had never been known to use such tricks to lure humans into a trap, like a timid snake he slowly slithered toward the banister to take a cautious look.

"Son?" the voice shouted again.

"Wiley?" Reza asked incredulously as he saw the old man crouching near the front door. "Is that you?"

"Lord of All, son!" he shouted. He gestured sharply for Reza to come to him. "Get your butt down here! We've got to get out of this place–"

A Kreelan warrior suddenly leaped through the damaged entryway, rolling with catlike agility to her feet.

In the blink of an eye, Wiley's finger convulsed on the trigger of his flechette rifle, hitting the Kreelan's torso armor with half a dozen rounds that killed her instantly. The impact flung her body against the wall. Her mouth still open in a silent snarl, she slumped to the floor, her talons twitching at the tips of her armored fingers.

With a pirouette that Reza thought should have been impossible for a man with one stiff, artificial leg, Wiley turned and fired another volley into the warrior's partner, whose shoulder armor had caught on the lip of the canted entry cylinder door and prevented her from raising her own weapon. Her head vanished in a plume of bloody spray and gore.

"Come on, boy," the colonel beckoned, "while we still have time."

Reza wasted no time in bounding down the stairs to the lower level, hurling himself into the old man's waiting arms.

"What... what happened?" he asked, looking up at the bloody smear on Wiley's forehead where he had knocked his head against the frame of the old truck. "I almost didn't recognize your voice."

The colonel's face broke into an ironic grin. "Seems God chose to give me back my marbles for one last game," he said, holding Reza to him with one arm while the other held the flechette rifle pointed at the entranceway. "Listen," Wiley said, "I don't know how long I'll be any good to you, son. This thing," he tapped his temple, "can short out at any time, assuming the Blues don't get us first." He reached down to grab the strangely contoured rifle the first Kreelan warrior had been carrying. "Take this," he said, passing the flechette rifle to Reza, keeping the alien weapon for himself. "All you have to do is point and shoot. Just don't hold the trigger down too long or you'll be out of ammo before you know it."

"Wiley," Reza whispered as they crouched down near the Kreelan's body, "what are we going to do? There are Kreelans all over the place. I saw them from the upstairs windows. I suppose the people in the shelter will be safe for a while, but–"

"Baloney," the old man spat. "Those shelters are the damned most foolish things anybody ever dreamed up. All they do is trap people in one place and make it easy for the Blues. It'd be better to give every kid a rifle and bayonet and teach them how to use it as they grow." He looked pointedly at Reza. "But who's going to give a planet full of orphans their own weapons?"

He suddenly closed his eyes and rubbed his forehead with an age-spotted hand.

Reza saw that hand shaking as a tear rolled down the old colonel's face.

"I'm starting to lose it, boy," he muttered, his mouth drawn in a thin, determined line. "Wiley the Clown is knocking on the door–"

A muffled boom that set the windows rattling and dust sprinkling from the ceiling stole away the end of his sentence. The two of them stared at each other in the silence that followed, wondering what the noise had been.

"Maybe the Navy..." Reza began, but a gesture from Wiley cut him off.

"The squids aren't going to hit a friendly site from orbit," he whispered hoarsely. "They'd send in Marines. Every ship bigger than a corvette carries at least a company."

Then they heard the spitting of Kreelan light arms fire and someone screaming, but while the scream was only from a single terror, it had many, many voices.

"Oh, my God," Wiley said, closing his eyes. "They breached the shelter."

Reza thought of Mary worrying about him, whether he would be all right by himself until he could get to the safety of the shelter. And now all of them – a thousand or more children and adults – were being massacred. Reza started to shake.

"Boy," Wiley said quickly, afraid that both he and Reza would lose their will and their wits if he waited but a moment longer, "it's now or never. You're going to have to make a run for it on your own." Reza opened his mouth to protest, but Wiley hushed him with a finger across his lips. "I can't go with you, son. I'm too old and too slow, and my brain's going to turn to mush again here pretty soon. I can feel it."

He took something out of his coat pocket, the one over his heart, the only one on his janitor uniform that had a button on it. It was an envelope, plain except for the Confederation Marine Corps seal at the closure.

"I wrote this the same night I wrote the one for Nicole," Wiley told him. "I knew you wouldn't need it for a few years, but when you have a noggin like mine, you do what you can when you can. Here," he said, pushing it into the boy's hands. "Read it."

Reza opened it to find a single sheet of paper inside. But the paper was by no means ordinary. In addition to the embossed Marine Corps emblem that showed through the paper when held up to the light, it carried the symbols of two Confederation Medals of Honor, the Confederation's highest award for valor in the face of the enemy. During the course of the war, only fifteen men and women had ever won two such honors; the Medal of Honor was almost always given posthumously. Colonel William Hickock had been one of those fifteen, and the only one who still lived. The words that were scrawled on the page were few and to the point:

To Whom It May Concern:

Being of sound mind and body as I write this, I submit that the young man bearing this document, Reza Sarandon Gard, be considered for acceptance into the military academy of his choice upon reaching the Confederation legal age of decision, that being fifteen years from his stated date of birth.

The Confederation Services will find no finer pupil for the military arts and the leadership on which the Confederation depends for its continued survival.

(Signed,)
William T. Hickock
COL, CMC (Ret.)

"Wiley," he began, "I don't know what to say..."

"It's the least I can do," the old man said quietly. "If it's what you want, that'll give you a little muscle to get past some of the stuck-up boneheads screening people for the academies." He looked around, as if he had suddenly forgotten something "But that's for another time," he said as he stuffed the envelope and its precious contents into a pocket in Reza's shirt. "You've got to get out of here, son." He looked hard at Reza, then pointed to the flechette rifle in the boy's hands. "Think you can handle that thing?"

"Yes, sir," Reza replied in a voice that sounded small and alone. "But–"

"No *buts*, boy," Wiley said gently, but firmly, leaving no room for argument. "This is it. For real. I'll try to create a diversion for you." He nodded toward where the screams from the breached shelter still rose and fell like pennants in a gale. "Besides," he went on quietly, his voice echoing memories from another life that Wiley the janitor had never known, "I want to die the man I used to be. Not as some senile broom pusher." His eyes pierced Reza. "You understand that, don't you?"

Reza nodded, biting back the tears he felt coming, remembering how he and his real father had parted a lifetime ago. *It's happening all over again*, he thought wretchedly. "Yes, sir," he choked.

"Do whatever you can to stay alive, son," Wiley told him softly. "If anybody can make it out of this, you can." He embraced Reza tightly.

"I love you," Reza said, holding on to his adopted father for the last time.

"I love you, too, son," Wiley said, stroking the boy's hair, fighting back his own tears.

Reluctantly, Wiley let go. Then he rose in a crouch, holding his artificial leg behind him like a kangaroo's tail for balance. "Good luck, Marine," he said.

This was how he wanted it, Reza told himself. He only wished it could be some other way. "You too, colonel," Reza said, snapping his arm up in a sharp salute.

The old man saluted him in return before making his way to the front door. After pulling the second Kreelan warrior's body into the lobby and clearing the exit, he squeezed through to disappear into the street beyond.

Feeling as if he were trapped in a holographic nightmare, Reza turned and made his way to the emergency escape at the rear of the library. Peering through the adjacent window, he saw that the area behind the library was clear, at least as far as he could see. The closest wheat fields were about two hundred meters away. Maybe a minute of hard running, he guessed. *Only a minute. Plenty of time to die.*

Holding the flechette rifle close to his side, he pushed open the door and headed outside, the door's emergency alarm blaring uselessly behind him.

* * *

Wiley crouched near the rock wall, not too far from the first group of soldiers that Reza had seen being wiped out by the attacking Kreelans. He had exchanged the alien weapon for a pulse rifle and a spare magazine from one of the dead soldiers. The pulse rifle was a bit heavier than the flechette guns, but had more firepower in its crimson energy bolts than a flechette could ever hope to boast. Unfortunately, their higher cost made them a low volume commodity on all but the best-equipped worlds.

He snaked forward along the wall, trying to get a glimpse of what was happening at the shelter. The firing had stopped, as had most of the screaming.

"What are you bitches up to?" he wondered aloud as he peered through a hole in the wall toward the admin building.

Kreelan warriors were clustered about the entrance to the vault, standing in two lines that extended from the vault's entryway where the great door had been blasted from its hinges, to where a vehicle resembling a flatbed trailer hovered in the center of the street. The warriors were passing objects from one to another, moving them from the vault to the carrier.

Bodies, Wiley thought. They're taking the bodies away.

The lone wail that suddenly pierced the air made his blood run cold. He watched as a child, five or six years old, emerged from the vault and was passed along the chain of warriors like a bucket in a fire brigade to where the other bodies were being stacked on the carrier. There, a Kreelan in a white robe – a type of alien that Wiley had never seen or heard tell about – did something to the child, who suddenly was still.

His eyes surveyed the carrier closely, and he noticed two things: there were no adults, only children, and the children apparently were not dead, just sleeping. Drugged or stunned.

The old man's mind reeled. There had never been a confirmed report of prisoners being taken in the war against the Empire. Sometimes, for reasons never understood, the Kreelans would leave survivors. But never had they taken prisoners.

Yet, here they were, making off with a few hundred children from this house alone. If they were doing the same at the other houses, they would be leaving with tens of thousands of children.

"I've got to get out a message, a warning," he whispered to himself.

But a presence behind him, a feeling that he was no longer alone, removed that concern from his mind forever.

He whirled in time to see a huge enemy warrior standing behind him, her form lost in the sun's glare, sword raised above her head. His old arm tried to bring the rifle around, his teeth bared in a snarl that matched the Kreelan's, but he wasn't fast enough. The warrior plunged her sword through his unarmored chest, burying the weapon's tip in the ground beneath Wiley's back.

His hand convulsed on the trigger of his rifle as he saluted Death's coming, sending nearly a full magazine blasting into the rock wall around them. And as the blood stopped surging through his arteries and his body lay still, he made a remarkable observation through his still-open eyes as the warrior knelt down to collect a lock of his hair: the Kreelan carried a scar over her left eye that was identical to Reza's.

* * *

Pushing his way through the chafing wheat, Reza heard the hammering of a rifle and stopped in his tracks. He knew that it must be Wiley, and that the old Marine would never have fired off a full magazine like that unless he was in dire trouble.

He hesitated, wondering if he should go back, desperately wanting to. He knew that Marines did not leave their own behind, and Wiley was one of his own. He felt the envelope with Wiley's letter burning in his breast pocket, and his indecision made him feel unworthy of it.

But he knew it would be too late. If Wiley were in trouble, there would be no helping him. And that was the way the old Marine had wanted to die, Reza reflected somberly. He silently hoped that he had taken out a dozen of the aliens with him.

Damn them all to Hell, he cursed.

Completely alone now, he continued on through the wheat, not knowing where he was going, no longer caring.

* * *

He had been walking for nearly half an hour when he heard the aerospace vehicle's screaming engines. He threw himself into the dirt just as its dark shape passed directly overhead.

"I think I've had it," he murmured, clutching at the flechette rifle as he lay still. He could hear the ship somewhere nearby, no doubt dropping off a hunting party. *Maybe more than one*, he thought glumly as he heard the ship move off to his left and hover again.

Then the ship left, its engines a muted roar against the wind, and Reza decided it was time to move. He got into a crouch and quietly made his way forward. Pushing aside some wheat stalks, he found himself face-to-face with a Kreelan warrior.

Death was literally staring him in the face.

With a cry of surprise, the Kreelan suddenly flew backward through the wheat, her body carried by the volley of flechettes fired from Reza's rifle. The reflexive spasm by his right index finger on the weapon's trigger had been the narrow margin between his life and her death.

Shaking like a leaf from the adrenaline surge, he quickly forged onward through the wheat, his heart hammering in his ears as his mind relived the brief battle a thousand times in the blink of an eye. He looked about wildly for more warriors, but with visibility of less than a meter, it would be another chance encounter, with the odds stacked well against him. Fate would not favor him a second time.

Unexpectedly, he burst onto an open quad. While he desperately wanted to cross over the clear ground instead of struggling through the wheat, he knew that to be seen was to be killed.

But the sounds of pursuit that suddenly arose above the wind and the whispers of the stalks as they caressed one another made his decision. There was no going back the way he had come. He pounded across the field at a full run, glancing back over his shoulder for signs of the enemy. The sound of his footsteps and his labored breathing thundered in his ears, as if his senses became more sensitive the further he went across the quad.

"No!" Reza shouted as the Kreelan ship suddenly shot overhead to hover directly above him. He raised the rifle and fired, but the flechettes merely ricocheted harmlessly, not even scratching the vessel's hull. He stumbled, dropping the rifle, then began again to run toward the safety of the wheat, which beckoned to him from the far side of the quad.

I might make it, he thought hopefully, as his legs pumped and his chest heaved. He bolted the last few meters to the waiting wall of golden wheat.

A Kreelan warrior, crouching unseen, suddenly rose up in front of him. The weapon she held looked incredibly huge. She squeezed the trigger.

For a moment Reza went blind and his ears rang from the buzz of a thousand angry wasps. But then he suddenly felt as if something soft and warm had embraced him, driving the air out of his lungs and the strength from his limbs. He crashed through the first few rows of wheat to land, unconscious, at the warrior's feet.

* * *

"These animals have all met the standards you set forth, priestess," the young warrior declared, her head lowered to honor her superior.

Tesh-Dar ran her eyes across the hundreds of human children arrayed like so much cordwood near the base of the shuttle, their bodies stunned and then drugged into a stasis sleep for the long journey ahead. Knowing – and caring – little about human physiological development, Tesh-Dar had set height as the main criterion for selection, as it was a convenient reference, easily measured. Any child taller than about one and a half meters was not acceptable. And therefore would die.

"Carry on, child," she ordered, returning her subordinate's salute and watching as they went about loading the human pups for transport to the great ship waiting in orbit. Across the planet, thousands of other human young were being collected for transport back home. Back to the Empire.

The sound of an approaching scout flyer drew her attention as it settled into a hover nearby. The clawed landing gear hummed from recesses in its belly and locked as it settled to the dusty patch of ground that served as their main landing zone.

Several warriors descended from the gangway before it had finished opening, bearing two bodies between them. The first, a small human, was deposited unceremoniously at the edge of the enormous pile of humans that would be left behind to die when Tesh-Dar's party took their leave of this world. Hundreds of them lay there, many long since crushed to death by the inert weight of those on top. Few, except for the adults who had been killed out of hand, bore any blast or penetration wounds. After being stunned and measured, they were simply discarded like trash.

The second body, Tesh-Dar saw, was that of a warrior, her chest armor riddled with the tiny holes made by the humans' flechette weapons.

Curious, nodding toward the dead warrior, Tesh-Dar asked, "What happened to her?"

The lead warrior, an elder as old as Tesh-Dar but far less accomplished, replied, "A young human killed her as he fled through the vegetation." She flicked a glance at the tiny human body, her cobalt blue face passionless. "Kumar-Etana was not fast enough, it would seem." She turned back to Tesh-Dar. "We stunned the animal, but it was not within your parameters, priestess."

Tesh-Dar nodded for the warriors to continue their duties, her mind idly pondering the likelihood of such a situation. She had noted the size of the human when they threw it onto the open grave, and it was far too small to have been trained as a warrior. Yet, it had killed Kumar-Etana, who had never been noted for sloth in combat, in what Tesh-Dar had implicitly understood to be a fair match.

Curious, Tesh-Dar allowed herself to be drawn to the mountain of dying humanity. Pitiful cries rose from the heaps of flesh as the effects of the stun wore off, for those humans who would not be leaving with her were not given the stasis drug.

Prodding one or two of the bodies with her sandal, she stepped to where her warriors had left the small human who had killed Kumar-Etana. It lay face-down, its frail form wrapped in clothing that was torn and battered. She hooked one powerful foot under the animal's left side and lifted, flipping the body over onto its back.

"The scar," she gasped as she saw the creature's face. Kneeling next to the human, she touched the scar over its left eye, wondering if it was possible for another human to have such a mark.

But, no, she decided, after studying the pup's face. The hair was darker perhaps than it had been that night, and the scar had lengthened as the skin stretched with growth. But on this creature she could clearly see the face of the pup she had nearly killed those few cycles ago. The one whose scar she shared.

Her mind probed into the human's spirit, examining the ethereal thing that lived within the shell of flesh as she might an insect pinned to a tree. It did not sing as did her spirit, but there was no denying that it was the same human.

"Much have you grown, little one," she said to the still form, fingering the human knife that still rested in her waist belt, a treasured curio she valued for the memories it brought to her. "And, perhaps, much may you yet learn."

Effortlessly, she picked Reza up in her arms and carried him to the healers who were preparing the other human children for transport. "This one shall go, as well," she ordered, setting him down next to a little African girl whose skin was as black as Tesh-Dar's armor. "Ensure that he survives."

"As you command, priestess," the healer replied as she continued her tasks. Tesh-Dar watched as the boy was drugged into stasis for his voyage to the Empire. As the healer worked, stripping everything from the pale body down to the skin before injecting the necessary potions, Tesh-Dar saw her remove a tiny object from around the boy's neck, tossing it toward the pile of human debris that would be left behind.

Effortlessly, the priestess snatched it from the air and held it up to the yellow light of the planet's sun. Its shape and manufacture intrigued her. It must have been of great importance, she thought, for the young animal to be wearing it around its neck.

"Curious," she murmured, glancing at the child, who was now being wrapped in amoebic tissue as if he were being rolled into the tight embrace of a pulsating, living rug. It would keep him alive for the long voyage ahead.

With a final nod to the healer, Tesh-Dar put the small cross of shiny metal into the pouch in which she collected her trophies before heading toward the shuttle's landing ramp to await the time of their departure.

* * *

The sun had not yet set when the Kreelans lifted from Hallmark with their human cargo. Once back aboard the battlecruiser *Tarikh-Da*, Tesh-Dar resumed her place on the bridge and began the final stage of their visit into human space.

The human survivors – those who were conscious – left behind on Hallmark rejoiced as the last of the Kreelan shuttles left for orbit. But their revelry was to be short-lived.

Seventy-seven black spheres, each about five meters across, were dispatched at precisely timed intervals from special bays arrayed along the *Tarikh-Da's* flanks. One after another, sometimes in pairs, they flitted away like melancholy balloons, seeking their orbital nodes with unerring accuracy to form a shell around Hallmark.

The last was launched from the battlecruiser only moments before the ship broke orbit for its jump point. As the *Tarikh-Da* sped away, a signal from the ship initiated the detonation sequence of the seventy-seven orbital weapons. In moments, Hallmark's atmosphere was transformed into a cloud of churning plasma, and the planet's surface temperature soared to that of molten lead.

Four hours later, when the lone Kreelan warship jumped into hyperspace, Hallmark had been scoured clean of all signs of life.

* * *

Nicole's flight bag was so full that she had to sit on it to get it to close. She had found half a dozen books for Reza and some chocolates for Wiley, and somehow had stuffed them all into the bag, along with her clothes.

Having won the battle with the flight bag, she appraised herself in the mirror. Trim and dashing in her dress black Navy uniform, her epaulettes carried the single thin stripe of cadet ensign, and her boots shone like mirrors. Even though the trip itself would take nearly a week – a third of her leave – she wanted to look her best for them from the start. For her friends. For her family. She got along well with the other cadets (even the upperclassmen) and the instructors, but Reza and Wiley were her only family.

She had half an hour to catch the shuttle that would take her to the orbiting freighter and on to the first leg of her trip to Hallmark. Hefting her bag, she had just started down the hallway toward the elevators when a voice caught her from behind.

"Carré!"

She turned to find three of her friends rushing toward her. They all looked as if they had just lost a close relative.

"*Oui, mes amis?*" she asked as an unpleasant tingle ran up her spine.

"Nicole," Seana, her roommate asked quietly, "have you heard?"

"Heard what?" Nicole asked, her throat constricting with foreboding. The three of them looked at one another in a manner Nicole had seen often enough. It was the unspoken vote as to who would break the bad news.

"What is it?" Nicole demanded.

Seana looked at her two companions and knew she was the one who had to do this. She was Nicole's roommate and the best friend Nicole had here. But this was a duty she did not want to perform. Nicole always talked about the orphan boy on Hallmark, referring to him as her brother (although Seana knew that Nicole was deeply in love with him), and doted on the old man – a Marine hero, she had said – who was her surrogate father. Sometimes all the talking about the boy annoyed Seana, who could not wait to get away from her own four brothers. But she could not deny the obvious love the girl felt for the boy and the old Marine, and she had come to find that listening to Nicole made her think more about how much she missed her own family.

And now this.

"Nicole," Seana said, taking a step closer to her friend and gently putting a hand on her shoulder. "A report came in across the op's desk. A week ago, something happened... on Hallmark." She paused, unsure as to how to continue, her mouth working as if she were chewing something unpalatable, indigestible.

"Dammit, Seana," Nicole lashed out, her heart thundering with dread, "what is it?"

"The Kreelans attacked Hallmark, Nicole," Seana said softly, ready to break down in tears herself. Then she went on with the brutal truth, knowing that Nicole would not tolerate any of the candy coating so many others needed to take with their dose of tragedy. "They used something – some kind of new weapon, or so the rumor goes – that burned away the planet's entire atmosphere. The surface..." She shook her head. "There was nothing left." Her voice had fallen to a whisper as she watched the blood drain from Nicole's face.

José finished it for her. "There were no survivors, and no record of what happened during the attack, except some debris from the orbital defense network. That's the only reason they're sure it was an attack instead of some bizarre natural disaster or something."

"That's enough, José," Seana told him. "I think she gets the picture."

Nicole did not hear her. The flight bag that she had been clutching so tightly in eager anticipation of her departure fell to the floor with an empty thud, the precious books and chocolates now dead weight without destination or purpose. The image of Hallmark boiled into her mind, the planet's atmosphere burning away, incinerating the surface as it blew off into space. Tens of thousands of human bodies swirled in its wake.

"*Non*," Nicole murmured, shaking her head slowly as first Reza's, and then Wiley's face swam out of the maelstrom, the flesh burning away until there was nothing left but a charred husk, the jaws locked open in an unending scream of agony. "*Mon Dieu, pourquoi?*" she whispered, her hands pressed tightly to her eyes to shut out the living nightmare. The only family left to her had been torn away like a tender sapling in a brutal whirlwind, spinning away into darkness. "Why? Oh, God, why?"

But God had no answer. He stood silently by as she collapsed into her friends' waiting arms.

FIVE

Reza awoke with a blinding headache, waves of pain pounding inside his head in a symphony of agony. He was not sure how long he had been floating on the edge of consciousness, but bit by bit he came to the conclusion that he was still in one piece, alive.

He tried to open his eyes, but his eyelids were solidly gummed shut. With a seemingly Herculean effort, he managed to pop them open with a sickeningly loud crackle. Mercifully, the light in this place, wherever he was, was turned down low, the features around him lost in shadow, blurry. He felt some sort of bedding underneath him, hairy and thick like an animal hide, its faint musky odor reminding him of the real leather coat he had seen Mary Acherlein sometimes wear to the library before she went out on a date.

As his hands probed his surroundings, he incidentally discovered that he was completely naked. Any other time he might have tried to be modest. Right now, however, he was still in too much pain, and the memories of the attack on Hallmark filled him with dread.

He sensed movement to his right. Much to his regret, he tried to turn his head. The resulting typhoon of pain threatened to render him unconscious again, but after a moment it began to subside. He stifled a groan and tried to keep himself from recoiling as the Kreelan who had been silently sitting next to him applied a cool, moist cloth to his forehead.

"Who are you?" he murmured at the blurred shadow with blue skin, the sound of his voice reverberating painfully in his skull. His forehead tingled from whatever the cloth had been soaked in. The Kreelan held it there for a few moments, watching him with the inscrutable expression of a reptile.

She reached to her side to pick up a wide-brim cup holding a foul smelling concoction. She lifted his head with one hand, careful not to scratch his skin with her talon-like nails, and put the cup to his lips. He vainly tried to turn his head away. The smell of the cup's contents forced him to the brink of vomiting.

"Drink." The alien's command, spoken in Standard with the husky voice of one used to being obeyed, caught Reza completely by surprise. He involuntarily gaped at her, never having heard of a Kreelan speaking in a human language, and she used the opportunity to toss the oily liquid down his throat. That left him with no choice but to swallow it quickly or drown. He decided to swallow, as his benefactress looked in no mood to try and resuscitate him.

"Ugh!" he croaked, trying with all his might to keep from throwing up. The alien pinned him with one silver-nailed hand and forced him to drink the dregs that remained in the cup. "Oh, God," he gasped, "what is that?"

Not surprisingly, she did not respond. Instead, she gave him a cup of water to chase down the offensive brew. After he had drunk it all, she released him, taking the cloth and wiping his face and neck free of the liquid that had spilled from his lips. She threw the cloth into a small earthen bowl and returned her gaze to Reza.

"What is your name?" she asked in eerily accented Standard, her white fangs glistening as she spoke.

Reza saw that her skin was as smooth and sleek as the handmade porcelain he had seen in a spaceport shop once, with lips that were a very deep red and lustrous as satin in the soft light. Her silver-flecked cat's eyes, perfectly spaced above a sleek nose that probably was much more adept at its job than his, were clear and bright, taking in everything in an instant. The talons on the ends of her fingers were short and silver, and stood in marked contrast to the gold-trimmed ebony neckband with its hanging pendants that was a trademark feature of every Kreelan ever observed by humanity. Had she not been the enemy, she might have been considered beautiful.

"Reza," he said, choking back the pain in his head. "Reza Gard."

She gave a quiet huff at the information. "This," she held up the cup that had held the horrible liquid, "will relieve your pain and allow you to begin soon."

"Begin what?" he asked. He looked around again. "Where am I? And who are you?"

His warden narrowed her eyes. Then she reached forward with one hand and flicked a single finger against Reza's still-throbbing skull. He gasped at the pain.

"Animals do not ask questions," she growled. But after a moment she went on – whether in answer to Reza's questions or as part of a prepared speech, he did not know – in near perfect Standard, spoken slowly as if Reza were a complete imbecile. "I am Esah-Zhurah." She considered him silently for a moment. "You, and those like you, were chosen by the Empress to come among Her Children, that you may be shown the Way, so that She may know if animals such as you have a soul."

For a moment, Reza was simply shocked, but then her words gave rise to anger. "Of course I have a soul, you–"

She flicked his head again, harder this time, and Reza let out a yelp of pain.

"That," she hissed, "you will have ample time to demonstrate, human."

She suddenly stood up. "You will rest now," she ordered. "When I return, you will be ready to begin. We have much to do." With that, she disappeared down a dim hallway, her black armor and braided jet hair melding into the shadows.

Shaken and confused, Reza wondered what new Hell he had fallen into, and if anyone else from Hallmark was still alive.

* * *

In the days that followed, Reza found himself clothed in animal skins and introduced to the "apartment" (he had no idea what else to call it) that was to be his world for the foreseeable future. There were no windows, nor could he open the door he thought might lead to the outside world, whatever it was. There was a single main chamber in which he himself slept, as well as an atrium (with walls too tall to climb) containing an open pit fireplace that served as a kitchen. The second door in the apartment led to the Kreelan girl's room. Both doors were kept firmly locked.

Air vents, much too small for his growing body to negotiate, were arrayed about the apartment and kept the air from getting stale, although it was always either too hot or too cold. This did not bother his keeper, and he decided not to let it bother him, either. He had lived through much worse in the fields, and even the Kreelan girl was more socially palatable than Muldoon had been.

Each day began with the same ritual, a portion of roasted meat brought to his bedside by the Kreelan (she apparently did not trust him in the kitchen) and however much water he chose to drink. She did not eat with him, but watched silently, as if she were observing a rodent in a psychology experiment, taking notes in her head. The only time he asked her if there was anything else to eat – vegetables or fruit, perhaps – she had grabbed his meat from him and disposed of it somewhere, refusing to feed him for the next two days.

He did not make that mistake again.

Once the morning meal was over, she sat him down in the atrium and began to teach him their language and a seemingly endless series of obscure customs and protocols, grilling him mercilessly on what he had been taught as they stopped for the mid-day ration of meat and water. The language came to him quickly, but many of the other things she tried to teach him –

so much of it based on a hierarchical symbology of Kreelan history that was often totally beyond him – were difficult to understand at all, let alone absorb and remember. But he tried, and quickly he learned.

During these inquisitions, her reactions to his answers varied from thoughtful contemplation to severe beatings that left him with bleeding welts and horrendous bruises that did not go down for days. He had learned to accept them quietly, as protest or complaint only seemed to make the treatment more severe, and he did not feel quite strong enough to challenge her. Yet. Survival was paramount, but his pride ensured that he looked her in the eye, even if he had to pry them open from the swelling to do so.

When the endless hours of study were over, she returned him to his room where she directed him to exercise. She did not care what he did, as long as he expended energy doing it. He did pushups, sit-ups, and chin-ups from the rafters in the ceiling, or just jumped up and down on the pad of skins that was his bed. He did this for as long as he had to, for to stop before she ordered was to invite anything from a scolding to a beating, generally depending on how well he had done during the preceding learning period.

After that, she made him wash himself from the cold water that dribbled from an open pipe in one wall of his room that provided water for drinking, washing, and sanitation. This was also when he discovered that modesty was something the Kreelans apparently did not believe in. After the first few times he had to stand naked under the frigid water and Esah-Zhurah's equally frigid stare, he stopped feeling embarrassed. His haste to get dressed was more to get warm and dry than to conceal his nakedness from her alien eyes.

Then there was the evening meal, consisting of yet more meat and water, after which he was allowed to collapse into an exhausted sleep.

He was able to keep this up for what he thought must have been several months before he realized that he was becoming ill, and he was fairly sure of its cause: malnutrition. He knew that his body could not survive on meat alone. While it was adapting as well as it could after the trauma of the voyage to wherever he was now, given enough time his present diet was as lethal to him as poison. He knew of rickets and other diseases caused by malnutrition, and knew that if he was to live for much longer, he needed more than just the stringy red meat served to him three times a day from an unclean plate.

The only problem would be to convince his keeper of these facts. With him being a mere animal in her eyes, that wasn't going to be easy. Reza had to act.

When the girl came in one morning with his hunk of meat and water, she found Reza already awake and clothed, standing near his bedding. She usually had to rouse him from his exhausted stupor with a rap on the head or leg, whichever happened to be protruding from the skins, and actually showed surprise that he was awake.

"So, my animal is eager this morning, is it?" she commented as she plopped the meat down on his bed and stood back to watch him eat. Reza did not glance at the meat.

"My name is Reza," he said firmly in Standard, an offense that itself warranted a beating, for he was only to speak in what she called the Language of Her Children, or not at all, "and I'm not your pet animal." He gestured at the smoldering meat. "My body needs more than just meat to survive. If you want me to keep playing your stupid little games, you're going to have to give me some fruit and vegetables and let me out of this hole to get more sunlight."

For a moment, she simply stood there, utterly stunned. Her eyes went wide and her fists clenched and unclenched at her sides.

When she finally reacted, Reza was ready for her. Another resolution he had made in the night while he contemplated his failing health was that he was going to make her earn the right to beat him, because if he waited much longer, he might not have the strength to defend himself at all.

She hissed an alien curse between her teeth and stepped toward him, her right hand reaching behind her to the short whip clipped to her back armor, the instrument she used to deliver the worst of the beatings she meted out.

Predicting her move, Reza rushed her the moment she was committed to working the whip's catch. Her surprise was such that she simply stood there as he launched himself into the air over the short expanse between them, bowling her over onto the floor where they struggled in a desperate embrace.

Reza held her from behind, pinning her arms so that she could not lash out at him with her claws, but he was unable to hold her for long. She was larger than he was, taller and stronger, and several times she bashed his head by flinging her own back and forth.

Realizing the precariousness of his failing grip, he let go and rolled away, barely avoiding her talons as they gouged the floor centimeters from his spine.

The two got to their feet, and Reza noticed that the whip lay on the floor near his bedding, practically at Esah-Zhurah's feet. But she had no need of it. Her claws were all she needed to kill him.

"Well, come on then!" he shouted, adrenaline surging through his body. He knew that if he died now, at least he would die fighting, which was better than many could ever hope for in this war.

Esah-Zhurah moved toward him slowly, her eyes fixed on his and her fangs bared in rage. Her nails were spread in a calculated pattern that would do the most damage should they make contact with her prey. The small room gave little opportunity for maneuver, and Reza saw his options evaporating with every cautious step she took.

But then he saw with slow-motion clarity her mistake, the mistake he needed. She stepped onto the hide rug, the edge of which lay at Reza's feet. Suddenly dropping to the floor, he grabbed the rug's edge and yanked it up and back with all his strength, snapping it like a magician pulling the tablecloth from under a full setting of priceless china.

Esah-Zhurah gave a startled yelp as she flipped backward, her arms flailing in a futile attempt to balance her fall. Her head made a sickening thump as it hit the stone floor, hard.

She lay dazed, moaning, and Reza snatched up the whip. Rolling her over and leaping onto her back, he wrapped it tightly around her neck above the neckband. He held the whip's ends in his hands and planted one knee in her back, putting his full weight behind it. As her senses returned, she began to struggle, weakly at first, and then with growing strength at the realization that she had been fooled. But Reza tightened his grip, forcing her to the brink of unconsciousness before she stopped struggling.

She lay there gasping, her hands reaching feebly for the black leather whip. Her eyes bulged, and saliva ran from her gaping mouth.

"Stu...pid animal," she rasped, straining against the dark clouds of unconsciousness that loomed over her.

Reza leaned close to her ear. "Listen to me," he said, his own breath coming in heaves from holding her at bay, his arms beginning to burn furiously from the exertion, "I want to live. But I'm not going to live as an animal in whatever experiment you're running here. I am something more. I need more to survive: more food, more light, more freedom, and you're going to give them to me." He tugged savagely on the whip, eliciting a gag from Esah-Zhurah. "And you're not going to beat me anymore. If you don't want to see me as your equal, that's fine. I know I am, and that's enough for now. But if you want to go on treating me like an animal, then just nod your head and I'll kill you now and take my chances." He paused a moment, catching his breath. "What's it going to be?"

She hissed and strained against him, and then finally gave up. She laid both hands on the floor, palms down.

"*Kazh*," she said softly, bitterness evident in her voice. "Stop."

"All right," Reza said warily. He let go of the whip with one hand, then uncoiled it quickly from her neck before she could get hold of it. "I think I'll keep this for now, if you don't mind," he told her, quickly backing away and making ready for a renewed assault, "as a reminder of the bargain you just made."

She made no move to strike out at him. Instead, she lay gasping for a few moments before finally rising to her feet, turning toward him as she did so. He could see that she was still dazed from hitting the floor, but she surprised him with what she did next. He thought for a moment that she was collapsing. Instead, she knelt to the floor, bowed her head to him, and crossed her left arm over her breast in an alien salute. Then she stood up, without lifting her gaze, and unsteadily made her way out of the room.

A few moments later he heard the thick door to her room open and then close behind her. Then all was quiet.

Reza collapsed on his bedding, too physically and emotionally drained to enjoy any thrill of victory he might have felt.

Damn, he thought, *how the hell am I going to make it here?* He had no friends, no allies, no one but himself. "I don't even know what planet I'm on," he whispered quietly as he rubbed his arms, the muscles aching and sore from fighting the girl. His entire body ached and shivered, and it dawned on him that he was starving.

"Breakfast," he sighed with morose resignation, "hurrah." He looked around on the floor of his room for the morning's meat, but could not find the plate. He frowned. He did not remember Esah-Zhurah taking it back when she staggered from the room.

Puzzled, he wandered into the atrium where the morning's fire smoldered in the open pit. There, balanced carefully on the pit's stone rim, was a clean bowl of what could only be some type of weird fruit. There were at least two kinds, one that looked something like a purple squash, the other of a bright orange color but no particular shape, as if it had formed in variable gravity without any genetic code governing how it should turn out. There were also a few strange cakes, off-white with darker flecks of brown, which perhaps had been made from some sort of alien grain.

Next to the bowl was a large metal mug that he had never seen before, containing something that, on closer inspection, smelled of alcohol. He tasted it carefully, and found that it had the bitter taste of what Wiley had called "ale," something he occasionally served Reza and Nicole from out of the back closet of his library apartment.

Reza took a long swallow of the ale and with his other hand reached for the fruit, curious as to how it might taste. He could only assume that Esah-Zhurah had taken his body chemistry into account. If she had not and the food was poisonous to humans, he might well be about to eat his very last meal.

He was half finished with his small bounty (he found that the orange fruit had a sour taste that he hoped meant it was high in vitamin C) when he heard her voice close behind him.

"Is it what you need?" she asked, her voice brittle. She stood in the doorway of her room, clutching at the frame. She obviously had not yet recovered from her encounter with the floor. She did not look him in the eye.

He looked around and stood up to face her. There were long black streaks down her face, as if she had rubbed charcoal from under her eyes down to her neck. *Kreelan tears*? he wondered.

"Yes," he replied quietly. He was shocked that she was treating him with such respect. "Thank you."

"*'In'she tul'a* are the words in the New Tongue, human," she told him, still looking down at the floor. "There is more food in there," she gestured to a previously empty cabinet under the hearth.

Reza nodded, wondering when the fruit and bread had been put there. Could she have somehow been expecting this?

"You will rest now," she said. Her voice was subdued, but there was no mistaking that it was still a command. "We will continue tomorrow."

With that, she turned and disappeared back into her room and was quiet for the rest of the day.

Reza did as he was told, but only after finishing off a second bowl of the fruit and dry tasteless cakes. His mouth salivated uncontrollably as he gobbled down the precious food, praying that his stomach could take it all.

When he returned to his room, he stretched out on the bristly hide and settled down to a contented, restful sleep, his first in he did not know how many weeks.

* * *

"*...karakh-te na tempo Ta'ila-Gorakh.*" Reza heaved in a breath, his lungs empty from reciting the first eleven commandments of the *Se'eln*, the orthodoxy that governed the equivalent of Kreelan public behavior and etiquette.

"You learn well the words, human," Esah-Zhurah commented. "But do you understand the meaning?"

Reza shrugged. It was one of the few uniquely human expressions that his ever-present companion had never punished him for. "Some," he told her in what she had told him was the New Tongue. He spoke without any accent, and could have passed for a native if he had been a female with blue skin. "I understand that status is shown by the pendants hanging from the collar, the length of the hair, the depth of the ridge above the eyes. I understand that one's place in life – the Way, as you call it – is measured in some kind of steps from the Empress's throne, but I have no frame of reference for that."

She nodded for him to continue.

"I understand that warriors always salute their superiors, but warriors who are seven steps below another are to bow their head in passing or kneel when they are stopped, together." He paused. "I believe that much is correct. As for the other things, I do not yet understand them."

Reza waited as she considered his answer. This had been going on for months now, endless hours of instruction in the Kreelan language and their customs, a veritable treasure trove for any of the xenospecialists Reza had read about in his other life before coming here. He thought of all those researchers who would literally have given their lives for the opportunity he had now. But it was an "opportunity" that had been thrust onto Reza's unwilling shoulders.

After their pact made over the issue of food, Esah-Zhurah began to treat him more like a sentient being, his defiance apparently having aroused a degree of grudging respect from her. The beatings became less frequent and severe, both because Reza gave her less reason to beat him and because she chose not to. He only tried to stave off the most damaging blows, and did not try to retaliate against her; he knew she no longer underestimated him and would never afford him an opportunity again as she had the first time.

All in all, they lived an endurable if uncomfortable coexistence. Reza was determined to live as long and as best he could, while Esah-Zhurah was burdened with an agenda she kept quietly to herself.

He folded his arms over his chest and looked at her. She sat there like a coiled snake, silently appraising him with her silver-flecked eyes, absently running a talon up and down her right thigh and cutting a shallow groove in the rough leather armor.

"We are through with this," she said suddenly. "Tomorrow will be different."

"How so?" Reza asked, curious and somewhat afraid. "Different" could mean too many things.

Her mouth curled around her fangs into what Reza thought might have been something like a smile. It was chilling.

"Patience, animal," she said, intentionally barbing him with the reference she knew he despised. "You shall see soon enough."

Six

Reza was jolted out of his sleep by a sharp rap on the bottom of his foot. Peering from beneath the warmth of his bed of skins, he saw Esah-Zhurah standing beside him, a short black baton inlaid with a complex silver design in her hand. He blinked his eyes a few times, trying to clear his head. She hit his foot again, harder this time, his nerves sending a sharp report of pain to his brain.

"Ow!" he exclaimed, drawing his foot away from her and under the comparative safety of the skins. "What is that?" he asked about the baton, never having seen it before. He spoke only in the Kreelan New Tongue now, only rarely having to resort to Standard.

She looked at him, head cocked to one side. "You tell me," she said, holding it up for him to see more clearly. About as long as her forearm and the thickness of Reza's thumb, the baton was a gleaming black shaft crowned by silver castings and a series of runes in silver that must have been incredibly ornate when new. But now only the ghostly impressions of the strange runes (they were obviously Kreelan, but did not match the character set he was learning to read) glimmered in the polished metal, untold years and hands having taken their toll.

"A Sign of Authority?" Reza guessed. It was the only thing he could think it might be. A Sign of Authority, Esah-Zhurah had once explained, was like a public symbol of an elder who had delegated both responsibility and authority to a subordinate. With such a symbol, the populace at large would have to treat the bearer with the same regard as they would the elder. The bearer had great power, but also carried the liability that went with it. Esah-Zhurah had made it abundantly clear to Reza in many lessons that personal responsibility was not taken lightly in the Kreelan culture. It was literally a matter of life and death, and he wondered if he would finally have the opportunity to see it in action.

"Very good, human," she said. "Get dressed now. We will be going outside this day."

His excitement matched only by his apprehension, Reza hurried to dress, lacing his skins on over his naked body. Pausing to relieve himself, he felt her hands working at the back of his neck.

"What–?" he exclaimed.

"Be still," she ordered as she removed his old leather collar and replaced it with a new one. Larger, thicker and made of cold metal, at least he no longer felt that he was being slowly choked to death. "You grow quickly," she commented, clipping a leash to the collar and giving it a quick yank to make sure it was connected properly.

"Why the leash?" he asked as he finished getting dressed.

"You are my responsibility," she told him, holding up the leash for him to see. It was made of a tight, dark metal chain, with a studded leather thong at the far end that was looped around her wrist. "You are unfit to walk among Her Children without proper supervision. It will help remind you of your place."

He was tempted to react to her taunt, but her expression and body stance – he could read her alien nuances now, sometimes – made him give in to caution. He elected to let the comment pass.

She led him to the door and stopped, turning around to face him. "You must listen, and do exactly as I say," she commanded. "You will not speak. You will not look directly into the eyes of another, especially those with special markings here." She pointed to the center of the collar that hung just below her throat.

Reza nodded, his stomach knotting in excitement. Whatever lay beyond these walls, he was eager to see it. He had been imprisoned here for far too long.

She opened the door and led him out. Much to his surprise, the door led to a long corridor lit by triangular windows set high in the arch that formed the corridor's ceiling. The light that filtered through was warm and bright, with the slight magenta hue to which he had become accustomed from the light flowing down into the atrium where the fire was kept. Reza could smell a faint odor that reminded him of an old stone house he had once known on New Constantinople: it was the smell of age and time, the smell of quiet strength. The walls, though, were smooth and seamless, without visible signs of having been hewn or carved.

As Esah-Zhurah led him toward the door at the end of the corridor, Reza could see that there were many other doors like the one they had left behind. But they were not evenly distributed along the hallway as they would have been in most human-designed buildings. Some were very closely spaced, while many meters separated others. And the doors themselves, apparently of some type of dark wood, seemed different from one another, not so much in dimension but in the pattern and tone of the wood, as if the doors themselves were of vastly different ages. All of them appeared unique, as if each had been made by hand.

Reza listened, but could hear no sound other than their footsteps and the occasional clinking noise of the chain that bound him. He watched the girl walking smoothly before him, and noticed that she had put the baton in a sheath that was part of her left arm's leather armor, the wand's silver head protruding near her shoulder. He also saw that she wore a weapon today, something he had never seen her do before. It was a long knife, almost a short sword, with an elaborately carved bone handle and, judging from the shape of the leather scabbard hanging from her waist, a blade that was as elegantly shaped as it was deadly.

Reza was amazed that so much of what he had seen appeared to be, by and large, handmade. The quality of the workmanship was incredible, he admitted, but where were the mass-produced items that virtually every human took for granted? Where was the technology? Computers, appliances, everything up to starships and even terraformed planets were trademarks of man's industrialization. The Kreelans obviously had the technology to reach out to the stars and wage war on a galactic scale, but it was certainly absent from this place. Of the little he had seen so far, they seemed to be living on a level close to that of lost colonies that had lost contact with the Confederation for decades, and survived with only the most rudimentary technology.

He was under no illusion, however, that this race was not capable of every technological trick imaginable, carved bone knife handles or not. They had mastered interstellar flight and the myriad intricacies of related engineering, and had shown equal brilliance and innovation in every other sphere in which they and humanity had come in contact.

Except for communication and diplomacy, he thought grimly.

They reached what he took to be the main entrance, a large two-sided door that conformed to the shape of the arched walls.

Esah-Zhurah stopped, and again turned to him, her eyes narrowed. "Remember what you have learned, human," she told him gravely, "for failure outside this door will not bring the pain of the lash. It will bring death."

"I understand," Reza told her firmly, reciting in his head the commandments she had taught him, cramming them into his consciousness until they came to him automatically, without thinking.

She opened the door and led him outside. The first thing he noticed was the air. It was fresh and clean, with a slight breeze and the mingling smells of alien vegetation and some mysterious fauna. He involuntarily took huge gulps of it through his nose, his system becoming inebriated on the flavors. His head cleared and his senses sharpened after a few breaths, and he felt his energy level soar.

He stood behind Esah-Zhurah on a stone terrace at what he mentally designated the building's front, and looked down the steps before him into a large area that looked like a garden. It was not of the food-growing kind, but had a variety of stunningly beautiful trees and flowers – none of which he had ever set eyes on before, of course – in a definite, though alien, pattern, the whole of it scrupulously maintained.

Further out, he saw several circular fields bounded by thin, closely spaced pillars of rough black stone with shapes, indistinguishable at this distance, carved into the tops.

Arenas, he thought absently. *They look like some kind of arena or training ground.* He remembered seeing holos of horses and other animals being trained in similar rings, and he instinctively knew that he would come to know the sand in those arenas very well, if he lived that long.

Beyond the fields lay a forest of emerald green and amber trees that rose many meters into the air. The tremendous golden spires of what could only be a city pierced the sky beyond, and his heart raced at the thought of going there.

A slight tug on his chain reminded him that he had been gawking. The girl was obviously eager to get on with whatever errand she had in mind for them.

As they walked down the steps of what had been Reza's home on this world, he saw that there were other, smaller buildings clustered near the one from which they had just emerged. A tremble ran through him as he recognized many similarities between the layout of this place and the House 48 complex.

He wanted to ask Esah-Zhurah so many questions, but bit his tongue. He did not want to spoil this, especially if there was any chance of escaping, although he held only slim hopes for that option. Alone, on a world inhabited by the enemy, where could he run? When he was locked up in the apartment, he had fantasized about somehow getting away from Esah-Zhurah and escaping back to humanity. But being outside and seeing the world around him put an end to that. He knew he was on an alien-occupied planet, perhaps even their homeworld. And a lone human boy simply was not going to get away unnoticed in a society of blue-skinned aliens, and females, at that: no human had ever seen a Kreelan male, and no amount of hypothesizing had been able to explain why.

As Esah-Zhurah led him down the smoothed earthen path that cut through the trees toward the city, he thought it odd that there were no other Kreelans about. While he had never heard any sounds from other tenants in the building where he had been held, surely there must have been someone else somewhere. Certainly they would not have dedicated an entire complex such as this solely for his benefit.

Or would they? What did he know of the Kreelan thought process? While he realized that he was now undoubtedly the human expert on Kreelan psychology (since no other human had ever been able to communicate with the Kreelans and live to tell about it), he still knew next to nothing about what lay behind their feline eyes and inscrutable faces.

But the further he walked into the shadows of the forest, the more convinced he became that his curiosity about the existence of other denizens was being rewarded. While he had never been in a real forest, he could tell that something here was not entirely natural, not quite right.

Suddenly he realized why.

They were here. He could not see or even hear them, but he was certain that there were Kreelans nearby. As he walked steadily behind the girl he became aware of at least ten sets of eyes following him from various points in the forest. He was not sure if the others were following them or just happened to be there as they passed, but the eyes watched. He was sure there must have been even more, deeper in the brush, moving like whispers, but he could not be sure. And he did not really want to find out.

A chill running up his spine, he picked up his pace, moving closer behind Esah-Zhurah.

On through the forest they went, and eventually they left the prying eyes behind. Reza occasionally heard an animal grunting off in the woods, or the screech of some unknown beast of tiny proportions lurking high in the trees. He did not notice any creatures flying through the air, but by now the dense forest canopy obscured much of the sky itself, and such creatures would have been beyond his view.

After a while, he caught sight of the city spires again through the tops of the trees. They were very near now, or seemed to be, and he was caught between the excitement of seeing something no other human had seen before and the anxiety of knowing that he probably would never have the opportunity to tell another of his kind what he was witnessing.

"What is the name of this place?" he whispered.

"This is Keel-A'ar," she told him. "It is the place of the First Empress's birth."

He wanted to ask her more questions, but he could tell from her tone that she was not inclined to explain the history of the place now, although he knew that she would later, if he asked.

The trees suddenly thinned away until he found himself standing on the crest of a hill overlooking the city. The spires were tremendous, rising from stout bases to soar hundreds of meters into the air, thinning to nearly invisible points in the sky. Each was translucent, each a different color than the others, shimmering in the sunlight. Among the great spires were huge domes of gold and crystal, with streets and boulevards running like sinuous rivers between the buildings. The city's layout held no apparent pattern, yet it seemed in perfect harmony, each structure complimenting the next. On the city's far side ran a river, whose last bend took it directly through the city, and the Kreelan engineers had made the river an integral part of the overall design, buildings and bridges gracefully spanning the water.

"It's beautiful," he breathed, his eyes drinking in the city's magnificence.

Esah-Zhurah, in what he thought an uncharacteristically thoughtful gesture, let him gaze about for another minute before ushering him onward.

Walking for over an hour without seeming to get any closer to the surrounding wall, Reza began to appreciate just how large the city was. He could now see Kreelans moving through a huge gate in the wall. He imagined there must be several such gates around the city, but this was the only one he could see. Most of the Kreelans wore armor, while some wore robes of various colors: white, deep purple, cyan, and others that he did not even have a name for. Some carried satchels of various sizes and types, while others carried nothing that he could see and had their hands folded inside the billowing sleeves of their robes. None but the warriors had ever been seen by humans in a century of warfare.

At last, in what he guessed was three or four Standard hours of fast walking from the tree line, they reached the great gate. It was embedded in the city wall, which stood at least twelve meters high and must have been at least five meters thick. He could not understand how it had been built, as there were no visible seams or cracks, not even the scratches and other slight damage that must come with time. It was smooth as a polished stone, its mottled gray exterior, like the scales of a sleek reptile, stretching off to his right and left until they curved away from sight.

There were many Kreelans here, and Reza felt distinctly uncomfortable under their unabashed stares. He recognized the *tla'a-kane*, the ritual salute, as the aliens passed one another, crossing their left arm, fist clenched, over their right breast and bowing their head. It was one of the aspects of their etiquette that he found baffling. An older Kreelan would salute a much younger one, even younger than Esah-Zhurah, and nearly every passerby might salute a particular individual of indeterminate age and social standing, regardless of whether they wore armor or the flowing robes. Their nearly instantaneous grasp of all the factors that made up an individual's standing within the caste system that determined their rank from the Empress on down astounded him the more he watched. It was only with the greatest of effort that he held his eyes downcast, for his curiosity to look at everything was overpowering.

But no matter where he looked, of all the people they passed or could see at any distance, all he saw were females. Reza had read that humans had never encountered any males, and it was a subject of endless speculation among xenobiologists. Kreelan females did not have any particularly exotic sexual traits, and were in fact quite similar to human females, which strongly suggested that there should also be a male of the species. Otherwise, how could they reproduce?

So where are the males? Reza wondered as he surreptitiously glanced around. *There certainly aren't any here.*

The palatial structures became ever taller the closer they moved toward the city's center, as if they were ascending a mountain made by Kreelan hands. All had intricate carvings and runes adorning their superstructures, written in a dialect of their language that he couldn't read, but that didn't keep him from trying.

Lost as he was in gawking at the world around him, he nearly ran into Esah-Zhurah when she stopped. She had been watching him and the citizens that passed by, most of whom were exhibiting more than a casual curiosity in the human, and had decided that a reminder was in order.

"Remember," she whispered, taking him by the neck with her free hand and whispering into his ear. Her mouth was so close that he felt one of her upper fangs brush against his skin, sending a chill down his spine. Her hand gave a firm squeeze around his neck to emphasize the single word. She looked him in the eye for a moment, and then turned to lead him further into her world.

Except for an occasional glance at the spires that towered above them, Reza now kept his field of vision limited to the ground, with only an occasional peek to see where they were going and what was happening around them. He noticed with growing concern that an increasing number of the city's inhabitants were stopping to stare at him. A few very young ones had even begun to trail along, as if they had never even seen an image of a human, let alone a real one. As he walked he began to feel the feathery pressure of small hands reaching out to touch him as if he were an animal in a petting zoo.

Many of the older ones, the full adults, stopped and stared for a moment, sometimes speaking quietly to one another before moving on. Others simply gawked, continuing to do so until Reza and Esah-Zhurah had disappeared from their sight. But none made a move to interfere or harass him or his young keeper, and they passed their way into the heart of the city unmolested.

The population seemed to rapidly increase in density as they moved inward, and soon they were passing through a very large but orderly throng moving about a gigantic central plaza. The plaza had several levels, and was bounded by four of the largest spires in the city. Despite having four corners, it was hardly a rectangle: the plaza flowed from one spire to the next in elegant curves. Everywhere, it seemed, the Kreelans had forsaken the angularity and symmetry so treasured by humans.

The bottom level was an enormous garden park that stretched several kilometers across, and at its center was a huge obelisk that towered to nearly a third the height of the surrounding spires. It had a crystal at its peak that looked like an enormous sapphire of deep blue that blazed in the sun. Reza could see a number of people strolling about or sitting on the intermittent grassy areas near the base of the obelisk. It was orderly, peaceful.

The edge of each higher level was set further back from the center than the one below, so that all of them were open to the magenta-tinged sky above, and every level was well adorned with trees and bright flowering plants. Reza could not see anything that looked like shops or businesses along the periphery; rather, it seemed like the entire plaza had been constructed simply because it formed an attractive and peaceful core for the populace, a gathering place for their people.

They wound their way down a curving avenue of inlaid stone into what looked like a marketplace. There seemed to be hundreds, perhaps thousands, of vendors selling their wares from stores set into the buildings or from small wheeled carts scattered about the square (which, of course, was in the shape of anything but a square). Many of the items that were being offered were completely unfathomable, but others were readily identifiable. Food, much of which did not appear very appetizing, was in great abundance here, and in a much wider selection than he had experienced in his meager diet. Weapons of various intriguing shapes and functions – knives, swords, and others that he could only guess at – were the subject of discussion and what he assumed to be bargaining.

But again, even here, he saw no real evidence of a high level of technology. There were no vid-screens or their equivalent, no appliances of any type, nothing even so innocuous as a hand-held computer. Even among the weapons, there were no projectile or energy weapons, only weapons that would have been recognizable on Earth during the Middle Ages. Everything he saw here was probably the same as it must have been centuries, or even millennia, before.

And as he looked at the people around him, he saw Kreelans that seemed to come from different places, groups, or maybe professions (if they had any other than slaughtering humans). But no matter the details of their outward appearance, they still broke down into two general groups: those with robes and those with armor. He did not see a single warrior type vending, the Kreelans in robes of several colors fulfilling that task. Nor did he see any robed ones with weapons.

As he passed the shops and stalls on his way to wherever the girl was taking him, he also noticed that there was not really any buying going on. He never saw any kind of money (so far as he could tell) exchanged, even when the would-be buyer walked off with the goods. Nor did he see anything like credit discs that were the standard in the Confederation, and he could not understand the process at work here. A Kreelan would walk up to a vendor, apparently choose whatever they wanted, chat with the vendor a moment and then walk away with the goods, the vendor turning to whomever was next in line.

While the buying process was a mystery, the order in which people were served was not: it was clearly defined by the rank protocols. What he took to be lowly individuals, usually girls about his keeper's age, but often older, sometimes stood a considerable time while others stepped up in front of them to do business. But he saw no sign of frustration or anxiety on the part of those who had to wait, only seemingly endless patience.

His observations were interrupted when he felt Esah-Zhurah's hand suddenly clamp down on the back of his neck. She forced his head down so far that his chin practically touched his chest, the cartilage in his neck popping in protest.

Out of the comer of his eye, he caught sight of a warrior's black talons. He remembered Esah-Zhurah's repeated warnings to avert his eyes, but his curiosity nearly overpowered his sense of self-preservation. The warrior's claws were jet black and shiny, like razor sharp obsidian, and were considerably longer and more lethal looking than Esah-Zhurah's. The owner's hand, arm, and lower body – that was all he could see – were all tremendously developed and obviously much more powerful than all the other warriors he had glimpsed. Her leather armor bulged with muscle, giving the impression of a champion bodybuilder and athlete.

But they moved on, the great warrior passing into the throng behind them.

Finally, they arrived at their destination. It was, at least compared to some of the other places they had passed, a nondescript aperture into a building adorned with the usual indecipherable runes.

Before mounting the steps, Esah-Zhurah stopped and hailed a much younger warrior, apparently chosen at random from among a group of similar minors. The young girl, maybe all of six human years old, saluted and bowed her head.

"See that the animal remains here," Esah-Zhurah commanded, handing the young girl his leash.

"Yes, Esah-Zhurah," the tiny warrior replied, bowing her head again.

Reza was not sure which was more shocking: that she would leave him under the care of such a young girl, or that they all seemed to know each other's names.

"Stay here," she told him, pointing at the ground where he stood. Without another glance, she turned and went up the steps, disappearing into the arched doorway.

As he watched her go, he idly noticed that this was one of the few buildings he had seen that had real windows. Many of the others just had what looked like slits randomly disposed about their exterior, shutters opened to the side.

He looked at the girl holding his leash. She seemed terribly young, but her face radiated a sense of authority and determination that few human children would ever boast, even as adults. She stood at a kind of attention, her cat's eyes never straying from him, her hand securely locked in the loop of the leather thong at the end of his leash.

"What is your name?" he asked her quietly, hoping his voice would not carry to the passing adults and arouse their attention any further than did the simple fact of his being there.

She glared at him, and he instantly realized his mistake. There was some key or trick to their names that Esah-Zhurah had not described, some way they immediately recognized one another, and to ask this girl her name must have been an insult.

He sighed in frustration and turned away from the glowering blue-skinned imp.

After a few minutes, Reza saw that more of the children, as well as adults, had taken time out from their alien day to get a closer look at him.

None made threatening gestures – at least from what he could tell; they all seemed threatening enough as it was – but the circle about him was rapidly growing in size and diminishing in distance.

His fear of being torn to pieces by an alien mob brought home the importance of his relationship with Esah-Zhurah. While he could hardly consider her an ally, much less a friend, she was the only link he had to life. Without her, he stood no chance at all of survival on this world, among these people, and he frantically wished she would come out of the building and lead him away from the overly inquisitive group forming around him.

At last, she emerged with a black tube about the length of her forearm clutched firmly in one hand. Taking the leash from the young girl, she started off again, Reza in tow. Flowing with the increasingly thick crowd of people, he occasionally bumped against warriors whose shoulders were above his head.

"What is that?" he asked Esah-Zhurah quietly, discretely pointing at the tube she carried.

"It is the priestess's correspondence," she answered. "It is a task certain of us undertake for her each day." She looked askance at him. "Consider yourself honored, human."

Reza raised his eyebrows in surprise. He had never been on a planet or known anyone who communicated by hard copy means, "the post" always having had an electronic connotation. But letters written by hand were akin to the books he had so treasured, and he began to believe that maybe the Kreelans were not complete savages after all.

"We will go to the bath," she told him as she led him around a tight knot of warriors arguing heatedly over something that he could not quite make out. "What is your saying?" She thought a moment. "*Nature calls?* Yes?"

"Yes," he replied earnestly. Although he had not had anything to drink for hours, he suddenly felt like his bladder was going to explode. Of course, he had been so preoccupied with gawking at the city that he hadn't noticed until Esah-Zhurah mentioned it.

She led him to a doorway along a street that looked no more or less unusual than the others cutting through the metropolis. Through the doorway was a large softly lit anteroom. Kreelans in dark blue robes, barely contrasting with their skin, were in attendance, and Reza was shocked to see that everyone else – Esah-Zhurah included – was stripping off their clothing.

She turned to him, naked now except for her neckband and the ubiquitous baton, and snagged his skins with one of her claws. "Off," she commanded tersely, wrinkling her nose in a sign of disgust. She gestured toward the robed attendant who already was holding Esah-Zhurah's armor.

Reluctantly following Esah-Zhurah's command, he stripped and gave his motley skins to the attendant, who took them as unwillingly as he parted with them before carrying everything away through another door.

Reza heard a growl behind him. Turning around, he found himself toe to toe with a warrior, her taut breasts – the left one carrying a terrible scar running from the left armpit to her stomach – a hair's breadth from his nose, so tall was she. Even though they were aliens, they still had more basic things in common with human females than not, and he felt his face flush with embarrassment. He also noted that Esah-Zhurah was observing his predicament with keen interest.

The other Kreelans in the anteroom stopped what they were doing and stared, as well. Most probably had never seen a human other than himself (or had only seen one long enough to kill him or her, he thought), and by their reaction they certainly had never seen a naked human, least of all a very young male. Most of their eyes were focused below his waist.

Determined to show some courage, he raised his gaze from the warrior's chest to her eyes and held her stare. From somewhere behind him, drops of water splashed, and he began to count them to mark what probably would be the last few moments of his life. He reached a count of eleven before he heard Esah-Zhurah's voice behind him.

"Enough, animal," she said, tugging him by his leash away from the still-staring warrior. "Combat is not permitted in the bath."

Without another word, she led him through another archway and past the staring patrons in the anteroom. They went down a corridor lined with some kind of mosaic scenes of swirling rune-like shapes before entering the next room.

Reza stopped in his tracks, just inside the archway. *This is too much*, he thought. It was a public bath, all right, as in bathroom. As in bodily functions. He sighed heavily and followed along behind Esah-Zhurah, who had stopped when she noticed the resistance on the end of the leash. His stomach churned.

This is really disgusting, he thought. He had never liked the open bathrooms of House 48. But at least there, even in an open bay bathroom, everyone had to endure the same level of public humiliation, and so it generally was not that big of a deal. And, if nothing else, everyone in the room had been human. And of the same sex.

After a moment's pause he followed after Esah-Zhurah, who took her place on a strangely shaped throne of dark green. He took the seat next to her and tried to keep his mind on what he was supposed to be doing, rather than what was going on around him.

Esah-Zhurah finally stood up (he had already finished, such was his eagerness to get out of this place) and took him through the next archway, where a cleansing waterfall cascaded over them from the ceiling. The water itself smelled different, as if something – a detergent or antibiotic agent, perhaps – had been added, but he noticed nothing different about the taste as it poured over his head. The water ran down through sculpted drains in the sides of the chamber to disappear below.

After passing through a short tunnel past the waterfall, they found themselves in a large chamber that was, in fact, a soaking bath. Esah-Zhurah led him into the water, its scalding heat making him hiss with pleasure as it crept up his body. She propped her back against the side of the large pool, and he stayed close to her; even her despotic company was welcome over the hostile faces that peered from the water like sea monsters wreathed in a steamy mist. He kept inching closer to her, until their shoulders and arms touched under the water.

After he was sure she was not going to push him away, Reza closed his eyes, shutting out the alien faces around him. He forced himself to relax, letting the water's heat penetrate his body. After a few minutes, and hoping he wasn't going to breach any codes of etiquette, he took himself all the way under the water, rinsing out his rapidly lengthening hair and washing the accumulated sweat from his face. He felt his pores opening up from the water's heat, and he sighed with the unexpected pleasure of actually having a real bath, a *hot* bath, for a change. Up to this point he had only the freezing water from the spigot in his room and a crude metal basin with which to wash. Blowing like a broaching whale as he returned to the surface, he met Esah-Zhurah's eyes with a smile. He figured she would not understand its significance, but it felt good to have something, anything, to smile about.

Esah-Zhurah gave him a perplexed look, but nothing more severe.

When they were finished, she led him out the other side of the pool to a large area open to the sky. There they settled onto comfortable mats among the many other bath-goers who were drying off in the warm sun.

* * *

Reza did not realize he had drifted off to sleep until Esah-Zhurah poked him with a claw.

"We go now," she said. They stood up, completely dry, and headed off down yet another corridor to the anteroom to retrieve their clothes. Reza noticed that his had been cleaned and smelled almost pleasant now.

As they headed through the main entryway, an incoming group of Kreelans made to enter, neither party seeing the other until it was too late. The ensuing confusion resulted in some unexpected jostling. But no one took offense, and Reza and Esah-Zhurah rejoined the throng of Kreelans moving through the boulevard.

Near the edge of the plaza, they happened to pass a group of older warriors in the undulating crowd. Reza, now used to the drill, lowered his head and averted his eyes, while Esah-Zhurah performed the ritual greeting.

But something went wrong. One of the warriors barked a question at Esah-Zhurah in a dialect Reza didn't understand. Surprised, Esah-Zhurah started to respond, eyes still lowered. But she stopped in mid-phrase, looking at her left arm.

The baton, the Sign of Authority, was missing.

Esah-Zhurah's hands flew across her armor in search of it, as if she might have accidentally misplaced it when dressing at the bath. Then she shot a questioning look at Reza, as if he might have had it. Her eyes were frantic.

"Reza," she gasped. It was one of the only times she had ever called him by name. "Reza, where is the Sign of Authority? What has happened to it?" Reza could see she was petrified.

It must have been at the bath, he thought. It must have fallen out when we ran into that group of warriors when we were leaving.

He was just opening his mouth to tell her this when the questioning warrior, quite formidable in appearance, spoke to Esah-Zhurah in a harsh tone using the same dialect she had before.

Esah-Zhurah was silent, her head hanging low in what Reza understood with a chill to be total, utter defeat. Without the baton, she had no authority and therefore had no right to claim him as her own. In this society, rank and authority were everything, and she had little of the first and none of the second in the eyes of the accusing warrior. The end result would be that the challenger could kill them both, or – even worse in Reza's mind – take him as her own, for purposes he did not care to contemplate.

His fears grew deeper as the warrior momentarily turned her attention from Esah-Zhurah to himself. From her belt hung what could only be ears. Human ears. There were least twenty pairs strung on a cord. He felt a hot flame of rage flare in his heart, a worthy companion to the chill of fear that ran down his spine.

The warrior turned from Reza and spoke briefly to her comrades, and they murmured a response. He couldn't understand the words, but he didn't need to: he and Esah-Zhurah were in deep trouble.

The warrior took one step closer to Esah-Zhurah and – without any warning at all – flattened her to the ground with a brutal open-handed blow to the side of her head, the rapier claws gashing the girl's scalp to the bone above her right ear.

Reza watched, wide eyed, as Esah-Zhurah yelped once and then crumpled into a dazed heap on the ground, dark blood pulsing from her wounded head. The warrior viciously kicked her over onto her stomach and then reached for a knife. Leaning down, the warrior grabbed Esah-Zhurah's hair and used it to lift up her head, exposing her throat to the knife the warrior held in her other hand.

Reza moved without thinking. He rushed the warrior from behind, kicking out at her with both legs in a flying leap. She grunted in surprise and went tumbling over Esah-Zhurah's prone form, nearly impaling herself with her own knife. But she recovered quickly, rolling deftly to her feet.

The other warriors and passersby gasped in astonishment, and a crowd instantly began to gather around the mismatched combatants. Their guttural comments merged into a buzz of curiosity as they formed a ring that marked the onset of what in their culture was an everyday occurrence: ritual combat. The only difference was that this would be to the death.

The warrior bared her fangs and roared a challenge at Reza. He backed up, trying to draw her away from Esah-Zhurah, who lay terrifyingly still. Reza thought frantically about his biggest problem: he had no weapon. Even if the advancing warrior had nothing but her talons, he stood no chance against her. Unless...

Acting quickly, Reza tore at the thin ragged animal skin that served as his shirt, coming away with a strip of thin leather that was almost twice the length of his arm. Then he quickly searched the ground for the other vital ingredient he needed: a simple rock. On the well-swept boulevards they had been on, he didn't hold out much hope, but for once Fate favored him: a small piece of chipped cobblestone lay only a few paces away.

Praying that the warrior's arrogance would give him a few more seconds, he dashed over and picked it up. Placing it carefully in the makeshift sling, he began his windup, wondering if the brittle leather would hold the sharp-edged projectile long enough before the sling came apart. The air filled with the whirring sound as he whipped it around his head, faster and faster.

The warrior stopped, regarding him with what he took to be bemused curiosity. Then she let out a harrowing bellow that was echoed by the other warriors surrounding them.

Ignoring the noise, Reza whirled the sling even faster, waiting for the right moment.

Now! he thought, releasing the stone just as the warrior stepped into the sling's line of fire. The cobblestone shard flew straight and true, its jagged edges mincing the Kreelan's right eye. Her scream filled the void left by the suddenly silent onlookers. Dropping the knife, she fell to the ground, clutching her injured face and wailing in agony.

Reza wasted no time. His lips pulled back in a snarl of rage, he dropped the tattered leather strip and grabbed up the fallen knife. Leaping onto the warrior's back, he entwined his left arm in her hair and levered her head back, exposing her throat to the blade clenched in his other hand, just as she had done to Esah-Zhurah.

The Kreelan went very still, as if she were expecting this and wasn't going to struggle.

Reza hesitated, his resolve suddenly cracking. What was he supposed to do? he wondered. He knew the woman's life was his for the taking, and he had no doubt that, were their positions reversed, she would have no compunction about killing him. Esah-Zhurah had not spoken of how such things were handled, perhaps in the firm belief that if Reza ever found himself in such a situation, either she would be able to get him out of it or he would simply be killed.

And yet, here he was.

This, he thought ironically, is what in a more lucid moment Wiley had once called a "command decision." There was no one from whom he could ask advice or consent. The burden of success or failure was on his shoulders and his alone.

The Kreelan, trembling beneath him from a kind of pain Reza hoped never to have to endure himself, waited with a patience grown through a lifetime of conditioning. Around them, the crowd of observers was deathly quiet, waiting for the contest to be resolved.

Remembering the sets of human ears hanging from the warrior's waist, he suddenly knew the course for his vengeance. Taking a handful of the woman's braided hair, he cut it off with the knife.

She screamed in agony, from a torrent of incomprehensible pain that Reza someday would come to understand himself. Esah-Zhurah had told him that a Kreelan's hair was her strength, her bond to the Empress, and he knew that it was as precious to them as it had been to Samson in the Old Testament of Earth. He didn't understand all of what Esah-Zhurah had told him, but it was enough that the Kreelans believed in the importance of their hair. And he had just deprived this warrior of a goodly portion of hers.

He left her, stepping away to where Esah-Zhurah lay bleeding. He carefully turned her over to look at her wounds. The four ugly gashes across her skull were deep, and there was a tremendous amount of blood in her hair and on the street.

"Oh, God," he whispered in Standard, wondering if she could be bleeding to death, or if her skull had been fractured. He had no idea what to do.

Her eyes fluttered open. She tried to focus on him and opened her mouth to speak, but no words came out before she passed out again.

The stricken warrior had stopped screaming. Now she glared at him, the blood and fluid from her devastated eye seeping down her face like a smashed egg. He watched her carefully, waiting for the next attack, the one he would not be able to stop.

Her face finally locking into a frigid mask of utter hatred, the warrior got to her feet faster than Reza would have thought possible. Her claws flexed like the talons of a predatory bird as she began to move toward him.

He moved between her and Esah-Zhurah, clutching the warrior's own knife in his hand as he made ready for a last desperate stand, his hopes of survival all but extinct.

A shadow suddenly fell over him and a huge hand with obsidian claws clutched his shoulder from behind, pushing him back down beside Esah-Zhurah with the irresistible strength of a mountain. He went perfectly still as a voice behind him, oddly familiar, spoke to the advancing warrior in the same dialect that Reza could not understand, but in a tone of unquestionable authority.

The warrior stopped. She listened intently to whomever was standing behind Reza. His opponent said nothing. She glared at him one final time and then, much to his surprise, she bowed to him, her arm across her chest. She reached around to her back and tossed him the scabbard for the knife he still held.

And then she slit her throat with her own claws.

Reza watched in horrified fascination as blood gushed from the ghastly wound and air whistled from her severed windpipe like someone blowing over the top of a bottle. The warrior stood at rigid attention until, as the flow of blood slowed to a trickle, her good eye rolled up into her head and she fell to the street, dead.

Reza vomited, but nothing came up. He simply knelt in the street, wracked with dry heaves. When he was finished, he felt the great hand on his shoulder again. Turning his face up, he looked at the woman standing over him, and his heart froze at what he saw.

Silhouetted against the slowly setting sun, standing at least a head taller than the tallest of the other warriors and with a frame whose strength could have matched any two or three of their kind, was the most powerful Kreelan he had ever seen. A great gnarled staff that Reza doubted he could have even carried was held easily in one hand. Her breast armor, a glistening black that seemed to have an infinite depth, boasted an intricate series of crystal blue runes inlaid into the metal that sparkled like diamonds in the sun. From her neckband hung several rows of silver, gold, and crystalline pendants, and the neckband itself had a cobalt blue rune at its center, a feature whose importance was evident by its uniqueness.

She was a priestess, he knew. This much, Esah-Zhurah had taught him.

Her eyes blazed at him from beneath the ridge of bone or horn that made up her eyebrows. The ridge over her left eye and the skin of her cheek had been cut, leaving an ugly scar…

…that was the mirror image of his own.

"No," he whispered hoarsely in the New Tongue, as the nightmare image from his childhood became the warrior priestess now standing over him. "It cannot be."

"And yet, so it is, little one," Tesh-Dar replied, speaking in the New Tongue so he could understand. Her eyes darted to his hand, the knife shaking in his quivering grip. "Do not raise your hand against me," she warned, "for I will not be so charitable as the time we first met."

Her words sank into Reza's skull, and he realized the ridiculous futility of even attempting to attack her. The scar that marred her proud face was the result of a fluke that she had taken with good humor. To try and repeat the feat would be nothing less than suicide.

Reluctantly, he held the knife out to her, handle first.

"No," she told him, her voice echoing her satisfaction that the young animal was not going to act foolishly. "It is yours, a prize of your first contest. Your resourcefulness and spirit have saved you yet again, child."

Turning her attention to Esah-Zhurah, she knelt down to examine the girl's injuries, delicately probing the gashes with her talons. Esah-Zhurah twitched, but she did not regain consciousness.

Tesh-Dar stood up, satisfied. After a moment of reflection, she leaned over and took hold of the thong on Reza's leash, and Reza wondered how he had not tripped over it during the fight. She put it around her wrist and spoke to Reza, gesturing toward Esah-Zhurah with the staff in her other hand. "Carry her," she ordered.

Reza knelt down and picked Esah-Zhurah up in a fireman's carry, the blood from the wound on her head occasionally dripping down his back.

Staggering under the load, he followed after the priestess as she strode down the street, occasionally tugging on his leash. The crowd respectfully parted in front of them, leaving eddies of conversation behind as they made their way out of the plaza and toward a different gate in the city wall.

They stopped just outside the gate at a corral that housed strange dinosaur-like creatures that Reza hadn't seen before. An attendant wearing a rough leather robe brought one of the animals, already saddled and bridled, to the priestess, who smoothly mounted the snorting beast. Then she turned it about, neatly plucking Esah-Zhurah from Reza's shoulders and laying her down across the animal's back, just in front of the saddle. Esah-Zhurah's head and feet dangled limply toward the ground on either side.

Tesh-Dar regarded Reza for a moment, wondering if she should let him ride with her. It was a long way to their destination.

"I will run," he told her without being prompted, his spirits buoyed by a sense of determination, even if he were to regret it later: he had no idea how far they had to go. He had already walked for hours that morning, but he was not about to ride with the creature that had killed his parents. His day for vengeance would come, he vowed to himself. Perhaps not this day, nor the next, but it would come. Until then, he would not give her the pleasure of seeing weakness in him.

"As you wish, little one," she said, wondering with some interest if he was up to the trek. If he were not, his carcass would feed the animals that roamed the forest. She had saved his life twice now. She would not do so a third time.

Or so she believed as she prompted her mount to a fast walk, Reza trailing along behind her like a hound following its master.

Seven

Reza sat alone under the shelter in the corral, watching the rain fall. He had no idea where he was, yesterday's journey ending well after dark. Nor did he know how far they had traveled, although it had been far enough that he could barely move his legs, they were so sore.

Upon their arrival last night, Kreelan girls had appeared to help the priestess with Esah-Zhurah. They carried her off into the dark, the priestess following them after dismounting her animal, entrusting it to yet another of the young warriors. Almost as an afterthought she had ordered that something be done with Reza, and some of the girls brought him into this stall and chained him up in what he had come to think of as the dinosaur pen.

He had already gauged his chances of breaking his chains and given up any thoughts of escape as hopeless. He was not too worried about water, as the troughs for the animals were full (although rather foul smelling). But food would soon become a problem. As would the vermin that had infested his scalp, he thought in frustration as he forced himself not to scratch the incessant itches that now plagued his head.

He watched as the strange animals – *magtheps*, they were called – nibbled at the coarse grain that had been dumped in their food troughs. Somewhat larger than a Terran horse, they had shaggy dark brown hair with black tiger stripes. Two powerful hind legs could propel the beasts at an impressive run, as he had observed from his rather unique vantage point the evening before, and each hind foot carried a set of talons that seemed obligatory for every species on this accursed planet. The front legs, diminutive in size, seemed well adapted for holding onto the fruit or leaves these creatures might have eaten in the wild. But despite their athletic build, their heads were nothing but homely, having short, droopy ears and incredibly large eyes set close over what looked like a beak with lips, and two wide nostrils on either side.

The beasts seemed almost to regard him as one of their own – something for which he was very thankful, considering their size and strength – and were nothing but gentle and reserved in their disposition toward him.

Sighing as he scratched one of the curious beasts behind an ear, he turned toward the morning sky and wondered what lay beyond it, in the depths of space. He fantasized that a human fleet was even now on its way here...

Then he sighed with resignation. There would be no Confederation Marines coming to his rescue. No Navy battlewagons were coming to save young Reza Gard from his blue-skinned alien captors. He was alone and would have to fend for himself. As it so often seemed he had.

He looked at the knife, the trophy from the warrior he had defeated. Only this morning, when there had been plenty of time to look at it, had he discovered that it was human-made: a Marine combat knife. Itself a grim reminder of his plight, it was the only physical link he had left to his own people. Everything else he had ever had, even the little silver cross that had been a gift from Nicole, had been taken from him. The knife's edge, while not as advanced as Kreelan blades, was nonetheless a testimony to human craftsmanship. It was razor sharp, exquisitely tailored for the act of killing another living being.

And that is what he had to look forward to, he knew. This race lived and died by a code of conduct based on the glorification of mortal combat, and he had to adapt to that code and make it work for him if he wanted to survive.

* * *

He awoke the next morning to the familiar smell of cooked meat, and opened his eyes to see a plate, a real china plate, sitting centimeters from his nose. It was loaded with properly cooked meat, fresh fruit, and the wheat cakes he had come to detest but forced himself to eat anyway. Esah-Zhurah, sitting next to him and watching him with her feline eyes, held a cup of ale for him.

Reza saw that the wounds on her face were all but healed.

"That is impossible," he breathed. He reached out a hand to touch her face, to make sure it was real. "How can your wounds be healed already?"

"Our healers make short work of such trifles," she said blandly, pushing his questing hand away.

Reza shook his head. Such a feat was well beyond anything he had ever read about for human medicine.

"How do you feel?" he asked, curious about her condition.

"Well enough," she said, bowing her head to him slightly in acknowledgment.

She looked into his eyes, her own glinting in the morning sun. "You must have fought well, human," she said, "for the priestess to take such an interest in you."

"What do you mean?" he asked, grabbing one of the tangy fruits and biting into it eagerly to satisfy his loudly-complaining stomach.

"Tesh-Dar, the priestess of this *kazha*, this school of the Way, has adopted you into the ranks of her pupils." She paused. "It is something for which there is no precedent. You should be very honored."

Reza glared at her. "How can I honor the one who killed my parents, who helped destroy my homeworld, who attacked yet another world to bring me here?" He broke a piece from the cake he held in his hands, half of it crumbling in his angry grip. "Maybe if I had not been so terrified," he muttered bitterly, "I could have rammed my father's knife into her brain instead of just cutting her face."

Esah-Zhurah leaned forward, her eyes wide. "You made the scar over her eye?" she whispered in awe.

Reza nodded, opting to stuff more food in his mouth rather than say anything more, trying to avoid those painful memories.

Esah-Zhurah silently pondered this newest revelation as Reza ate. When he was finished, she asked another question. "Why did you not let the warrior kill me?"

Reza stifled a bitter laugh. "If I would have let her kill you, where would that have left me?" he asked. "Alone on this world, without a single friend or ally, I cannot even blend in with your people in some vain hope of camouflaging myself, for my skin is not blue, nor do I have talons or fangs." He gestured at her chest. "Nor am I female."

"There is more to your actions," she said, her eyes noting the small nuances in his body language that she had been studying for so long.

He sighed at her probing of his motivations, but did not think it worthwhile to try and avoid answering her. "I do not consider you a friend," he said, looking her in the eye, "but you have kept me alive, for whatever reason. And for that, perhaps I am in your debt, and maybe by taking care of you I might increase my own chances of staying alive," he looked away, "until I can return home."

"That, human," she said slowly, "you shall never do." She swept her arm about her. "This is your home, now, for however long you may live. You shall never venture far from this place, and certainly shall never leave this world."

"Then what am I doing here?" he asked angrily, his hopes of a future fading to a dim, lifeless gray. His finger traced the edge of the china plate, now empty, that carried the words *C.S.S. Arizona* stenciled around the edge, and had the old battleship's crest emblazoned in the center. The *Arizona* had been destroyed in a horrendous fleet engagement near Kyrie the day Reza had been born. There had been countless fleet battles during the war, but that one had made it into the school history books. The irony was not lost on him.

"From this day on," she said, "you are to learn of the Way, as if you were to become one of us."

Reza opened his mouth in protest, but she silenced him with her own words, having anticipated his response. "You need not worry about serving the Empress, human," she said derisively. "We do not ask your allegiance to the Way, for you are not of it. You are here to satisfy Her curiosity, to see if animals such as yourself have a soul." Her voice left little doubt as to her own beliefs. In her mind, Reza was as much a spiritual being as the snorting magtheps in the stalls behind them.

"You do not believe I am your equal, do you?" he said. It was more a statement than a question as his mind grappled with the implications of what she was saying.

"No," she responded curtly. "I do not."

Reza smiled at her, baring his teeth as he had seen her do sometimes. "You will," he said, "even if I have to prove it to you." He leaned closer to her, his eyes burning fiercely. "In fact, I will prove that I am better than you. All you need is the courage to give me the chance."

The girl grunted, unimpressed. "That," she said, "the priestess has already granted." Her mouth crinkled in a Kreelan grin. "You will have ample opportunity to demonstrate your superiority, animal."

She gathered up the plate and cup in one hand and took Reza's leash in the other as she stood up, signaling an end to the conversation.

"Come," she ordered, leading him out of the barn. "You smell like the animal you are." Her nose wrinkled in disgust. "It is time for you to learn civilized ways."

* * *

Reza spent most of the morning trying to wash in the freezing water of a nearby stream under Esah-Zhurah's steady gaze. Modesty had long ceased to be a factor in their relationship, whatever it might otherwise be called. Esah-Zhurah gave him some kind of soap that he put in his hair to kill off the mites that had attacked his scalp, but the stuff burned his skin so badly that he almost would have rather left the tiny parasites in peace. When he finished, he stumbled out of the water, looking for the skins he had washed earlier and hung up to dry in some nearby bushes.

They were gone.

"Where are my clothes?" he asked her, shivering with cold, the breeze against his wet skin making him even colder than he had been in the water.

"You will need them no more," she replied cryptically. She stepped close to him and ran a hand over his chest, marveling at the blue cast of his skin. "Why do you change color?"

"Because I am freezing!" he answered testily, rubbing his hands over his arms to get his circulation going again. "No blood is reaching my skin," he explained through his chattering teeth. "That is what changes the color." He was less than amused by the inopportune disappearance of his clothes, but he forced himself to have patience. His keeper often worked in mysterious ways.

She *humphed* to herself and led him naked from the stream. He had never had anything on his feet since coming to this world, and now it seemed that the rest of him would go naked, as well.

"Damn," he cursed under his breath, too low for Esah-Zhurah to hear.

After a short brisk walk they found themselves at the entry to one of the many buildings of the kazha, a school that was as large as most human universities, ensconced here in the forest.

As Esah-Zhurah opened the arched door and ushered his naked, shivering body inside, he saw that it was an armory. Weapons ranging from short stilettos to pulse rifles and many others that he had never seen before were arrayed in orderly rows in racks on the walls flanking the well-lit main corridor. She led him down to the second archway on the left, and Reza temporarily forgot the cold that had been wracking his body. He saw nearly a dozen figures robed in black, fitting armor to several young female warriors, each of whom was clad only in the thin black gauzy material he had seen under his keeper's armor.

But this armor was not the same as that worn by the Kreelans in the city, Reza saw. It had no adornments of any type, no scrollwork or runes. It was completely utilitarian, and the robed Kreelans, the armorers, fitted each piece with exacting skill and precision. This armor was going to be used for its intended purpose, and their honor was at stake in its fitting.

Two of the girls were finished at the same time. After bowing to the armorers, they brushed past Reza with a hiss and bared fangs.

Esah-Zhurah bowed and then spoke briefly and rapidly with the senior armorer, gesturing toward Reza. The woman disappeared from the room.

"Stand here," Esah-Zhurah ordered, ushering Reza toward where four other armorers waited. Hands clasped inside the fabric of their robes, they eyed him – particularly his maleness – curiously.

"What–"

"Silence," Esah-Zhurah said sharply. "You will answer any questions they may put to you, but you will not ask any and interrupt their work. They must concentrate, or your armor may be less than perfect." She paused. "That would be an unfortunate situation in the arena."

While Reza worried about the ominous reference to the arena, one of the armorers unclipped his leash with her clawless hands, a trait Reza had not noticed before. Others began measuring his arms and legs with what looked like nothing more impressive than an ancient-style fabric tape measure that some human tailors still preferred to use.

After interminable measuring, one of them disappeared into another room, emerging an amazingly short time later with one of the black undergarments for Reza while the others continued their tasks.

"My thanks," he said fervently. He was grateful to finally have something to put on over his freezing skin.

They then measured him again, after which they began to test fit various pieces of leatherite armor, taking away the ones that were not perfect for reworking and refitting.

After several hours, Reza stood in a full complement of matte black leatherite, including sandals with wraps that came nearly to his knee. They had very tough soles and were without a doubt the most comfortable footwear he had ever worn. It was ironic that here, among the enemy of his race, his clothing and footwear was custom made; in House 48 he could never have even dreamed of such a luxury.

He flexed his hands in the black gauntlets that fit as if they were a second skin, feeling natural despite the metal claws that had been added to the fingers to even the odds against his naturally-endowed counterparts. Standing in this armor made him feel like he might have a chance of survival after all.

The armorers finally stepped away, except for two who bore the breast and backplates that shielded the wearer's vital torso area. Reza had fully expected to have two conic projections on the breastplate, such was the pervasiveness of the female form. He was amazed to see that, like everything else, the armorers had crafted plates just for him. They fit his chest perfectly.

Finished at last, the girl saluted the armorers, and Reza bowed his head to them, omitting the crossing of the arm. It was a ritual mandated by the many commandments they followed, but since he was not of "the Way," it did not apply to him. Yet he still wanted to show his respect.

The armorers, apparently somewhat less apprehensive or bigoted toward the alien among them than were the warriors, returned his gesture with no discernible malice.

"Come," Esah-Zhurah beckoned, leading him away by the arm. The leash had been left behind in the fitting room. Their trust in him to obey – and his understanding of that trust – was now implicit.

Once outside, she guided him to a secluded patch of grass in the midst of a stand of trees. They sat down, cross-legged, facing one other.

"Tomorrow," she told him, "you will begin a new life. All that has gone before, all that you have known and believed must be pushed aside, purged from your mind, if you wish to survive. There will be little margin for error, and no allowance made for weakness. You asked for the chance to prove yourself; so shall you have it.

"From now on," she explained, "you will learn to live and fight as we do, as have the warriors for the last twenty-seven thousand generations who have passed through the gates of all the kazhas such as this one. You are about the size and strength of those entering the intermediate combat training that is taught here. Thus you will be handicapped, for you have not had the training given the young ones, and you will be given no allowances for this shortcoming. Do you understand?"

"Yes," he said, wondering just what kind of nightmare he had fallen into.

Satisfied, Esah-Zhurah continued. "You will be taught in the ways of the Desh-Ka, the order of the priestess who brought you here. And I," she said with audible resignation, "am to be your *tresh*, your... partner."

"My partner?" he asked incredulously.

Esah-Zhurah shrugged. "There is no better description of it that you would understand, human," she said contemptuously. "The bonds of the tresh are much deeper than mere partnership or your concept of *friendship*. It is beyond your understanding. Besides," she added, "I doubt you will survive long enough for it to become an issue."

"We shall see," he said coldly.

Esah-Zhurah went on as if he had remained silent. "You no longer have a leash, yet you must be with me always, and I with you, unless I tell you otherwise. This is not because you are human; it is simply the way of the tresh. We will eat, learn, fight, and live together."

I am so looking forward to it, he thought sarcastically.

"For at the end of every cycle," she went on, "all of the tresh take part in The Challenge, a competition among the peers that begins the process of our adult ranking in the Way. Those who do well, rank highly. Those who do not... sometimes do not survive. Those tresh who die leave their partner standing alone, for tresh are bound for life to one another, come what may."

That thought hit Reza like a slap to his face. "So," he asked tentatively, "what would happen to you should I die?"

"I would be left alone," she said bitterly, "as I have been since my real tresh died two cycles ago."

"And what would become of me should you die?" he asked quietly. "What is to prevent one of the peers from taking any opportunity to kill me outright?"

"My death would be consistent with the Way: you would be left to fend for yourself, alone. It is an unenviable existence for any tresh, but especially for you, human.

"As for the peers trying to kill you, it is very unlikely unless they become careless or overzealous in the arena. The priestess demonstrated the good will to bring you here, and has given you armor from her stores, food and drink from her commissary." She gave him a hard look. "You do not understand the honor that she has accorded you, human, but perhaps you will learn. I do not believe she would look kindly upon anyone who killed you without just cause. Your life rests under her authority now, and it is much more powerful than any power I shall ever boast. Why she has intervened in your life is something she will reveal at a time of her own choosing, if she chooses to at all."

She leaned closer to him. "But beware," she warned, "for while her benevolence has kept you alive, it may just as easily get you killed. Death comes easily in the Way of my people. From my studies, I do not believe you will find life pleasant here. You will suffer extraordinary physical pain and exhausting hardships with little to hope for but to take yet another breath."

She leaned back. "Our training begins each day at dawn and ends at dusk. You will be subjected to tests of the body and the mind, and the price for failure will be pain or, worse, humiliation before the peers. And, like all things among the tresh, your partner will suffer with you until your learning is complete or one of you dies. I will suffer pain gladly," she said, "but do not humiliate me, human. Ever."

Reza could not believe how much today differed from yesterday. Then, he had been something between a slave and an animal, and now he was to learn how they lived, had been given a chance to survive. He did not care about the girl's warning of hardship and pain. He welcomed it. He had hope, tenuous though it might be, that he might someday, somehow, get back to humanity again.

But he was nagged by a persistent thought: would he still be human?

"If you teach me well," he told her, "I will not fail you, or myself."

Her eyes gleamed at the challenge in his voice. "Then let the new day come forth," she said, her fangs reflecting the red glow of sunset.

* * *

Reza lay awake, unable to sleep. His mind drifted from one thought to another as he pondered the coming dawn. He had asked Esah-Zhurah to explain more about what would happen, but the details she would not say.

He rolled over in his hide blanket to look at her, asleep nearby. What humiliation must she be enduring, he wondered, to be the tresh of a human, an animal? How must she feel, having to sleep outdoors in the forest rather than in the shelter of the dormitory buildings because Reza was unclean, and she was bound to him?

He glanced up at the stars. Somewhere out there were people he had known, going about their daily business. Maybe one of them paused now and again to think about the child with dark brown hair named Reza Gard, the one who loved to read for endless hours, the one who entertained the little children reading stories about princes and princesses from ancient times. Perhaps, Reza thought, Wiley Hickock's face suddenly surfacing in his mind, there was a Marine Corps recruiter somewhere asking if anyone knew the whereabouts of one Reza Gard, whose pre-draft requirements had come up. Maybe one of the billion specks of light in the cloudless sky was a human ship, a battleship, about to rake an enemy vessel with its fiery broadside. Or perhaps it was Nicole in her fighter, tight on the tail of a Kreelan destroyer.

He listened to Esah-Zhurah's deep, steady breathing next to him, and wondered what Wiley would do if he were here. That thought brought about a wave of guilt. Was Reza collaborating with the enemy simply by wanting to stay alive? And what would people think – if he ever did return to human space – when they discovered that he slept with the enemy, ate with the enemy, and had learned to think and speak like the enemy? Would he not become the enemy himself?

He tried to force the thoughts from his mind. He would become an alien to survive while he lived among them, but he would not let go his roots. The Kreelans had taken away everything else that he had known, but he would not give them his soul, a soul they did not even believe he possessed.

He looked at her again. Now that he thought about being her partner, he rapidly came to the conclusion that he could have done a lot worse. She seemed tough, but not as brutal as some of them appeared, and she was obviously extremely intelligent. She had treated him fairly well, considering her origins. He found that he did not want to disappoint her, did not want her to be humiliated. He wanted very much to survive the things that lay ahead, but he wanted to do it with dignity and honor, something that these people did not believe he had.

Her eyes suddenly flew open, startling him. He had been looking straight into her face.

"Reza," she spoke quietly, "you must sleep now. Tomorrow will come of its own accord. You must be rested. Sleep."

He stared into her silver eyes, lit by the enormous moon – the Empress Moon, he reminded himself – that shone high above. Of all the things about her and her kind, it was the eyes that captivated him. He held them for a moment longer, mesmerized by their beauty. His mind warred with itself, guilty for feeling such thoughts, but unable to deny them.

Finally putting off that particular battle for another time, he nodded to her, and she closed her eyes.

After a few minutes, his own eyes closed as he fell into an uneasy sleep.

* * *

Reza awoke as the Kreelan sun cast its first rays over the valley. Surprised that he had arisen before his keeper – his tresh, now, he reminded himself – he took the opportunity to enjoy a brief moment of this alien planet's natural wonder as the sky sparkled in vivid hues of crimson and yellow. But the transition lasted only a moment before the odd magenta shade of the daytime sky began to claim its territory from the dawn.

He put on his armor and was preparing their usual morning meal – dried meat for her and some fruit for himself – when at last Esah-Zhurah began to stir.

"Good morning," he said.

She only looked at him as she stretched and began to put on her armor.

Reza shrugged. *She's never been a morning person,* he thought. He handed her the strips of stiff dry meat he had cut off the hunk in her pack. She accepted them without comment and began to tear them up with her canines before swallowing the pieces almost whole. That was unusual; she normally chewed her food carefully and took her time.

"Is something bothering you?" he asked.

"Yes," she answered without hesitation.

"Well," he prompted after she remained silent, "what is it?"

She sighed. "There will be a ceremony today," she said, "the most important one a tresh will ever attend. For you, it probably will also be the most difficult. And if you fail to perform it, I will be forced to kill you." She paused briefly. "And myself."

Reza sat down, suddenly serious, suddenly angry. "Why did you not tell me of this before?"

"I was forbidden," she told him. "In any case, it does not matter. What is important is that you must take what you would call an oath," she told him slowly. "Not to declare your honor to the Empress," she said, "but as a sign of your responsibilities as a tresh. Even for you, an animal, the priestess believes this important. And you must do it freely, and with conviction. You must consider this carefully, human." She glanced at the rising sun, calculating the time. "When the sun is there," she gestured with her arm to a point where the sun would just be fully over the tree line, "it will be time."

"And if I refuse?" he asked.

"If you refuse, you will die. And after you have breathed your last, then so shall I. It is your choice."

He unsteadily rose to his feet and began to pace, occasionally glancing at the sun as if to slow its inevitable rise into the sky. He did not have long. If he died, here and now, he thought, who would know of it, and who would care? Certainly not these people, to whom he was a mere beast. But neither would humanity, he told to himself. To them he was almost certainly dead and gone, a memory at best, a forgotten burden on society at worst, never having had the chance to make a small mark on the universe. Perhaps Nicole would think of him from time to time, but only in the past tense, as another casualty of the war, an element of the past in her own tragic life.

Reza wanted so much to go on living. He would not sell his soul for an extra minute of life, but he was willing to suffer for it. He had been suffering for his next breath for most of his life, and if he had to declare himself willing to submit to their rules of life in order to live, he would. That was not a question of loyalty; it did not make him a traitor in his mind.

And even his loyalty, he decided at long last, was not really to his race. It was to certain people, the people he had known and loved, even if they only lived on in his memory. Wiley, Mary, and the few others he had called friends, all from Hallmark, all probably dead. All except Nicole, the girl he had loved, and still loved. But the rest of human society, he knew from bitter experience, had treated him little better than the Kreelans had, and in some cases, worse. To them he owed nothing.

"You must not accept if you cannot pledge yourself sincerely, human," Esah-Zhurah counseled. "By accepting, you accept all that is the Way: the physical, mental, and spiritual things that bind my people together. You must, in effect, become one with us, if you can. If you feel incapable of this, it would be better to die now as the alien you are, rather than inflict dishonor on yourself and on me. If you are not sincere, the priestess will know. She can see what is in your heart."

"And if I did make it through all of this, would your people accept me?" he asked sharply. "Will I ever be anything but an animal to you and the peers? Or will I endure all that you inflict on me, only to be killed at the end of this grand experiment?"

Esah-Zhurah stood and walked over to him. She grasped his arms in her hands and leaned very close. "Should such a thing ever come to pass," she said quietly, "should you survive all that is to come, and the Empress judge you worthy of the Way, you will receive one of these," she touched her collar with a silver talon. "This signifies your entry into Her family, and endows you with more than what you would call citizenship. It is your badge of honor, the signal of the Empress's blessing. Any who would not accord you every tribute due your standing would be shamed in Her eyes, something that is intolerable to all among Her Children. For this," she tapped the collar again, "is not easily earned, is not given to all who are born into this life." She ran her nail along the several rows of pendants hanging from the collar. "But first, human," she said, "you must prove that you have a soul, that your blood sings the melody of the Way."

"I do not understand what you mean," he said, confused. "How can my blood sing?"

"That is what we have yet to discover," she replied cryptically.

Reza pursed his lips, his concentration easing as the inevitable conclusion presented itself. "I agree," he said simply, bowing his head to her. There was no other choice.

"Very well," she said, her voice echoing barely concealed doubt, whether at his intention of fulfilling his part of the bargain or at the likelihood of his survival, he did not know. She looked quickly at the steadily rising sun. "I must teach you the words of the ceremony. We do not have much time."

Under the gathering dawn, Reza began to learn the declaration of his acceptance of an alien way of life.

* * *

When it was time, Esah-Zhurah took him to one of the arenas where several hundred other young warriors were gathered. Many were arrayed around the edges of the circular field. These Kreelans all had neckbands. Those gathering within the arena itself were without, and several senior warriors were putting them into orderly rows.

"You will be on your own for this, human," Esah-Zhurah told him. He nodded that he understood, and she gestured for him to enter the arena.

He walked forward through the dark sand to where the others were gathering and made toward one of the warriors arranging the neophytes for their proclamation of faith. She took him roughly by the arm and escorted him to a point of the hexagon that had been marked in the sand that was well away from the other neophytes. The warrior then resumed her place at the front of the group that now numbered about two hundred. She turned to the assemblage.

"*Ka'a mekh!*" she bellowed, and the young warriors knelt as one, crossing their left arms over their breasts in salute and lowering their heads in submission. Reza knelt, but did not salute; in their eyes, he was not yet worthy. The warrior turned around, her back to the neophytes, and knelt herself.

Then the priestess, Tesh-Dar, appeared from among the warriors surrounding the arena. She strode to a position well in front of the kneeling throng before her, the early morning sun gleaming from her ceremonial armor, her long braided hair swaying to her gait. She stood before them, feet planted shoulder width apart, head held high, and she began to recite the preamble to the rite of passage.

"Oh, Empress, Mother of our spirit, before you kneel those who would seek the Way–"

"–to become one with their ancestors," Reza heard himself murmur in time with the others, "to become one with their peers, to become one with all who shall come after."

"Those who kneel this day seek the privilege of The Challenge–"

"–to learn to fight and die in the flesh, that the spirit of Thy Children may grow ever stronger, that our blood may sing to Thee."

"Bound shall they be from this day forward–"

"–to the honor of the collar, the symbol of our bond with Thee, the badge of our honor–"

"–to be worn unto Death," the priestess finished.

One of the elder warriors stood and ordered the young neophytes to stand. Once they had done so, she led the priestess through the rows on what appeared to be a rank inspection.

When Tesh-Dar reached him, he bowed his head as the others had done, averting his eyes from her gaze. She stood there for a moment, perhaps a bit longer than she had in front of the others, before she moved on.

Finally, she returned to the front of the formation and spoke a few words to the accompanying warrior. She, in turn, ordered the neophytes to kneel again, and the priestess departed without another word. Then, with a final order, they all stood once more, and the Kreelans surrounding the arena let out a horrendous roar of approval.

Reza stood quietly, unable to dispel a feeling of despair that had deepened with every word. No matter what Esah-Zhurah had said, what he had taken was still an oath of fealty to the Empress, for to follow the Way – whatever that truly meant – was to follow her.

"You did well," Esah-Zhurah said as she came to his side. "Your words were clear among the voices of the peers, which speaks well of your commitment."

"For all the good it may do me," he replied somberly.

"Come," she said, taking him by the arm, apparently uplifted by his depressed mood, "we have much to do this day. It is time to begin your training." She guided him toward one of the smaller arenas where a number of other neophytes had gathered, eyeing the two of them with great curiosity. "It shall be a day you will long remember."

Reza shot her a sideways glance. "I have no doubt."

* * *

He lay that night in an aching heap in his bedding of soft skins. Esah-Zhurah had told him that the first step to the Way was to build a sound body, but what he had endured in the arena that day had been brutal.

After the ceremony and until the sun set and the huge gong at the kazha's center rang to sound day's end, the tresh ran, jumped, sparred, and wrestled with one another. The routine was broken three times by the appearance of three different senior disciples, who instructed them on different weapons and techniques that they put into practice immediately.

Reza, not having had the benefit of any such training when he was younger, had been hit and battered by the blunt ends and edges of the training weapons so many times that his body felt like one enormous bruise. His lip had been split open, he had a deep gash above his right ear, and his legs had been pounded so much he could barely walk. Esah-Zhurah had to help him hobble back to their little camp in the woods where a healer tended to his wounds. But even after she had finished, his body remained an ocean of pain.

But he had never cried out, nor had he complained. No matter how many times his legs were tripped from under him, no matter how hard the other tresh – particularly Esah-Zhurah – struck him, he staggered back to his feet so he could take some more.

He rolled over to face the fire that burned brightly in their little camp near the stables, biting back the urge to groan at the throbbing pain. He watched Esah-Zhurah as she unbraided her hair, meticulously combing it out with her talons once it was free.

Reza idly considered the condition of his own hair as a diversion from his aching body. Now shoulder length and dark brown, it was festooned with knots and mats, for he had nothing to comb it with. On impulse, and despite the gnawing pain, he decided just to cut off most of his hair with his knife. He had always liked his hair cut short, and it would be much easier to care for.

He sat up, hissing through his teeth at the pain of simply moving. He tossed aside his hides, letting in the evening chill. The black gauzy material that formed his undergarments was incredibly comfortable, but was not a very effective insulator against the cold. He probed with his fingers through the thickening thatch of hair over his skull, trying to get an idea of where to start. In the end, he simply grabbed a handful at random and reached for his knife with his other hand.

The blade was just biting through the first strands when he was tackled from behind, Esah-Zhurah wrenching the knife from his hand.

"No!" she cried, flattening him against the ground.

"*What the hell?*" he sputtered in Standard. "What is wrong?" he demanded in the New Tongue, struggling against her weight.

She rolled him over on his back, flashing the knife in front of his eyes. "Never do that!" she exclaimed. "Why would you do such a thing?"

"What?" he asked, utterly confused. "Cut my hair? It is matted and snarled, and I prefer it short. I–"

With a growl of frustration she plunged the knife's blade into the ground, burying it nearly up to its handle.

"You must never cut your hair," she told him. "It is one of your most sacred possessions. Have I not told you this, fool? The only ones who follow the Way and have short hair are those who have been disgraced and been denied suicide. It is the worst punishment among our people. If you follow the Way, you must let your hair grow, for it is the only mark of longevity for my race. Except for those like the ancient mistress of the armory, our bodies do not age in the same fashion as do yours. Our skin does not decay, nor do our muscles weaken until we are very near death. By the hair and by this," she tapped her collar, "are you judged by the peers."

Reza sat back, confounded. "Well, if I have to grow it, I will need something to comb it with."

"You use these," she said in frustration, as if Reza were a slow-witted child, holding up her hands and wiggling her fingers. "Have you not seen me use them for this purpose?" The firelight shone on her silver claws as they danced to and fro. Then she pointed at his gauntlets with their imitation talons. "Here," she said, grabbing them, "I will show you." She made Reza put them on. Then she sat up behind him and began to comb his hair with her own claws, skillfully ferreting out and eliminating the snarls with only a rare painful pull.

"Now," she said after she had done most of the difficult work, "you try."

He put on the gauntlets and began to work their claws through his hair, but was so clumsy she felt compelled to grab his hands before they had gone more than an inch past his hairline.

"Be careful," she warned. "You will cut yourself badly. You must do it like this." Her hands guided his through the gradually aligning strands, and she soon left him to do it himself.

He only scratched himself once or twice by the time he had combed everything out to his satisfaction. When he was done, it felt much better, although the hair that hung over his eyes remained a problem. He tried to brush it back, but it stolidly refused, instead sticking out at all angles as if he were carrying a hefty charge of static electricity.

Esah-Zhurah leaned over his shoulder to get a look at his face, and she burst out in what he thought must be laughter. Brief though it was, she had never made that sound before.

"Are you laughing?" he asked skeptically, watching her face closely. "Do you think I look...*funny* with my hair like this?"

"Perhaps that is what you would call it," she answered. "I do not think it is quite the same for my people. But yes," she said, considering the question, "you do look *funny*."

Without warning she reached toward his face and grabbed the hair in front of his eyes. She cut it off cleanly with one of her claws in the time it took him to blink.

"This, you do not need," she informed him. "Only that which flows down your back." She regarded him for a moment, then nodded in approval. "Your hair is yet too short to braid. That will come later." She ran a hand through his hair, her touch sending a pleasant tingle down his spine. "You must groom well every day. Your hair is thick, but will foul easily." Then she turned her attention to the lock she still held in her hand. "May I keep this?" she asked.

"If it means something to you," he told her, "you are welcome to it."

She bowed her head to him and carefully placed the hair in a pouch that hung on her waistband, nearly identical to the one the priestess – and all the other warriors, he realized – carried.

"We should sleep, now," she told him. She banked the fire and returned to her bedding.

Reza followed suit, stifling a groan from his protesting muscles.

"Tomorrow shall soon be upon us," she murmured as she lay down.

He did not need further prompting. He buried himself under the thick skins, and was asleep as soon as he closed his eyes.

* * *

The days became weeks, then months, and Reza's body grew toward the man he might one day become, if he lived long enough. He had already outgrown three sets of armor, and the seams on the newest were stretching at the shoulders.

Esah-Zhurah, too, was gradually changing as the shadows slowly lengthened toward winter in the planet's extended seasonal cycle. Her body was filling out and becoming more powerful, her arms and legs rippling with lean muscle. She moved with the grace of a dancer, and he did his best to emulate her, learning how to move quickly and quietly. Her black hair grew ever longer. The beads attached to the ends now reached her waist, and the protuberances that were her eyebrows had formed into a graceful arch over her eyes.

After the furious hours of their normal training, the two often walked or ran long leagues under the ceaseless sun and cool, fresh air, and Reza felt himself growing stronger day by day. They silently challenged one other in undeclared races through the forest or up a hill, and while she often won, the margin was an increasingly small one.

As time went on, he and the other tresh began to build on the foundation that had come with the endless exercises and mock combats. Reza discovered with some surprise that they had something akin to team sports, with hardwood poles serving as swords, and he played them just as aggressively as his blue-skinned companions. While he often spent the nights nursing welts and bruises, increasingly he was able to compete on their terms, and his Kreelan counterparts were beginning to show him some degree of respect.

However, as Reza one day discovered, there was more to be found at the kazha than endless hours of fighting practice and nights filled with pain.

Late one evening, he and Esah-Zhurah were in the armorers' chambers having their weapons and armor checked. While the duty armorer and her apprentices were busy with Esah-Zhurah, Reza happened to notice a lone armorer sitting alone at a small stone table in an adjoining room. She was quite old, judging from the length of her hair and the slight palsy that caused her neck to twitch. She bent close to her work, her eyes perhaps having grown weak from countless years (he still had no idea how long Kreelans could live) of such painstaking labor. A lamp hung close to the table's surface, and he caught sight of what appeared to be a brush of some kind in her hand. His curiosity mounted as he watched her make a stroke on whatever was serving as her canvas, dipping the brush in a small container, then continuing to paint.

Without conscious thought, he wandered over to where the old woman worked, curious as to what she was doing. Lying on the table was the metal that would become a warrior's ceremonial breastplate, and on it she had traced a design whose origins and meaning were beyond him, one of the runes in what he knew was the Old Tongue, but which he could not read. But the beauty and intricacy of the woman's craftsmanship were universal. It was an ice-blue rune, arcing its way across the metal surface like an ancient scimitar, the colors used in its creation precise to render an effect that was almost three-dimensional, each shade and hue regulated and blended to perfection.

He stood quietly behind her as she slowly filled in a segment that would be the design's center, fascinated by the steadiness of her ancient hand.

"If your hands hold the interest of your eyes, little one," she said in a soft voice, startling him, "yours is it to try." She looked up at him, her eyes milky with cataracts, so old perhaps that the healers could do no more for her. Or perhaps she did not want their help.

Reza, dumbfounded, nodded stiffly. The woman rose from her stool, her joints creaking loudly, and gestured for him to sit. She handed him the brush and proceeded to guide his hand along the trace of the rune with one hand, while supporting herself on his shoulder with the other. When she judged that the brush needed more dye, she guided his hand toward the appropriate vial. There were dozens of them, Reza saw, as well as a seemingly endless variety of hues the old woman had created by mixing other colors, placed with exacting care on the palette next to his elbow.

Time was lost to him for the rest of that evening. He had forgotten everything except the glowing design that was assuming its final form under his hand, with the old woman's help.

At last, it was done. He had finished the last quarter of it by himself, with only occasional prompts from the woman. His hand was cramping from holding the brush, but he felt oddly triumphant. He had helped create something of beauty, and had not had to fight or be beaten to do it.

"Good is your work, little one," she said as he held the breastplate up to the light for her inspection, her tired eyes still somehow able to see. "The priestess shall be pleased."

"The… priestess?" Reza stuttered.

"Of course, young tresh," she said, her nearly toothless mouth curling into a kindly smile. "Did you not notice its size?"

"No…" he said, shaking his head. But it was immediately obvious, now that she had pointed out the fact. The plate was nearly twice the size of his, if not larger. "No, I did not."

"More observant should you be, then," she advised. "Short is a warrior's life, otherwise."

"Of course…" Reza paused, looking at her helplessly. *Her name*, he thought. *I should be able to figure out her name. But how?*

"Pan'ne-Sharakh," she said, as if reading his mind. "Her Children know each other by blood, human," she said cryptically. "But it is also written here," her fingers pointed in sequence to five of the many pendants that hung from her collar, "in the shape of the stars that are brightest in the sky when the Empress Moon is directly above. Look at the sky this night, and you will know the ones of which I speak. Their names your tresh shall teach you. They are the key."

"Thank you, Pan'ne-Sharakh," he said gratefully, bowing his head. "Thank you for your kindness."

"I serve Her in my own way, little one," she answered softly, patting his shoulder gently before turning back to her work.

He turned to leave, and found Esah-Zhurah standing in the doorway. He realized with a shock that she must have been standing there for hours.

She brushed past him to greet the old woman, bowing with reverence, and spoke quietly with her for a moment. Then Pan'ne-Sharakh slowly shuffled from the room, her back bowed with age.

"She seems to feel you have a talent for such work," Esah-Zhurah told him, obviously surprised. "You shall develop that skill in addition to your others, but not in their stead. Should you have the time," she added dubiously. She gestured impatiently toward the exit. "Let us go."

He followed her back to their little camp, looking at the stars in the sky.

And there they were, as the old woman had said they would be: the five bright points of light that would frame the Empress Moon when it hung directly overhead, the key to the names of Her Children.

EIGHT

The sword flashed down in a savage arc, the sun's glow blazing from the metal as if the weapon itself was made of light.

Reza pitched himself to the right, dodging the blade, then kicked out with his left foot, his thigh like a massive piston that drove the air from Nyana-M'kher's lungs and flung her to the ground. The few seconds of surprise his parry had given him was all he needed. Smoothly drawing the black shrekka from its holder on his left shoulder, he hurled the hand-held buzz saw and watched with satisfaction as it buried itself in the ground five centimeters from Nyana-M'kher's head, showering her with sand from the arena's floor.

"Enough!" called the arena's umpire, a stocky warrior by the name of Syr-Kesh. A gesture of her hand made Reza's victory official.

Reza collapsed on his knees into the sand next to Nyana-M'kher, who was also trying to get her breath back. She struggled to her knees, and the two of them bowed their heads to Syr-Kesh, Nyana-M'kher saluting as she did so. Then they both knelt there for the brief time that was allowed for meditation after one combat and before the next, a mental cool-down that the Kreelans considered an essential part of their routine.

Reza closed his eyes as his mind made the rounds of his body, sounding it out for damage and weakness, evaluating and relaxing each muscle in turn. Their combat had taken an unusually long time – nearly ten minutes, so evenly matched had they been – and his shoulders and legs ached fiercely from the duel. It had been the third one today for both of them, and this one had been Reza's only win. He had lost the first match to a senior tresh in a spectacularly one-sided – and decidedly brief – engagement, and the other to a very young tresh who felled him with a lightning-swift cut to the legs that would have crippled him for life had the sword carried any edge.

In these moments, when he turned inward like this, he was amazed at how much control he was gaining over his body and his mind. With a handful of exceptions, notably in his mid-back and feet, he could flex each muscle individually, leaving those around it totally relaxed. His breathing and heart rate, too, were gradually coming under better control, and he found that he could hold his breath for nearly three minutes before he felt compelled to take a breath. Even then, he could force himself to breathe normally and keep his heart rate at a steady cadence, rather than take huge gulps of air as his heart raced to get oxygen back into his system and to his brain.

His fighting skills, while hardly impressive by Kreelan standards, had improved to the point where he was no longer the punching bag he had been when he had arrived. While he returned with Esah-Zhurah to their tiny camp each night bruised and often beaten, those who faced him in the arena treated him with respect for his cunning and tenacity, if not for his neophyte fighting skills. The days of underestimating the human, the human many of them had been convinced would simply wither away and die in those early days, were over. Reza had quickly come to understand the soul-deep importance of combat to the Kreelans, and had devoted himself to its study. He observed and mimicked the others, especially Esah-Zhurah, and invented his own tactics. He went over moves in his mind, awake and asleep, before putting them to the test in his waking hours.

And after the combat was finished for the day and they had eaten, Esah-Zhurah would lecture him for hours on the ways of her people, on the Way itself. Gradually, he came to understand that the Way was not just an ideology, a set of abstract concepts meant to structure their lives such as the laws of humankind sought to do, but it was also a physical thing. While he did not yet understand just how it worked, the Way was intertwined with their racial bloodline: when Esah-Zhurah described her people as the Children of the Empress, it was – literally – true. There was some physiological thread that bound them together in much the same way that ants or bees of a particular colony identified themselves and their functions as part of a much larger whole. But how this worked, he did not yet understand. Nor, surprisingly, did Esah-Zhurah.

"It simply is," she had told him once. "Her will is as fundamental to us and as evident as is the air we breathe. I do not hear Her voice in my mind; I am not a telepath. But I sense in my blood that which She seeks for us, and I know my place in Her design."

Reza had pondered those words many times since, with a vague sense of loneliness, and perhaps even jealousy, clouding his heart. For he did not know Her will, and he feared his own destiny within the strands of the web the Empress wove for Her people.

"Time," Syr-Kesh called, and Reza's reflection disappeared like sea mist blown clear by the morning wind. He bowed his head once more to Syr-Kesh before getting to his feet, walking to where Esah-Zhurah stood waiting for him near the entry to the arena. Behind him, several tresh frantically raked the sand smooth for the next contest.

"You did well, my tresh," Esah-Zhurah said as he approached, and he bowed his head to her in respect. "Much better than I expected, especially without the sword on which you have so heavily depended to this time." Reza ignored the barb, a ritual habit of hers that never failed to annoy him, but about which he could do nothing. A part of him hated her deeply, but another part, what he often hoped was the most human part, wanted her respect, wanted her to be proud of him. "But these practice sessions are as nothing compared to the Challenge you will face in four days. Your opponents here do not show all of their skill or their strength, they do not waste their energies here, as do you, but save them for the time when they will need them most."

"What does it matter?" he asked angrily. "I can only do my best. If I am beaten in the first match of the first Challenge, then so be it." He shrugged out of his armor, letting Esah-Zhurah open his black shirt to apply one of the writhing living bandages to the creased welt on his shoulder. Nyana-M'kher had brought her sword down on the joint between his shoulder armor and the metal backplate, pinching a hand's breadth of Reza's flesh into a puckering tear that had proved incredibly painful for the rest of the extended combat. "But one day," he said, more to himself than to her, "I will stand in the final arena with the winning sword in my hands."

"That," Esah-Zhurah said as she massaged the oozing mottled mass of the bandage into the wound on Reza's shoulder, her voice tinged with sarcasm that sounded all too human, "is a day I wish not to miss."

Reza flinched as she pressed at the wound. A shudder of revulsion swept through him as he felt the amoebic mass of tissue begin to merge with his flesh, mysteriously healing it. It would leave a sculpted scar in its wake, a trophy of his tiny victory. He knew that whatever the thing was, however it and the things like it were made – or bred – it was infinitely beyond any comparable human technique he could imagine. The scope of wounds and injuries, even diseases that it could treat was apparently limitless. But having another living thing pressed into his flesh, and knowing that it would become a part of him, a perfect symbiosis, left him yearning for the cold touch and electric hum of the instruments and analyzers, the smells of ozone and alcohol, of the little clinic of House 48.

The pain made him think of the last, and worst, time Esah-Zhurah had punished him for anything. The only thing among the countless subjects they discussed that she adamantly refused to reveal to him was if there were any males in their society, and if so, where they were. On this one subject he could get nothing out of her other than, "You shall know when the time comes, if it comes," and the subject would be considered closed.

The one time Reza had tried to push her on it, the last time he had asked about it, she had turned on him like a lioness defending her cubs. She had beaten him so severely that he missed nearly three days of training, spending most of that time in the care of the healers as they reset the five ribs and one arm that Esah-Zhurah had broken in the course of his punishment. The healing process had been nearly as bad as the beating itself, especially when they held him down and forced his mouth open, pouring a wet mass of the undulating healing gel down his throat. It slid across his tongue like a wet oyster before pumping itself into his airway and then his lungs. In the moment before it stilled the pain of the jagged edges of the ribs tearing into his lungs and made breathing easier for him, he thought he would go mad at the thing churning within his body. Esah-Zhurah had chastised him afterward for being a coward, shaming her before the healers with his squeals of revulsion. Her words had burned themselves into his heart and mind as he lay in the infirmary for the next three days with her sitting next to him, back turned, silent. If she had heard him call her name, or felt his tentative touch, or sensed the silent tears he shed, she did not show it. Only when the elder healer had cleared him as being well and he had risen from the bed of skins had she addressed him, and then as if nothing had happened.

"There," she said, closing his shirt. She helped him get his torso armor back on, the bandage throbbing uncomfortably. "Come. You have completed your three obligatory matches for this day, and I have something for you."

"What?" Reza asked, his mind alert to the mischievous undertone in her voice.

"Patience," she said, her eyes laughing at him. "You shall see."

He followed her, and was surprised when she led him to the stable where the magtheps honked and snorted as they stomped about their enclosure. Reza's nose quickly filled with their musky smell, a smell he had become quite accustomed to in his first few days here, when he had to sleep with the animals, chained to a post.

"What is this about?" he asked her.

"Tomorrow we begin our free time before the Challenge," she told him. "From sunrise tomorrow to sunset the second day after that, we may do as we please."

"So?"

She turned to him. "I wish to take you somewhere," she told him, "and, unless you wish to run to the mountains," she gestured to the distant peaks on the northern horizon, "you will need to learn to ride."

Reza's heart suddenly began to beat faster. "You will teach me this?" he asked, his voice betraying his hopefulness. How long had he been here, he wondered. A Standard year, perhaps? Two? And this would be the first time he would ride one of these fascinating animals, rather than running along behind them like a dog.

Esah-Zhurah smiled, mimicking a human, her lips parting to reveal her ivory incisors. "I will provide you an animal," she said. "The rest will be up to you." She paused a moment, watching Reza's face turn from hopeful excitement to wary reservation. "It should be interesting to see one animal ride another."

"Where is it?" he asked, forcing himself to be calm, forever wondering why he continued to hope for some kind of real respect from her, or even a little genuine warmth. *Without doubt*, he told himself cynically, *you are the galaxy's greatest optimist*.

"Come," she said, beckoning him to follow. She led him around the enclosure, stopping in the low-ceilinged tack room at the far side of the stable where she retrieved a riding harness and a light saddle, which she gave to Reza.

When he followed her around to the far side, he found himself standing at the gate to a large, individual enclosure that he had not seen before.

"This is the animal," she told him, pointing into the enclosure.

A single beast stood there, a young bull that was larger than any magthep Reza had ever seen. The animal stood alone, except for the scrub rats that darted across the enclosure, searching for food. Its eyes were fixed on Esah-Zhurah and himself, and Reza could see that the animal was uneasy at their presence by the way it perked its floppy ears and nervously shifted its weight from foot to foot. The talons, grown too long on this soft ground without a trim, raised small clouds of dust from the parched soil. Its hide was dirty and unkempt, and Reza could easily make out the whitish tracks of scars that crisscrossed the massive animal's back and withers.

"This animal has been mistreated," he remarked coldly.

Esah-Zhurah snorted. "That is not so," she protested. "It simply refuses to be tamed. The scars you see were left by riders when thrown from its back. It has never been beaten as punishment."

A clear advantage over my social status, Reza told himself sourly. "If no one can ride it," he asked, "why is it kept in the stables? Why not let it run free or kill it for meat?"

"Because," she said, "there are those who find such challenges entertaining."

"And those," he finished for her, "who are entertained by watching someone as they are thrown and then trampled."

"Here," she said, pointedly ignoring his comment as she gave him the bridle, the leather saddle already in his other hand.

He was about to mention the fact that she had not bothered to show him how to attach the saddle and bridle, but decided against it. Both of them were relatively simple devices that he had already seen on other animals, and he was sure he could figure them out. The major problem, he thought, was going to be getting close enough to the snorting magthep to put them on. And, until that was accomplished, he did not have to consider the prospect of being thrown. He only had to worry about being trampled and then shredded to pieces by the hooked talons on the animal's feet.

As he pondered his first move, a glint of green near his sandal caught his attention, and he saw with surprise that he was standing in a patch of *yezhe'e* plants, which he knew magtheps liked. Looking at the beast's enclosure, he saw that he was standing on the edge of a green border that marked the magthep's reach beyond the wooden bars, everything closer to the fence having already been plucked from the ground and eaten.

Gathering the saddle and bridle in one hand, he leaned down and pulled as many shoots as he could hold. Reza noted with satisfaction that the prospective food had not eluded the magthep's wary eye. With cautious steps and flared nostrils, it moved slowly toward him.

Reza motioned for Esah-Zhurah to open the gate. Once inside, she closed it behind him, the squeak of the wood jangling his nerves. He let out his breath quietly, forcing himself to relax as the beast came closer, its large almond-shaped eyes and their yellow irises fixed on him. He decided to leave the riding gear behind for the moment, setting the bridle and saddle down slowly so as not to startle the animal. If he could not gain its trust, he would not need them. Then he took off his gauntlets with their gleaming talons and hooked them onto his belt, hoping the touch of his bare hands might be more reassuring than the lethal weapons his fingers became when encased in the armored gloves.

Now armed only with the tempting plants, he began to slowly walk toward the magthep, calling to it quietly. "Easy, boy," he said in Standard low enough that he knew Esah-Zhurah would not hear, and thus take offense. "Take it easy."

Esah-Zhurah watched as Reza began to play out whatever strategy he had decided upon, and was not surprised when other tresh began to take an interest in the proceedings. They came to cling to the fence like iron filings to a magnet, eager to see the outcome of the human's fourth combat of the day. For a moment, a streak of an unfamiliar emotion passed over her heart like a wisp of cloud before the sun: guilt. She had not told him that the scars on the animal's back had been left not by simple riders thrown by an unruly beast, but by the best trainers in the kazha who had all tried – and failed miserably – to train the magthep, to make it a riding animal. One of them had even been killed after the animal had become enraged, tearing the helpless fallen rider to pieces. But even after that, no one had suggested that the animal be killed. It was a challenge to be conquered, a mountain to be climbed, and those were the things on which her species thrived. But the others who sought to try their hand knew the animal's history. Reza did not.

It did not matter, she told herself firmly. The animal – Reza – would not, could not long survive in her world, among her people. His death would come soon. If not today under the magthep's feet, then a few days hence during the Challenge, when there were few rules and death was an unfortunate, if infrequent, consequence. And if not then, her mind went on as she watched him come under the animal's nervous shadow, there was always the Challenge of the next cycle, and the cycle after that...

Reza and the magthep had come as close as either dared for the moment, each eyeing the other warily, alert for any sudden or suspicious movement. Reza could see that the bull was a very young adult, its tiger-striped fur thick and lush under the coating of dust and grime, the hair around its wet muzzle still dark, with no sign of gray. But its size was nothing short of extraordinary, its powerful shoulders well over his head. The beast's nostrils flared at his scent, but he saw the animal's attention inexorably drawn toward the plants he held in his hand, their scent a powerful distraction. Carefully, slowly, Reza took one of the shoots in his free hand and extended it toward the magthep, palm up and open to avoid losing his fingers should the beast try to snatch it away.

But the animal would have none of it. Snorting furiously, it backpedaled several paces, then whirled in a circle, prancing on its taloned feet as the smaller arms on its shoulders made random clutching motions, as if instinctively grasping for the plants he held.

"Take it easy, boy," Reza murmured, standing absolutely still. *Be patient*, he told himself. *Take your time.* "It's all right. I won't hurt you." He continued to hold his arm out, the light breeze carrying the scent of the plants to the magthep. Again, it came closer.

Closer. Craning its neck so far that Reza could hear its vertebrae popping, the magthep stepped forward just close enough for its prehensile upper lip to tug the shoot out of Reza's hand. Instantly, the plant was sucked into the animal's mouth. It backed away again, but not as far as the first time, and not quite as fast, while it enjoyed its treat.

Slowly, Reza took another shoot in his hand, holding it out to the animal. Again, the ritual was repeated, the beast slowly coming forward to take the offering. And again. And again.

By the time the shoots in his hand were gone, the magthep no longer backed away, but stood towering over Reza, patiently waiting for its next treat as Reza spoke to it quietly, calming it with the sound of his voice. After the animal had swallowed the last of the plants, Reza held out his empty hand. The magthep leaned down, smelling the scent of the plants, and began to lick Reza's hand, then tried to grasp it with its questing lip. As it did so, Reza slowly raised his other hand to the animal's muzzle, and then slightly higher, stroking the front of its head very gently.

"Good boy," he whispered softly as he moved his hand around the beast's head, scratching lightly, trying to show that he meant it no harm. Taking it very slowly, he began to run his hands through the animal's fur, scratching and petting it, letting it get used to him. He moved his hands over its head, neck, and shoulders as high as he could reach, then across its flank and back toward the tail, always maintaining eye contact with the animal as it turned to watch him, careful not to make any sudden moves.

Sometimes the magthep would get unnerved and dart away from him, but it always came back. It was not accustomed to such attention, and it seemed to be intrigued by Reza's smell, something it had never been exposed to before, and the taste of his skin.

The salt, Reza thought to himself. Esah-Zhurah had explained to him once about how precious salt had been in the ancient times. Reza remembered how he used to sweat in the fields, and how the white salt crusts would form in his boots around the ankles and in the wrinkles of the clothes pressed tight to his skin. Here, when the days were hot, he would sweat so much in his leatherite armor that parts of it would turn gray and then white with salt from his sweat before the armorers insisted on remaking it.

He let the magthep lick his hands with its coarse black tongue as much as it liked, pulling his hand away only when the beast became overzealous and reached out for him with its grinding teeth. Then he began to pet and scratch the magthep again.

His shoulders burning from holding them high enough to scratch or touch the animal everywhere he could, Reza made his way back once more to the magthep's front and then down the opposite flank, choosing not to try and cross around the animal's rear and the powerful legs. Then he started all over again.

"There," he murmured, unconsciously switching back to the Kreelan tongue as he finished the third and last go around. He was filthy from the dust and dirt that had spilled from the beast's coat, and his hands were dark brown with oil and grime. But when he looked up into the animal's face, he saw that he had accomplished something. The ears seemed to be poised in a posture of attentiveness, rather than fear, and the animal's eyes seemed to look at him with curiosity rather than mistrust. "Well," he said to the magthep, "what now?"

For lack of any better ideas, Reza walked back to where he had left the saddle and bridle, and was pleased to hear the magthep's quiet footsteps close behind him. It was so close, in fact, that its head was poised almost directly over Reza, the massive skull blocking the hot sun like an umbrella. Looking at the bridle, Reza considered his chances for any further success. He had never ridden any animal, let alone one of these alien creatures, and had no idea how it might behave if he tried to control it. He felt that the magthep no longer really distrusted him, but he knew that could change very quickly if he did the wrong thing at the wrong time. The scars on the animal's back attested to its willingness and ability to rid itself of unwanted cargo, and Reza did not want to push things too fast. But how fast was that, exactly? How long should it take to turn one of these things into a riding animal? An hour? A day? A whole cycle? He just did not know.

Looking away from the animal for a moment, he saw that the fence behind him was lined with his would-be peers, three or four deep, as they watched one animal try to tame another. He saw Esah-Zhurah, her face caught in something between a grin and a sneer. She knew how badly he wanted to get away from the kazha for even a little while, to see something other than the hundreds of blue, hostile faces that greeted him each day as he learned how to fight and kill. And bringing this magthep to heel was the only way he could do it, the only way he could escape this great cage for a day or so. He felt a wave of anger boil up as he swept his eyes over his unwanted spectators, and channeled it into determination. He reached down for the bridle.

The magthep suddenly snorted and began to back away, and Reza stopped. He straightened up, the bridle still on the ground.

So, he thought with resignation, *it seems we will have to do this the hard way*. He knew that the beast had probably been tricked more than once into wearing the bridle, and would not fall for it again. He stepped toward the beast, palms out. It did not back away, but stood to sniff at his hands, then lick them tentatively, attuned for any trace of the hated bridle. Reza scratched the magthep's ears, and once again, it seemed to accept him.

Moving again down the beast's flank, Reza started to lean against its side, patting it, stroking it, then pulling on its hair, lightly at first, then harder in hopes of sensitizing the magthep to his presence. He found a particularly good spot to scratch, and the magthep elongated and twisted its neck in pleasure, its upper lip reaching out to flip at the air.

Holding on tightly to thick hanks of the animal's fur, Reza suddenly leaped up. Twisting his right leg over the animal's back, he planted himself in the wide, shallow valley between its shoulders and hips. His hands curled around the longer hair further up on the animal's neck with a grip that bled his knuckles white, anticipating the pounding he was going to get when the animal reacted.

Esah-Zhurah held her breath as Reza mounted the animal. Around her, the other tresh gasped, waiting for the beast's savage twisting and bucking that would send the human flying.

But nothing happened.

Reza watched, wide-eyed with surprise, as the beast's head slowly turned toward him on its graceful neck. It blinked its eyes twice as if to say, "Oh, it's only you." Then it turned away and began to amble toward the shelter that housed its water trough, Reza clinging to its back like a confused tickbird.

"In Her name," Esah-Zhurah heard someone beside her whisper, an oath that was repeated many times up and down the rows of onlookers.

"How is it possible?" someone else asked, and she felt a tug at her arm. "Esah-Zhurah," asked Amar-Khan, the most senior among the tresh of the kazha, "what trickery is this? Is it so that one animal may speak to another? How can the human do this, when our best riders and trainers have failed?"

"I..." Esah-Zhurah began, her gaze torn between the tresh's angry eyes and the sight of Reza, scratching the magthep's shoulders with both hands, seemingly oblivious to any danger of being thrown. "I do not know. I do not understand their Way."

Amar-Khan let go her arm, baring her fangs in a grimace. "Their Way," she hissed. "You give animals a great deal of credit, Esah-Zhurah. Perhaps you, too, would speak with the magtheps?"

Esah-Zhurah felt a surge of fire in her blood, and the rational thoughts of her mind boiled away as her hand sought the handle of her knife.

"Enough!"

The tresh parted before Tesh-Dar, who came to stand beside Esah-Zhurah, dismissing Amar-Khan with her eyes.

"Offense was given, Esah-Zhurah," the priestess said quietly, "but I bid you pay it no heed. Neither Amar-Khan, nor the others – myself included – understand the life you have accepted as Her will, and you will encounter such ill-conceived notions from time to time. Your blood sings to Her, but your mind must control the fire in your veins."

"Yes, my priestess," Esah-Zhurah said, grateful for the older warrior's understanding. She sheathed her weapon, feeling a chill run through her body as the fire faded from her veins.

"He again surprises me," Tesh-Dar murmured thoughtfully, stroking the scar over her left eye as she watched Reza begin to communicate his wishes to the magthep in an as-yet uncoordinated signaling of hand and foot. "Already the beast acknowledges his commands," she said. "And without a bridle, without a saddle." She paused for a moment, cocking her head, as if listening. "He speaks to it."

"I hear nothing, my priestess," Esah-Zhurah told her. She could see Reza's mouth moving slightly, but they were many strides away, far beyond Esah-Zhurah's hearing. "What does he say?"

"I do not know," Tesh-Dar replied, shrugging. "It is in the human tongue so many of them use." She sensed Esah-Zhurah bristle at the knowledge. It was one thing about which she had been adamant: Reza was to speak only the language of the Empress. To speak any human language was to summon fast and furious punishment. "Allow him this one day to speak as he would," Tesh-Dar suggested, commanded, sensing Esah-Zhurah's reaction. "If he can tame such a beast with this," she tapped her foot at the base of a mound of yezhe'e plants, "and alien words and thoughts, then he has earned such a privilege. Our own ways fared not nearly as well."

They both looked up at the sound of the rhythmic pounding of clawed feet in time to see Reza bring the magthep to within a meter or so of the fence and stop. The beast flared its nostrils and bared its flat, grinding teeth at the Kreelans. The young human warrior sat erect on the dirty back of his mount, his hands resting on his thighs, arms shaking from the exhaustion of his intensive acquaintance with the animal. But his eyes did not waver as he looked over the crowd. His gaze lingered on Esah-Zhurah, making sure that she saw and understood the contempt in his own eyes before he sought out the priestess's gaze. He bowed his head to her.

"This," he said proudly, "is *Goliath*."

Nine

After a hasty breakfast of barely cooked meat and a handful of small fruits, Reza and Esah-Zhurah joined the hundreds of other tresh who were making their way from the kazha to wherever they had chosen to spend their free time. Some would go to the city, many to the forests and mountains, and still others to places Reza did not yet even know of. Only the priestess and some of the more senior warriors would remain behind.

The weather that morning was magnificent, the sunrise breaking over the mountains to fill the valley below with the promise of a warm day under a clear magenta sky. The cool air was crisp and filled with a cornucopia of scents that Reza had come to subconsciously accept as the smell of home.

As he rode beside Esah-Zhurah, towering above her on Goliath's back, he found that he could hardly wait to get away from the suffocating closeness of the peers. They treated him with more respect than they had when he had first come among them, but he was still the lowest form of life on this planet, lower even than the simpleminded animals raised for meat. Ironically, it was Esah-Zhurah who had consistently proven the most difficult to sway, her arrogance virtually undiluted from the day he had first awakened to her scowling face.

Yet, he was increasingly unsure if her behavior was entirely sincere. Sometimes he awoke to find her staring at him, her eyes flickering in the glow of the low fire they kept to ward off the night's chill. The look on her face was always thoughtful, contemplative, rather than the perpetual sneer he was used to seeing during the day. But always, as soon as she realized he was watching her, a cloud passed over her eyes, and she would roll over, turning her back to him.

The way he had seen her interact with the tresh also made him wonder. As the months had come and gone, she had become less and less tolerant of the other tresh making derisive comments about Reza or bending the rules in the arena just far enough to try and do him serious injury, something he had thus far managed to avoid. For just a moment he would think – or at least wistfully hope – that she was acting on his behalf. But the hope died as soon as he saw the look of conceit on her face or heard the arrogant tone in her voice, and the anger and loneliness that were his heart and soul would pierce him like a white-hot knife. Hot and cold, hard and soft, she was at once one thing and yet another, gently applying a bandage to a wound one minute, brutally punishing him the next.

"What are you thinking?" She asked, eyeing him closely. "I have learned that expression you now wear, that tells of your mind contemplating alien thoughts."

Her thigh brushed his as they rode side by side, and he felt a sudden rush of heat to his face. He reflexively guided Goliath on a slightly divergent path.

"I was thinking about you," he said.

"Oh? And what great thoughts are these, human?"

"I was wondering," he said, "if you really care as little for me as you would like me to think? Is all of your conceit and arrogance genuine, or just a façade to conceal your true feelings?"

He suddenly found himself talking to empty space. He turned around to find the girl and her magthep stopped, her hands clutching the bridle tightly, her face as still as the eye of a hurricane.

Touché, he thought.

She was quiet for a long moment, her expression completely unreadable to Reza, who had never before seen her like this. Had she been a human, he thought, she might have been about to cry.

"I applaud your powers of deduction, human," she told him quietly. "But what I feel, and for whom, is not the business of an animal whose existence is measured in terms of the charity the Empress has chosen to bestow upon you. Never will there come a day when you shall be privy to the workings of my heart and mind."

With a less than gentle kick, she started her magthep walking again.

Reza bowed his head to her, bringing Goliath alongside her mount, reining his beast in slightly to match the smaller animal's slower pace. He claimed the round as a tactical defeat against himself, but a strategic victory of sorts. Despite her emotional screen of anger and, perhaps, embarrassment, he knew that he had touched on a nerve, and could not resist one final thrust. "Among my people," he said, "there is a saying: *Never say never*."

"My eternal thanks for the wisdom of your people," she replied acidly, kicking her magthep in the ribs and pulling away from Reza and Goliath at a gallop. "Follow if you can, animal!" she shouted.

Reza took up the chase, disappearing into the cloud of dust behind her as the two of them raced away from the thinning caravan of tresh, heading toward the distant mountains.

* * *

The sun had just passed its zenith by the time they departed the great plain on which the city and most of the forests stood, and began to move into the range of mountains that lay beyond. Reza had never imagined he would find such color or beauty here. When viewed from the kazha, the mountains always seemed shrouded in darkness, their details lost in the distance and an ever-present crown of water-laden clouds that obscured the jagged peaks for all but a few precious minutes of nearly every day. But the deep purple granite around him sparkled and shimmered as the rock's tiny facets reflected the sunlight like millions of tiny diamonds. The ancient canyon walls, severed and shifted by eons of irresistible pressure from beneath the planet's crust, revealed bright mineral veins that wound their way through the host rock like glittering rivers. The ground that passed beneath the magtheps' feet was virgin soil, for all Reza could see, the hard earth revealing no signs of any previous traveler's passage.

As they rose higher through the canyons toward wherever Esah-Zhurah was leading him, Reza saw tiny oases of startling violet flowers whose petals waved in the air, beckoning to the insects that hovered and flitted near the ground, that they might bring life-giving pollen to the flowers.

Still higher, the violet flowers gradually became a seamless background to the other species that began to appear. Reza saw everything from tiny lichens clinging tenaciously to rocks, to enormous ferns that towered above the two riders on their animals, their house-sized fronds waving ponderously in the light breeze that swept up the mountainside.

"How much further is it?" Reza asked, his eyes wide with wonder at the sights that surrounded him.

"Not far," Esah-Zhurah called back as she maneuvered her magthep through a particularly dense stand of vines and ferns. Behind them, Goliath plowed straight through the plants, his muzzle snatching occasional mouthfuls as he went, a bad habit that Reza had not yet figured out how to cure.

"Here!" she called at last, reining her beast to a stop and smoothly dismounting onto a carpet of iridescent orange moss that had appeared like a welcome mat.

Reza nudged Goliath to a stop as he gawked around him. They were on a ledge, halfway up one of the mountains of the range that ringed the plain. Through the ferns and moss-covered boulders he could just make out the shimmering spires of the city far in the distance, and the forest in which lay their kazha. To the other side, a mountain lay very close by, like a wall that rose straight up as far as he could see, disappearing into the clouds that danced in the winds. Everywhere the purple granite had disappeared, replaced by the vibrant greens and oranges of the plants and mosses that were dominant here.

"It is beautiful," he whispered in awe.

"You have not yet seen beauty," Esah-Zhurah said quietly. "Come. Gather your things, for we have not yet reached our destination."

The two of them stripped the magtheps of their riding gear and released them to wander and eat as they pleased.

"Will they run away?" Reza asked as he let Goliath go.

Esah-Zhurah looked at him. "Why do you ask? Are you afraid of walking back?"

Reza frowned, not enthused at the idea. But watching Goliath devour the nearby plants eased his mind. Unless something frightened him, he would stay here where there was plenty of food.

They left the saddles in a convenient enclave of dry rock and forgot about the feasting animals. Hefting the packs of supplies that Esah-Zhurah had made up for them, they began to climb higher up the mountain face, scaling their way along a natural stairway in a huge crevice that split the mountainside like a mischievous, toothy grin.

They had climbed only a few minutes before they came to a tunnel that disappeared into the mountain. Esah-Zhurah waited for Reza to join her before she stepped off into the near darkness of the tunnel, feeling her way along, her talons lightly scraping the tunnel walls. Reza was fascinated by the echoing sounds of their footsteps and the smell that is peculiar to ancient stone places that have never seen the full light of day. But after a few paces his ears pricked at something new: the rushing sound of water.

"Esah-Zhurah..." he said tentatively, a trace of fear in his voice as his mind conjured up an image of the two of them being swept down the mountainside by a sudden torrent of water erupting from the mountain's bowels.

"We are nearly there," came her voice from the darkness, and Reza felt her hand take hold of his forearm to lead him along; she could still see clearly in the dark, while he could barely see a shifting shadow where she might – or might not – be.

The rushing sound grew into a roar, and Reza was opening his mouth to speak again when suddenly, as if dawn had broken within the tunnel, light began to return.

He found himself standing on a ledge overlooking paradise.

"*My God*," he whispered, his eyes lost to the wondrous sight before him. Esah-Zhurah overlooked his comment in his old tongue, forgiving him as she herself embraced the scene.

They stood overlooking what had once been an ancient volcano. It was a tremendous crater whose walls rose nearly vertically to a height of hundreds of meters to the clouds that swept along the crest. Mosses and lichens covered the walls like tapestries of fire, their reds and yellows swirling like the surface of a gas giant. Leafy green plants also flourished, clinging insistently to the ledges protruding from the sides like tiny green outposts in the midst of a desert of rampant color. And on the far side from where the two of them stood was a waterfall that roared its existence, born from the tap of a stream far above them to fall into a crystal pool that lay at the bottom of the ancient caldera, forming a beautiful grotto. The surface shone like the shimmering mirror of some great telescope, the falling water leaving behind a gentle mist that floated in the air as if by magic.

"Come," Esah-Zhurah said, tugging on Reza's arm. Had he looked down at just that moment, he would have seen the trace of a smile on her face as she saw the wonder on his, but it passed swiftly, as if stolen by the steadily setting sun.

He wordlessly followed her toward an enclave whose overhang kept the rock within dry.

"This," Esah-Zhurah said as she set down her things, startling a small lizard that disappeared into the vegetation, shrieking, "shall be our home until we return to the kazha, and the Challenge."

* * *

Reza awoke the next morning to the sound of a group of lizards, perched somewhere high above, trumpeting their territorial claims to one another like a brass ensemble gone mad. The sun had not yet risen high enough to reach the bottom of the caldera, but it would: on this day, unlike most, the clouds that normally concealed the grotto's inhabitants from the piercing rays of the sun, leaving it instead in a soft glow of filtered light, had parted. Already some of the more adventurous – and boisterous – inhabitants had gathered to await the arrival of the warmth that would come from above.

He was reluctant to shed the musky skins that had protected him from the slight chill of the night, but his stomach was insistent. Dinner had been light the previous evening, as neither he nor Esah-Zhurah had wanted to spoil the sunset and twilight with cooking chores, and both of them had gone to bed early, lulled to sleep by the steady roar of the waterfall.

Reza listened to the tumultuous sound of the water and thought that it would be nice to see if he could manage a swim later on in the pool below. Reluctantly, he tossed aside the covers and began the ritual stretching the tresh were taught early on to perform, readying his body for whatever lay ahead during the day.

"Late do you rise, my tresh," Esah-Zhurah called from a few meters away where she was cooking him something to eat. It was a seemingly incongruous task that she took upon herself, despite his protestations.

Perhaps, he thought cynically, she only does it so she can burn the meat.

"And soundly do you sleep. The lizards," she pointed to a place high on the far side of the grotto, "have long been calling to you."

"Perhaps," he said, starting to pull on his black pajamas, as he had come to think of them, "they were simply keeping me informed about what you have been doing while I slept."

Esah-Zhurah looked at him, then at the lizards, a look of considered suspicion on her face. "Is such a thing possible?" she asked him finally.

Reza shrugged, trying to keep his face straight. "It is something for you to think about, is it not? You believe I talk to magtheps. Why not lizards, as well?" He sat down next to her at the fire, quietly enjoying her mental squirming as she tried to figure out if he really could talk to the animals.

Finally, she looked at him sharply. "I do not believe you can speak with the beasts," she said. Then she paused, unsure. "Can you?"

Finally, he could stand it no more, and he burst out laughing at the serious expression she bore. "No," he admitted as he saw her face cloud over with anger for laughing at her, "I cannot. Please," he told her, bringing his laughter to a swift end, "forgive me. I did not mean to make you feel a fool."

In reply, she only scowled at him before turning away, thrusting his meat deeper into the coals where it sizzled and popped, then finally caught fire.

"Here," she said, thrusting the stick that held the flaming meat into his face. "Eat."

Dodging the flames, he took the stick like the baton in a relay race, snatching it quickly from her hand before she dropped it or impaled him with it, and then blew out the torch that was his breakfast.

"Thank you," he said quietly. "Esah-Zhurah," he said after a moment. She paid him no attention, focusing herself on paring strips from the raw hunk of meat that was her own morning meal. He reached out and gently touched her arm. She did not pull away. "Please forgive me," he said quietly. "I meant you no harm. It was only meant as humor, a joke, nothing more."

"Do not do it again," she said after a moment of silent consideration, her eyes still focused on her food as her talons tore it to shreds. "I do not like it." Reza nodded, letting her go. "I forgive you," she added softly.

Reza sat back, stunned, his mind seeking a precedent for this development. There was none.

After a few moments he asked, "What would you like to do today?" He was unsure if the free time before the Challenge brought with it some kind of unannounced itinerary.

"Today I would bask in the sun, as do your lizard friends," she said. "To lay upon that rock," she pointed to a peninsula of moss-covered stone that jutted into the pool, "and become one with the earth is my sole desire for this day."

"A more noble ambition there has never been," he said, tearing the meat with his teeth.

It was not long before the sun's trace began to work its way down into the grotto. The chorus of the lizards – dozens of them now – grew louder as the sunlight dropped deeper into the caldera. He and Esah-Zhurah were finally compelled to put their hands over their ears as the animal shrieks reached a shattering crescendo. But then, as the light reached the bottom and struck the pool, almost at once the trumpeting and chirruping ceased, the animals now mollified by the sun's warmth.

"In Her name," Esah-Zhurah breathed, "such a noise they make!"

As she made her way down to the pool, Reza went and opened his pack, rummaging around near the bottom for what he sought, his hands curling around a thin-skinned case that was roughly as big around as his chest, but not nearly so thick. Pulling open the top flap, he looked to make sure that everything inside was as he had put it. The old armorer, Pan'ne-Sharakh, had given him his own palette of dyes and brushes, and he had eagerly taken up dye-setting – painting – as his escape from the brutal life he had been forced to lead. He used whatever metal he could scavenge for canvas, usually damaged backplates that the armorers deemed unworthy of salvage. He hammered them as flat as he could and put them to use for his own designs. The images he had made did not have the texture of real paintings, being dyes on metal, but his interpretation of the Kreelan art lent them a depth and perspective that made the images almost three dimensional, surreal. He did not consider himself to be a modern incarnation of Monet or Da Vinci; he was content to be himself. It was the only thing he had that, for a few moments of each of his hellish days, allowed his soul to go free.

Turning around, the satchel in hand, he saw that he would not have to search far for a subject. Against the backdrop of a misty rainbow born of the waterfall, Esah-Zhurah lay nude on the chaise of stone that protruded into the pool, her blue face to the sun, her braids hanging toward the pool below like ebony streams. Her eyes were closed; she was probably already asleep. One hand was draped over her torso, lightly cupping her left breast, and the other lay at her side.

Reza's heart suddenly thundered in his ears as he looked at her. The hot pulse sent a jolt up his spine as he suddenly found himself smitten with the beauty of this alien girl, this young woman, who was at once his ally and his enemy, his savior and would-be killer, all rolled into one. In that blink of an eye, he wanted to reach out and touch her, to hold her against him. He wanted to feel her warm lips on his, remembering how it felt when Nicole had kissed him goodbye when she left Hallmark. He could remember that kiss like it was yesterday. But he could barely remember what she looked like now.

He tore his gaze away. He knew his body was on the edge, or even through, the age of puberty and all its attendant changes, and resolved to blame this treacherous feeling on the hormonal pranks of his growing body. Still, he could not deny the heat that blazed in his core at the thought of how closely he and this alien girl lived together, despite how far apart they would forever remain.

As if in sympathy, thin gray clouds drifted over the caldera, muting the dazzling sunshine reflecting from the pool below and softening the light to an even glow.

Blinking his eyes clear, he quietly arrayed his arsenal of colors and began to paint.

* * *

The morning stretched into afternoon, and at last Esah-Zhurah stirred from her long nap, stretching like a cat. Reza, his hands and upper body tired from his tender labors over the canvas of metal, surveyed his handiwork as he began to put his things away. Looking at the traces he had made, the first shadings now setting into the blackened metal, he smiled. It would be the best work he had ever done, he thought, the best by far.

"Do you paint your friends, the lizards?" Esah-Zhurah called to him.

Reza looked up to see her lying on her side, watching him, one hand lazily stirring the water lapping at the rock. A thin sheen of mist covered her nude body from head to toe, making her glisten like an unearthly siren beneath the waterfall's rainbow.

"It is my time to do with as I please," he told her, knowing that she did not really approve of his undertaking of the old armorer's craft. "And if it is a lizard that I paint," he went on, sealing the etching into the satchel, "it is a lizard that speaks in Her tongue."

"How amusing," she replied sarcastically as Reza made his way down to the water's edge and began to take off his clothes. "What do you intend to do?"

"I..." He could not think of the word, and resorted to one of his few acceptable uses of Standard, to explain what words or phrases he did not know in her language. "I wish to go... *swimming*." He carefully folded his black underclothes, putting them on top of the pile of metal and leatherite that was his second skin before stepping gingerly into the water, expecting it to be freezing. Much to his delight, it was warm against his skin, a wonderful feeling after having bathed so many times in the ice-cold stream that ran near the kazha, barred as he and Esah-Zhurah were from the normal bath facilities because of his being human. "This is wonderful," he sighed as he moved into deeper water, wading in past his waist.

"Be careful," Esah-Zhurah said suddenly, kneeling over the edge of the rock and watching Reza with wide eyes.

"Why?" he asked, suddenly wary. His eyes darted to and fro, searching the crystalline water. "Is there some beast in here that I should know about?"

"No," she said firmly. "But do not go in above your head."

"Why not?" he asked, puzzled at her concern. "What happens if I do?"

She snorted. "You will drown, fool. This even a magthep knows."

Reza laughed at her and then leaped backwards, disappearing in a huge splash that drenched Esah-Zhurah.

"Reza!" she cried, jumping to her feet in a panic. She crawled as close as she dared to the edge of the rock and peered into the water, desperately searching for his body.

She did not see the shadow directly below her. As Reza's head broke the surface, she shrieked, drawing back in surprise as he spouted water on her like a cherubic fountain.

"What," he asked, trying desperately to hold back his laughter at her reaction, "are you so afraid of?"

"I do not like the water," she said angrily. "And you should not be so quick to disobey me when I warn you of something."

"You cannot do this – swim – can you?" he asked, treading water next to the rock.

"No," she admitted quietly. "Very few of my people can do this." She told him the Kreelan word for *swimming*, one that she had never used with him before. "It is not considered a high priority for the learning period of youth."

Reza swam up to her and clung to the rock with one hand, sweeping the other through his soaking hair. "Let me teach you," he asked hopefully.

She looked at him and saw nothing but sincerity in his eyes, but there had always been something about water that troubled her, and sometimes she had dreams. They were nightmares about cold black water that closed in around her, filling her lungs as Death closed its icy fist around her heart, leaving her soul trapped in a lifeless body that would be forever spinning, spinning beyond the reach of Her light, Her love.

"No, my tresh," she told him, turning away so he would not see the fear on her face. "I know you mean well, but I do not wish to."

"Is there–"

"I do not wish to," she said again, facing him now, her eyes hard.

Reza nodded. "Very well," he said, his heart sinking like a stone. He had so much wanted for her to say yes.

Pushing her from his thoughts as he kicked away from the rock on which she stood, he turned and began to explore the wondrous pool. He probed through the shallow water, imagining himself as one of the ancient mariners about whom he had read once upon a time, the men and women who had explored the great seas of Earth.

Esah-Zhurah watched him swim and dive like the aquatic creatures she had occasionally seen in the river that flowed through the city, faintly envious of this ability of his. He appeared to be enjoying himself tremendously, blowing water into the air and then taking a breath before diving back down again to observe some unfathomable sight at the bottom of the pool.

Something that I will never see, she lamented quietly to herself, unconsciously drawing away from the water's edge and the waves kicked up by Reza's frolicking. She saw him wave to her as he swam under the waterfall, and she managed a halfhearted gesture in return, still uneasy at being able to see only his head above the water. And then even that disappeared as he dove under once more.

Perhaps for the first time since he had been brought to the Empire, Reza felt completely free. Alone in this tiny world of water, where even his tresh feared to come, his heart seemed to unfold. The horrendous load on his mind and soul that sometimes threatened to crush his sanity lightened, fading away to nothing in the warm embrace of the grotto pool. He watched with fascinated eyes the grotto's creatures – none of them overtly threatening – as they swam, crawled, or scuttled about the pool. Brightly colored fish stared at him with wide black eyes from their tiny holes among the rock clusters that dotted the pool's bottom, and tiny crab-like things tussled amongst themselves on the bottom, raising a tiny cloud of sand as they dragged one another in a miniature tug of war.

Beneath the waterfall itself, Reza found a darker world. Having taken a deep breath after waving to Esah-Zhurah, he descended into the maelstrom of the waterfall. He emerged on the other side, the light fading and swirling in time with the roiling water behind him. He was about to leave when he spotted what looked like an underwater tunnel in the rock behind the waterfall. Without thinking, he dived into it to find himself swirling down a subterranean passageway that ended in total darkness.

* * *

Esah-Zhurah clicked her nails on the rock in growing apprehension as time passed and still Reza did not reappear.

"Reza?" she called, finally giving in to the mounting tension that was constricting her chest like a metal band. "Reza!" she shouted again, standing on the rock so she could better see out over the pool.

Nothing. There was no sign of him, only the darting shadows of the grotto's fish as they went about their business. She had been thinking of asking Reza to try and catch some for their dinner, but that thought vanished as her concern grew. It had been too long.

Gingerly, she made her way into the water, venturing in up to her waist, then up to her breasts, the muscles in her belly clenched tightly with fear as she made her way deeper into this unfamiliar, and potentially deadly, environment. "Reza," she whispered hoarsely, "where are you?"

* * *

Spots were dancing before Reza's eyes, bright stars in the blackness of the tunnel he had ventured into. His lungs burning for want of oxygen, he groped in the darkness with his hands, seeking a way out of the trap he had gotten himself into. He cursed himself for following the tunnel until the light was gone. *I've got to find a way out,* he thought frantically. He waved his hands across the water-worn rock ever faster in hopes of finding his way back.

Suddenly, his left hand found an empty place, and he quickly followed it to find smooth rock leading upward through the darkness. He kicked hard, driving himself through the water in a desperate race for air, his muscles tingling with the pricks of invisible needles and his lungs threatening to explode with pain.

He suddenly burst from the water into blessed air. He stayed where he was for a moment, treading water while sucking in deep breaths of the cool damp air that caressed his face. He thought he might have gone temporarily blind, for when the dazzles cleared from his eyes, he could see nothing at all. But after a moment he did see something in his peripheral vision, a dim reddish glow that had no particular shape and did not move, but hung suspended in space above the water to his right. Swimming slowly toward it, his foot struck a submerged ledge and he let out a startled cry of pain.

More carefully, he moved closer to the glowing thing. The bottom of what he now took to be some kind of cavern rose higher until it finally broached the water's surface like a boat landing, and Reza found himself standing on dry rock in a low chamber.

Putting his hand out, he touched the red glowing thing that was brighter now as his eyes became accustomed to the darkness. His hand touched something soft and spongy, yet resilient enough that nothing stuck to his fingers when he pulled them away. The thing pulsed more brightly for a moment, then returned to its earlier state. *It must be some kind of plant*, Reza thought, unconsciously rubbing his hand on his naked thigh, vaguely repelled by the way the thing had felt to his touch.

Putting his hands to the walls, he moved about the chamber until he came to a large fissure that led upward, toward where he heard the waterfall's roar more clearly. Carefully placing his hands and feet, he climbed into the fissure, plenty wide for his lean body, and began working his way upward.

He had only gone a few meters when light began to trickle down the shaft, growing steadily stronger as did the sound of rushing water. Suddenly he found himself standing in another cavern, much larger than the first tiny vestibule: it was like an open balcony that lay directly behind the waterfall, a vertical crack in the caldera's face forming a window from which Reza could see the water cascade past as it fell to the pool below.

"Incredible," he whispered, awed by the miraculous luck that had brought him here. The cavern itself was completely dry except for some spray that coated the edge near the waterfall. He walked over and put his hand out to intercept the falling water, bringing a handful to his mouth and drinking.

"Reza!" he heard a voice call, barely audible over the crashing of the waterfall. "Where are you?"

"Esah-Zhurah!" he shouted, peering through the waterfall to try and catch a glimpse of her, but he could see nothing past the shimmering blue and green wall of water. "Up here!"

"Reza!" he heard again. The concern in her voice was unmistakable, and he quickly decided to return to her, eager to tell her of his discovery.

"I am coming!" he shouted, hoping that she would be able to hear him.

* * *

Daring to go no further into the water, Esah-Zhurah stood breast-deep, calling repeatedly to Reza. Once, she thought she heard his voice, but after that there had been only silence.

Finally, overcome by a sense of anguish that she would never dare admit to any but the priestess or the Empress herself, she turned and began to trudge back to the shore, convinced Reza was dead.

Such then, was her surprise when he burst from the surface near the waterfall.

"Esah-Zhurah!" he cried excitedly after he drew in a single deep breath to replenish his lungs. The return trip had been much easier than had been the way in, and he had reached the grotto pool long before his lungs had begun to burn. "I found a way behind the waterfall! You will not believe it!"

Her heart hammering with relief, she waded back into the water and took him by the arms as he swam toward her.

"Never do that again," she scolded him, trying to conceal her relief with an angry façade. "Never! I forbid it."

"But," Reza stammered, totally confused and ignorant of the thought that she might actually have been concerned for his welfare, "it is incredible. You must see it." He pointed to the waterfall. "Up there, there is a cave that–"

"It matters not," she said sharply, cutting him off. "The priestess would be angry with me if I let you perish during the free time before your first Challenge. You will not disobey me again." Her eyes carried the look that Reza had come to understand well: punishment was close at hand. And both of them knew she was his physical superior.

For now, Reza thought coldly. His spirits wilted like flowers put to the torch, and he lowered his gaze. He swiped angrily at the water with one hand, sending a flurry of droplets out into the pool.

"Yes, Esah-Zhurah," he murmured, trying to contain his anger and disappointment.

"If you would like," she went on, satisfied that he understood that she was serious, "you may try and capture some of the swimming things; I think I can prepare them in a way you would find acceptable. The ones with red stripes and yellow tails are good to eat, as are the violet sponge plants. The others are poisonous to us, and probably to you, also." She looked at the fading light in the caldera as the afternoon drifted toward evening. "You must hurry, for they hide in the rocks at night."

Nodding, but saying nothing, Reza swirled past her on his way out of the pool, stomping onto the beach to retrieve his knife. He returned to the water, but did not look at her. His knife held tightly in his hand, he swam through the water, hunting alone.

* * *

Esah-Zhurah lay against the side of the rock enclave that served as their camp within the caldera. She silently observed Reza as he stared off toward the waterfall, which now was backlit by thousands of tiny iridescent flora that made the water glow topaz in the absolute darkness within the grotto.

After their dinner, of which Reza had eaten surprisingly little, he had quietly excused himself and taken up a seat on the far side of the enclave from her, and said nothing since. It was a stark contrast to most of the nights they spent together, when Reza would ask one of his ever more complex questions about Her people and the Way. They were questions that were becoming increasingly difficult to answer and challenged Esah-Zhurah's own understanding of her culture. Sometimes they would spend hours this way after their training day had ended, stopping only when Reza's seemingly insatiable curiosity at last was put to rest, or Esah-Zhurah forced him to go to sleep, postponing the session's completion until the following evening. It was a ritual she had come to secretly enjoy, so different was it from the normally quiet and contemplative lives of the initiate tresh. And since Reza had begun to speak the Empress's tongue well, he constantly asked questions, wanting to know more, to learn.

But tonight he had been silent as the stone around them, and it concerned her for a reason she could not quite identify.

As if anticipating her question, he suddenly turned to her, the low fire dancing in his green eyes.

"Would you tell me just one thing?" he asked softly above the murmur of the waterfall.

"If I am able," she said carefully, kneeling closer to the fire, and to him.

"When I step into the arena, to face my first Challenge," he said evenly, "do you hope I will die?"

The question caught her completely by surprise. She opened her mouth, but no words came forth, for she truly did not know at that moment how she might answer him truthfully. She snapped her mouth shut, her face twisting into a mask of concentration.

Is that what I wish? she asked herself. *Do I honestly hope that he will die, this creature with whom I have spent so long, this animal with whom I have lived and suffered, to whom I have betrothed myself as a tresh?* Despite all the things she had ever imagined or been taught, she had come to feel a sense of pride in Reza, a pride that was more than one should feel for teaching an animal tricks, as the handlers were sometimes wont to do. She knew that he must hate her, must despise her entire race, and she often sought to use that as a weapon against him, to break him down, to make him fail.

But he had only become more determined, rising unfailingly to every test she put before him. His success or failure was, at that stage, immaterial; he consistently made the attempt, and that is what counted, all that mattered. Gradually, his perseverance had paid off. Many of the peers were discreetly jealous of her tresh, if that was possible. She herself had become possessed of a strange fondness for him, despite the revulsion she felt toward his species, despite the continued irrepressible urge to force him to her will, to show her own superiority, a superiority that she knew was fading as he grew stronger, quicker. *If only his blood would sing*, she often cried to herself. If only his spirit – if he possessed one – would show itself, all could be... different, in a way she was afraid to fully imagine.

If only his blood would sing...

Turning back to meet his glowing eyes, she knew in her heart that he must someday die, that he would – no, that he must – never leave the Homeworld alive. But she could not find it in herself to wish it upon him.

"Reza..." she said, trying to find a way of saying what she felt without exposing the weakness she had developed toward him. "The oath you took when you were brought into the kazha, the oath by which you bound yourself as a tresh, I also have taken, though long before you came to me. It is an oath taken only once in life, but it lasts for as long as the heart beats, as long as two work together as one, as tresh. The one to whom I was bound, cycles ago, died in a... training accident, you might call it. But my obligations to her honor were passed on to you when I was called upon to become your tresh. Your teacher. And in that capacity, I can be nothing but pleased, for you have learned well, animal – human – or no." She looked away toward the water, struggling to admit what she had to say. "There will come a day, my tresh, when your blood will soak the sands of the arena," she told him, her claws digging silently into the rock as she willed the words forward, as if her throat was suddenly too small to contain them. "But I shall not rejoice in it."

She could see relief wash over Reza's face. She was surprised how well she could interpret his body language, not because she could understand that of the humans, but because the language of his body had become Kreelan.

"Esah-Zhurah..." he said. Then he stopped, not sure how to continue.

She watched as he struggled with himself for a moment, until the strange strength that dwelt within him surfaced, washing away the creases of doubt on his face.

"There is much for which I feel compelled to hate you, to hate your kind," he explained, his eyes drawn to the fire as if in search of the meaning of his fate. "For the deaths of my parents, at the hands of the priestess herself. For the destruction of the world of my birth, and the many lives that perished there. For the destruction of the planet from which I was taken, a world I often hated, but which I had come to call home. And for all of the death that has been wrought upon my people, on a scale I will never be able to understand, and will never truly be able to feel in my heart." He looked up at her, his face betraying an open vulnerability that shocked her as strongly as if she had been doused with freezing water. "For all this, I cannot find it in me to truly hate you, my tresh, my teacher. There are many among my kind who would condemn me to death as a traitor for those words, but they are nonetheless true, and to deny them, or leave them unspoken, would be to lie to myself." He looked back to the fire, helplessly. "There was a time, not so long ago," he whispered, "when I wanted to beat you, to destroy you, to make you feel pain a thousand times what I felt every time you beat me. But..." he shrugged. "But I found, after a while, that I wanted your respect, your trust, more than anything else." He fell silent for a moment. "The greatest fear I have," he went on, "is that I will fail you, will bring shame upon you. And that... you will shun me."

Esah-Zhurah did not know what to say. Never had she thought such a time as this would come, when this human, so full of fight and anger, would reveal such a thing to her, something that could be exploited as a terrible weakness.

But that was the point, she told herself. He had laid himself open to her, in hopes that she would not turn his words against him, that he could trust her. And, in a decision that shocked the part of her mind that carried the xenophobic character of her race, a race that had exterminated over a dozen sentient species in past millennia, she committed herself to guarding his trust.

"I will not abandon you," she said simply, openly. "Whatever the Way brings us, we shall share in it together."

* * *

Later, after they had banked the fire and lay down for the night, Reza remained awake. His mind was consumed by thoughts that swirled and circled like wolves around a stricken deer, darting just to the edge of focus before they faded into the shadowy darkness once more. The more he watched them, the more they seemed to carry the faces of people he had once known, some of them of a kind his people called "friends," a relationship that did not exist among the society that had kidnapped him.

One of the wolf faces, an old man with the eyes of a young warrior, especially troubled him. The eyes did not accuse, but Reza could not help but feel that he had somehow betrayed the being that lay behind the mask that lunged and retreated within his mind.

Wiley, he suddenly thought, wincing at the foreign sound of the name even as he breathed it in his mind, *am I a traitor?*

"*Do whatever you can to stay alive, son*," the old colonel had said that day so long ago, "*If anybody can make it, you can...*"

Wiley, Reza cried to himself, *must I become one of them to make it? Do I have any choice?* For just a moment, he bitterly resented the old man's leaving him, going off to die himself as Reza was taken by the cruel fate that had pursued him since the fall of New Constantinople.

But the moment blinked away into nothingness, just as the wolfish thought-face blurred into oblivion. Wiley had been wise enough to know when it was time to die, and had done so with the dignity of soldiers throughout history who had made one last, hopeless stand against the invaders of their homeland. And, aside from the admission letter he had given Reza for the academy, the old man had left Reza with the only other gift he could give: a chance at life. And Reza knew then that if he chose to trust this alien girl, to allow himself that vital weakness before her, Wiley would understand.

Slowly, the beasts in his brain retreated into the darkness, only their glittering eyes remaining, flickering in the glow of the fire.

He blinked, but the glowing eyes remained. Suddenly, he realized that he was seeing the silvery glint of Esah-Zhurah's talons. Her hands lay on the skins near her face, the ebbing firelight making them twinkle like stars against the satiny glow of her deep blue skin as she slept. Reza felt another sudden twinge of guilt at the thought of how much he had come to need her, to rely on her. Worse, he found that he was beginning to like her.

What might things be like, he thought, should she someday come to lead her people? Would her association with him have any effect, make any difference in how they viewed humanity? It was difficult for a boy, struggling simply to remain human, let alone to become a man, to comprehend the fact that he was an ambassador, of sorts, to these people. While this particular course of his life had not been chosen willingly, he was nonetheless determined to make the best impression he could, to do whatever he could to help the people of his own blood. Who could tell, he asked himself, if the girl who lay asleep an arm's length away might not someday sit on the throne that commanded the Empire? The thought settled onto his brain like an insistent ache, an itch that insisted it be scratched.

"Esah-Zhurah," he said quietly, hating to disturb her, but unable to put off the question until morning.

Her eyes flickered open and she looked around, confused. "What is wrong?" she asked, one hand instinctively reaching for the knife that lay nearby.

"Nothing is wrong," he told her, ashamed now for awaking her. But the question in his brain pounded against his skull. "Nothing. It is just that... I have to ask you something. I am sorry, but I did not think it could wait until morning."

Ah, she thought, *he is back to his normal inquisitive self. Good.* Even after the revelations earlier in the evening, he had still remained uncharacteristically quiet, and this urgent need for information reassured her that all was yet well. She knew that he would have to discipline himself against the urgency of his curiosity, but this was not yet something she thought fitting to punish or dissuade; in fact, it was a vice she found enjoyable. "What is it," she asked, "that cannot wait for the light of the sun?"

For a moment, Reza was almost afraid to answer, suddenly realizing that she had taught him virtually nothing about the succession rites, that his question might put him on perilously thin ice culturally: matters regarding the Empress were not to be addressed lightly. It was something they'd never talked about before.

"I was wondering," he began, swallowing as he forged ahead, "how... the Empress is chosen. I mean, could you someday become Empress?"

Esah-Zhurah's expression clouded, became unreadable. Reza feared that he had made a major blunder.

"No, Reza," she told him after a moment. She spoke not with anger, but with sadness. "Of all the things I may accomplish in my life, I may never become Empress." She paused. "Never."

"Why?" he asked, rolling onto his side, propping his head up with his arm to look at her.

"It is because of what happened long ago," she began, "in a time when our Empire was of one world, when warriors – male and female – answered the call of their blood." She rolled over on her back, her eyes focusing on the far distant stars. "Mine is a very old race, Reza, far older than your own. We live now in the time of the First Empire, which began over one hundred thousand of your Standard years in the past. But the earliest records of our civilization go back much, much further, perhaps as far as five hundred thousand of your years. And it is in the twilight ages between those times that the legend of the First Empress was born, in the days when the Old Tongue was widely spoken and unbridled warfare was rife across the land.

"Before the First Empire was founded," she explained, "the legends say that rival city-states vied for dominance, for power. We rose to the pinnacle of civilization time and again during the course of many generations, only to be plunged into renewed dark ages by frenzied, uncontrollable warfare. Many times, leaders banded their nations together with strength and cunning to lead us out of darkness, but when they fell the land was plunged into chaos once more.

"But there came a day," she said, her voice filled with awe, "when a child was born in the city of Keela'ar, born to a great queen and her consort. The child, whose hair was white as the snow atop the mountains and had rare red talons, was named Keel-Tath.

"Keel-Tath's parents, as was the custom in those days, entrusted their daughter's training to one of the warrior priestesses of the Desh-Ka, and in time she took the reins of her mother's domain into her own hands.

"Cycles passed, and time saw her expand her domain across the face of the known world. And before her hair had grown long past her waist, she stood before her entire race as Empress: the leader of all, the first to unite our world.

"In the cycles after the Unification," Esah-Zhurah went on after a moment of silent reflection, "Tara-Khan, a male warrior who was the greatest of his kind, perhaps the greatest who has ever lived, won her heart. He had slain her enemies upon the field of battle just as he now warmed her bed with his love. In time, she was with child, a child who would be born with white hair, who would someday become her successor upon the throne. The two were happy, so say the legends, and the Empire prospered in Her good graces.

"But there came a warrior who sought to usurp the power of the Empress, a warrior whose name has long since been stricken from the Books of Time in the darkest of disgrace. For he was Tara-Khan's tresh, and he betrayed his brother of the Way. As the Empress lay in her chambers, giving birth to her child, the usurper lured Tara-Khan away from her side, telling him of a plot within the palace to kill the Empress and her child. The usurper led Tara-Khan into a trap, where the betrayers and his followers fell upon him. Many did Tara-Khan slay, but he did not count on the treachery of his companion; the usurper's blade pierced Tara-Khan's back, and so did he fall.

"When the deed was done, the usurper and his mistress, the high priestess of one of the ancient orders, now long forgotten in the depths of its disgrace, led more of their followers to the Empress's chambers, killing all present save the Empress and Her child. 'Give me the child,' the usurper demanded of the Empress, 'and I shall spare its life, and thus shall Your daughter live as mine own.' For the great priestess was barren, and longed for what the Empress had, but she could not; and for his twisted love for this woman did the usurper demand the Empress's child.

"'And what of Tara-Khan?' demanded Keel-Tath as the evil ones surrounded Her. 'His body feeds the wo'olahr of the forest, as yours shall feed my desires,' the usurper spat in reply as he moved to force himself upon her in a grotesque consummation of his lust and greed."

Reza's skin crawled at the thought, his long-forgotten memories of Muldoon's diseased cravings suddenly surfacing in his mind.

"But he was never to touch her," Esah-Zhurah continued. "Her heart broken at the death of Tara-Khan, Her blood burning in blind rage, She invoked the Curse that has vexed us to this day. The conspirators did Keel-Tath curse, calling upon the powers that lay deep within Her, powers that could change the very shape of our nature.

"First was cursed the usurper who had betrayed Tara-Khan and threatened to defile Her. Such was the power of his lust, Keel-Tath told him, that lust is all that would remain. And not just for him, but for all his kind. And in moments the warrior began to writhe in agony as his body withered to half its once-proud size, his head shrinking to house a brain that knew only of mating, and could never be home to another treacherous thought. But then she decreed that the urge would be satisfied only once, whereupon he would die in horrible agony. The legends say that on the day following her judgment, there were no more male warriors to be found in the world, only shells that were nothing more than breeding machines that could function but a single time. Only her imperial guards were spared this fate."

Reza shuddered at the thought. Even a boy such as he knew that legends were often no more than empty fairy tales, no more real than the Tooth Fairy. But Esah-Zhurah told the tale as if it had happened only yesterday, not millennia – *a hundred millennia* – before.

"Then," Esah-Zhurah went on softly, and Reza had to strain to hear her above the waterfall, "she cast judgment upon the usurper's mistress. Her punishment was equally terrible. Keel-Tath decreed that the woman and all who shared her bloodline would have what they so desired: to be able to bear children. The usurper's mistress would be fertile and forever intertwined with the usurper and those like him, now a mere animal in search of a female in heat. Her punishment was that she must breed every cycle of what we now call the Empress Moon, or she would die in terrible pain. She must embrace her lover once, then watch him die in agony. And so she would never forget that she had been barren, one daughter of every two would be infertile, and born with silver claws as witness. The claws such as are upon mine own hands."

She turned to face Reza, silently wondering what this alien, this outsider, could think at the misfortune of her race.

Shocked, Reza understood. She was barren, disgraced by a nameless woman who died millennia ago, and only those who could bear children could sit upon the throne of the Kreelan Empire.

"And what of the clawless ones?" Reza asked quietly, not wanting to dwell on Esah-Zhurah's tragic fate. "Did they play a role in this?"

Esah-Zhurah shook her head in the Kreelan way. "After Keel-Tath had delivered the curse upon the usurper and his mistress," Esah-Zhurah went on, "She summoned the priestesses of the other orders and bade them to kneel before her. Handing the first her knife, the knife that had belonged to her mother, she commanded the eldest priestess to deliver up the talons of her hands, the very badges of warriorhood, as a sign of loyalty. And the priestess did this, cutting her talons from her fingers, one by one, and dropping the bloody claws into the urn the Empress held forward to receive them. The knife was passed from priestess to priestess and the ritual repeated. After the last had tossed her proud talons into the urn, Keel-Tath cast a spell upon them, that the children of their bloodlines would be born without talons, and would be known forever as those most loyal to Her will."

"What happened to her?" Reza asked softly. "To Keel-Tath?"

"The legends say that she was stricken with grief at the death of her lover. That very day She gave up her child to the high priestess of the Desh-Ka, for her to bring up the child and teach her the Way as tradition demanded. And then Keel-Tath plunged a knife into her own heart, destroying the life in her body. Such was her sorrow, that her spirit did not seek a place among the Ancient Ones; instead, she sought out the Darkness to dwell in grief for all the days of Time."

Reza thought for a moment that the terrible tale was finished. But he could tell from her expression that there was something else, a final tragedy on that horrible day so long ago. And then he knew what it was.

"Tara-Khan was not really dead, was he?" he asked.

Esah-Zhurah's eyes focused on him, her eyes gleaming as they reflected the fire's flames. "And thus do you surprise me once again, Reza," she told him before continuing her tale. "He made his way back to the palace, more dead than alive, driven by his love for Keel-Tath. But when he arrived, he found her slain by her own hand, and the infant Empress in the hands of the Desh-Ka, its young spirit crying in grief and incomprehension. He lay down beside his lover, and with his last breath did he vow to protect Her evermore from those who might travel beyond this world to seek Her power in the name of evil. And thus did he die. After that, no one knows exactly what happened to Her. Legend has it that Her body disappeared, Tara-Khan's body and the imperial guard with it. No one knows where they may have gone.

"Over time," she said, drawing her tale to a close, "the bloodlines were said to merge, and now those of the black claws and those with none must mate every cycle, or death will take them. Of the children, those who bear these," she held her silver claws to the light, "are only spectators to the continuance of our people, forever barred from the throne by sterility. And tradition demands that the Empress must be possessed of white hair, a direct descendant of Keel-Tath."

Reza didn't believe in what sounded like magic in the legends, but with a race this ancient, who could know? Regardless, he felt sick. Despite the horrors he had suffered at the hands of these people, despite the untold suffering of humanity before their attacking fleets, he pitied them. With his entire heart, he pitied them. Such a wonderful and proud race, violent though it might be, doomed to such a horrible fate.

"Esah-Zhurah," he stuttered, wanting to offer something, but not really knowing what to say. "I am... sorry. For all of you."

She looked at him closely for a moment, and he thought for just an instant he saw punishment looming in her eyes. But it vanished with the shifting of the dying flames, and her beautiful cat's eyes softened again.

"Save your sorrows for your own people," she told him. "The Children of the Empress need not your pity." With that, she turned away from him, drawing her skins tightly around her as she fought to ward off the chill of the night and the visions of Keel-Tath's legacy to her people.

And as sleep stole upon her, she thought of something that never would have occurred to her, never in all her life, had not Reza asked his question this night.

What would it be like, she thought to herself as she drifted away into the land of dreams, *to become Empress, the Ruler of Eternity?*

* * *

Reza's eyes snapped open. His heart was tripping like a hammer, and he found himself breathing rapidly, as if he had been running for leagues. He looked around cautiously, but could see only the ethereal glow of the moss that lined the bottom of the grotto, twinkling in the mist from the waterfall. Other than that and the light from the stars, it was completely dark. The night was yet full.

Had he been dreaming, he wondered? After a brief inspection of his body's condition, he decided that no, a dream was not the cause of his unease. He had awakened from the combat reflex that was slowly but surely becoming an integral part of him, his senses having warned him through his subconscious that something was wrong. But he did not yet know what.

Esah-Zhurah continued to sleep peacefully, her body turned away toward the grotto beyond the shelter of the alcove. He found it difficult to believe that whatever had awakened him had failed to do the same to her, but he was even more skeptical that the hairs standing on the back of his neck were a mistake.

His eyes darted about their limited field of vision as his nose and ears searched for clues as to what was troubling him. He lay perfectly still, searching. He had learned long before that to move before isolating a hidden threat was often a fatal mistake. One did not have to be a veteran of the Challenge to know that.

There. The cry struck him like a blow. It was the sound of the magtheps outside the entrance to the grotto, screaming in fright.

"Goliath!" he said, throwing aside his blankets and getting to his feet. He had no idea what was out there, but his instincts – even bred as they were from a different order of evolution – were crying out in alarm. He bolted toward the rocky trail that led to the opening to the side of the mountain where the magtheps had been grazing.

"Reza!" Esah-Zhurah called, grabbing his arm. "Wait!"

"But–"

"Listen."

And then he heard it, a basso growl that ripped across every nerve in his body like a twisted, clawed hand. He had never heard such a frightful sound before, but he knew it was close. Too close. Even in the darkness, he could tell that Esah-Zhurah's skin had paled. Her hand was gripping his arm so hard she had drawn blood. She was terribly frightened.

"What is it?" he breathed.

"Genoth," she whispered hoarsely, her body beginning to tremble.

Reza looked at her, the word meaning nothing to him. "What does that mean?"

"It is terribly dangerous, Reza," she said, drawing herself closer to him, dropping her voice even further. "It is a... a dragon, a great carnivorous beast."

Reza looked up toward where the magtheps' cries had echoed through the portal, but could see nothing. The sounds had faded without any squeals of pain.

"Goliath and your animal must have fled down the mountain," he said, relieved that they might be safe.

The growl came again, louder this time, and Reza realized with sudden dread that the sound had begun to echo. *It was in the caldera.*

"It is in here," he whispered, stepping carefully beyond the alcove's overhang, scanning the walls around them.

"Reza, do not–" Esah-Zhurah's voice caught in her throat as she saw the shadow atop the far side of the grotto, a great dark blob of matter that seemed to consume the stars in the sky. "There," she whispered, pointing to where the beast sat, perched atop the grotto's rim.

Of all the ways to die, this was the one that Esah-Zhurah feared most of all: to be eaten by another creature that was ignorant of all things but hunger and primal instincts.

The creature remained dormant for a while, and the two young warriors waited through minutes that seemed like ages, waiting to see what it would do. Hoping beyond hope that it would turn and leave them alone, they knew with the certainty of those condemned that it would not; that it would, at long last, begin its fateful descent.

Reza's mind was working frantically. Somehow, there had to be something they could do, something better than an offering of token resistance that would not even serve to annoy the beast as it gobbled them up. He had never seen what one of these creatures looked like, but from the silhouette on the grotto's rim he could tell that it was huge, and Esah-Zhurah's fear was an indicator of how fierce it must be. He cursed himself silently, tearing his eyes from the beast to search the grotto, thankful that the sound and mist from the waterfall seemed to have protected them from detection thus far.

They were trapped, he thought desperately, trapped in a tomb of beauty, but a tomb nonetheless. If only–

The waterfall...

–there was somewhere–

The waterfall...

–they could hide.

"The waterfall," he murmured, his eyes fixed on it now. And then he knew. "Of course," he said. "The cave!"

"What?" Esah-Zhurah asked, barely able to shift her attention from the mesmerizing form of the beast as it sat, waiting. Watching.

"We have to get to the water," he told her.

"Why?" she asked, pulling on his arm as he tried to creep forward.

"Do you not see?" he asked, roughly pulling her to him, his face so close to hers that their noses touched. "We will be safe in the cave behind the waterfall!"

"No," she said, trying to pull away from him, her fears doubled now at the prospect of having to swim in the dark water. She would rather face the genoth, a fear and enemy her heart and mind could cope with, not like the shadowy darkness of the water, which perhaps was the water of her nightmares. "I cannot. I–" A roar that shook the entire grotto drowned out her words. The black shape that was the beast shifted and became smaller, then disappeared against the darkness of the side of the caldera.

"It is coming down the wall!" Reza hissed, knowing now that it had spotted them. "Come on!"

Pulling Esah-Zhurah behind him, he half led, half dragged her toward the edge of the pool, stumbling and tripping over the rocks that were only shadows upon shadows. Guided more by the sound of the falling water than the dim glow of the moss illuminating the pool, he suddenly felt the cool water lapping around his feet, and he surged forward.

"No!" Esah-Zhurah cried, pulling her arm away, turning to run back toward the shore.

Reza cursed in frustration. His eyes caught a glimpse of a dark form slithering down the wall as his ears picked up a faint *click-click-click* as it came for them.

He grabbed her by the shoulders and whirled her around to face him. "Esah-Zhurah," he said quietly, holding her with all his might against her struggling, hoping that she would not decide to impale him with her claws, "you must trust me. Please." She broke his grip and raised her hands toward him, ready to strike. "I trusted you this night," he said hastily. "Now it is time for you to do the same."

She paused, his words echoing in her mind, echoing with the sound of truth, of wisdom. Then her eyes caught sight of the genoth as it casually scaled the grotto's wall toward the bottom. Toward them. Her eyes wide with fear, she nodded assent, and Reza quickly turned and began to splash further out into the water, holding her hand like a child's.

"Here," he told her, turning to hold her with one arm crossing over her breast and up to the opposite shoulder. "Just relax and let me do the swimming," he said.

Panic-stricken as he pulled her backward into the water, Esah-Zhurah grabbed at Reza's arm, cutting him badly, as she tried to get away.

"Trust me!" he shouted, grimacing in pain as her talons again raked his forearm. "Be still!"

With a monumental effort, she did as she was told, and let Reza propel them through the water with powerful kicks of his legs, his free arm guiding them toward the sound of the waterfall.

Reza had lost sight of the genoth, but it did not matter. Either they would make it to safety, or they would not. Of the many gray areas life presented, this was not one: they would survive or they would die. The pain in his arm left by Esah-Zhurah's talons boosted more adrenaline into his circulatory system as he swam. He picked up his pace, surging through the water.

"Do you see it?" he cried above the waterfall's roar. "Where is it?"

"It is nearly to the water!" she shouted back, her talons again pressing into his flesh as she watched the beast – a huge animal, larger than any she knew to be on record since times long past – scale the last few meters of rock and lichens to reach the pool. Without missing a step, it slid its dark form into the water, the phosphorescent wake of its reptilian body arrowing directly toward them. "It is in here!" she screamed, struggling to escape, still with her hand clamped firmly to Reza's arm.

"Hold your breath!" Reza shouted, turning her around to face him. "Do you hear me? Hold it!" He caught sight of the animal bearing down on them. It was so close now that he could smell its alien musk through the cloud of dark water that hung about them like a cloak. He heaved in one last breath before plunging beneath the surface, dragging Esah-Zhurah with him into the blackness.

Esah-Zhurah was beyond fear as she clutched Reza's arm, her mind pulsing with terror of the thing that must even now surely be right behind them, ready to lash out with its tremendous jaws at their frantically kicking feet. While she was terrified beyond her wildest imagination, she found herself trying to match the urgent rhythm of Reza's strokes with her own powerful legs, letting him guide them deeper into the maw of the dark cave.

Her head suddenly crashed against an unseen rock, and she let out a cry, more of surprise than pain. But the effect would have been the same. She involuntarily inhaled some water, and she began to drown.

Reza felt her sudden panic and the spasms of her body as water began to fill her lungs. With one final, desperate kick of his legs, his hand made contact the smooth surface of the stone floor. In a motion born of terrible need, he launched himself and his choking companion into the life-giving air of the lower cavern.

Esah-Zhurah began to writhe, still conscious but unable to get the water out of her lungs. Pulling his own shaking body from the water, he hauled her away from the water's edge and into the crevice that lay above.

"Hang on," he panted. "I have you."

He had acted none too soon. A huge geyser exploded from the underwater tunnel as the genoth thrust its head through the too-narrow canal in a last ditch effort to retrieve its coveted meal. The water doused the two of them, but there was no sign of the creature, its colossal head too large, its neck too short, for the tunnel. They were safe.

Turning his attention back to Esah-Zhurah, vainly trying to shake off his own terror, he quickly turned her on her stomach and pressed against her naked back, hoping to expel some of the water that had found its way down her throat. She struggled weakly, then began to gag as water came gushing out her mouth.

"Reza," she managed before she vomited into the water, her shaking body steadied only by his bloodied arms.

"Hush," he said, holding her tightly to him, his eyes desperately probing the darkness for some sign of their nemesis, wondering if even now its head hung above them in the cavern, poised like a cobra ready to strike. "We must get to the next level," he told her. "I do not think it can come through the tunnel, but..."

In the dark, Esah-Zhurah nodded weakly as her hand sought to wipe the foulness from her lips and chin.

Reza wrapped an arm around her waist and helped her to stand. "Can you make it?" he asked.

"Yes," she told him, although her body was trembling like a leaf before the wind. She put her arm around his shoulder, careful to keep her talons from his tender skin, and together they made their way up the narrow fissure to the balcony that overlooked the grotto.

Behind them, the black waters stirred once more, the act of a behemoth denied. Then all was still.

* * *

Reza watched the swirling barrier of the waterfall as it gradually grew lighter, more vibrant. The sun was finally rising. He suddenly remembered his father asking him once what he thought might be on the other side of a waterfall. And now, seemingly a lifetime after his father's death, he knew the answer: sanctuary. Life.

He closed his eyes, acutely aware of Esah-Zhurah's warmth as she slept beside him. Her face was buried in the hollow of his neck, one of her hands covering the deep cuts in his arm as if in apology. It had been almost impossible to get any rest, as the cave was terribly cold and the night beyond the waterfall was filled with the genoth's frenzied grunting and squealing as it cursed their escape in its own language. Neither of them had been wearing any clothes, a habit of sleep long since established, and had taken flight only with what nature had endowed them and the collars about their necks. A fortunate coincidence for swimming, Reza had thought, but a terrible burden as the cold rock leeched the heat from their bodies. He had taken to standing near the lip of the cave's mouth, listening to the genoth as it rampaged in the water below. A curious chattering sound drew him back into the cave, fearful of some new menace. But it was only the sound of Esah-Zhurah's teeth clicking together from cold, as she lay inert on the cave's floor. Her body was spent and her mind numbed from facing so many private fears in so short a time.

Giving up on the genoth as an immediate threat, he lay down next to her. Gently, so as not to wake her from the exhausted, frightened sleep into which she had fallen, he put his arms around her, cradling her against what warmth his body could provide as he waited for the dawn.

Now, hours later, the genoth was quiet, having grown tired of its fruitless search. But Reza knew it had not yet departed, for the animals of the grotto had sung not a single note. The lizards that only yesterday had clung to the grotto's walls and heralded the coming of morning were ominously silent. Only when they sang again would Reza believe it safe to walk beyond the safety of the water that fell beyond the cave's mouth.

His body was settling into sleep again, the filtered sunlight warm against his face, when the infant light of morning was beset by a shadow that eclipsed the water cascading past. It did not take much imagination for Reza to know that it was the creature's head, a triangular killing machine whose maw could easily swallow his body whole. It hung suspended, perched somewhere on one of the rock outcroppings that lined the waterfall's passage, swaying like a hangman's noose.

Without warning the creature vomited a huge pile of reeking debris from its mouth, voiding its stomach into the pure waters of the waterfall with such force that some of it blasted through the perilously thin barrier of falling water to spatter inside the cave. The stench of the creature's expectoration was almost unbearable as it flooded through the chamber.

Esah-Zhurah stirred beside him, and he carefully put a restraining hand over her mouth, lest she suddenly come awake and cry out.

The genoth retched again, sending out another torrent of indigestible material, some of which clattered about the cave. Some debris that bore more than a passing resemblance to crushed and shattered bone fragments tumbled hollowly about before coming to rest. It was then that Reza knew the animal was not sick. It was simply purging itself of those items that its digestive system could not accommodate.

Esah-Zhurah lay frozen against him, her eyes wide with horror. She waited for the terrible beast to peer beyond the curtain of water at which its tongue now lapped, a giant pink worm piercing the veil of the waterfall.

But it did not. With one final heave, the thing's shadow disappeared as it scaled the walls of the caldera to find a better hunting ground.

Their attention turned to what the genoth had left behind, and Reza nearly vomited himself at what he saw. Strewn about the cave by the genoth's explosive heaves were parts of what had once been at least one young Kreelan warrior. Reza could clearly see the metallic glint of the remains of a collar and some of its pendants. There was torn and twisted chest armor. Unidentifiable hunks of partially digested bone were scattered among the dreadful refuse, along with the remains of the warrior's claws and fingertips. He heard Esah-Zhurah suck in her breath as she recognized the remains.

"Chesh-Tar," she murmured, having determined the nature of the collar's design from the pitiful fragments. Unsteadily, she got to her knees and saluted her dead fellow warrior. "Great is my grief," he heard her whisper. "May you be one with the spirits of the Way, Chesh-Tar."

Reza did not know what to say. It seemed so incongruous, that a member of a species that was founded on war, on killing, could show the grief that he beheld on Esah-Zhurah's face.

"I am sorry," he said. It was all he could think of to say.

Esah-Zhurah nodded, as much at Reza's sincerity as at the meaning of his words. "No longer may she serve the Empress in this life," she said quietly. "That is my sorrow, human." She turned tired eyes upon him. "She was a very skilled hunter," she said quietly, moving closer to better see the remains that lay before them like a carnal banquet. She wanted to take the collar in her hands, but she knew it would have been unwise – and horribly painful – to walk through the stomach acid the genoth had vented. Luckily, the falling water created a natural draft that pulled the rancid air out of the cave. Otherwise, she would have been overcome with uncontrollable retching even now. "This must be an extraordinarily cunning beast to have outwitted her."

"What do we do?" he asked, pointed at the pile of chewed and melted debris.

"We leave it," she replied. "There is nothing we can do, now. The priestess will send a party to attend to her last rites."

Reza only nodded, then turned away from the oozing mass that had once been a young woman. Kreelan or not, Chesh-Tar had suffered a fate he would not have wished upon anyone. Together, he and Esah-Zhurah huddled together for warmth that was spiritual as much as physical as they waited for the fullness of the new day, fearful that the creature might be lurking further up the caldera's wall in the growing light.

Soon, much to their relief, the animals of the grotto began to emerge. At last Reza heard the sound he most wanted to hear: the boisterous warbling of the grotto lizards.

TEN

Twelve Years Later

Cold was the wind that howled in Reza's face, and he struggled to more tightly bind the furs that protected his head. He peered ahead over Goliath's powerful shoulders as he gripped the reins in his gloved hands, his body moving in time with the beast's undulating gait as he plodded through the deep snow. Through the tiny slit in the fur wrappings protecting his face, Reza could see little more than glaring whiteness and the occasional gray shadow of a withered tree. Although the dim light from the sun penetrated the white shroud that clung to the earth, the line where land and sky met was all but obscured.

Beside him, Esah-Zhurah rode her magthep, an unnamed cow much smaller than Goliath's aging bulk. Despite their hardiness, even the Kreelans eschewed the cold of deep winter, when the kazha conducted its training in the few indoor facilities dedicated to the purpose.

But there were times when the tresh were sent forth on missions, and this was one of them. The priestess had dispatched the two of them to the city to retrieve her correspondence, a similar errand that had brought him under Tesh-Dar's influence some dozen human years earlier. Their errand was certainly not the first of its type for Reza, but it was certainly the first time he had become genuinely concerned for their safety, and with every passing moment his sense of worry deepened.

They had reached the city and conducted their business there without incident, leaving the black tube that contained the priestess's outgoing correspondence and picking up its counterpart to return to her. After a quick meal in a public hall, where the two of them had perched comfortably next to a huge pit of glowing coals, they had begun their journey back.

The first part of their return trek had been entirely uneventful, with nothing more than a light snowfall and playful breezes. But soon the winds had become threatening, and even the magtheps – as well-protected against winter's perils as they were – had begun complaining. They shook their heads to throw off the heavy coating of ice from their eyes and ears, all the while muttering to each other in their own way. The horizon had closed in around them, finally disappearing in a total whiteout of heavy snow.

Above all else, Reza knew it was taking them much too long to return from the city. He had spent enough time on this world without any chronometer save the sun, Empress Moon, and stars to know that they had been traveling half again as long as they had that morning to reach the city.

"Esah-Zhurah," he shouted through the furs and the wind, "I think we are lost."

"Nonsense, Reza," she told him. "We are on course," she said, holding up a circular device about the size of her palm with a pointer in the center: a compass. "We are only delayed by the winds and snow."

"Then why have we not seen any markers for the last few leagues?" he asked, referring to the tall stone cairns that lined the roads that spread outward from the city like spokes on a wheel, serving to guide travelers in conditions just such as this. "There is nothing out here but us, and I do not recognize any of this."

Esah-Zhurah ignored him. It annoyed her that he, the tresh who had in some ways become the envy of many of her peers, appeared to be losing his courage and his faith in her. But her pride would not allow her to admit that the seeds of doubt had sprouted in her own mind, as well. The lack of familiar landmarks – the peninsular forest, the three rock outcroppings that lined the road to the kazha like lonely sentinels, the stone pyramid markers – was troubling.

But I have followed the compass unerringly, she told herself. Again she checked that the needle was precisely in the position it was supposed to be. It showed three points left of north, pointing directly toward the kazha from the city's center. "We are going the right way," she said again with finality, spurring her magthep into a faster gait in a demonstration of her resolve. "If you do not accept it," she told him, "you may choose your own direction."

Reza sighed, saying nothing. He did not want to antagonize her needlessly, especially since he was not quite sure of their situation. The compass had been pointing in the right direction. But the conditions they were in were unusual, even for this time of year. Prodding Goliath to move on after his tresh, he tried to silence the alarms in his mind.

Time passed, hours measured by Goliath's bounding stride, and with each step Reza's concern grew. The winds were blowing furiously, and the snow had become a curtain of shrieking whiteness that cut visibility to less than two full strides of Goliath's powerful legs. At last, he could hold himself back no longer.

"Stop!" he shouted suddenly to the shadowy form ahead, his voice strangely muted by the whipping snow around them.

"What is it?" Esah-Zhurah called back, reining in her magthep. Reza heard anticipation in her voice, as if she expected him to be pointing to the kazha, about to tell her he saw something he recognized.

"Esah-Zhurah," he said, moving close to overcome the howling wind, "you must face it: we are lost. Night will fall soon, and we must find a place to make camp or we will freeze to death."

"For the last time, Reza, I say we are going in the correct direction," she said, her voice tight. Her own fears had been eating at her like a maggot feasting on rotting flesh, and Reza's words only served to fuel the parasitic beast. But her pride concealed the extent of the rot, providing her a false shield of self-righteousness. Inside, she wanted to protect him, to do what was right. But the prideful froth that beat against her brain, the fact that he might be right, was too much for her still-xenophobic mind to grapple with. "It is just that the winds and snow–"

"We are lost!" he suddenly shouted, grabbing her by the shoulders and spinning her around in the saddle to face him, finally losing control over his anger and fear.

It was a mistake. Using his own leverage against him, she reflexively rammed her right elbow into the side of his head. He was unprepared for an attack, and he toppled from the saddle as if struck with a lance. He landed on his back, the fall cushioned slightly by the layer of snow on the ground, but not enough to prevent the wind from being knocked out of him.

Esah-Zhurah watched with hooded eyes as he struggled to his knees, gasping for breath. "I am sorry, Reza," she said, anger ruling her mind, a cheap substitute for reason. "If you do not wish to accompany me, I will not keep you."

She prodded her magthep with her feet, sending the cow galloping away into the curtain of white.

"No, wait!" he croaked, forcing air through his still protesting lungs. He staggered to his feet, only to fall again, his head whirling from her unexpected blow. He crawled to Goliath's side, the claws of his gauntlets grappling with the saddle as he struggled to his feet. "Esah-Zhurah! Wait!" he cried again, finally clearheaded enough to lunge into his mount's saddle.

But it was too late. He watched helplessly as she sped into the wall of snow, swiftly disappearing from sight.

* * *

Esah-Zhurah did not how long she had been going at a full gallop. Her anger at Reza, a demon that had struck with the suddenness of lightning, had been so all-consuming that she had completely lost track of time. But from the magthep's labored breathing, she knew that it was time to let it rest. Forcing herself to relax somewhat, she eased it to a slow trot, then a walk.

She looked yet again at the compass, but she was not entirely consoled by what it told her. As much as she hated to admit it to herself, Reza had been right about one thing: even as bad as this weather had been, they certainly should have reached the kazha – or at least one of the outer ring roads – by now.

Stopping her magthep for a moment, ignoring its hungry mewling, she peered intently into the snowy world around her. She looked for landmarks, but there was nothing. Not a single feature stood out. Not a rock, not a tree, nothing. She found that in itself curious and disquieting. There was not a single lump or disturbance in the ground within the confines of her limited visibility; the ground under the snow seemed to be as smooth and flat as a pane of glass. She looked again at the compass. The needle still pointed insistently three points left of north, exactly as it should. It had not deviated since they started from the city.

As she fumbled with the flap of the compass pouch, she suddenly stopped as those four words echoed in her head. *It had not deviated...*

With a feeling of sickening certainty, she took a close look at the compass, already knowing what she would find. Indeed, the needle still pointed as it always had – no matter which way the device was turned. Holding it close to her face, peering through the driving snow, she saw that the tiny air bubble under the glass face was locked in position, the liquid inside the compass frozen solid.

Baring her fangs and roaring with anger at her own stupidity, she smashed her fist into the fragile face of the device. She hurled what was left of it into the snow with all her strength, watching it disappear as it sailed into the bleak whiteness that had encircled her.

And only then did the magnitude of her predicament become apparent. Having abandoned Reza, she may well have forfeited her own life. Her people ventured into the Homeworld's winter harshness in pairs at least, for one terribly vital reason: one body alone, even in the emergency shelters they always carried, could not produce enough heat to overcome the freezing temperatures of the night. The magtheps were insulated well enough that they could burrow into the snow to shield themselves from the wind, and thus survive. But without Reza's body heat to combine with her own, she would almost certainly die of exposure.

Worse than the thought of death, however, was how she had tainted her honor before Reza with her pride and arrogant self-confidence. She had breached the trust he had vested in her that day in the grotto, now a lifetime ago, yet only yesterday. So much had they shared in the cycles that had passed, and only now did she understand the depth to which their relationship had grown. She accepted that he was not an animal, but a being worthy of her trust and the mercy of the Empress. Of all the things in her life of which she could be proud, he was the first and foremost. Death she could accept. But dying without a chance to redeem herself to Reza – that she could not.

She saw that the snow was beginning to fill her magthep's tracks, slowly obliterating them and marking the time before she might have to lay down to sleep one last time and await Death's cold embrace.

"Reza," she cried, reining the magthep around to head back in the direction from which they had come, "what a fool I have been!"

There was no answer, save the mocking howl of the wind.

* * *

Awkwardly, sometimes stumbling where the snow deepened unexpectedly, Goliath loped along the trail of giant bird-like footprints left by Esah-Zhurah's mount. He was guided as much by his own instincts as by the half-blinded human on his back. Reza knew that normally Goliath could keep up this pace for hours without becoming overly tired, but the deepening snow was slowing him down. Slowly but surely, the great beast was tiring.

But even with Goliath, it would be impossible to catch Esah-Zhurah unless she had at some point slowed to an easy walk. Following her magthep's spoor was becoming more difficult by the minute. The blowing whiteness around him had turned a dull, lifeless gray as the invisible sun began to set, and it would soon give way to the icy depths of night, beset by temperatures that would freeze exposed flesh in a matter of seconds. The wind that drove the snow over the tracks he desperately sought to follow also was attacking his body, impaling him with tiny needles of cold that lanced at his nerves before they disappeared from his sense of touch altogether. Already, he had lost most of the feeling in his toes; a residual tingling was all that remained. If he could not find Esah-Zhurah soon he would suffer from frostbite, his flesh perhaps permanently damaged if he could not reach a healer in time. If he did not find her at all, they both would die.

He was running out of time. Each newfound footprint was shallower than the one before it, covered by the massive snowfall that had reduced

Reza's world to a few paces of his own legs. Goliath's stride was almost that long when he was moving quickly, and if Esah-Zhurah made a sharp turn somewhere up ahead as she followed her faulty compass, Reza could easily miss it and lose the trail even before the snow covered it completely.

Cursing under his breath to any god that might be listening, even the Empress, Reza urged Goliath on, driving him as fast as he dared.

* * *

Esah-Zhurah had slowed her mount to a dull plod as she squinted in the dying light to see the spoor her magthep had left coming the other way. She had not realized before how far she had come since leaving Reza behind, but backtracking was leaving her with little hope of finding him. The tracks were all but gone, mere dents in the featureless gray landscape, and the blinding whiteness of the snowy cloak around her was quickly giving way to the deadly darkness of night. If she did not find him soon...

She carefully guided the magthep along the fading trail, but her skill could not forestall the inevitable. The last visible track behind her now, she saw only falling snow, a dark gray curtain ahead of her in the rapidly fading light. The trail was gone.

"Reza," she murmured, "what am I to do?"

* * *

"Well," Reza said to himself, batting his arms against his torso to keep his blood flowing into his numbing fingers, "the hunt is over." After passing an indentation he took to be a footprint, he had found himself surrounded by snow, snow, and more snow, without any further sign of the other magthep's trail. Even Goliath had lost the scent of the other beast, and stood snorting into the freezing air. With a morbid curiosity befitting a cynical embalmer, Reza wondered how it would feel to freeze to death. The accounts he remembered from his fading memory of things human described it as feeling terribly cold, then warm, and at last falling asleep, never to reawaken. "That is not so bad," he sighed. There were plenty of worse ways to die, he knew. But this was fundamentally wrong to him in a way that he was at a loss to explain.

He stared into the snow, where the horizon should have been, but he was not looking at what his eyes were seeing. He was listening to a voice that spoke deep within him. It did not use words, or even images, like in a dream. It was more a feeling that pulsed from his core, a flame that had been kindled in his soul as he slept one night, perhaps. He did not know exactly when it had first come to him, or what it might have been, but he accepted it now as an ally. It was not simply the voice of his will to survive. It was like a living thing within him, an alter ego that played the role of guardian angel by giving him the strength he needed to live. Alien or human, it did not matter. It was with him.

Esah-Zhurah was somewhere close by, the voice seemed to say. And Reza believed. He knew it was true. It must be.

As he drew on that source of inner strength, a rush of adrenaline suddenly surged into his system. Taking the furs from his face, he cupped his hands to his mouth.

"Esah-Zhurah!" he shouted as loud as he could, his diaphragm ramming air into his throat like a turbine, stretching the last syllable until his lungs had no more to give.

Without the tiniest trace of an echo, the wall of snow around him consumed her name.

Closing his eyes, he listened.

* * *

Esah-Zhurah was just about to dismount and set up the shelter when she heard something above the howling of the falling snow. It sounded like a faintly audible note that might have been a voice coming from her left. It grew for a moment into a steady tone that suddenly ended.

"Reza?" she whispered. "Reza!" she shouted, "Where are you?"

Nothing.

"I did not imagine it," she said aloud, sitting ramrod straight in her saddle, as if her body could act as an antenna to gain some additional clarity should the note be repeated.

Beneath her, the magthep threw its head from side to side, growing restless for no reason Esah-Zhurah could fathom. It mewled quietly, stomping its feet, waiting for Esah-Zhurah to make up her mind.

There! The sound came again, and she was sure it was her name being called, and was not simply a wishful hallucination.

"Reza!" she shouted with all her strength. "Over here!"

Her heart thundering with relief, she wheeled her magthep around and began to gallop in the direction of his voice, thanking the Empress that Reza somehow had found her, and that perhaps all would yet be well.

* * *

He was about to call out to her again when he heard a thunderous boom. Goliath suddenly sprawled forward, catapulting Reza over the beast's twisting neck. Reza's arms and legs flailed like a doll's as he spun through the air, his mouth gaping open in horrified surprise.

In the moment he was airborne, surprise gave way to terror as he saw a jagged black chasm yawning beneath him where only snow had been before. Freezing water lapped hungrily at the serrated edges of the broken ice, and welcomed Reza with a frigid embrace that stole the scream from his lips as he plunged into the river.

* * *

The sound hit her like a shot from a rifle, echoing through the air and reverberating through the ground at her feet.

"What is that?" she whispered, peering in the direction from which she had heard Reza's voice.

She could see nothing. Her ears, however, had no difficulty in picking out sounds she recognized instantly: a magthep's terrified squeals mixed with the sound of splashing water.

The river! she realized. We have been traveling along the river. And Reza and Goliath must have fallen through...

"No!" she cried, kicking her magthep in the ribs and sending the beast racing as fast as she could toward the frenzied thrashings. "Reza, hang on!" she shouted into the wind. "Hang on!"

Suddenly, as if someone had whipped a curtain aside, Esah-Zhurah found herself plunging toward the gaping black fissure in the ice where Goliath had broken through. The great magthep was now pawing and kicking desperately at the edge, his tiny forearms grappling pitifully at the icy wall that rose nearly a meter above him.

As she watched, more ice tumbled down into the black waters. The layer that had covered the river was treacherously thin and hollow between the surface of the water and the bottom of the ice. The magthep screamed in terror, his rear legs and tail thrashing as he sought to escape.

"Reza!" she shouted over the magthep's braying. Her eyes scanned the water, hoping to spot him alive among the drifting chunks of ice, or – better by far – somewhere near the edge, out of danger. She would have taken her magthep closer, but she was already dangerously near the snaking web of cracks that spiraled outward from where Goliath lay struggling.

Leaping from her mount, she moved as close as she dared to the crumbling edge. "Reza!" she called again, her voice cracking with the effort.

"Esah-Zhurah," came a hoarse cry, barely more than a whisper it seemed, from somewhere in the water, "here."

Desperately, Esah-Zhurah searched the water for him, edging ever closer as she sought to pierce the undulating shroud of darkening snow.

Without warning, there was another tremendous boom from the ice, and her magthep plunged into the frigid water. Esah-Zhurah was flung clear by a huge chunk of ice that catapulted her into the air like a springboard. Rolling to her feet in the snow, she turned to find Goliath finally struggling to safety, having at last gotten a grip with his rear feet on stable ice. The beast shook himself mightily, flinging away the water that had not yet frozen to his fur. Retreating a short way from the fissure, he turned to bray at his companion cow, now struggling for its life. Lacking Goliath's enormous strength, the smaller animal was doomed.

"Call again!" Esah-Zhurah shouted, "I cannot see you!"

"Here," came the voice, weaker this time.

Her eyes were drawn to two black streaks across a large chunk of ice. They suddenly resolved into Reza's arms, the claws of his gauntlets thrust into the ice. Just before the snow obliterated the scene, she saw his head lolling just above the water.

"I see you!" she shouted. "*Do not let go!* Do you hear me?" she cried. "Hang on!"

She turned to Goliath, the problem of how to retrieve Reza without killing herself consuming her thoughts. Since the day in the grotto, she had learned from Reza how to swim, but she had never tried anything like this, nor had she ever been in water this cold.

"You are going to have to help me, Goliath," she said, grabbing some rope from where it was lashed to the saddle. She shook the ice and snow from it, the fibers crackling as she began to unwind the sturdy hemp. She tied one end through one of the stirrups on Reza's saddle, then dropped the rest to the ground. Bracing herself against the cold, she ripped off her metal chest armor. She would have taken off the rest, but there was no time.

She took up the rope and stood on the thinnest ice that would still support her weight. She knew now that her destiny had arrived. This was the source of her dark dreams, the nightmares that had plagued her since she was young. This was the dark water that would steal her breath away, that would still her heart, that would take her life. She might have laughed at the sudden memory of her fear of the waters of the grotto that night, as Reza struggled valiantly to convince her that lying in a genoth's belly was indeed worse than diving beneath a waterfall. "Have faith," she told herself softly, gritting her teeth. "Be strong."

Gripping the free end of the rope in one hand, she ran toward the water, praying that her body would be able to stand the shock. She leaped into the air just as the ice gave way beneath her and dived head first into the water, arms outstretched, with the rope trailing away behind her like a harpoon's lanyard.

Her thoughts and her breath were ripped away as she hit the water, the cold stabbing into her body like an icy sword. She was sure her heart stopped for just an instant. But then, almost reluctantly, it began to beat again, counting down the few minutes she had before the cold would claim her. She began to swim toward the small berg to which Reza had anchored himself. From land, it seemed like it could only be a dozen meters. But now, in the freezing water, every stroke seemed like a league. She could feel the cold sucking the life from her, the water a much more insidious opponent than the air above. Her heart thundered as it tried to keep warm blood flowing from her weakening core to the straining muscles in her legs and arms.

Without warning, she felt herself jerked up short. Only after a moment of confused turning in the water did she realize what had happened: the rope was not long enough! Hesitating for a precious moment, she finally let it go and kicked away, leaving it behind to sink into the darkness. She had been depending on Goliath's brute strength to get them out, but now she was on her own.

She turned her head just in time to see Reza slip beneath the surface. His hand trailed limply behind him like a periscope until that, too, vanished beneath the roiling water.

"No!" she screamed, kicking madly toward where he had gone down. Frantically, she swam to where she had last seen him clinging to the ice. She dived below the surface and swam in a circle for as long as she could, finally coming up for a gasp of air. She could see nothing, feel nothing in the murk below. How was she to find him in the black water? Which direction was the current flowing? She dived back down, searching with her hands. But all that her numbed nerves reported was the deathly cold water. She swam back to the surface again, her hopes for finding him dying with the light of the sun.

"Please," she prayed to her Empress through her violently chattering teeth, "please let me find him. Do not let it end this way. Please."

Then there came an odd tingling sensation, as if a frail *grensha* moth were fluttering along her nerves, and Esah-Zhurah suddenly felt a comforting warmth spreading through her chest. She knew she must be falling over the edge into hypothermia as her body lost its core heat. But somewhere within her, a flicker of knowing flared into a low blaze, and she saw Reza in her mind, saw his limp body, trapped against an outcropping of ice somewhere below her.

Gathering air in her lungs until she thought they might burst, she thrust herself down a final time, her body following a set of directions her mind did not understand, but dared not ignore. She swam beneath the ice, entering a world of complete darkness, where not even the brightest light could shine through, had there been any such light remaining in the world above. She knew that if she did not find him now, both of them would be dead, food for the swimming things that teemed in the river during the spring season after the spawning.

Her fingers touched something. Desperately, she latched onto it, for there was nothing else to sustain the hope that dwindled with the last of the oxygen in her burning lungs. She grappled with the unseen thing, and finally was rewarded as Reza's lifeless form came free from the inverted ridge of ice where he had been trapped by the slow but irresistible current.

Perhaps infinity was a concept best not dwelt upon by a young warrior still untested in battle, but Esah-Zhurah thought she came to understand it well as she struggled through the water toward the surface. Distance and time merged into numbing agony and fear as she fought for every stroke against the current that had helped her find him, but that now threatened to doom her to the same fate. She clamped her arm harder around Reza's chest to keep his armored body from sinking like leaden ballast. She turned to look at his shadowy outline, wondering if he could even still be alive.

No matter, she told herself. She was determined not to leave him behind. Not ever.

The flame that had burned so brightly within her, the power that had somehow shown her where to find him, was flickering like a candle flame surrounded with mist. Her heart was beginning to slow as her body temperature fell, and the numbness in her limbs was overshadowed only by the intense burning in her cramping muscles as their strength swiftly ebbed.

A hideous apparition suddenly flew at her face from the darkness, teeth bared behind savagely drawn lips, ebony eyes bulging from its unearthly face. Claws appeared, reaching for her...

Esah-Zhurah almost screamed into the frigid water at the sight, but her panicked brain understood – barely in time – that it was only the corpse of her magthep. Its struggles against the water now over, its ragged shell was bound for the ocean that lay far beyond the great wastelands.

Just then, her head shot through the water into the frigid air above, and Esah-Zhurah gasped at the shock of it, the taste of life in her mouth. She fought to get Reza's head above the water, even though she knew he was not breathing, and had not been for she did not know how long. She tugged and pulled with her legs and free arm, propelling herself toward the craggy outlines of the ice rim.

But it was not enough. Just at that moment, her struggling legs failed.

As her head went under for the last time, her free hand touched something, and instinctively she grabbed hold of it.

The rope!

Biting her tongue, the pain forcing one last surge of adrenaline into her arteries, she managed one more kick, pushing her head above the water.

Managing to loop the rope around her free wrist, she screamed a last command to the faithful beast above before the water jealously pulled her back. "Goliath, *drakh-te ka!* Pull!"

Nothing happened. As she began to sink, her legs having given their last, she sucked in one final breath before her head went under

Her arm was nearly pulled from its socket as the slack in the rope suddenly vanished. Obeying the command that Reza had once taught him as a useful trick, Goliath hauled them out with his mammoth strength, running headlong away from the fissure. Esah-Zhurah clung desperately to Reza as the two of them swept through the water like porpoises, leaving a rooster tail of icy water showering behind them.

Ahead of them loomed a wall of ice, the edge of the collapsed ice dome through which Reza had fallen. The top of the ice was nearly a meter above the surface of the water, and Esah-Zhurah visualized the two of them being smashed senseless against it as Goliath pulled them blindly onward.

She opened her mouth to tell Goliath to stop, to slow them down before they hit. But a monstrous roar drowned out her voice as the entire ice dome around them collapsed into the water. They were now surging toward a part of the fissure that was in the shape of a V, spearheaded by the rope that had sawed through the thinner ice under Goliath's power. A tidal wave crashed over them, and then they were smashing through sheets and blocks of jagged ice. Frantically rolling to one side, she tried to use Reza's armor as a shield for her own body as they scraped and bucked over the razor-edged floes. Had her arm not been entwined with the rope, she would have lost her grip and fallen back into the water.

Then they were free, their bodies plowing through the snow as Goliath pulled them at a full gallop. Esah-Zhurah let him go for a while until she thought it might be safe to stop.

"Goliath," she called wearily, hoping the animal would hear her through the still howling wind. She had visions of herself and Reza, frozen to death, twirling on a rope behind the animal until it, too, finally died of exposure. "*Kazh!* Stop!"

The rope went slack.

Esah-Zhurah wanted to lay there in the snow and rest for a long while, but she knew that to do so would have brought Death calling. Reza lay next to her, his body still. She had to act quickly. She gained her feet, staggering like a drunkard, and was met by Goliath's steamy muzzle. Petting the beast with dead hands, she worked her way to the saddle and grappled with the lashings that held the shelter, slashing the frozen bindings free with her talons. It fell into the snow. The small brown roll, about the diameter and length of her thigh, immediately began to grow, quickly assuming a hemispherical shape that was nearly as big around as Goliath was long. A tube extruded itself from one end as the whole thing changed color from a leathery brown to a heat absorbing black. As an afterthought, Esah-Zhurah pulled the saddle from Goliath's back, leaving him free to seek his own shelter.

She pulled Reza into the tube, the shelter's sphincter-like entrance dilating open to accept them as if they were crawling back into the womb, then closing behind them. Groping wearily in the darkness of the vestibule with her numbed fingers, Esah-Zhurah cut away Reza's frozen armor, the ice shattering as she peeled it away like the hardened chrysalis of some exotic species of insect. She tore at his clothes, quickly throwing everything to one side in a frozen heap. Then she dragged him into the main part of the shelter and turned him on his stomach. Doing what he had once shown her, she straddled his back and began forcing the water from his lungs with her hands, pushing down with all her weight on his back.

Beneath her, she could hear the sickening gurgle of water as it gushed from his mouth onto the floor of the shelter. Push, release, push, release, until the water fell to a trickle, then stopped. Then she hurriedly turned him over. She bent down, putting her ear to Reza's naked breast, listening for a heartbeat through the pounding of her own that reverberated in her ears. For eight beats of her heart, there was nothing. Then, she heard a faint *lub... dub* through his flesh.

The sound energized her with the power of hope. She bent over him, praying that she could remember the things he had taught her when she was learning to swim. "*Mouth-to-mouth resuscitation*," he had called it in his native tongue. She had laughed at him at the time, finding the thought of doing such a thing to another Kreelan – let alone a human – repugnant.

But the humor of that day was now replaced by desperation as she took his head in her hands. With one hand cupping his head and the other clamping his nose, she put her numbed mouth over his and began to force air into his waterlogged lungs. She took another breath, then blew again. Her body shook from sheer exhaustion and cold, and her heart beat so fast that she knew it must soon burst. But she refused to give up.

Suddenly, he began coughing. He spouted water everywhere as his lungs received a signal from his dazed brain that they were to begin functioning again, and they sought to clear out the last of the offending fluid. Esah-Zhurah shuddered, praying her thanks to the Empress.

After a few minutes, his breathing became ragged but steady. Undoing her own armor and shedding her clothing, she held him close, wrapping her quaking arms around him. Beneath them, the shelter absorbed the icy pool of water from Reza's lungs. It left behind only a soft, dry bed that already had begun to warm them, reflecting their flickering body heat inward.

Cradling his frigid body to give it what little warmth her own had to offer, she spiraled into a dark, dreamless abyss.

* * *

Tesh-Dar stood at the great window in her quarters, watching as the muted light of day faded into the cold clutches of deep winter's night. She did not need a thermometer to tell her that the temperature was plummeting, and that any organism directly exposed to the night's ministrations would not long survive.

"All of the tresh are accounted for, save Esah-Zhurah and the animal," her First reported quietly. The task they had been given had been a simple but vital one, carried out by generations of tresh for eons as a service to the priestesses of the kazhas. The journey to the city and back, even in deep snow, should have taken only three-fourths of the day's light. But dusk was now upon them, and the young pair still had not returned. "Perhaps," she went on in the silence left by Tesh-Dar, "the human did something..."

The priestess waved her hand impatiently, dismissing the First's veiled accusation. "Had he wished to do something in that vein," she said, "surely he would have done so before this day. No," she said, turning away from the window, "it is not that. Perhaps they remained in the city through good judgment. I do not know."

"If there is nothing else, my priestess, I shall retire for the night," the First said, saluting before she turned to leave. "If the weather allows, I will send out search parties tomorrow to find them."

"No," Tesh-Dar told her. "If they are alive, they must find their own way. If they have perished, there is no need to risk the lives of others to find frozen corpses. Many lives has the winter claimed in this way, and I will not willingly add to its toll."

"Then it is in Her hands," the other woman observed. "Sleep well, my priestess," she said, softly closing the door behind her.

Turning again to the window, a grimace kissed Tesh-Dar's lips at the First's parting words, for no sleep would she find this night.

Closing her eyes and straining to hear and see with senses far beyond what her body boasted, Tesh-Dar began to wander through the endless cold of the night, searching for her missing children.

* * *

Reza was not sure if he was awake or simply in some kind of strange dream. The world was cloaked in velvety darkness, and his skin tingled in a strange, yet familiar way. After a moment, he realized it was the sensation left by the healing gel as it worked its strange miracles. He lay against something warm and smooth, his face pressed against a firm pillow. His nose relayed a gentle smell he recognized as the alien musk to which he had become so accustomed, the smell of Kreelan skin. Esah-Zhurah's skin.

"Esah... Zhurah?" he rasped, his tongue a flaccid lump of flesh in his parched mouth.

"Yes," came her voice from somewhere in the darkness, accompanied by the cool touch of her hand on his forehead, gently brushing his hair back. "I am here, Reza." When she had awakened from the nightmare that had finally come to pass, she had found Reza lying next to her, shivering and burning up with fever. The shelter had done as best it could to save the frostbitten flesh, automatically coating Reza's skin with healing gel, but there was nothing it could do for whatever raged within his body. Esah-Zhurah had despaired for his survival as she did what little she could to keep his temperature down, comforting him in the few lucid moments the fever had allowed.

"Are you... all right?" he asked.

"Yes," she told him, her heart swelling at his concern for her. He tried to move, but Esah-Zhurah held him back. "Be still, my tresh," she commanded softly, her hands holding him firmly in place against her side, his head cradled between her breasts. She put her hand against his forehead again, reassuring herself that it was only warm, and not hot. "Your body is yet weak."

"Where is Goliath?" he asked.

She smiled. Reza was forever concerned with his animal friend. "Goliath lies buried next to us in the snow, keeping warm in the way of his kind. He, too, is well; complaining of hunger, but alive."

"How long..." he asked. "How long have we been here?"

"The sun has risen and set twice since I awakened, and now it is night," she told him. "I do not know how long I was unconscious before that." She felt Reza's eyes close, the brushing of his eyelashes a pleasant tickle against the skin of her breast. Thinking he had returned to the quiet of sleep, she said no more.

But he was not asleep, only thinking. "Esah-Zhurah," Reza said, breaking the silence, "why are you still here?"

"What do you mean?" she asked, puzzled.

"The storm has long since passed, has it not?" Outside, the only thing to be heard was the muted sound of Goliath's breathing and an occasional groan as the beast voiced its hunger.

"It is so," she answered cautiously, unsure where his thoughts would lead.

"I was as good as dead, drowned in the river," Reza went on, his voice a gentle but unrelenting probe, exploring her motivations. "You could have left me behind. You could have taken the shelter and Goliath and tried to make it on your own. Why did you not?"

She shifted uncomfortably beside him. "I shamed my honor with my arrogance by abandoning you," she said, her voice low and measured, each syllable a self-punishment exacted by her conscience. "I could not abandon you again. You are strange, and not of our Way, but you... are special to me, in a way I do not fully understand." She paused. "I could not bear the thought of losing you."

His hand found hers. There was no need for words. She held him tightly, feeling the warm wetness of his tears upon her breast. In her heart there was a quiet jubilation that they were both alive, and that this day they were something more than they had ever been before.

As their bodies melded together in the deepening cold, she found herself murmuring softly in a prayer to the Empress, asking if perhaps this human – just this one – might indeed have a soul and a place among Her Children.

* * *

When Reza again awoke, it was to a sensation of rampant thirst the likes of which he had never known. Esah-Zhurah had done her best to give him what fluids she could against the fever that had taken him, and had drained all of the shelter's normal liquid supplies. But it had not made up for what he had lost, and the debt the fever had left in its wake had finally caught up to him. The inside of his mouth felt like it was sewn together from sun-baked leather.

"Water," he croaked.

"Here," she said, holding a small clump of packed snow to his lips.

He opened his mouth eagerly, but found the icy snow, taken from a small pile Esah-Zhurah had brought in for the purpose, to be like acid in his mouth. It burned in his throat as it grudgingly metamorphosed into its liquid form. Even so, his thirst was so overpowering that he began to suck on it greedily, and was rewarded with a fit of coughing as water found its way into his trachea, choking him.

Esah-Zhurah held him steady as his coughing subsided into ragged breathing. He was still terribly weak.

"Wait," she told him, gently rolling him onto his back.

He heard her scoop up some snow from wherever she had it sequestered behind him, and then she was silent for a while.

"What are you doing?" he asked, staring into the darkness.

Then he felt one of her hands reach down to cradle the back of his head, lifting it up, while the other gripped his lower jaw and gently forced it open. With shocked surprise he felt her lips press against his, and then cool water was spilling into his mouth from hers. For a moment, he did nothing, disbelieving that she was actually doing such a thing – the rough equivalent among her kind of a human kissing a dog in the world he had once known – and wondering if he should be thankful or repulsed by her touch.

But then her lips pulled away, and he forced himself to swallow the water she had shared with him, having melted the snow in her mouth with the heat of her body. With a detached, almost shameful sense of curiosity, he found himself analyzing the water for any trace of her own taste that might be there, noting with mixed emotions the lack of anything unpleasant.

"More?" Esah-Zhurah asked. She had discovered that actually carrying out the idea that had struck her had been... pleasant. It was not at all like when she had pressed her frozen mouth to his to force air into his lungs. In fact, it had excited her in a way. She wondered what it must have been like before the reign of the First Empress, when male warriors walked among her race, and there were no clawless ones, no sterile mules like herself. Did they perhaps lie quietly next to one another like this on cold winter nights, speaking only with the beating of their hearts and the touch of their bodies? This was the stuff of legend, of fairy tales, or so many peers thought, and undoubtedly it was so. The ancient tales and songs of those times struck a hollow chord among the Empire's warriors. For they knew that the males of their race were nothing more than instruments for the propagation of their species, and it was hard to imagine they had ever been anything more. Some, like Tesh-Dar, truly believed the ancient legends as historical truth. But many had their doubts. Esah-Zhurah tended to believe that the legends were only stories. But something in her mind, a tiny race memory left in the wake of the long evolution of her people, left her thinking that perhaps the peers, the doubters, were wrong.

Licking the tiny bit of moisture that had spilled on his lips, Reza nodded in the darkness. "Please," he begged, his thirst now completely awakened, a ravenous thing trapped in his parched mouth.

Esah-Zhurah repeated her performance four more times, until her tiny stockpile of snow was gone. She noted with a twinge of alarm that touching Reza this way was beginning to seem more than just pleasant. As she gave him the last of the water, the stream between their joined mouths now spent, she pulled away from him, pausing with her lips a hair's breadth from his, her heart beating like thunder in her ears.

"Thank you," he whispered, his lips brushing hers as he spoke the words, sending a jolt of emotional electricity through her. He reached out, running his fingers across her cheek, through her hair, before drawing her down to him. Like strangers whose destiny was to become fast friends and more, their lips touched in a gentle kiss that left them both breathless. When their lips parted, he only had time to utter her name before she kissed him in her own turn, carefully lowering her body onto his, her breasts pools of heat against his chest.

Reza felt a stiffening at his groin that he had experienced before only in his sleep. It was something he had never experienced in human company. He moaned softly as his erection pressed against the smooth, taut flesh of her belly, and he felt her shiver as his hands moved down her back to stroke her sides, his fingers tracing invisible patterns against her skin.

Esah-Zhurah was nearly lost to a power she had never even dreamt of, something that had not been experienced by a member of her race for thousands of generations: physical love. Her mind sought vainly to understand what her body instinctively knew, and she felt the first stirrings of a part of her that – as a mule – normally would have remained dormant her entire life. The fire that had begun in her veins when their lips touched had worked its way downward, and the wetness she felt in the furnace that burned between her thighs both exhilarated and terrified her.

"Esah-Zhurah," Reza whispered, reluctantly parting from her kiss, "is this even possible?"

"Yes," she answered huskily, gently running her fingers over Reza's face. "Our bodies... are similar enough to a human female's, but..." She shook her head and began to pull away from him, but he held her back.

"What is it?" he said, holding her face in his hands. "Tell me."

"I must not do this," she rasped. "It is forbidden me to mate, and to do so with one not of the Way..." Her whole body trembled suddenly, as if she had been taken by a wracking sob, and Reza held her tightly against him, ignoring the pain in his body. "We could be punished by death, Reza. Even for this."

The words tore at his heart, but he understood now what was at stake. He would not sacrifice her, or himself, for this desire that threatened to consume them. They had come too far to throw everything away for a single touch that might easily deny them a lifetime together.

"Listen to my words," he told her softly. "There will someday come a time when that will not be so. In this I believe. The day shall come when we may be as one, and until that day dawns, I shall wait for you."

She kissed him again, softly. "I pray to Her that it shall be as you say." She kissed his face, her lips and tongue caressing him with a tenderness he had never imagined possible for her. "You must rest now, my tresh," she said. "Rest, and grow strong again."

Esah-Zhurah pulled him close, her arms wrapped around him, her musky scent strong in his mind. He closed his eyes to the bitterness that welled up in his soul at the unbidden remembrance of terrible things now long past, things that had happened to a human boy who was fast becoming a man among an alien race. Shutting out those images and the guilt they threatened, he focused his thoughts on her hand as it ran through his hair, and the tingling sensation that stirred at the passing of her fingers.

His body swiftly gave in to the need for rest. And as sleep quietly crept upon him, he uttered the question that had been floating in his mind, hidden by the alien code of honor that bound him during his waking hours, but which carried no weight in the world of dreams.

"Do you love me?"

The answer would have pleased him, had he heard the whispered word before he slipped away into the waiting embrace of sleep.

"Yes," came Esah-Zhurah's soft voice. This warrior, who had once pledged her honor to break this human's will, now found her soul bound to his by something her race had not known for millennia. She lay silent, cradling him against the cold of night and the unknowns of the future, wondering if her world would still be the same come the dawn.

* * *

The First strode through the door, snow fluttering from her fur cape as she shook off the cold. "The sentries report that Esah-Zhurah and the human return," she announced. She was obviously amazed that it was possible for them to have survived six days in the wilderness in winter, alone.

"I know," Tesh-Dar told her from where she sat on the floor, legs curled under her, head bowed. She did not tell her subordinate that she had known their whereabouts since Esah-Zhurah had dived into the water after Reza. Her mind's eye had watched her pull him from the water and give him life with the touch of her lips upon his. She had kept watch periodically over the following days as she tended to her own business, wondering if they indeed would survive.

But her wonder had turned to shocked disbelief, as she witnessed from afar the emotional whirlwind that had swept over the two during the following nights. Her hours had been spent in deep meditation since then, with her mind's eye focused on them as they made their way back to the kazha with the coming of the sun and first light this day. "Have their mount taken care of, and bring the two young warriors to me."

"Yes, my priestess."

Time, being a very relative thing to one so old as Tesh-Dar, passed quickly. She opened her eyes to find Esah-Zhurah and her human consort before her on their knees, waiting.

"Greetings, priestess," Esah-Zhurah ventured quietly, unable to gauge her elder's mood. Reza remained silent, his eyes fixed to the smooth stone of the floor.

"You have something for me?" Tesh-Dar asked, as if the two had never been missing at all.

"Yes, priestess," Reza said quietly, holding forth the black tube that held Tesh-Dar's correspondence. Fortunately, it had been strapped to Goliath's saddle, and not to that of Esah-Zhurah's ill-fated mount.

Tesh-Dar leaned forward and took the tube – still cold to the touch – from Reza's hands, noticing that they did not shake, but were firm, confident.

"You have done well, young one," she told him, setting the tube aside. "Go now to the healers and let them tend to your injuries. Then go to the hall to eat. No more do I have for you this day."

"Yes, priestess," Reza told her, bowing his head. He got up from his knees and headed for the door. Esah-Zhurah made to get up to follow him.

"My business with you," Tesh-Dar said ominously, "is not yet complete."

Esah-Zhurah dropped back to her knees, hearing the door open and close quietly behind her as Reza – much as he hated to leave her alone – carried out Tesh-Dar's orders.

"Look at me, child."

Trained from birth to show respect by averting the eyes, it was a difficult thing for her to do. That the priestess had asked this of her drove home the seriousness of whatever matter the elder warrior had on her mind. Warily, Esah-Zhurah met Tesh-Dar's gaze.

"This I will say only once, for I will forgive it of you only this once," the great priestess said. "I cannot prohibit the feelings in your heart for the human. But I now remind you that to show those feelings toward one not of the Way with a touch, a caress," her voice strained as she fought off the shivers of disgust that swept through her at the things she had witnessed, "is forbidden, bestial in Her eyes. No more shall there be, or you will find yourself bound to the Kal'ai-Il, the Stone Place, in punishment." The Kal'ai-Il was an ancient monument to the discipline of the Way, a stone arena where only the most serious wrongs were punished. It had stood for millennia as a symbol of the price to be paid for the Empress's honor by a warrior fallen from grace. "You, like the others in this grand experiment, were chosen for this task because of your strength and spirit, your knowledge of their alien tongue and ways. Do not disgrace yourself in Her eyes again."

Lowering her head nearly to the floor, Esah-Zhurah cringed in shame, her fears realized. No feeling, no thought, no action was beyond the knowledge of the priestess. Esah-Zhurah felt like a tiny grain of sand, infinitesimal, before her gaze. But deep in her heart she felt the forbidden desire burn even brighter, a flame that she could never escape.

"It shall be so, my priestess," she whispered, the words sounding hollow and empty on her lips.

Tesh-Dar nodded, noting the deep turmoil in the child. She frowned, knowing that the coming cycle, Reza's last unless his blood was heard to sing, would be terribly difficult for Esah-Zhurah. Tesh-Dar knew that the child would likely wish to take her own life when the human's came to an end. It was a most unfavorable prospect for such a promising warrior. Worse, Esah-Zhurah was more than just another young warrior to her. Far more. Tesh-Dar would have to watch her carefully. "I will say no more of the matter," she told Esah-Zhurah gently. "Go now in the footsteps of your tresh and rest, for the sunrise shall again call you to the arena to train."

"Yes, my priestess." Saluting, Esah-Zhurah departed.

Tesh-Dar stared after her a moment, wondering at the intensity of the feelings she had sensed in the two of them. Was mere punishment, even shaving one's hair, enough to deter such things?

Then Tesh-Dar thought of the Ancient Ones who had watched over Esah-Zhurah as she had struggled to free Reza from the clutches of the river's icy waters. Never had Tesh-Dar known them to be interested in such affairs. What stake could they possibly claim in the matter of a warrior and her animal tresh? Tesh-Dar did not understand their motivations or what precisely they had done that night, but she had clearly felt their presence, guiding the girl through the water to find the human. She knew from the power of their song that they had not been mere bystanders in what had taken place.

Pondering this thought, Tesh-Dar opened the black tube that had been the catalyst for their tribulations. She began to read the long-delayed correspondence from the Empress, knowing that she must seek an audience with Her to discuss these unforeseen developments.

ELEVEN

"And there is only the one who remains, priestess of the Desh-Ka?" the Empress asked. The two of them walked side by side in the Imperial Garden. It was a paradise of flora from every one of the Empire's ten thousand worlds. The number and variety of plants were such that, had Tesh-Dar the luxury of time, she could have expended a complete cycle walking about the great greenhouse, strolling for several hours each day, without ever seeing the same tree or blooming flower twice. The aromas that caressed Tesh-Dar's sensitive nose were an endless source of delight. The one time she had dared touch one of the plants – only with the permission of one amongst the army of clawless ones tending to their welfare, of course – her fingers had thrilled to a song of life that was unlike anything she had ever felt before. Primal and pure, it was a feeling she deeply cherished.

But now, walking beside the Empress, even the great garden could not lift her spirits. She felt an acute sense of disappointment at the results of the great experiment that had begun what seemed like only yesterday. But over a dozen years had passed since the raid on the strange human settlement that had been populated almost entirely with their young. Tesh-Dar would have thought that such planets would have been plenty, for that is how their own young were raised. After giving birth at the nurseries, the mothers departed soon after their recovery, leaving the infant children in the care of the Wardresses who would tend to their needs and train them until they were ready to join the kazhas. It was not uncommon for a mother never to see her child again after its birth, and the code of the Way ascribed even the naming of the child to the Wardresses. The only link from generation to generation was the passage of the *Ne'er-Se*, the ritual verse each mother left the Wardresses to teach her child, an oral trace of the females in the mother's bloodline. The males, of course, were not included; they were never even given a name, and those born lived, bred, and died at the nurseries. Thus it was a surprise to Tesh-Dar to learn that the human planet they had raided had been an aberration, a purgatory for the human young who had been forced to live there.

The priestesses of the other kazhas who had participated in the raid had been equally shocked. They should have been walking here with the Empress, as well, save they had no reason to come: in the cycles that had passed since then, all of the human children who had been taken had died on the terrible path that was the Kreelan Way. By disease, overzealous punishment on the part of the tresh, accidents, suicides, and from countless other causes, many never fully understood by the priestesses and the healers. The answer to the Empress's original curiosity had been unavoidable: the humans had no soul. Yes, Tesh-Dar had conceded, some of them rose well to the thrill of battle, the crash of sword upon sword, the sting of the enemy's claw; but still, their blood did not sing. Many times she had seen fire in one or another's eyes as she had traveled through the kazhas spread across the Homeworld and the Settlements, but she had never once heard a single note of the song that united each of Her Children unto the Way. Their voices among the spirits – the Ancient Ones – to which she especially was attuned, had remained silent these many cycles. The plants around her now were more vocal in spiritual song than anything she could detect from the humans, save the occasional insight into their torrid emotions.

Yes, she thought to herself grimly, *they all had died.*

All but one. Reza.

"Yes, my Empress," she replied to her ruler, her twin sister by birth, "there remains only one." In an ironic twist of fate that was so common among her people, Tesh-Dar had been born with silver claws. Her twin sister, whose given name had never been spoken since she assumed the leadership of her people, had been gifted both with black claws and the white hair that tradition demanded of one destined for the throne. Tesh-Dar flexed her claws, black as night now. The color, as well as her tremendous size and strength, had come with the changes wrought during an ancient ceremony performed among the Desh-Ka, the bonding of one soul with another. The one to whom she had bonded herself had long ago died in battle, and Tesh-Dar's heart had ached with emptiness ever since. "The one of my kazha, whose tresh is thy daughter, Esah-Zhurah, yet lives."

"And how," the Empress asked, turning to face her sister, "does it fare?"

"He fares well, my Empress," Tesh-Dar replied, unconsciously substituting the pronoun she herself used for referring to the human. She had long before stopped calling Reza "it." Tesh-Dar would have died before admitting it openly to the peers, but she had become fond of him with a depth that bespoke her respect for the child. Rarely did she miss the chance to watch him fight in the arena, sparring confidently with those of her own race. His first Challenge, fought after he and Esah-Zhurah had returned from the mountains with the fantastic tale of the great genoth, had been less than auspicious, she remembered. The two of them had returned from their free time exhausted and spent from their ordeal, and two days later was the Challenge. Tesh-Dar pictured Reza in the arena that first time, pitted by the draw of the lottery against Chara-Kumah. It was a pairing that Tesh-Dar had considered a fairly even match, at least in terms of size, for the human child.

But the match was hardly even. Chara-Kumah expertly humiliated her opponent, toying with him, drawing him in each time to receive a blow to the legs or shoulders, inflicting pain but little damage. And Reza reacted as if he had never had a moment's training in the use of staff or sword, as if he were still the tiny spirited human pup who had lashed out with his father's knife at a Desh-Ka priestess so long ago. Tesh-Dar had seen the flames in Reza's eyes, and she had found herself hoping beyond all hope that her mind would catch a note – a single peal – of the song she sought to hear. But there was only the grunting and crash of weapon against armor, the cries of pain as exposed flesh was bruised and beaten. Reza lasted for two turns of the timeglass before Chara-Kumah tired of his company. She felled him with a brutal blow to his carelessly exposed legs, then quickly delivered another strike to his head before Tesh-Dar called an end to the affair. Half-carried by Esah-Zhurah, who made her own way to the fourth set of contests before falling to a young swordmistress, Reza staggered from the field, bloodied and beaten.

But he had never allowed himself to suffer such a humiliation again. During the next cycles, he improved tremendously, so much so that Tesh-Dar felt compelled to let him act as a weapons master, a teacher for the neophyte warriors coming into the kazha. His last performance in the arena had been little short of astounding, winning all of his matches to the fifth level, two short of the final match that determined the overall winner of the single-round elimination combats that made up the Challenge. Esah-Zhurah, too, had improved more than Tesh-Dar ever would have been able to believe for one whose collar had been earned as a child on the space-going kazha for those called to serve the Imperial Fleet.

She thought again of Reza. Were his skin different, had he claws and fangs and raven hair, had he been female – one would have believed he was Kreelan. And perhaps, Tesh-Dar thought, he was. In spirit, if not in body. Yet his blood did not sing, and it pained her greatly.

"It is my belief," she said, "that – barring accident – he will survive the rigors of the kazha, my Empress. Well does he fight, and well does he seem to understand the Way, as Thy daughter has taught him."

"Yet," the Empress asked, "his blood does not sing?" Tesh-Dar heard it as a statement, not a question.

"It is so, my Empress," she replied woodenly, for she knew that her words sealed Reza's fate as surely as if she had thrust a knife into his heart.

The Empress looked thoughtfully upon her sister. Tesh-Dar had served Her well, as she had the Empress who had reigned before. And among all the countless warriors who now lived and breathed, Tesh-Dar stood highest among the peers, upon the second step from the throne. Many scars did she carry from innumerable Challenges, and then – after the humans had come – from the battles she had waged against those who were not of the Way, contests fought to the thrill of the Bloodsong that was the will and spirit of their people. To live in Her light, with Her blessing, and to die honorably in Her eyes: these were the things to which all aspired, and no better example existed than the woman who now stood beside Her.

Yet, there was a melancholy about her that the Empress did not understand. About this one thing, this human child whom Tesh-Dar might once have killed simply to sharpen her talons, was the warrior priestess distraught. To the Empress, it was a simple matter: the animal's blood did not sing, therefore it had no more soul than a steppe-beast or winged *gret-kamekh*, and would be killed when it proved of no further interest. But she could feel the blood that coursed through her sister's veins, and knew that her mind was not at ease in the matter.

"Tesh-Dar," she said, lifting her hand to the great warrior's chin, tilting it gently so that their gaze met, "what is it that troubles you so? Surely, if the humans are the soulless creatures we believe them to be, their hearts and blood silent to the ears of the spirit, the life of this one individual, this child, could not mean so much? What trouble is there, to such a warrior as yourself, to taking its life?"

"My Empress," Tesh-Dar said, averting her gaze in deference and embarrassment at what she felt compelled to ask, "I beseech Thee to let him live until the seventh great cycle of his learning is complete. Five cycles has he lived among us, two more remain. I..." she paused, grasping for the words to explain the strange things that ached in her heart. "I have heard whispers from the Ancient Ones," she said at last, "that at once seem clear in my mind, but which have no meaning for me." She looked into the eyes of the one who commanded the lives and aspirations of countless souls, wondering what worth a single human life might hold for Her. "They know of him, Empress," she said slowly. "They do not speak his human given name, as do we at the kazha, but they watch him through our eyes. They watch the human and Esah-Zhurah as if they were one, and they wait. They helped her to save him from death in the Lo'ar River."

The Empress looked away into the garden for a long moment, Her eyes focused on places and times that were remembered now only through crumbling stone tablets and withered parchments. For Her memory was that of all those who had gone before Her, who had worn the simple gold band that now adorned Her neck. Accepting the ornaments of the Empress was to accept the spirit and knowledge of the thousands who had once walked in the Garden, and to know the thoughts and feelings of countless billions. All bowed to Her will. "I, too, have heard these whispers," She said slowly, "and many times have I beseeched them for their meaning. But I cannot believe the answer that I hear."

"Then it is true," Tesh-Dar said softly. "He may be the fulfillment of The Prophecy."

"The thought is a most absurd one," the Empress replied, but Her voice betrayed Her own growing suspicion that She could not rule out the possibility, however faint.

The priestess kneeled, humbled by the Empress's remark, but nonetheless determined in her conviction that it could be true. "Yes, my Empress, but it is a thought I am unable to banish from my mind."

The Empress recalled the words that made up The Prophecy. It had been passed down from generation to generation since the death of Keel-Tath, millennia long past. It gave hope that someday their atonement might be made, but nothing more. None knew if the First Empress had spoken it, for She had gone away into the Darkness, and Her people had to live on as their Way demanded. So long had it been, that even the Ancient Ones had long ago given up any hope of redemption, believing Her Children to be cursed for all Eternity. Until now, perhaps.

And as the Empress thought of where the Way had taken Her people over these many generations, the nearly forgotten words of a passage from The Prophecy came to Her:

Of muted spirit, soulless born,
in suffering prideful made;
mantled in the Way of Light,
trusting but the blade.

Should this one come in hate or love,
it matters not in time;

For he shall find another,
and these two hearts they shall entwine.

The Way of sorrows countless told,
shall in love give life anew;
The Curse once born of faith betray'd,
shall forever be removed.

Shall return Her love and grace,
long lost in dark despair;
Mercy shall She show the host,
born of heathen hair.

Glory shall it be to Her,
in hist'ry's endless pages;
Mother to your hearts and souls,
Mistress of the Ages.

The Empress turned away, looking down the path they had been following, Her eyes tracing the smooth cobblestones. Each stone, like the plants around them, had been brought from a different planet in the Empire. Set into the paths that wound their way through the garden, they formed a galactic mosaic beneath the Empress's feet, the richest mineral collection among the ten thousand suns that were home to Her Children. The Empress knew precisely how many of Her predecessors had walked down this path and had stopped in this very spot, deep in contemplation. Better than anything else, She thought, the stones that She paced each morning of Her life represented the strange thing that was their Way: countless pieces of stone or flesh, it did not matter, for they were all bound to Destiny. It was Destiny, She knew, that eluded even Her vision, just as did the path, turning behind a grove of trees with crimson flowers, a relic of a planet that had long since been turned to dust, the onetime home of an enemy of the Empire.

She could not see the future. But Tesh-Dar's concerns, and the interest of the Ancient Ones, She dared not ignore. If they watched the human child and his tresh, the daughter of Her Own blood, there was good reason. She herself could not hear their voices as clearly as the Desh-Ka priestess who stood beside Her. But she trusted Her blood sister's judgment with all Her ageless soul.

"I grant your wish, priestess," She said to Tesh-Dar. "The human child is yours to do with as you please, unto the seventh – and final – Challenge.

"But if by the eve of that Challenge, when the tresh set upon their time of contemplation, the animal's blood does not sing, its life must be spent upon the arena's sands." She paused, looking at the Homeworld as it hung high overhead, a great blue and crimson orb shining through the windows of the palace garden. "And," She went on, "if by some miracle it should still emerge victorious, Esah-Zhurah is to take its life, and bring its hair to me as a testament to her strength and will."

TWELVE

The force of Esah-Zhurah's attack thrummed down Reza's arms as he parried with his own sword, the clash of razor-sharp metal ringing in his ears like a church bell. He dodged to one side and pirouetted, tensing for a thrust against her midsection. But his blow, in turn, was deflected. The two contestants circled each other warily, their breathing coming in controlled heaves, before they crashed together again, continuing the combat that had begun nearly an hour before.

Tesh-Dar watched them from atop the arena's dais, her eyes and ears following the course of the combat in intimate detail. Watching these two had become a ritual for her over the last cycle when other duties did not call her away. She had observed the evolution in their skills since the day Tesh-Dar had informed Esah-Zhurah of the Empress's wishes regarding the human. Her young disciple had been visibly crushed, but had offered no argument as Tesh-Dar had expected. Instead, she had mercilessly driven herself and her human tresh toward technical excellence in the arena and in his knowledge of the Way. Watching them now, Tesh-Dar had no doubt that both of them would be serious contenders in the upcoming Challenge; they would be the ones setting the standards for the rest. And Reza's understanding of the Empire rivaled that of any of the other tresh, and many of the senior warriors, as well.

The priestess had not clearly understood Esah-Zhurah's motivations for some time, but she finally saw that the girl's only hope of saving the human's life was to find a way to make his blood sing, to prove that he had a soul. And for the Children of the Empress, the Bloodsong was never louder than in the rage of battle. Standing here, the girl's melody was clear and pure to Tesh-Dar's spiritual ears. It was a thunderous symphony that was unique in the Universe. But from the human, she felt nothing. Nothing at all. She could see the fire in his eyes, could sense the power of his body and the intellect of his mind, but of his spirit there was no trace.

She glanced at the setting sun, rapidly disappearing behind the mountains and the shining emerald of the Empress Moon as it rose to take its rightful place in the nighttime sky. An end must soon be called to the match, and when it was, the human's fate would be sealed. She felt a great sadness in her heart at what must be done.

Looking at him, she saw a man where once there had only been a boy, a tiny cub she had once held by the neck before he had struck the unexpected blow that had earned him her respect and these years of additional life, only now to perish. She had held such high hopes that she would receive some morsel of proof that he had a soul, for she wished with all her heart to watch him continue to grow, to see what the Way might hold for one such as he.

But it was not to be. As the top of the sun disappeared over the horizon, she called an end to the match, another deadlock. It was the final page in Reza's own Book of Time.

"*Kazh!*" she boomed. She watched with satisfaction as their swords stopped in mid-swing, as if frozen in time. Lowering their weapons, they turned and knelt before her. "Again, children," she told them, "it appears that your only equals are one another. Your final contest before the Challenge is concluded."

Reza bowed his head nearly to the ground, his breathing already easing to its normal deep rhythm. He felt tired but exhilarated, because he knew he was good. *They* were good, together, a force to be reckoned with, possessing combat skills that rivaled those of any of the tresh around them. When he raised his head after rendering the priestess her due, he looked proudly at Esah-Zhurah, but she did not return his gaze.

Instead, she asked, "My priestess, I would speak with you." Tesh-Dar nodded, and then Esah-Zhurah turned to Reza. "Go to our camp and rest," she told him. "I will return shortly."

Reza, understanding the set of her expression, simply nodded without asking what concerned her. It was not at all unusual for her to ask for a private audience with the priestess, and he had come to respect her privacy in such matters when she chose not to tell him what transpired. But something in her eyes made him uneasy, and even in the fading light he thought he could see the trace of mourning marks under her eyes. Bowing again to the priestess, he got to his feet, collected the four shrekkas the two of them had ineffectually hurled at one another, and headed back for their camp.

Esah-Zhurah watched him disappear into the woods in which their tiny home had been nestled since the first day they had come to the priestess. How many nights had they lain there, next to one another under the Empress Moon? Through the calm of the warm season, the chill of winter, the raging storms of spring when even the Stone Place, the Kal'ai-Il, shuddered at the power of nature's fury, they had remained under the stars and the great moon that was their sleep time canopy. She thought of how terribly difficult many of those nights had been since she had first touched Reza on the lips, had tasted the wonderful saltiness of his skin and the sorrowful longing of his tears. Since that wonderful day, that terrible day, she had rearranged their bedding so that they could lie close to one another. Sometimes, when her courage allowed, she extended a hand to touch him, reveling in the pleasure even this merest contact gave her. There were times when the urge to press her lips to his and do other things with him that would be unthinkable to another of her kind was nearly irresistible. Nonetheless, she had not broken her vow to the priestess. To do otherwise would have spelled an end to her honor, and to their lives.

But those were thoughts of the past. It was time to turn her attention to the future, or what little remained. Forcing herself toward the dais, Esah-Zhurah sensed that her Way had suddenly become short, very short indeed.

"What is it, child?" Tesh-Dar asked, already knowing what troubled the young warrior.

Esah-Zhurah knelt at Tesh-Dar's feet, her head lowered to her chest. "Priestess," she began, "must it be this way? Cannot you implore the Empress for more time–"

"For what?" Tesh-Dar snapped, more from her own anguish than any anger at the young woman kneeling before her. "Think, child," she said more gently. "The human has been among us for seven full great cycles now. How much longer must we wait for him to show his inner self, for us to hear his Bloodsong? Do you know?" Esah-Zhurah slowly shook her head. "Nor do I. And do not forget that the Empress already has given him one reprieve. Were it not for that, his bones would have been reduced to ashes two cycles ago." She ran a hand through Esah-Zhurah's hair, thinking how much she had come to think of her as a daughter, though Tesh-Dar had never given birth. The metamorphosis of the ritual that had changed her talons from accursed silver to beautiful ebony and given her the strength of five warriors had done nothing to alter the barrenness of her womb. "It is your destiny, child," she said softly, sensing the trembling of Esah-Zhurah's heart. "And his."

"If he survives the Challenge, or if I must face him in the arena under the code of *Tami'il* – a fight to the death – I... I cannot do it, priestess," Esah-Zhurah said, looking into Tesh-Dar's eyes, pain etched on her face. "I cannot kill him."

"Listen to me well, young one," Tesh-Dar said coldly. "Your soul, as are the souls of all those who are of the Way, is bound to the will of the Empress. Her will is clear in this matter, you can feel it pulse in your veins as well as I. If you cannot do as you are bidden, your hair will be shaved and your soul left in the barren shadows of Eternity." Her eyes softened. "I have heard the cries of those sent to that place, child, the agonies of those fallen from Her grace. It is a fate I bid you to avoid." She paused. "If you face one another in the arena, the human must die. If you both refuse to fight, I will decide the matter myself, and your soul will suffer accordingly." *You do not know the grief that would bring to my heart, my daughter,* Tesh-Dar thought. "And ritual suicide is not an alternative."

"Yes, my priestess," Esah-Zhurah replied woodenly, her body suddenly numb and lifeless. Even the release of suicide had been taken from her, condemning her to live in a lonely, loveless purgatory. "I understand."

Tesh-Dar paused a moment. "Esah-Zhurah," she said softly, noting the black streaks that poured from the child's eyes as her heart cried out its mourning, "I grieve with you. Long have I thought about the coming of this day, and long have I dreaded it, for both of you. Many nights have I lain awake, wondering what could be done, listening for the song of his blood, but there is nothing. Even the Ancient Ones, who once watched the two of you, have gone silent, no longer interested, I fear. They do not hold sway over Her, for She rules even in their ethereal domain, and Her word has been given. Our Way shall be as She wills it."

"Yes, my priestess," Esah-Zhurah intoned, her thoughts now dark swirls of hopelessness.

"Go now, my child, and spend wisely the time that remains," she told her, gesturing for Esah-Zhurah to rise. "Go in Her name."

Esah-Zhurah blindly made her way back to their camp where a fire burned brightly among the forest trees. Her feet trudged along the ancient cobblestones that wove their way about the kazha like a system of great roots, embracing everything. It was a seemingly infinite path that, in the end, led nowhere. As did her Way. She suddenly stopped in her tracks and gripped the handle of her knife. She saw in her mind the image of her plunging it into her chest, feeling the blade part her ribs with its serrated edge, the tip piercing her heart, and the blood in her veins suddenly growing still. It would be the end of life, of suffering against the unknown, of what she knew to be her future. To kill Reza would be to kill a part of herself, a part that she had come to value above all else, save her love for the Empress. And even that...

"Troubled are you," came a husky voice from behind her. Esah-Zhurah whirled around, only to find the ancient Pan'ne-Sharakh, the mistress of the armory, staring at her with her half-blind eyes. She bared her fangs in a friendly greeting, exposing the once magnificent incisors that were now faded yellow with age, worn down so far that she would soon starve, unable to tear her meat properly. Tesh-Dar was old even by Kreelan standards, but Pan'ne-Sharakh was older still: she had been fitting armor to warriors since long before Tesh-Dar was born. There would be much mourning on the day she departed for the Afterlife and her deserved place among the Ancient Ones.

Esah-Zhurah bowed and saluted. "Forgive me, mistress, but you startled me."

"The body is old," Pan'ne-Sharakh said, "but the mind still quick, and the foot light upon the earth, by Her grace and glory. You shall walk with me." Pan'ne-Sharakh held out her hand, and Esah-Zhurah dutifully took it, gently cradling the antediluvian woman's bony fingers in her own armored gauntlet, careful not to let her talons mar the mistress's translucent skin. "Tell me of what troubles you so, my child. For even these old eyes can see the works of sorrow woven upon the tapestry of thy face."

"Mistress... I..." Esah-Zhurah stuttered, not knowing how – or if – she could tell the ancient mistress what she knew, what she felt. But suddenly the words came, slowly at first, but then in a torrent that surprised Esah-Zhurah. It was as if they were not spoken by her own tongue, but by a force that lay within her, beyond her control. She laid bare her heart in a way that would have shamed her into punishment in the Kal'ai-Il had her words become known among the peers or reached the ears of the priestess. But to this quiet ancient who now shuffled slowly beside her, she told everything. Her feelings, her desires, her shames and fears. Everything.

Her words carried them over a path that eventually wound its way to a secluded overlook that took in most of the great plains and the mountains beyond, a place of private meditation frequented by the priestess, although she did not declare it as her own domain. It belonged to Her, the Empress, as did all things that lived or did not live, as far as the eye could see, as far as the stars above, and beyond.

Pan'ne-Sharakh stood silently for a long time, staring into the distance. Her milky eyes, their vision useless a mere meter beyond her face, were still able to peer into a vista of hard-won wisdom that had come with the many cycles of her life and the mystical thing that pulsed in her veins, the spirit of their Way.

"Dearest child," she said, still focused on whatever it was that she saw in her mind, "much have you suffered for this creature, this human, and more are you willing to endure, it would seem. I would caution you against such things, but you are far beyond that, now. Far beyond."

She let out a resigned sigh, and Esah-Zhurah became afraid that she had been foolish to tell the old woman anything. But the look on the mistress's face was nothing if not compassionate. "Long have I walked the Way, my child, and many strange and wonderful things have I seen. But I have never beheld such a wonder as are the two of you, the warrior and her animal tresh. He is still a stranger among us, but his heart and mind have become one with the Way. You have led him that far."

"But his blood does not sing," Esah-Zhurah lamented, wishing she could see something on the horizon other than darkness. Death.

"No," Pan'ne-Sharakh answered, "it does not." She looked up at the young woman beside her. "But still, the Ancient Ones wait. I have heard the priestess speak on the matter, and she believes they are no longer interested in the goings on at our humble kazha. I believe differently."

"How, mistress? What is to be gained by their silence?"

"They wait, child, as if holding their breath, as if a single whispered word would snuff out the candle that flickers here, beneath the Empress Moon. They wait for you." Seeing that Esah-Zhurah did not understand, she went on. "Why, child, does the human's blood not sing?"

"He is not of the Way," Esah-Zhurah replied. "He is not of Her blood."

Pan'ne-Sharakh smiled as if Esah-Zhurah had just explained the answer herself. "That is so, child. He is not of Her blood. And what is there to do about such a thing?"

Esah-Zhurah shrugged in the Kreelan fashion, pained frustration showing on her face. Her patience was wearing thin, mistress or no.

"Do you remember, child, the history of this order, the Desh-Ka, since the times even before the First Empress?"

Esah-Zhurah shook her head. She had been born into and raised in another order, the Ima'il-Kush. Her knowledge of the Desh-Ka, the oldest order known among their people, was far from complete. "No, mistress," she said. "Little is taught of those times, for it is said that the Empire and the Way have always been one, and that what was then, remains as now."

Pan'ne-Sharakh waved her hand in a dismissive gesture. "Long was the Way before even the First Empire, child. But no matter. In those times before Keel-Tath and the Unification, before the curse She later wrought upon our blood, the Desh-Ka were the greatest of the warrior sects that lived on our world. Many outsiders aspired to come among them, but few – terribly few – were ever chosen." She took Esah-Zhurah's hands in hers. "Once there was a ceremony, long since forgotten in the minds of most, which was the mark of one's acceptance into the Desh-Ka. And even over the thousands of generations since Keel-Tath's birth, every warrior bearing the great rune of this order has also borne a scar," she explained as she ran a callused finger across the palm of Esah-Zhurah's right hand, "that marks their acceptance by one who has gone before them."

"This is the ritual of Drakhash," Esah-Zhurah said, remembering, "the passing of honor from one warrior to another. But what does it have to do with me? I am not of the Desh-Ka, nor is..."

Of course, Esah-Zhurah thought, the truth striking her like a bolt of lightning. It was not just a passing of honor, *but of blood as well.*

Pan'ne-Sharakh nodded as she saw the dawning of understanding on Esah-Zhurah's face. "Now all is clear to you, is it not, my daughter?" she asked.

Esah-Zhurah slowly nodded. Her eyes were wide with surprise, and they opened still wider when Pan'ne-Sharakh brought a sheathed knife from within the folds of her robe.

"This," she said reverently, carefully placing the weapon in the young warrior's hand, "I have saved for many, many great cycles, from when I was almost as young as you are now. It was the first weapon I made for a young warrior of that time, a mere child I could have bounced upon my knee, who one day would become the flesh and blood of the Empress Who now reigns."

Esah-Zhurah's hand trembled as her fingers closed around the weapon, about as long as her forearm, the curved and ornate blade perfectly balanced against the weight of the handle. It seemed to burn her palm, even through the thickness of the armored gauntlet she wore as a second skin.

"After the Ascension," Pan'ne-Sharakh went on, her eyes misting with the memory, "She called me unto Her, and gave me this as a gift, a token of Her love and remembrance. I have kept it safe and hidden from my own extravagances, knowing that there would come a time when it would be needed. And last night, in the dreams possible only for one whose Way is coming to an end, I knew that the time had come, and to what use it must be put." Reluctantly, she took her hands away, her fingers brushing over the ancient metal one last time. "The next step," she said quietly, "is up to you."

* * *

Reza heard Esah-Zhurah coming long before he could see her, especially now that the fire had died down to glittering coals of deep cherry red and amber. He was startled that she was not walking as she usually did, using the nearly silent step that was now his own, but was treading the earth as if afraid of nothing, as if stealth were alien to her. The unease that had been building in him since earlier that evening had reached a feverish peak.

"Esah-Zhurah," he called softly, knowing that she would be able to hear him easily, "what is wrong?"

She knelt down next to him, a shadow in the darkness, and wrapped her arms around him, pulling him close.

"Do you trust me?" she asked, her face close to his. He nodded once. Words were unnecessary. "Then do as I ask this night, and sleep. Rest, that we may leave early tomorrow for our free time. And then I shall explain all. I dare not here."

He suddenly felt her lips pressing hungrily against his, parting to release the warm tongue that set his body aflame. She lingered for but a moment that was itself an eternity in Reza's mind. Then she drew away, leaving him breathless and flushed with a mad desire to hold her, to touch her in ways that came to him with force of instinct, but with the tenderness of the love he felt for her.

"Esah-Zhurah," he rasped, reaching for her, holding her close. She knelt close to him, but did not let him kiss her again. It would have been too much to resist, such was the pounding in her breast and the desire working between her thighs at the thought of what could be, what must be, in the days ahead.

"No, my tresh," she told him, gently but firmly pushing him back down on his skins, running a hand across his forehead before laying down next to him, a painful moat of distance between them. "Patience is a warrior's virtue. There is much about which we must speak, but it must wait until tomorrow."

The word echoed in Reza's mind as he lost himself in the wondrous pools of starlight in her eyes.

Tomorrow.

* * *

Reza sat with his legs crossed, his arms draped over his knees. He stared past the mouth of the great caldera whose edge lay just beyond his feet, his thoughts lost in the sprawling horizon that lay in the distance. The faint rumble of the waterfall was broken only by the whispers of the wind and the rustling of the lush ferns that covered this part of the mountain like a vast forest.

The ride to this place, the grotto that had been their refuge and escape each cycle since coming to the kazha, had been a long, silent one. Reza sat upon old Goliath, with Esah-Zhurah beside him on her mount. Their only contact had been an occasional brush of thigh against thigh, and once he had reached out to take her hand, squeezing it in reassurance. She had refused to tell him what was on her mind until they arrived at their destination. But the mourning marks that streamed from under her eyes, the marks that had been hidden in the darkness of night, did nothing to lift his spirits. After they had arrived at the grotto and set up their camp, she had taken him by the hand and led him here to the overlook, a ledge jutting out into space from which one could see forever.

But to Reza, forever had been reduced to three sundowns hence. For, according to what Esah-Zhurah had just revealed in a halting, agonized voice, he would be dead upon the sands of the arena by the time the sun set upon the day of his seventh Challenge.

"And if I should win?" he asked quietly.

She looked away. "If you win, I am to take your life and your hair to the Empress." Her whole body seemed to tremble. "Reza," she whispered, "easier it would be for me to tear my beating heart from my breast than to spill a drop of your blood this way. I would gladly spend eternity in the Darkness to spare you, but I am forbidden even that. I must wait for death until the Way brings it to my doorstep."

He took her hand in his, and gently turned her face so that he could look into her eyes. "It is Her will, my tresh," he told her, the sincerity in his heart echoed on his face. "If that is what the Way holds for us, then it must be so. I am only grateful that, should I have the honor of winning the Challenge, yours will be the hand that sends me from this life." He stroked her face, smiling with a confidence that came with his acceptance of his own mortality. "It shall be as it must."

She pulled him close and wrapped her arms around his neck, holding him tightly. "When you are ready," she said, her voice muffled as she pressed her face into the hollow of his shoulder, "come to me. There is something we must attend to, something that can wait no longer." Pausing only long enough to kiss him lightly on the cheek, she stood up and began making her way back down the mountain. She did not look back.

After Esah-Zhurah had gone, Reza turned his attention back to the horizon, concentrating not on the future, which had already been written by another's hand, but the past which none could deny him. As if reading a most treasured book, he turned the pages of his life, reviewing the memories held in the storehouse of his mind. He paused on the few remembrances he had managed to keep alive from before he had come to the Empire, saving them as treasured icons of an existence long since past. But even those visions that he had labored to keep fresh seemed to be from another person's life, yellowed and faded with time, the faces now indistinct and the names awkward to his tongue. Yet, they were a part of him, and the feeling the ancient images engendered in his heart warmed and comforted him as the evening breeze swept over the mountain and the sun fell toward the far horizon.

But the humanity left in him was merely a vestige of a human boy who had metamorphosed into a Kreelan warrior, alien to his heritage in nearly every way but the very flesh of which he was made. The imprint of any human society on a prepubescent boy was simply not enough to hold back the cultural onslaught to which Reza had been subjected. And now, reviewing in his mind the few mental tokens that remained of his previous life, he discovered that he could not remember the last time he had really thought of himself as being human, of having descended from the people of Old Earth. Even though the peers called him "human," or "animal," he had come to think of himself as a Kreelan, and that perception of himself had grown ever stronger the closer he had come to Esah-Zhurah. There had been a time when he would have feared the loosening of his grip on what had been human in him, the part of him that was now little more than an afterimage in his mind. But that had passed with his acceptance of the code by which he had lived most of his life; the code by which he would soon die.

He thought for a while about what death would be like. Death, a force that had pursued him relentlessly for most of his young life, would finally get its due. Like an old relative who had dropped by many times to visit, only to miss Reza by a shard of time, it would at last embrace him and welcome him into whatever lay within its dark domain. Reza had never been terrified of death, but had evaded it because he had loved life enough to suffer for it. But now he found death a welcome thing, for then his greatest quest would be over, the search for the answer that was the very reason for his coming here: to discover if he had a soul. Long having forgotten the Christian teachings of his childhood, he now wondered only what the Bloodsong must sound like, the thing that united the Children of the Empress to Her will. But he had never heard it, neither from himself nor the tresh around him. He did not even know what to listen for, or if it was really a "sound" at all. All he had was question upon question, all without answer as long as he lived and breathed. Did he have a soul, or was he merely an animal, as the peers believed? Was he nothing more than animated clay fashioned into human form by Her hands? Would he pass through the portal of Death to something beyond? Or would he simply cease to exist, turning to dust and ash as Esah-Zhurah set his body ablaze in a funeral pyre that was the tradition of Her Children? It seemed that only in death would he discover the truth of what Her Children knew from birth.

As the sky above turned from the pastel magenta of day to the inky darkness of night, he welcomed the stars as they emerged from their celestial slumber, and made a silent wish upon the five stars of Her name.

He wished for a soul, and that all would not end when his body suffered the final blow.

* * *

When Reza returned to the grotto, he found Esah-Zhurah kneeling, her pensive face turned to the fire that burned beside her, the flames licking quietly at the air as if afraid to disturb her thoughts. Slowly, as if breaking herself away from a hypnotist's swaying talisman, she looked up at him, and his heart skipped a beat at the black marks that swept down from her eyes, a window to the pain in her soul.

"Kneel," she said, gesturing to the skins that formed the floor of their makeshift abode.

Reza took his place before her, his knees just touching hers, his hands spread, palms down, on his thighs.

"There is an ancient tradition," she began, "that predates even the First Empire, that was part of our Way before Keel-Tath ascended to the throne, before we became what we are now. It was not a tradition of all our people, but of the Desh-Ka. It was begun from the first day their rune was engraved in the stone of their temple, and which all Desh-Ka have followed throughout the ages. It is the rite of Drakhash, the blood bond.

"In those days, as now, the blood of the tribe was considered most sacred, and to share it with another was both a great honor and a great responsibility, often with terrible consequences during the Reign of Chaos. So legend tells us." She paused, reaching beside her for a knife that lay unsheathed near the fire, a blade that Reza had never seen before, but whose exquisite workmanship was unprecedented to his eyes. "You, Reza, of human birth and blood, have shown the skill and fire that are the marks of our warriors. You, whose blood does not sing, who cannot hear the Bloodsong of Her Children, are as a stranger to our tribe, our people, yet worthy of our respect and trust." Holding the knife between them, the dagger blade pointed at the sky, she said, "Although I am not Desh-Ka by birth, I am a True Daughter of the Empress, born of Her womb, blessed with Her very blood. And thus I may speak without falsehood, for my will is Her will, and it shall be done."

Taking off his gauntlets, as she had her own, she took his hand in hers, clasping it tightly as her other hand kept the dagger aloft, still pointing skyward. "I ask you only this: do you accept Her in your heart of hearts, that you shall follow Her will unto death, that the Way of our people shall be the Way of your heart, of your mind?"

Reza's mind was spinning at the enormity of what his tresh was doing. He knew that the priestess would have categorically forbidden such a thing, yet Esah-Zhurah could not go against the Empress's will. In whatever incomprehensible way these people were bound together, he knew that to be impossible as surely as he could not spread his wings and fly from this mountain to the plains below. But his thoughts were preempted by the words spoken by his heart. "With all my heart, Her will is mine, the Way of Her Children is the Way of my soul. To die for Her honor is to die for Her grace and Her love. So has it been, so shall it forever be."

Esah-Zhurah nodded. Wordlessly, they raised their clasped hands into the air, and she placed the knife between them, the flat of the blade cool as it rested against their palms.

"With this knife, forged long ago for one who would ascend to the throne, wielded by Her in battle, are we now joined." With a slight twist of her knife hand, the blade's razor edge broke the boundary of skin between them, drawing a deep line of blood as she pulled it downward, the weapon slipping from their joined hands like a newborn infant from the womb. Esah-Zhurah set the knife aside, then wrapped her free hand around their joined fist. She felt the warm pulse of her blood, and his, as their wounds sought each other out, mated.

Reza's hand was tingling as if Esah-Zhurah was sending electric currents through it, and as they knelt there, face to face, the sensation began to spread up his arm, then his shoulder. And looking into her eyes, he could see that she felt it, too.

"I must tell you something," she said, her cat's eyes pools of glittering fire, stars in the blackness of mourning that besieged her face. "I feel fear, Reza, such as I have never before felt. I fear losing you, losing your voice... your scent... your touch. In my language, even the Old Tongue that you have not been taught, there are no words to describe these things I feel for you." Slowly, she placed her free hand over his heart. "The only hope of my soul is that the blood now in your veins may sing to Her, that She may know thy voice."

"Esah-Zhurah," he whispered, "I love you." She leaned close to kiss him lightly on the eyes, her fingers in his hair. "Had I my entire life to do over," he told her, "I would change nothing, would suffer anything, that I could be with you."

She kissed him softly on the mouth, and then slowly rose to her feet. He made to rise also, but she gently pushed him back to where he knelt. "Stay," she whispered huskily. "I have learned the tradition of the Old Ways, before the Curse," she told him, her breath warm against his face, "when male and female touched in desire, not desperate need. So it was then, so shall it be now."

The tingling sensation still spreading through his body, she separated her bloodied hand from his. Slowly, she began to undress. She undid the belt that carried her weapons, letting it slide to the ground. Then she began to unfasten her armor, placing it in an orderly stack beside her. Her black undergarment disappeared in the shimmering firelight, then her sandals.

Reza watched, enraptured, as she discarded the last of her clothing. Her blue skin glowed as she stood before him, backlit by the flames. Her muscles were taut in anticipation, and he could see the gleam of wetness between her thighs. He could hear her quickened breathing, the rapid beating of her heart. Her musky scent touched him, teased him, arousing him to the point where he was sure he would explode without her ever touching him.

She knelt down to straddle his body. He reached up to touch her, but she deflected his hands away, neither of them concerned with the blood and pain from their wounded palms, the spiritual consummation of their commitment to one another.

"Do not move," she whispered, running her nails along the side of his face, just touching the skin. "Lie still." Her hands ran down his neck and chest, sending shivers through his body. She began to undo his clothing, slowly exposing his skin to her touch. The armor seemed to simply melt away under her strong hands, and suddenly she was pulling the upper garment over his head and tossing it aside, never taking her eyes off of him. Her hands glided over his skin, sending shivers up his spine as they worked down lower, lower. She undid his waist belt and the lower part of the undergarment, pulling them away. With the agility and grace of a cat she moved away from him to remove his sandals, then returned to her former position, her face only a few centimeters from his.

He leaned forward to kiss her, but she drew away, her lips trembling in restrained urgency.

"No," she whispered. "Not yet." She gripped his shoulders with trembling hands and began to kiss his eyes, his face, carefully avoiding his lips. She continued on to his neck, her fangs lightly scoring the skin.

Reza moaned and closed his eyes, clenching his fists so hard that his knuckles cracked like wet wood on a fire. He had trained so long to heighten his senses, his perception of his surroundings and his own body, that her touch was overwhelming him, burning in his brain as her mouth moved along his body.

Her hands, now running along the inside of his thighs, convulsed slightly. She straightened up with a deep sigh, a shuddering breath. Her eyes were misty, far away. She kissed him hard on the mouth, her incisors nearly cutting into his lower lip. Then she raised herself further and brought his head to her breasts with one hand, the other now supporting her body above him.

"Soon," she gasped.

He took each breast in turn to his mouth, savoring the slightly bitter flavor of her smooth skin with his tongue. His hands caressed her body, moving across her taut belly to her thighs to linger in a cautious exploration of what lay between.

Without warning she pushed him down on their bed of hides. She took hold of his wrists and moved them clear of her body.

"It is time," she whispered. Her breath now came in rapid, shallow heaves. She was at once tormented by need and alight with pleasure. She took his throbbing erection in both hands, drawing an excited gasp of anticipatory pleasure from his lips.

With one last look between them, she slowly impaled herself on him. Both of them cried out at the flame that suddenly surged as their bodies joined. Her nails pierced the flesh of his shoulders, but there was no pain. His mind was in sharp focus, and its point of interest lay nowhere near his shoulders.

Involuntarily he began to move his hips, holding onto hers with his hands, his fingers pressing deeply into the tensed flesh as he drove himself into her.

"No, Reza!" she cried. "Lay still, my love. Lay still."

He managed to regain control of himself, using every bit of willpower he had gained as a warrior to do his lover's bidding. He wrapped his arms around her and held her to him, and they lay entwined, their breath coming rapidly in the night. Her eyes had become unfocused, her oblong pupils dilated wide open, far more than the fire-lit darkness demanded.

He was becoming concerned that something was wrong when he felt the first pulse. Some mysterious mechanism in her body began to stimulate his own, and he felt the same sensation as he had on his tentative thrust, but without moving himself. The pulses, the strokes he felt inside her, came slowly at first, but their tempo built quickly, the intense sense of pleasure obliterating reality.

He cried out as he came inside of her, his body arching upward in blind ecstasy that engulfed him for a few brief seconds that seemed to span eternity. He was lost in waves of sensory overload in an act that had once merely been a part of procreation, but that now meant so much more.

As he regained his senses, he realized that her pumping had not ceased with his own climax, but had grown even more frenzied, her body twitching to the music that boomed inside her. Her eyes were closed now, and her head slumped to his shoulder.

Without warning, she cried out, her voice reverberating off the grotto's dark, invisible walls. He fought her hands to keep her talons from slashing his sides as she thrashed about in the ecstasy that had taken her. Her mouth was open wide, her fangs gleaming white in the fire's glow, and for a moment he was afraid that she would simply plunge them blindly into his throat.

But she did not. The storm left as suddenly as it had come, and her climax left a quiet denouement in its wake. Her mouth closed after a moment more of straining in concert with her body, and then she seemed to relax and laid herself back down on top of him, her whole body shuddering as if she were freezing. Her hands twitched, and he held them in his own, holding them against his sides. Her breathing slowed, and he knew from the rhythm that she must have passed out, gone to sleep. He held her tightly to him, running his hands through her dark braids and across her back. Tears sprang from his eyes as his love for her filled his heart. And for one of the few times in his life, they were tears of joy, not of pain.

After a few moments, he gently rolled her over on her side and lay next to her, lost in her warmth, their union finally broken by his body's flagging bridge. The fire kept him company, and he watched it with the fascination that had captivated his kind for millennia. He lost himself to the flame, until he felt a stirring beside him.

She was looking at him with eyes hooded by the inexorable hold of sleep, but troubled by a terrible sadness. "I grieve for my race, Reza," she whispered. "Most of my people mate. They must to survive. But they do not love. They have never felt this," she stroked his face with her hand, "since the death of Keel-Tath." She pulled him to her and kissed him. "I will carry this with me always, my love, forever as I walk the Way."

"So shall I," he whispered softly. "In Her name, so shall I."

* * *

The Empress dreamed.

It was a dream She had never had before. This might have been less of a curiosity had it been anyone else, but there was something uniquely peculiar about Her dreams. They were not the dreams of the woman who had accepted the simple white robe and band about her neck that were the only adornments allowed the leader of the Empire. At least, not entirely. That woman's dreams were a part of what was now cascading through the sleeping monarch's mind, but only that. A part.

For the rest of Her mind was devoted to the thoughts and dreams of those who had gone before Her, those who had inherited Her body as She had inherited their spirit and wisdom. The woman who lay quietly in her chambers within the Imperial Palace was not simply the flesh that wore the crown of Empire. She was the Empress; She was all who had ever lived since the Unification, save one. Keel-Tath's voice had never come to the Empress of the Flesh, the vessel of the Way, nor to any Empress who had come before Her. The spirit of the First Empress, the most powerful of all, lay forever in darkness. Waiting for Her people to redeem themselves, to prove themselves again worthy of Her love.

And that is why this dream seemed so strange. The knowledge of twenty-seven thousand generations was at Her beck and call, asleep or awake. The visions, the sensations of all those who had worn the very collar that hung loosely from her aging neck were as vivid as the day they were experienced by the Empress of the Flesh in some earlier time, from whence the memory came.

But not this one. All that She was, all the thousands of spirits clustered in Her soul, bound together as one, watched like fascinated spectators in the arena as the vision unfolded in Her mind.

She saw herself kneeling before a young human, a human that She had never seen before but felt She knew as well as Her own blood. And then She saw their clasped hands, Herself and the human, joined together as tightly as the enormous polished stones that made up the wall of the Great City far below the Empress Moon. The words that were spoken She did not hear or understand in the dream, but there was no need. The ceremony was well known to Her, even though Her own hand did not bear such a scar.

There was a silence between them, and then She undressed, at last standing nude before him.

Then came the first touch. The Empress shivered in Her sleep, a moan of surprise and unexpected pleasure escaping Her lips at sensations She had never before felt. Higher and higher She flew, riding the crest of a wave that seemed as vast and powerful as the Empire itself. And when the warm spear She felt within Her erupted in its fury of passion, She cried out in surprised ecstasy.

She suddenly found herself awake, curled on Her side, staring into the wide and terrified eyes of Her First.

"My Empress," the elder warrior gasped, one hand curled around the handle of her sword. She had never seen the Empress awaken in such a state. It had simply never happened before. Ever. "Are you well?" she asked, clearly frightened. Not that the Empress would die, for that was simply not possible but for the vessel that embodied Her spirit. No, she was afraid that the Empress might have been frightened by something. "Empress?"

The Empress lay there for a moment, catching Her breath and waiting for the spasms in Her loins to stop. Never in Her mating years had She known such feelings as this dream had brought upon Her, nor had Her body been thrilled as it had during those few immeasurable moments. But pleasurable though these sensations were, the unknown nature of their cause disturbed Her greatly.

"Empress?" the First inquired again, with increased alarm. So much so that she laid a hand on her monarch to steady Her shaking body.

"I am well," the Empress replied at last, thanking the First for her concern with a shaky caress of the younger woman's hair. "It is past, now." She thought for a moment, the remnants of the dream that seemed to be more than a dream swirling through Her mind, tantalizing Her body with a few more spasms. "Tell me," She asked, Her voice carefully controlled to conceal the quivering of Her chest, "did I speak in my sleep?"

The First bowed. "Yes, Empress."

"What did I say?"

"Only one word, one I did not recognize as being of either of The Tongues," the First replied. No other language besides the Old Tongue and the Tongue of the First Empire had ever been uttered in the palace before this day. "You cried *reza*."

Thirteen

The storm clouds that were gathering around the mountain like anxious horsemen intent upon some unimaginable apocalypse were a vision into Reza's soul as he and Esah-Zhurah worked the magtheps down the steep slopes toward the darkening valley below, leaving their beloved grotto behind forever. Since the night they touched, they had scarcely risen from their bed, making love or simply holding one another as the sun rose and then set once more. They had spoken precious little, for there was little to say between them that could or need be expressed by mere words. And there was no time for idle banter, for this time together would be all they would ever have. A caress or a kiss said so much more, and time was valuable to them beyond measure. "Forever" had taken on a very literal meaning for the lovers, for it was now weighed in the trifle of sunsets remaining before Reza was to die.

But the Way was not known for its magnanimity, and their tiny allotment had been cut short by the hand of Nature. The sudden storm that had charged into the mountains would bring heavy rains, rains that would make the tiny mountain streams impassable torrents that would keep the two young warriors from their appointed destiny in the arena. While the thought had come to both of them that it could be used as an excuse to delay, an opportunity to stretch the inevitable just a bit further away, the notion had never been voiced. They were no longer children, and both of them knew their responsibilities as followers of the Way. Reza wore only the collar of a slave, but his soul was no less devoted to the ways of his adopted people. If the Empress willed his death, then it would be so.

He smelled the rain, the peculiar musty smell that bathed the land long before it was touched by water, and knew that they would have to hurry. The almost supernatural senses that his years of training had given him told how long it would be before the first drops would fall; it was a measure of time that could not be expressed in terms of hours or minutes, or angle of the sun, but was nonetheless precise. Esah-Zhurah sensed it, too, and together they picked up the pace, old Goliath lumbering with the gracelessness of age next to Esah-Zhurah's younger and more nimble beast.

Around them the land and sky had grown dark, the bright colors muted to a cold, glaring gray, broken occasionally by the angry brilliance of lightning bolts that struck at the land with the heat of a dozen suns. The echoes of the thunder that shattered the air drowned out the howl of the wind that rose and fell as it chose its fickle path among the canyons and arroyos through which the travelers made their way.

Had the day been clear, perhaps they would have seen or smelled the bloody mass of gnarled steel armor and shredded leatherite that had once been known as Ust-Kekh, now carefully hidden behind one of the lichen-covered rocks jutting from the canyon wall. Or perhaps they would not have simply passed by Ami-Char'rah's severed head, sitting near the side of the trail like a macabre sentinel. Her skull had been an unappetizing tidbit to the otherwise remorseless mind that had been the instrument of her demise.

But the lightning blinded the riders to these dark shapes that now stood silent vigil, and the shifting winds robbed them of the coppery scent of blood that even now dripped from the torn veins of the hapless victims. In the swirling night, they did not see the demonic face in whose eyes their reflections danced in time with the lightning hurled from the angry sky above.

Pan'ne-Sharakh had once told Reza that the day of his birth, as measured in the way of the Kreela, had fallen on the day of the Great Eclipse, when the Empress Moon had shielded the Homeworld from the light of the sun. It was an event that occurred only once every fifteen thousand and fifty-three Earth years, and was considered a day of wondrous promise for those born under its shadow. It was an omen of great battles to be fought, a sign of special love from the Empress. It was the closest thing the Way allowed for what humans might consider being lucky.

But Reza did not feel lucky when a shadow suddenly detached itself from the canyon floor. With startling speed, it grew in size until it blotted out the sky above, towering before them like a dark, angry mountain.

As Reza opened his mouth to shout a warning, his hand grabbing desperately for the battle ax strapped to his saddle, he felt the impact of the mammoth claw against his chest, a horrendous blow that hurled him from Goliath's back. Only his armor – now bent and torn like tissue paper – had saved his life. Reza's ears filled with the sound of crunching bones before his eardrums rang with the monstrous scream of hungry rage that muffled Goliath's squeals of agony. Reza hit the ground hard, but quickly rolled to his feet. And in a flash of lighting he saw it, standing over Goliath's struggling form, a nightmare of fangs, horns, and talons.

He gasped in awe at the thing that had transformed itself from mimicking silent rock into moving, living tissue in but an instant. Its head was larger than Goliath's body, with rows of razor-sharp teeth covered by a scaly lip to conceal them while the creature lay in wait. Horns sprouted from the thing's triangular head, and its blazing yellow eyes were cold and inscrutable. Its body rippled with strength, from the talons on each of its six legs to the needle-like crystalline tip on the end of its whip of a tail.

It stood above Reza like a colossus, an enormous gargoyle that had suddenly come to life. Before he could turn and run, it lunged down at him, its maw gaping wide, its fetid breath enveloping him with the stench of death's promise.

In that instant, as Reza watched death come, the mortally wounded Goliath snapped his powerful jaws shut on the genoth's vulnerable underside, close to its tail. The magthep's teeth were broad and flat, typical of the Homeworld's herbivores. They could not rip and tear as could those of the genoth, but they were powerful enough to grind the tough leaves of the hearty *suranga'a* bush into paste. Goliath's jaws clamped shut like a vise, crushing the unarmored flesh of the genoth's underbelly.

The dragon's teeth snapped together less than an arm's length from Reza's face before its mouth opened in a roar of agony and rage at the insolent magthep's attack. Ignoring Reza, it turned its attention to Goliath, who stubbornly clung like a giant parasite to its underbelly.

Reza whirled and ran to a nearby rock outcropping. Behind him, the genoth made short work of the wounded magthep. With a final squeal, Goliath was silent. Having disposed of its tormentor, the beast turned to reacquire its prey.

It found Esah-Zhurah.

Bearing her fangs in fear and rage, Esah-Zhurah raised her pike toward the creature in what she knew was a hopeless gesture. She had seen Reza get away, but had lost sight of him in the darkness. She desperately maneuvered her terrified magthep around to find him, not thinking of how vulnerable she was while riding her terrified beast. Suddenly, one of the genoth's forelegs lashed out, flinging her out of the saddle. She landed on the canyon's dusty floor with a muffled thud before scrambling to her feet, backing away from the apparition slowly, the pike still in her shaking hands. Her magthep, miraculously uninjured, shrieked in terror and fled into the gathering storm.

The genoth homed in on the young Kreelan woman. The animal had acquired a taste for Kreelan flesh over its many cycles, and it had chosen a most opportune time to come from the great wastelands beyond the mountains, through the ineffective barrier that proved little more than a nuisance to its great armored body. Already had it dined on five of the morsels this season, and now two more had come into its territory. Cautiously, for the tiny creatures were quick and could sometimes inflict pain, the genoth advanced on Esah-Zhurah.

Reza breathed a sigh of fear. He had to help her. *In Her name*, he thought, *what can I do against such a thing?* The ax weighed heavily in his hand as he moved from his cover of rocks, running in a crouch toward the beast's flank as it closed in on Esah-Zhurah, boxing her into a narrow cut in the canyon that was far too steep to climb.

Coming abreast of the beast, just out of its range of vision, Reza readied the ax for a throw. He cocked his arm behind his head and tensed his body to send the heavy weapon on its way in what he knew would be a futile attack at this range against such an opponent. But it was all he had.

Esah-Zhurah's attention was fixed on the beast until she saw the shadow of Reza's form standing to the thing's side, ax at the ready.

"Hurry, my love," she whispered, simultaneously baring her fangs at the thing now towering above her. The creature was maddeningly slow, advancing a step at a time, in no rush to tear her limb from limb, and she was growing impatient. "Throw it," she hissed at her tresh, though he could not hear her. "Throw it now."

Her eyes widened in disbelieving horror as she saw Reza suddenly drop the ax to the ground at his feet. With a startled cry, she looked up to see the beast's slavering jaws descending toward her.

* * *

Tesh-Dar was finishing her letter to the Empress when she sensed it. She was so surprised that she dropped her stylus, ignoring it as it rolled across the parchment, spreading ink over her neat script before clattering noisily to the floor.

"Priestess," Syr-Kesh, who had been awaiting an audience with her, asked, "is something the matter?"

Tesh-Dar merely stared into space, her eyes unfocused, her hands flat upon the writing tablet, utterly still.

Syr-Kesh was about to ask again, concerned that something was seriously wrong with the kazha's most senior warrior, when she felt it, too. It was a tiny warp in the fabric of the Way, a small voice crying out for the first time like a newborn babe. "It is not possible," she whispered, her eyes bulging with disbelief.

The priestess's head slowly traversed so that her eyes fixed the swordmistress like an insect upon a pin. "So have we always believed," she said slowly. "But so it obviously *is* possible." She paused a moment, listening to the spiritual transformation that was taking place, and to which she and all her kind would be witness. She only hoped that it was not too late. The Empress had never before reversed a decision such as She had cast for the human, for there had never been reason to. Reza was still scheduled to die in two days, his blood to be spilled upon the sands of the arena, and Tesh-Dar could not allow that to happen if there was any other way.

She turned to Syr-Kesh. "Fetch my shuttle here," she commanded. "I must seek an audience with the Empress immediately."

As Syr-Kesh fled to carry out her task, Tesh-Dar closed her eyes and searched with the eyes of her soul for the one whose blood had begun to sing.

* * *

Reza stood perfectly still, momentarily entranced by the prickling, burning sensation that was sweeping his body. Quickly, as if it were water spilled from a breached dam, he felt the fire in his blood crescendo into a roaring cascade of power that washed over his mind and flesh in a surge of raw, primal might.

Suddenly, in a flash of insight as illuminating as the lightning that sought to blind him, he knew what to do. Dropping the more cumbersome ax, he reached for the leather sling that was carefully, lovingly attached to his waistband. He quickly undid it and probed his fingers into the small pouch in which he carried the carefully prepared stones that armed the weapon. He found only two, but decided they would be enough. Placing a stone in the wide cup of the sling, he began to whirl it around and around, moving closer to the genoth.

"Here!" he shouted at the thing. "Come to me!"

The genoth whirled around at the sound of his voice, seeing another culinary treat with its glowing, multifaceted eyes. It paused for a moment, calculating the better of the two morsels to devour first. It was just what Reza had been praying for.

The sling circled faster and faster, the stone within gaining more and more energy. Reza's heart pumped in time with the weapon's rhythm as the enemy glared at him with its baleful eyes, perfect targets even in the darkest pitch of night. And suddenly, as if ordered by the Empress Herself, the wind was stilled for just one precious moment, and the tiny missile took flight, propelled with greater force than Reza had ever before mustered behind it.

As with the ancient tale of David and Goliath, the stone hit home. The round projectile blasted the genoth's left eye into pulp, exploding it like an overripe fruit that cascaded down the beast's face. But unlike David's foe, the genoth was not to die under such an attack.

The beast reared up, a shattering shriek of pain echoing down the canyon, humbling even the thunder above. It clawed at its face, at its obliterated eye, roaring in agony and rage.

Esah-Zhurah rushed forward with her pike, her own blood burning with the Bloodsong that was sustenance to her people as surely as the meat they ate each day. She buried it in the genoth's side, the weapon's point piercing the flesh just behind the middle right leg where thinner scales covered the creature's belly. Pausing only to ram it home with all her strength, she retreated, leaving it jammed into the dragon, with half of the pike's shaft buried deep in its flesh.

"Run!" Reza shouted, "Get back!" She needed no prompting from him. She ran as fast as she could, but it was not fast enough. The genoth's good eye caught sight of her, and the beast turned with astonishing speed to trail after its tormentor. Its slow, confident pace had all but vanished.

Its talons lashed out, and Esah-Zhurah was pitched into the air, flying head over heels. She hit the ground with a sickening thud, her metal breast armor screeching along the rocks that studded the canyon floor. Then she lay still.

"No!" Reza cried, running after the monster, now clutching his ax in his right hand. He realized with a sinking certainty that he could not reach her in time. The creature, grunting in its own pain and anger, was nearly on top of her, its jaws widening to crush her body into pulp.

Not realizing the strength that now lay within him, he was still trying to think and react as he always had, quickly, but not fast enough to avert the fate of his lover as the beast's open jaws descended on her.

But he discovered that the Bloodsong was more than a mere voice. It was a portal to things that would have taken Reza many more years – years that he did not have – to understand. His eyes narrowing in concentration, he focused his mind on the ax and projected an image of it buried in the left side of the creature's head. For a split second he felt his body and mind merge in a perfect union, as he were being guided by an unseen hand, and the ax flew with precision and power that he never would have thought possible.

The genoth's scales channeled the razor sharp edge of the heavy weapon as it struck the monster where its head and sinewy neck came together. Blood erupted in a spray as the weapon sliced its way deep into the genoth's flesh, the blade now buried up to the handle.

The creature stumbled forward, stunned, cracking its front teeth on the stone inches from Esah-Zhurah's head.

Reza's fierce battle cry was lost in the genoth's trumpeting of pain. He dashed forward, drawing his sword as the beast whirled about, thrashing with its forelegs in a futile attempt to dislodge the ax whose cutting edge was creeping ever closer to the animal's spinal cord. All thoughts of the prey on which it had been about to feast were forgotten as it fought against a new source of misery.

The genoth's tail whipped to and fro, beating the sand and dirt from the canyon floor in its blind search for a target. Reza paid it no heed, heading straight for the beast's exposed belly as it stood on its hindmost legs, the other four clawing uselessly at the air.

The Kreelan armorers would have been proud of the quality of their workmanship had they seen Reza's sword cleanly cut the left middle claw from its parent leg as he ducked under the genoth's belly. The beast mewled in pain and brought its head down to snap at him, but he whirled away, carried on the rising tide of power that flowed through him, slicing the genoth's belly open in a wide arc. He danced clear of the creature's remaining claws as its bowels spilled out onto the ground in a steaming deluge of viscera and blood.

The genoth whirled, its insides trailing after it like meaty chum from an ancient fishing vessel, and fixed Reza with its remaining eye. Its legs tensed to leap upon the tiny thing that had done it so much injury, and Reza knew that he could not escape. But he felt no fear, and readied his sword in a last act of defiance.

But it was not to be. In a starburst of flesh, the creature's remaining eye exploded as Esah-Zhurah's shrekka struck, sawing its way through the thinnest portion of the beast's skull to embed itself in the genoth's brain.

Relieved of its guidance mechanism, the body fell to the ground with a great thud, shuddering for a moment before its lungs exhaled a final, mortal sigh.

The genoth was dead.

Reza was not sure how much time passed between that moment and when he realized Esah-Zhurah was standing next to him, holding him by the shoulders and repeating his name.

"Reza," she said again, "answer me."

His eyes struggled to focus on her, and it dawned on him that he had been lost to the strange melody that flowed through him, something terribly alien, yet wondrous in its undiluted strength.

"Esah-Zhurah," he rasped, finally lowering the sword. "Are... are you all right?"

Her armor was dented and scored from where she had been tossed by the genoth, and there was a thin trickle of blood down the right side of her face where one of its talons had nicked her. It had been that close.

"Yes," she answered, steadying him now as he began to tremble violently. She took his sword before it dropped from his hand. "My tresh," she said, her eyes full of wonder, "it is within you. Your blood sings."

Numbly, Reza nodded his head. The thundering in his body had abated to a basso thrum. He fell down to his knees, his system reeling. "I have a soul," he whispered, his eyes lost in hers. "I have a soul."

Esah-Zhurah kissed him long and hard, then held him tightly as her own soul rejoiced at what they now knew, at the melody that had suddenly burst forth from her lover. Every soul ever born of Her blood that had not fallen from Her grace had its own voice, but Reza's was different from all of the others in a way that she could not define, but that she accepted as Her blessing in their final hour.

But joy was not the only emotion to be found in the falling rain.

With Esah-Zhurah's supporting arm around his waist, Reza made his way to the formless heap of flesh that was all that was left of his beloved friend.

"Goliath," he breathed as he knelt next to the stricken animal. Taking off his gauntlets, he ran his hands over the fur of the old beast.

"I am sorry, Reza," Esah-Zhurah said softly. "He was a noble creature. I grieve with you for his loss."

Goliath had been much more than a simple beast of burden or a pet. He had been his friend. Reza had often spent long hours talking to him when he was lonely, in the days when even Esah-Zhurah treated him as an animal, in the days when he had no one. No one except Goliath, who had always been there, who would listen to his troubles without complaint, contentedly munching on the plants Reza gave him as a treat. The quiet tears Reza shed for his fallen friend mingled with the rain, watering the earth with his sorrow.

"We must go soon, Reza," Esah-Zhurah said gently.

Reza nodded. "Good-bye, old friend," he whispered.

"There is something we must do first," she told him. Getting to his feet, instinctively replacing his gauntlets, he followed her to where the genoth's head lay stretched upon the rain- and blood-soaked ground. "I hope we are not too late."

"Too late for what?" Reza asked.

Esah-Zhurah did not answer him directly. Instead, she took out the knife that had brought them together, the blade once held by the Empress, and pried at a strange-looking scale above the genoth's blown-out eye. After digging it out of the dead animal's flesh, she held it out to the rain, letting the falling drops cleanse it before handing it to Reza.

"It is an eyestone," she explained. "You cannot see it now, but it should be brightly colored when held up to the light, like a mineral stone. Only this species is known to have them, one over each eye. They are terribly rare, for the beast must be only freshly killed for the colors to remain visible. It does not show while alive, nor after the animal has been dead more than a few moments." She was already moving to the other side to remove the remaining stone. "Long ago, they used to be valued greatly among our people as signs of courage. They are still terribly valuable in such a sense, but the Empress forbade the ritual killing of these beasts long ago, that they may continue to live in honor of the old ways."

"You mean," Reza said, "that the wastelands are filled with them?"

"Yes, according to Her laws. The wastelands are given to the creatures that dwell there. For us, it is a place forbidden. But this one," she gestured at the dead genoth, "trespassed upon our domain, and so is rightly ours to claim." She put the stones in a pouch and then held her face up to the rain for a moment, luxuriating in the cool water. It would quickly become a nuisance on the long trek home on foot.

"Come," she said. "It is time to return home."

Yes, Reza thought. *Destiny awaits.*

FOURTEEN

E'ira-Kurana was the first to spot them. "There!" she cried, pointing toward the two ragged figures trudging toward the kazha.

Tesh-Dar stepped forward, her eyes narrowed into tight slits against the glare of the sun. The human's Bloodsong had grown in strength as the night had worn on, clearly audible to the senses of her spirit. Only with the greatest of difficulty did she restrain herself from signaling for the two to come to her on the run.

Tesh-Dar's fists were clenched tight in anticipation, the muscles standing out on her arms like bands of steel as the two young warriors passed through the ancient stone gateway. As they made their way through the throng that had gathered to meet them, Tesh-Dar felt at once proud and afraid. Proud that she had taken a weak human who had had nothing to give but his life, and made him into a warrior respectable in all ways save his blood. And afraid that the origin of the song in his heart was not entirely of human origin, and what must happen if this was so.

As the two came near, dropping to their knees to salute her, she knew the truth. All of it. She could smell the human's scent on Esah-Zhurah, and she knew instantly that she had disobeyed Tesh-Dar's orders and touched the human in a way that she found entirely repugnant. And her mind did not have to probe far into the young warrior's soul to discover the rest of it; she did not have to ask Esah-Zhurah to know that there were matching wounds on their hands from the ceremony Esah-Zhurah had performed. For a moment, the priestess was overcome with the temptation to kill them both outright, but she reluctantly stayed her hand. Other things were already afoot, and to kill the two now would not make the situation any brighter.

"Greetings, priestess," Esah-Zhurah ventured.

Tesh-Dar's eyes were hard and her mouth was set in a grim line that reminded Esah-Zhurah of the faces carved in the entryways to many of the buildings in the City. The great priestess was not at all pleased.

"What am I to do, child?" she asked, her voice barely audible above the light breeze. But it was not a solicitation for advice. "Have you cast aside your commitment to the Way, to the Empress?" Her eyes were stony, accusatory. One of her duties was to dispatch justice in the name of the Empress, and it was not one she accepted lightly. Esah-Zhurah was to be given every chance to defend herself, but the evidence against her was already overwhelming. Esah-Zhurah opened her mouth to speak, but Tesh-Dar cut her off with a sharp gesture. "Silence," she hissed, pondering how she would handle the matter. "I would see you in my chambers, now." Both of them got to their feet and turned to go, but Tesh-Dar put a massive hand roughly on Reza's chest. "Not you, human."

Reza bowed his head. "Yes, priestess," he whispered, trembling inside. It appeared that his fate would not be so clean-cut after all, and he was terribly afraid that Esah-Zhurah had sacrificed her own future, as well.

In Tesh-Dar's quarters, Esah-Zhurah kneeled and told the priestess everything. She would not, could not lie.

Before her, Tesh-Dar paced in a seething rage. "I do not understand, child," she was saying, speaking more to herself than the fearful young woman. "You used a sacred ritual of another order – of *my* order! – to give this human that which we hold most dear, the blood of our race. Then you... you mated with him as is written in the legends from the Books of Time? And then you are set upon by a genoth the likes of which has not been found for nearly twenty generations, and the two of you alone are able to slay it?" She shook her head violently, sending her braids whipping around her torso. "Madness this is!"

"Reza carries the eyestones in the pouch I gave him," Esah-Zhurah whispered, any fear she had for incurring Tesh-Dar's wrath drowned in the shame she felt at the priestess's sense that she had been betrayed. But there was no shame in Esah-Zhurah for loving Reza, for doing what she had done. It had all felt... right to her, and had she to do it all again, she would change nothing.

"Have you anything else to add," Tesh-Dar said stonily, "before I pass judgment upon you?"

"Yes, my priestess."

"Speak, then."

Taking a deep breath, Esah-Zhurah told her, "Priestess, his blood not only sings Her glory – be it by my doing or the work of his spirit alone – but he has also invoked the name of the Empress, in his heart. He believes. And..." she heaved a breath, "...never did I deviate from the Way, my priestess, in binding our spirits through the flesh. My blood sang as it mingled with his, and never was there a dissenting note in the chorus that bound us together."

Tesh-Dar silently considered the implications of what the girl had said. If it were true, there was far more to these two than she had ever suspected. But how could it be? Sighing silently in frustration, she told Esah-Zhurah to leave. "You will be summoned when I pass judgment upon you."

"And what of–"

"His fate," Tesh-Dar cut her off angrily, "shall not change for the better with your meddling. Leave me now."

Esah-Zhurah withdrew quietly, leaving Tesh-Dar to fume in a miasma of anger, sadness, and fear. She recalled the sight of Esah-Zhurah's hand, the diagonal cut across the palm, still crusted with blood, a bridge the child had built between her own race and the alien youth. The song from the human's heart as he fought the monster in the valley played through her mind, and she frowned in consternation. She could not make the wrong decision now, for all might depend on it later.

"Oh, child," she exclaimed softly, "what have you done?"

* * *

Reza waited quietly in the priestess's chambers. Kneeling on the floor, head bowed and eyes closed as he waited for the priestess to return, he thought of the rapidly healing scar that marked where he and Esah-Zhurah had exchanged something more than words. He let the pleasant memories of the night occupy his mind while his exhausted body rested.

"You are lax, child."

The voice snapped him awake, and he found the priestess standing near the enormous window that encompassed most of the far wall, looking out toward the mountains of Kui'mar-Gol. "Slayers of the genoth should not become inattentive, even in sleep. Were I of a mind, I could have killed you all too easily."

"Were you of a mind, my priestess, there are few you could not kill," he replied quietly, his eyes on the floor. "Even in my dreams, my strengths could never challenge yours." He noticed that the pouch that had been bound to his waist was missing.

Tesh-Dar instantly sensed his feelings. *How strange*, she thought, *to be able to touch the child's spirit as I can those of my own people. Finally, after all this time.* "It is here," she said, holding the pouch up in one hand without looking at it. She had already surveyed the contents: two eyestones of extraordinary size and color. She held one in her other hand before the window so the light shone directly into it, filling the room with a blaze of cobalt blue that Reza could see reflecting from the floor.

"While alive," she said, almost as if he were not there, "the eyestone warns the genoth of the presence of prey by their heat, and is nearly indistinguishable from the other scales that coat the creature's body.

"But when the genoth dies, if the blood and fragile tissue are destroyed and drained rapidly from the eyestone, it becomes a thing of great beauty, an ornament much sought after, but rarely won in the contest between sword and claw. If not prepared quickly enough, the eyestone becomes opaque as milk, ugly and useless."

She turned to him, slowly twirling the sparkling gem in her fingers. "This one is of the rarest color, human. Only two other sets are known to exist in the Empire. This is the third – and greatest in size." Most eyestones were little more than a finger's breadth in diameter; these were as big as Reza's palm.

She set the prize down carefully, reluctant to part with it, admitting her own vanity at seeing colors the hue of her own skin sparkle and dance with life. She prayed that the stones were a sign from the Empress, symbols of the two young warriors who had come to mean so much to her, despite her anger at their unfathomable actions. Perhaps, as with the eyestones, it was their time to change, to metamorphose into the most precious of jewels, things of value and beauty. Or to die. Esah-Zhurah had said that Reza believed in the Empress, that he had truly accepted the Way. She had to know.

Her cloak whispered as she crossed the floor and knelt in front of Reza. Their eyes met. "It seems a lifetime ago," she said quietly, remembering the day she had first met him as a tiny, terrified boy, "that we once faced each other this way." She took his face in her powerful hands, the tips of her talons meeting at the back of his skull. "I must ask you this, Reza, and on your answer much depends: do you accept Her in your heart, and the Way of our people as your own?"

Reza no longer had to consider the answer to such a question. He met her gaze steadily. "I do, priestess," he said, feeling the pressure from her hands as they pressed gently against his cheeks.

After a moment, she released him. His heart was true. "It is so," she replied, standing up once again, returning to the window.

"This is a difficult day for me, Reza," she said, "as it will be for you, and for your tresh." She paused. "You exchanged blood, an acceptable tradition among certain of our people. But such a thing is only to take place after the final Challenge, and is always decided by the Empress Herself, or the head priestess of the Desh-Ka. It was the greatest gift Esah-Zhurah could give you as one who follows the Way, but it may prove her own undoing. She breached many of our codes to give you what you now possess."

Reza looked up, concern spreading across his face like cracks wending their way across a lake of ice. "My soul," he said quietly.

Tesh-Dar nodded. "Or its voice. Perhaps we will never know. Regardless, by giving you her blood, she imparted unto you her honor, and made you something more than you were before. But the fact of her transgression remains, and it has tainted you in turn," she went on. "I am left with no alternative but to punish you both." She saw Reza's grim expression. "You will both be bound to the Kal'ai-Il for punishment with the *grakh'ta*, the barbed lash. Six strokes for each of you, this day, upon the rise of the Empress Moon."

Reza's relief was enormous. Esah-Zhurah would be spared a humiliating death or the shaving of her hair. The pain of such punishment would be torturous, but it was endurable. He did not have to consider his own chances, however. Six lashes with but a single evening in which to heal would leave him a cripple in the arena for the final Challenge.

It did not matter, he told himself. Whether he died in the first combat or the last was immaterial; at least it would not be Esah-Zhurah who would have to suffer the pain of killing him. She would still have a chance at life, a chance to cleanse her honor. "My thanks for your leniency, priestess," Reza offered humbly.

"I wish... things could be otherwise, Reza," she said softly. Her anger had burned itself away at the thought of him dying in the arena, now to die with the bloody welts of his shame fresh beneath his armor. She knew that the punishment was unforgivably lenient, but there was no force behind the thought that they had done something wrong, as if the wrongness were merely a symbol upon a parchment being consumed by fire. The Ancient Ones were still and quiet. They did not call for blood, as they were wont to do in the rare cases when one of Her children strayed from the Way. Tesh-Dar only knew that they watched still, and their sightless stares into her soul made her wary of her footsteps in this matter. And then, she thought, there was the Empress.

"I thank you priestess," he said, "for everything." He paused, wanting to say something more, even reaching out his hand toward her, a tentative bridge over the rift that had always existed between them. They probably would never speak again, for the punishment would be rendered soon, and the Challenge would begin with the rising of the sun tomorrow, and Reza would be dead soon thereafter. He wanted to tell her that the malice he had felt toward her for what had happened to his parents was gone, that he had forgiven her. She had, he finally admitted to himself, become a surrogate mother to him, and perhaps something more, something beyond his ability to understand.

A quick rapping on the door startled Reza, and he turned to see a tresh enter and kneel. "They have found the genoth's body," she reported, looking askance at Reza. "The tale is true." She paused. "They also found the mutilated bodies of Ust-Kekh and Ami-Char'rah."

The priestess looked at Reza, noting the sad surprise on his face. "We never saw them," he said.

Tesh-Dar thanked her, and the warrior left. She and Reza looked at each other, the moment Reza had been searching for now lost.

"Go now," she told him, "and fetch me Esah-Zhurah, that I may inform her of my judgment."

Reza saluted and left, hoping that at least the final hours before their punishment could be spent quietly together.

Tesh-Dar watched him go. She was saddened that she would never know the words to the feelings she had felt flowing from him.

* * *

Esah-Zhurah was distraught, but not because of her own punishment.

"Priestess," she asked in a determined voice, "is it not possible for one of us to accept the punishment for both?"

"Do not be foolish, child," Tesh-Dar admonished, summarily dismissing the idea. Or trying to. "The punishment of one is suffered by the other. That is the code of the tresh. You have known this. You must withstand six times of the grakh'ta, and so must he, for I can give no fewer, and have not the heart to give more." She stopped her pacing to face Esah-Zhurah, whose own eyes were downcast. "Child, he is to die in the Challenge on the morrow. Is it not better that he be allowed to share in your pain?"

Daring to look Tesh-Dar in the eye, Esah-Zhurah shook her head. "I would rather have him stand a fair chance in combat and die at my hand or yours with the honor he has earned among us, rather than let him be speared like a meat animal, crippled and helpless with injury." Their punishment would be received without the usual support from the healers. If Reza was whipped with the grakh'ta, he would be so badly injured that he would die in the first round of the Challenge, if he lived even that long. "If I were to receive twelve lashes," she pressed, "must he also be punished? Must he, priestess?"

"There is precedent, Esah-Zhurah," Tesh-Dar reluctantly conceded. "It is terribly rare, and has never happened in my lifetime. But..."

"Then it can be done," Esah-Zhurah finished for her. "It is within your power to grant."

"Esah-Zhurah..." Tesh-Dar's voice died, for she did not know what to say. She turned away to look toward the mountains in the distance, hiding the feeling of impending loss that she could no longer conceal, for the mourning marks had already begun their march down her cheeks. Inwardly, she cursed the unforeseen turn the Way had taken. She had held such high hopes for these two, believing that Reza would survive to become something that had never been in all the history of the Empire: one not born of their race, but who might wear the collar in the name of their Empress, with Esah-Zhurah at his side. To see him perish now was a tragedy she mourned with a strength she would never have admitted. "If you must," she said in a despondent voice. "I will let it be so."

Tesh-Dar turned to her, the elder's face unreadable but for the mourning marks that now flowed openly down her face like ebony streams against a twilight sky. "Go now and prepare, child," the priestess told her, "for when the light of the Empress Moon shows in the referent of the Kal'ai-Il, it will be time."

* * *

Reza waited impatiently for Esah-Zhurah to return. Already the Empress Moon was rising above the twilight horizon, and their Way together grew shorter by the minute. He had no illusions about his future: his life would end tonight, save for the stilling of his heart by the sword or shrekka of one of the peers come morning. But he had accepted it as his Way and Her will, and knew that the Bloodsong would carry him from this place to yet another.

He held the knife he had won as a prize in his first combat the day Esah-Zhurah had taken him to the city so many cycles ago, the day that the priestess had taken the two of them under her wing. Carefully, he laid it aside. It was his gift to Esah-Zhurah. It was his most prized possession, and he wanted her to keep it in remembrance of him.

Suddenly he sensed that she was coming, and turned to greet her.

She was not alone. A healer accompanied her through the perimeter of trees that were the only walls to their home-in-exile, the clawless one's robe flowing like water in the light breeze.

"Are you prepared?" Esah-Zhurah asked quietly, kneeling next to him.

Reza nodded, wanting to reach for her and take her into his arms one last time. But the healer hovering nearby gave him pause. "Why is she here?" he asked.

"I asked her to come, my love," Esah-Zhurah said softly, wrapping her arms around Reza's neck. "She is here to take care of you," she whispered in his ear.

He felt a light sting on the side of his neck as Esah-Zhurah pressed a tiny patch against his skin, injecting a tranquilizer the healer had prepared into Reza's carotid artery. His eyes flew wide in surprise and he made to grab for Esah-Zhurah's hands. But it was too late, the drug already rushing through his system, robbing him of control over his voluntary muscles. He fell limply into Esah-Zhurah's waiting arms, asleep, before he could say a word.

"Forgive me," she begged, holding him tightly for what she knew would be the last time. "It was I who brought punishment upon us, and it is I who must answer for it," she told him, knowing that he could no longer hear her. "In exchange for my pain, you will have a fair chance in the arena on the morrow, a chance to win. Perhaps even a chance at life, should it be Her will." She tenderly kissed his sleeping lips. "That is my gift to you, my love. Should I be gone when you awaken, remember that I will always be with you, until the day the voices of our souls shall be one." She placed the Empress's blade, the gift from Pan'ne-Sharakh, in his waist belt. "This is now yours," she said. "Go thy Way in Her name, my love."

Esah-Zhurah kissed him one last time, then gently lay him down upon their bed. Two more healers came from the trees, and Esah-Zhurah watched as they carried Reza away to their chambers to watch over him.

High above, the Empress Moon rose.

* * *

Esah-Zhurah looked up from her meditation as Mara'eh-Si'er, Tesh-Dar's First, approached. The time had come.

"I am ready," Esah-Zhurah told her, standing up and forcing her mind away from Reza to the painful trial ahead. She followed the First toward the Kal'ai-Il, the Empress Moon shining full overhead.

Standing in the center of the kazha, the Kal'ai-Il was an ancient edifice whose worn granite pillars dated back to before the birth of the First Empire, from a time remembered only in legend. Forming a circle, the gray slabs that covered the ground radiated from the central dais to meet two concentric rings of pillars, themselves capped with purple granite blocks weighing hundreds of tons that bridged the tops. Every other pillar of the outer ring, thirty-six in all, supported staircases in the form of flying buttresses; the inner ring, comprising eighteen pillars half the height of those in the outer ring, had simpler stone stairways rising from the circle bounding the massive central dais. It was the largest structure in the kazha, but in all Esah-Zhurah's time here she had never seen it used. She had only walked through it once, at Reza's insistence as he asked her about its purpose in their lives. She had never considered that she would be the first one of the ancient kazha to be punished here since long before she was born.

"In all the kazhas throughout the Empire," she had explained, "there exists one of these. In ancient times, as now, the Kal'ai-Il was where the most severe punishments were carried out. In our early schooling, we are punished lightly, but in a large group. The transgressions of one are suffered for by many, and it is a terrible dishonor to bring shame upon any but yourself. As we grow older, we are placed in smaller and smaller groups, the last being as are you and I, as tresh, before we enter the Way as individuals.

"But," she went on pointedly, "the punishment becomes ever more severe for a given act. What a small child suffers lightly, an adult may well die for. At last, the warrior may find herself shackled in the Kal'ai-Il for offenses that demand public ceremony and atonement." She paused for a moment and looked at Reza, trying hard to make him understand the importance of what she was trying to tell him. "The only worse punishment is to have one's hair shaved and be denied death for a cycle of the Empress Moon, to wander among the peers in shame as one's name is stricken from the Books of Time, to die without honor, without a legacy among the peers, and to live for all eternity in the darkness beyond Her light."

Now, walking behind the First, Esah-Zhurah saw that the tops of the two granite rings were crowded with the peers, who stood two rows deep facing the massive, worn dais, their heads bowed and eyes averted.

Her escort stopped as she reached the two massive pillars of the entrance, sheared midway from the ground like two enormous tusks, broken off in an ancient battle and never repaired.

"Remember," Mara'eh-Si'er said quietly, leaning close to her, "you must pass this portal by the twelfth tone after your punishment has been rendered and you are released from the bindings. It is a test of your spirit above and beyond your atonement. It is a demonstration of your will to live in honor among your peers. If you do not pass this point," she gestured toward the glittering ebony stone marker that was set in the floor of the entrance like a buffer between two different worlds, "the priestess is obligated to kill you, for that is the Way of the Kal'ai-Il." She gestured for Esah-Zhurah to step forward to the ancient dais. Then she turned to join the elder warriors gathered on the inner ring.

Esah-Zhurah walked onward, her pace slow, the odd bit of gravel crunching under her sandals, loud as thunderclaps in her ears over the stillness of the wind and the silence of those around her. She noted with detached curiosity that nothing grew from the cracks in the slabs, some wider than the palm of her hand; the normally fertile ground was lifeless and dull, like mud from a dry lakebed baked into clay by a searing sun. It seemed that even the earth had forsaken those who trod this path.

Before her was the dais, a huge, ponderous structure that reflected the unyielding rigidity of the code under which she and her people were fated to live. The circular platform was overshadowed by a thick stone arch that looked like a natural formation, not something made by Kreelan hands. Two thick chains, their copper sheathing green with age, hung from the arch. Each chain had a metal cuff for the victim's hands.

She could see the priestess waiting for her, Tesh-Dar's black armor glistening in the dual light of evening. The fading sun, just falling below the horizon, was grudgingly giving way to the glow of the Empress Moon, huge now in the sky directly overhead. As she mounted the stairs, one of the tresh lit torches that made the top of the dais into a ring of fire, providing light for the peers to see by.

Having reached the top of the dais, three times Esah-Zhurah's own height, she knelt before Tesh-Dar.

"Remove your clothing," the priestess ordered quietly. Esah-Zhurah did as she was told, taking off her black cloth garment and her sandals, folding them carefully into the prescribed bundle and placing them at the edge of the stairway. Completely naked now except for the collar she wore about her neck, she moved forward to the center of the dais, extending her arms upward.

As if with a will of their own, the chains descended. One of the tresh locked the bronze shackles, the metal rough and pitted with age, around her wrists and fastened them tightly with bolts as big around as Esah-Zhurah's thumb. The young warrior did the same for the shackles on the floor, anchored to the dais by a short piece of chain, attaching them to Esah-Zhurah's ankles; their bent flanges bit into her flesh. The tresh then placed a strip of thick leather in Esah-Zhurah's mouth. It was something for her to bite down on, to help control the pain that was to come. Esah-Zhurah's eyes thanked the girl, for it was a mercy she had performed, not required by the code of punishment.

Then the girl stepped away. Unseen warriors in the bowels of the dais pulled the chains taut, lifting Esah-Zhurah clear of the floor. Her arms were stretched out above her and away from her body, her blue flesh now a glowing crucifix in the flickering light of the torches.

Tesh-Dar stood by silently, eyes closed as she listened to the clatter of the chains, the tired squeaking of the bolts as they were driven home, and then the gentle groaning of the ancient wheels as Esah-Zhurah's body was lifted above the dais. A memory flashed through her mind, a dark and painful one that had rarely surfaced over the years, of her own body being suspended in these very same shackles. It had been many, many cycles before Esah-Zhurah had been born, before the war with the humans had begun. It was strange, she thought, that she could not remember what she had done to earn such a punishment, so deep an effect had it had on her. She vaguely recalled that it was something terribly stupid, something even a magthep would not have concocted. But it would not come to her, and she let it rest.

She ran her eyes along the list of names of those who had taken punishment here, carved into the stone floor of the dais. Some were so old that they were nothing more than shapeless indentations in the stone. But the more recent ones were clearly legible, and she noted that hers was indeed the last before this day. The Kal'ai-Il was generally a silent pillar in their lives, but when it spoke, its words echoed for a long time, indeed.

She gripped the grakh'ta in her right hand as if it were a serpent trying to escape, the seven barbed tendrils that grew from the thick handle, nearly twice as long as she was tall, wrapped around her arm in the customary fashion. It was one of her favorite weapons in battle, but all it brought to her now was a foul and bitter taste at the back of her throat. The lashes she was about to deal out now would be more than she had given in punishment over her entire life, and it sickened her that she had no recourse. Her heart felt wooden, dead.

"All is ready, priestess," the young warrior reported from behind her.

"Strike the first tone," Tesh-Dar ordered, her mind turning to the task at hand, no matter how reluctantly. The tresh saluted, then made her way to the far side of the dais where a huge metal disk hung suspended, its upper edge at the same height as Esah-Zhurah's eyes from where she now hung. The center was well worn, for it sounded once per day as a reminder to the tresh of what lay here. The runes that decorated its surface were in the Old Tongue, a language that had died out in common usage before the First Empress Herself had been succeeded.

Esah-Zhurah watched as the warrior hefted the huge hammer, then cringed as she slammed it into the disk's center. The sound washed over her like a blast of chill air, setting her body vibrating like an insect caught in a spider's web. All around her, the eyes of the tresh lifted to watch the punishment, for it was a lesson for them, as well.

As the sound of the gong began to fade from Esah-Zhurah's ears, she heard a sound behind her like the rustling of leaves in the wind. It grew into a shrieking roar as the priestess flailed the grakh'ta with all her incredible strength.

Esah-Zhurah closed her eyes, waiting for the first strike to fall.

* * *

Reza's eyes flew open. He had been awakened by something, but he could not remember what it was. Looking around to make sure he was not dreaming, he saw the healers clustered about the window that looked out over most of the kazha, their backs stiff under their robes, their hands gripped tightly. Uncharacteristically for healers, who tended to be a garrulous group, they were completely silent.

"What is happening?" he asked, startling them. They had thought he would remain asleep for some time yet. "Why are you..." He suddenly remembered what had happened, what must be happening now.

Crack! A sound like a gunshot echoed across the kazha.

"Esah-Zhurah!" he shouted, struggling against the anesthetic, his body an immobile leaden weight. "Esah-Zhurah, no!"

"No, child," the senior healer, a woman nearly as old as Tesh-Dar, said as she and the other healers gathered to restrain him, "there is nothing to be done. The priestess ordered that you must wait here."

Reza, ignoring her and growling like a trapped animal, continued to struggle against the numbness, trying furiously to regain some control over his deadened body.

"This was a command, child!" the healer hissed, and Reza, shocked by the iron tone of the woman's voice, came back to his senses. There was nothing he could do.

Crack!

"How... many?" Reza choked. "How many must she take?"

They looked at one another, as if taking a silent vote as to whether they should tell him.

"Twelve lashes," the elder replied quietly, her voice brittle. For she knew well the terrible damage that the weapon could wreak on a body, particularly when wielded by the priestess, and she had her own doubts as to the chances of even the most seasoned warrior surviving so many strikes.

"How many remain?" he asked in a small, tortured voice, hoping that he had not come awake with the first lash.

Crack!

"Eight, now," came the reply.

Reza lay back and closed his eyes, tears cascading down his face as he fought to keep from screaming out of helplessness.

* * *

Crack!

Esah-Zhurah's eyes bulged as if they were about to explode from their sockets, so horrific had the pressure within her body become to resist the urge to shriek in agony. Her teeth had ground halfway through the hard leather in her mouth; she would have long since bitten off her tongue had it not been for that small kindness the young tresh had shown her.

Crack!

She groaned finally, but still did not cry out. There was no feeling in her body now, no sensation but stark, blinding pain as she felt the flesh being flayed from her back. Her head hung limply, a stray strand of the whip having stung her on the neck just below where the spine met the skull. Her lungs labored fitfully as the muscles along the front of her rib cage sought to take up the slack of those along her back that had been battered down to the bone. She hung still now, even when the lash struck, for the muscles facing the weapon had lost their strength for so much as a nervous twitch. She heard the whistling behind her and desperately sucked in her breath, clamping down on the leather in her mouth as she anticipated the next blow.

* * *

Crack!

Reza moaned in empathic suffering as he listened to the steady barrage of lashes onto the body of his tresh, his soul mate, and felt her keening Bloodsong. He could only cry silently as the gunshots of the grakh'ta echoed across the kazha.

Crack!

He flinched, then went on with his prayer to the Empress. It was the most emphatic he had ever made in his life, praying to give Esah-Zhurah the strength and courage she needed to survive. He waited for another strike, but it did not come. He was relieved to find that he had miscounted somehow, that the last he had heard had indeed been the twelfth. After a moment, the mournful tone of the gong sounded, informing all who could hear that the ordeal was over.

Almost.

Waiting silently with the healers, now clustered around his bed save one with sharp eyes who watched the dais, Reza counted the beats of his heart as he lay waiting for the next tone. It rang when he had reached fifty.

"Can you see her?" he asked urgently of the healer peering through the window. "Has she moved?"

The healer, a young woman who was also the senior by skill here at the kazha, signed negative. Her eyes were like those of a bird of prey, and she could see the dais clearly except for the floor, which was concealed behind the wall that ran waist high around it. But Esah-Zhurah clearly had not emerged. "She has not."

"Esah-Zhurah," Reza said under his breath with all the force of his soul, "get up. Get up and live."

The third tone sounded.

* * *

Her eyes flickered open at what her body reported as a spurious vibration, but which meant nothing to a mind that bordered on madness. Something told her that it was important, but she could not seem to remember why.

She looked around, swiveling her bloodshot eyes, and found that she was looking at someone's foot, very close up. Her hands lay in front of her, inert, bloody rings where the manacles had been. She was laying in something sticky, but did not know what it was, nor did she really care. She was tired; she wanted to sleep.

She closed her eyes again.

Suddenly, as if from very far away, she got the peculiar sensation that someone was calling her name, wanting her to do something, but she could not hear it clearly through the ringing in her head, the numbness.

The sound, the vibration, came again, and all at once she felt Reza with her. She could hear the song of his blood crying out for her, trying to give her strength.

"Reza..." she muttered thickly with jaws exhausted from biting the now-crushed piece of leather that she managed to spit from her mouth, "cannot... hurts..."

But his Bloodsong would not be still, would not be silent. It was a tiny force to set against the agony assaulting her senses, but its power grew, would not be denied.

With a tortured groan, she rolled over on her stomach, gasping at the effort. Her mind began to clear slightly now that she had a mission for it, and she was thankful that she was not paralyzed with pain. But that would come soon enough after the shock she was experiencing now wore off. She shook her head to clear her vision. She saw that she was pointing the right way, toward the break in the wall that surrounded the dais and the torches that ran along both sides of the stone walk leading to her destination.

She tried to stand, but without the muscles in her back to help lift her body, it was impossible. She slowly scrabbled forward using what leverage her biceps and quivering chest muscles could afford her, pushing weakly with her legs toward the stairs that led down from the dais, leaving a slick trail behind her like a giant, bloody snail.

Tesh-Dar, having finished with the grakh'ta, had moved to stand astride the ebony bar that marked Esah-Zhurah's goal, silently urging her on as the battered young woman met the stairs. Finding it too difficult to pull herself downward, the friction of the stone against the length of her bare body far too great, Esah-Zhurah pushed with her legs until she was parallel with the stairway, then rolled herself down. The priestess ground her teeth together in empathic agony as the young warrior flailed like a rag doll as she plummeted toward the bottom.

* * *

"She has left the dais," the healer reported, "but now lies still." She did not have to say that she did not feel Esah-Zhurah's chances of survival were very high. Her voice reflected a distinct lack of optimism that Reza found infuriating, yet he managed to hold his tongue.

The other healers waited silently. They had little to do, for it was forbidden to give aid to one punished in the Kal'ai-Il. They would make her as comfortable as they could, but that was the extent of the care they could render. The girl's life was entirely in Her hands.

The gong rang yet again, and they looked at each other, hope fading from their eyes. Half of Esah-Zhurah's time had passed, and she had yet far to go.

* * *

She lay there, panting, blinded by the white flashes that flared in her vision. The roll down the stairs had left her unconscious again, and she had no idea how much time remained to her, nor did she care. Her world was pain, only pain.

But the melody of Reza's song in her blood was insistent. Once again rolling onto her stomach, she began to crawl toward the portal, following the glare of the flickering torches. Her hands clawed at the unyielding slabs of rock, her talons fighting for purchase on the ancient stone as she desperately pulled herself forward.

The gong rang again. No good, she thought weakly, no good to crawl like a sand-worm. I have to stand, to walk.

Pulling her legs underneath her as if she were on her knees, bowed over in prayer, she set one foot forward. Then, balancing precariously with her hands on the extended knee, she pushed herself upward with all the strength she could muster. She managed to stand up, and her free foot wavered over the walkway as if blind before it finally found a place that sustained her balance. She made her way forward, swaying to and fro like a drunkard, praying she would not fall. For to fall now was to die.

Fewer and fewer were the torches before her, and she suddenly had a terrible thought: what if she was headed the wrong way?

No matter, she told herself. It would be too late to go back. At least her suffering would be swiftly ended with a blow from the priestess's sword. She nearly paused at the thought, the notion of a quick, painless death suddenly tempting. Her mind dared not contemplate the agony she would endure in the coming hours before she would die of shock and loss of blood.

Another step forward toward the darkness that stood at the portal, and another, and finally her foot touched the ebony bar.

Tesh-Dar caught Esah-Zhurah in her arms as she fell forward, her legs and back finally giving out completely. The final sound of the gong pealed behind her, signaling the end of the punishment. She struggled weakly, fighting Tesh-Dar's grip and moaning unintelligibly.

"You are safe, Esah-Zhurah," the priestess said as she held the girl gently, doing her best to avoid touching the devastated flesh of her back, her own heart a cold shard of steel in her chest. "It is over."

The healers in attendance looked at the young woman and exchanged glances that Tesh-Dar had seen many times before, and her hopes sank at their unvoiced thoughts.

"I will carry her," she told them, and they made no move to interfere.

* * *

Reza could only turn his head when he heard the door to the infirmary burst open; he had feeling through most of his body now, but no control. He watched as Tesh-Dar, followed by a train of healers who Reza knew would not be able to apply their craft, swept through the room carrying Esah-Zhurah's limp form. The sight sent a blade of ice through Reza's heart. He had felt her pain in his blood as she hung upon the Kal'ai-Il, but the sight of her lacerated body was far worse. He struggled upward, fighting against the useless muscles and nerves that stolidly refused his call to duty. But at last he was sitting upright, then was crawling on his knees.

"Is she alive?" he gasped in the direction of the group huddled around the raised dais where her body lay. Staggering to his feet, he caught a glimpse of the bloody mass of tissue that had once been her back, framed by a series of zebra stripes where the white gleam of bone shone through the tattered flesh. "Esah-Zhurah!" he cried, hurling himself forward, reaching for her.

Tesh-Dar materialized suddenly before him, embracing him in an iron grip and turning him away from the sight. "No, Reza," she said. "You can do nothing for her. Let the healers do what they can–"

"Esah-Zhurah!" he cried again, trying to wrench himself free. His anger boiled and madness threatened to take him. All at once he felt it again: the fire in his veins and the melody that hammered inside his skull, a tidal wave of power that he couldn't control, but welcomed now in his grief and rage. "Let... me... go!" He wrenched to one side so quickly and with such force that he broke free of Tesh-Dar's Herculean grip. Before his mind could react, his armored gauntlets were streaking toward the priestess's face, aiming to tear her eyes from their sockets.

But at the last instant, Tesh-Dar's hands rose to break his attack, and with the speed born of the special powers she had inherited from those who had gone before her, she smashed Reza to the ground with a double blow to his shoulders.

"No more, Reza," she commanded, carefully controlling the forces inside her own spirit that clamored for release, to join in combat.

Reza knelt before her, stunned by the blows, the fire burning hotter than before. But before the fire could take him again, he was once again in Tesh-Dar's arms. The elder warrior had sensed the new wave of power surging into the human and had elected to put a stop to it before she could lose control of what lay within herself. She held him so tightly that his armor began to give way, popping and denting with the pressure, and she continued to squeeze until Reza was panting desperately for breath, his arms nearly broken at his sides. At last, she felt the Bloodsong within him abate. When it had ebbed toward silence, she released the pressure, her arms around him more for support than restraint.

"I am not your enemy," she whispered to him, her own senses awash in the emotions pouring from this young alien, from the young warrior she looked upon in her heart as her adopted son. "I did as she wished, Reza. She begged me for this, to give you a fair chance in the Challenge. Do not disgrace her sacrifice this way."

She released his arms, and Reza wrapped them around her neck. For a long time he clung to her like a child, vainly trying to fight back his tears, as she held him. And on his face and hands, where they had touched Tesh-Dar's armored breast, was Esah-Zhurah's blood. So much blood.

"Forgive me, my priestess," he told her in a trembling voice. "My life, my honor a thousand times over is not worth this."

Tesh-Dar said nothing, but gently rocked him as she might a small child.

Behind them, the healers had done all they could, all they were allowed. They had arrayed the flesh and skin as well as possible and covered the ghastly wounds with sterile blankets, but that was all. They could give her nothing for the pain, put an end to the persistent bleeding, or disinfect the wounds. The chief healer saw the signs of internal injuries, as well, the force of Tesh-Dar's blows having driven the whip's barbs into Esah-Zhurah's lungs. But there was nothing she could do. Ordering her peers to stand away, she signaled to Tesh-Dar that they were finished now, except for the waiting.

"Go to her now, child," Tesh-Dar whispered. "I shall be here should you need me."

Reza nodded against her shoulder, then shakily turned around to look at what had become of his love, to see the price she had paid to give him a few more hours of life. She lay on her stomach, her arms at her sides. Her head was turned to one side on the thick pile of skins that served as both operating table and patient bed. A tiny bead of blood made its way from the corner of her mouth, pooling in the soft fur near her ear. Her beautiful blue skin was horribly pale, almost cyan, except for the brutal bruising that peered from beneath the black velvet bandages the healers had spread across her back, and the ebony streaks of mourning on her face. He knelt next to her and took off his gauntlets, dropping them to the floor. Carefully, afraid that his mere touch would cause her more pain, he ran a hand gently across her face, caressing her cheek.

Her eyes flickered open, and he felt her move.

"Be still," he whispered hoarsely. "Do not move, my love. I am here."

"Do not... leave me," she sighed. Her eyes were glassy with the onset of pain that was burning through the massive shock her body was experiencing.

Reza took her hand in his and squeezed it gently. "Never," he said with a strength that came from the core of his being. He wanted to shout at her, to ask her why she had done this, when his life was forfeit anyway. But he did not have to, because he knew. She loved him, and would have suffered a thousand-fold what she had today for his sake, and nothing more. "I love you," he told her softly, and he kissed her on the cheek.

She gave him a weak smile. "Fight well, my tresh, come the dawn. I will be with thee. And... may thy Way... be long... and glorious." Her grip relaxed as her eyes rolled up into her head, the lids closing over them.

"Esah-Zhurah?" he whispered. Her face was still, and with dread in his eyes he looked at the chief healer. "Is she dead?" he asked woodenly.

She shook her head. "Not... not yet," she told him, averting her eyes, knowing that it would not be long.

"Will she live to the morning?" he asked, his eyes pleading.

"I do not know, Reza," she answered truthfully. Life was a strange thing, and was often incredibly adept at cheating Death. For a time. "There is nothing more we may do."

Tesh-Dar stood close by, shrouded in the storm that tore through her heart. She was well acquainted with the process of death, and already she could sense a change in the melody of Esah-Zhurah's spirit. Very few were as perceptive of such things as was Tesh-Dar, and there was no mistaking it. The child's Bloodsong would soon come to a close, be it in the next moment or a few hours from now. But soon.

For all her life she had welcomed the event and celebrated it for others as she hoped they would someday do for her. It was an occasion for joy, when one passed from the field of honor to the spirit world beyond, where the Ancient Ones dwelled forever in Her light. It was the day for which the warriors of the Empire lived and breathed.

But the tortured lump of flesh that lay dying nearby brought her nothing but anguish, for to die this way was a horrible thing, especially for this child. Esah-Zhurah, born of the Empress herself, had sacrificed her formative years to study this human in the course of Her will, while her own peers sought glory against the alien hordes. And in the end, she had disobeyed a high priestess to lay with him, an act for which Tesh-Dar could have sentenced them both to death, but uncertainty had stayed her hand. The two of them, the whole that they formed together, was something unique in Tesh-Dar's experience, and the strange quiet that had descended over her ancestors in recent times had left her acutely aware of the consequences of the decisions she had to make regarding their welfare.

In the pair of young warriors she had discovered a new force within the Empire, something that before had only existed in legend, when a warrior could feel passion for another, and not all of one's heart was devoted to Her. She had heard Esah-Zhurah speak of love for Reza, but she understood now its true strength. The power that united these two former enemies was beyond Tesh-Dar's ken, and she vainly struggled to understand the force that had driven this young warrior, her pride and joy, to sacrifice herself for the one she had once called "animal," for the one who now lived clothed in the armor and beliefs of Her children, for the one who now knelt, weeping at the child's side. Esah-Zhurah's death would not bring glory to Her name; it would simply be a tragedy, and perhaps not for the two of them alone.

She walked to where Reza knelt and stood close to him, her great hand, still covered with Esah-Zhurah's blood, resting upon his shoulder. "The Challenge comes soon," she said softly. "You must prepare." She did not need to remind him that every combat in which he fought – as many as fifteen – would be to the death. No arena judge would preside, for the only rules governing each battle would be those of survival.

"I cannot leave her," he whispered absently, his hands gently folded around hers.

"Your armor is ruined, your weapons are not ready, nor is your mind," Tesh-Dar went on. "You must do these things or death will find you quickly. Esah-Zhurah paid a dear price to give you this chance to fight the rarest of contests, and the most honored. Do not forfeit her faith in you." She squeezed his shoulder firmly. "I will wait here, her hand in mine, until you return. I cannot hold Death at bay. But should her time come while you are gone, she will not face it alone." *As must most of our people*, she added silently, wondering if someone would be at her own side when her Way came to its end. "Go now, child."

Reza nodded heavily, as if once more he had been inflicted with the strange anesthetic Esah-Zhurah had used upon him, his body a vast numbness to his mind. "Yes, my priestess," he whispered. With a last kiss upon Esah-Zhurah's still lips, he rose and walked stiffly through the doorway, disappearing into the darkness beyond.

* * *

The Empress stood silently over Esah-Zhurah, with Tesh-Dar kneeling at her monarch's side. Not long after Reza had gone to prepare for the coming Challenge, the Empress had appeared. Her arrival was without fanfare, without a Praetorian Guard; She was a part of all Her Children as surely as were the hearts that beat in their breasts, and so was a familiar part of their lives, even to those who had never seen Her in the flesh. She needed no guard, for all the Kreela were Her guardians and protectors.

"I believe that she is The One," the Empress spoke at last.

"My Empress," Tesh-Dar asked, awed by the possibilities invoked by those words, "how is this possible? Her hair is black as night and she was born of the silver claw, barren as myself. How can we know that it is truly... She?"

"I do not know, daughter," the Empress replied. "It is a feeling – a certainty – that refuses to leave me."

"Then what shall be done?" Tesh-Dar still held Esah-Zhurah's motionless hand. The child's heartbeat was becoming erratic, and she would soon – long before dawn broke over the arena – pass from this life. "How may one be sure?"

"If the human is victorious in the Challenge this day, we shall have our answer. He shall bear the burden of proof," She told Tesh-Dar. "For I have realized that this is what the Ancient Ones have been awaiting, priestess of the Desh-Ka."

"Could it truly be?" Tesh-Dar murmured to herself. If what the Empress believed came true, the Curse of the First Empress might someday be undone. Her great spirit had been silent for ages, and Tesh-Dar could not imagine the impact upon the Way were Her voice to join the chorus of all those who had come after Her. The most powerful Empress who had ever walked the Way, whose spirit had vanished as Her body withered in death, in legend was said to be awaiting a host worthy of Her spirit. And it could be Esah-Zhurah.

Tesh-Dar shook her head. The possibility was simply too staggering. "If this is so, my Empress," she said slowly, "then I shall be to blame for failure. I ordered the child's punishment, and her Bloodsong grows weaker by the hour, by the minute." She looked up to her sister. "She shall die long before the combats of the day even begin."

The Empress frowned. "It shall not be so." Gently placing a hand on Esah-Zhurah's face, She closed her eyes. Her head leaned forward, nearly to Her chest. She spoke no words, no incantations, but Tesh-Dar could sense the power that flowed from Her as one could feel the heat of an open flame. The child shuddered, drew in a sharp breath, and then relaxed into a stronger, steady rhythm. Tesh-Dar could feel the spirit in her grow stronger. "Her spirit will remain with her body until I release it," the Empress said quietly, stroking Esah-Zhurah's face lovingly. The Empress had borne many children from Her Own body, and had forgotten none of them, even the males, who had never even received a name. And this child, above all others, did She hold most dear.

Tesh-Dar's eyes widened. She knew from legend that such things were possible, but no Empress in the last thousand generations had ever done such a thing, commanding a spirit to remain with the body past the time that Death should have its due.

"Are you to stay for the Challenge, Empress?" she asked, her tongue finally returning to the control of her brain.

"It shall be so," She replied. "Long has it been since I have seen the tresh fight, and longer still since combats have been fought to the death. I need to know, to feel the human's strength of spirit and will do so firsthand. If Esah-Zhurah is The One, then he must be completely worthy of her, and able to take the next step." Tesh-Dar looked up. "He must accept the collar of the Way," the Empress said quietly. "He must become one with our people."

FIFTEEN

Morning came, and the horizon shone a brilliant ruby red that would gradually lighten to the pastel magenta of full daylight. The wind was still, and probably would remain so throughout the day, keeping the ripe odors of the magthep pens away from the arenas.

But on this day, even the most malodorous emanations would not have concerned the throng that now gathered in and around the five arenas of the kazha, for today was a special day indeed.

For the first time in many cycles, the tresh would have the opportunity to face an opponent without the intercession of a judge; victory would be measured only by who survived the match. Not all of the combats were to be fought thus, only the ones in which the human was involved. But that alone served to sharpen the competition in the other combats, the other tresh battling for the honor of facing him in the arena. To kill him before the watching eyes of the Empress would be a tremendous honor, and to die by his hands would only be slightly less so. For few of the tresh who had trained with him considered him an animal any longer. He was a formidable warrior in his own right, and had even trained many of the novices.

The Empress stood now on the dais of the central arena. This arena hosted the first and last combats of the Challenge, with the other four arenas coming into play as needed. Thousands of onlookers were gathered, coming from kazhas all over the planet. Even warriors from the Fleet and the Settlements had come to see the spectacle, having received word that a human was about to fight in this, the last Challenge a warrior faced before her spiritual and societal coming of age. And as the mighty gong of the Kal'ai-Il sounded the first tone of the day, thousands watched a lone figure step onto the packed sand of the central arena to face the Empress.

Reza's stride was controlled, precise as he ventured forward toward where the Empress stood upon the elevated stone dais. He stopped before Her and thrust the sword he held in his right hand into the sand before he knelt and bowed his head to Her. He wore not the standard matte black combat armor that had always protected him in the Challenges he had fought before this day, but glistening ceremonial armor, no less functional than its less-enchanting counterpart, that the Kreela wore on special occasions. The cobalt blue rune that signified his kazha glowed from the swirling blackness of his breastplate, and the silver metal talons of his gauntlets, polished to perfection, glittered in the sun's growing light. His hair, drawn into the intricate braids demanded by custom, was entwined about his upper arms like coiled serpents, with enough slack to allow him full movement.

Beside him, the sword towered from the sand like a sharp-edged obelisk, the dark runes inscribed on the broad blade by Pan'ne-Sharakh's ancient hands telling the tale of his life since coming to the Empire, of the love he and Esah-Zhurah shared. Perhaps to give his despairing soul a glimmer of hope, much of the sword's blade still was bare, begging perhaps for the tale of their lives to continue, for more verses to be added to their own Book of Time. The golden hilt blazed like bloody fire from atop its tower of living Kreelan steel.

After checking on Esah-Zhurah one last time, giving her a final kiss as she lay sleeping, Reza had asked the priestess if he might be allowed the honor of fighting in the first combat, foregoing the normal random selections. Tesh-Dar had agreed, and now he waited for the lottery that would call forth his first opponent.

Another tone sounded from the Kal'ai-Il, and Tesh-Dar reached into the massive clay urn at the center of the dais to draw out the first name in the lottery that would begin the single-round elimination combats. Without looking at it, she passed it to the Empress.

"Korai-Nagath," She called in a voice that commanded countless billions of souls across the stars, "enter the arena."

A murmur of disappointment went up through the gathered crowd as the peers discovered they would have to wait for their turn at the human.

In the meantime, a warrior who stood half a head taller than Reza, and whom he had been training in swordcraft over the last cycle, entered the arena. Her pride was evident in her posture and the measured cadence of her stride. It was her third Challenge.

She knelt next to Reza, facing the Empress, and planted her sword and pike – her favorite weapons – in the sand beside her as she saluted her monarch.

The Empress nodded Her head in acknowledgment, then looked upon the assemblage. "As it has been, and so shall it always be, let the Challenge begin."

"In Thy name, let it be so," the throng echoed with its thousands of voices, their fists crashing against the breastplates they had worn nearly since birth.

Reza and Korai-Nagath stood and retrieved their weapons from the sand, then proceeded to opposite ends of the arena and turned to face one another.

"Begin," the Empress commanded.

The two warriors stood for a moment, sizing up one another, trying to match their own strengths against the other's known or suspected weaknesses. Each was heavily armed, in part because the savage battles that were fought on these sands were seldom decided by a single weapon, but also because the weapons first carried into the arena were all that could be used throughout the Challenge. Should a sword or knife break, or a shrekka miss its mark, there would be no replacement. Likewise, except for stanching the flow of blood from one's eyes, there was no medical treatment unless the challenger wished to forfeit the match. And that was one option none of the combatants today would have accepted.

Reza had no choice in the matter.

After only a moment's consideration, Reza hefted his sword and began a wary advance, his quarry doing likewise. She had favored her pike, as he knew she would, and was now moving forward to meet him.

Reza's heart began to thunder in his chest, his blood liquid fire in his veins as the sword became as light as a feather in his hand. The melody that had burst forth while he was fighting the genoth was back now, and he seized upon it quickly before it could overwhelm him. He channeled the energy as he moved forward, and his eyes gleamed with the cold flames that had taken him.

Korai-Nagath suddenly whirled, releasing a shrekka directed at Reza's chest. Rolling to the ground, Reza heard the weapon slice through the air a meter away and restrained the impulse to respond in kind. He had only three of the precious weapons, and once used, they would be gone. Korai-Nagath fought well for her stage of training, but Reza knew that she was fatally outclassed.

He spiraled in closer and closer, and only when he was within range of her pike did she realize her mistake in choosing it rather than the sword that now stood far behind her in the sand like a headstone. The pike, lethal in experienced hands and the right situation, was far too flimsy to parry the slashing attacks of Reza's sword. With nothing left in her hands but an arm's length of useless pole, she charged Reza with a knife in one hand and bared talons upon the other, a cry of passionate fury upon her lips.

The cry ended as Reza's sword pierced her breastplate directly over her heart. The two held each other for a moment in a macabre embrace, the scarlet stained steel of Reza's weapon protruding from her armored back, glistening in the gathering light before he gently laid her upon the sands. Silently, he pulled his weapon from her breast, drawing the flat of the blade across his other arm, a signal of his first kill.

Turning to the Empress, he kneeled. "May this one forever dwell in Thy light, my Empress," he said, energy still surging in his body, his mind so aware of his surroundings now that he could distinguish a dozen different heartbeats among the crowd behind him, "for in Thy name did she follow the Way."

"And so may it always be," thousands of voices echoed around him, completing the ages-old litany.

The first combat had ended.

* * *

The day alternately flashed and crept by. The periods of waiting as others battled their way through the arenas were precariously balanced against the blinding spells of combat that stretched for an eternity, then were gone in the blink of an eye. Each of the tresh fought and rested, fought and rested while others fell to the sand in defeat, or were killed by Reza's hand. As the day went on, the weaker and inexperienced ones were quickly weeded out from among the serious challengers. The pitched battles fought in the five arenas became ever fiercer as those with cunning and endurance slashed and clawed their way toward the final battle.

Despite his acknowledged skill, Reza did not go from combat to combat unscathed. Hour by hour, his body became host to a multitude of injuries. Individually, they were nothing for him to notice, but over time they began to take their toll. Blood seeped from a dozen wounds hacked through the tough leatherite covering his arms and legs. His beautiful chest armor was horribly dented and scarred, the breastplate a moonscape of bare, pitted metal. A poorly executed fall while avoiding a hissing shrekka had cost him the use of his left hand, the wrist broken. His face, cut and bruised in a snarling hand-to-hand struggle with Lu'ala-Gol, was barely recognizable for the blood and sand smeared across it. One of his eyes remained its natural, nearly violent green, while the other glared at the world as a crimson orb, the blood vessels ruptured during a hard blow to his head.

But the expression he wore was serene. This, he knew, was what he had been born to, no matter that the womb from which he had been born had not been of their race. To tread the Way, to know that She watched over one's soul, to fight for Her glory: this was all that mattered. This was what

Esah-Zhurah had suffered so to give him, and he was determined to win, to honor her, as well as the Empress. He could hear the song of Esah-Zhurah's heart, faint though it remained, and it heartened him and gave him strength, for it meant that she was still alive.

But he knew that on this day he would draw his last breath, as would she. His only prayer was that Esah-Zhurah would be waiting for him on the other side of this life, on the bridge that led to the everlasting Way, and that they could spend eternity together.

And then it was again time. He strode into the arena, waiting for the call to begin. Size up the other combatant. Move in close – shrekka! – drop, roll, attack. Parry. Attack once more. Thrust, block, slash. Close in... closer... strike! Move away, regroup.

He fought with the Bloodsong roaring fury and might in his heart, and in his mind were visions of Esah-Zhurah chained to the Kal'ai-Il, suffering for him, dying.

On and on it went, the sound of crashing metal and cries of fury and of pain shattering the air, until the sun began to wane. At last, as twilight crept upon the kazha and hundreds of torches around the center arena were lit, there were only two challengers remaining. Alone now, save for the hushed stares of the thousands watching and waiting for this moment, the two faced each other from opposite sides of the arena.

Blinking the blood out of his right eye, Reza took stock of his final opponent, Rigah-Lu'orh. He had watched her fight during his periods of rest, and had guessed since her second combat that she would be among the final challengers, and so she was. She stood taller by half a head, and was broader in the shoulders. But despite her greater size, she was incredibly nimble. She had performed a number of violent ballets throughout the day that had left two of her opponents dead and the others seriously injured. Her determination was visible even now, her distant eyes burning like tiny coals with the reflected light of the torches. She wanted his head, and wanted it very badly.

Reza wondered as to his opponent's energy reserves, but knew that he would not be able to gauge her strength until they crossed swords. His own body was nearing the end of what even the power pulsing within him could force from it. Even standing still he trembled, and the pain of moving his body with the speed required to survive was becoming intolerable, a constant screeching in his nerves and muscles. The great sword, its razor edge now dented and nicked from hammering and piercing so many breastplates, was like an enormous stone in his hand, his other hand hanging useless at his side, broken now in three places.

The Empress and the priestess stood upon the dais as they had all day, without pause or rest, watching him kill the best of the kazha. Now only this one, Rigah-Lu'orh, remained.

"Are you prepared, human?" the Empress asked, her voice easily carrying the distance across the arena.

Reza kneeled and bowed his head. "Yes, my Empress."

"And you, disciple of the Desh-Ka?" She asked of Rigah-Lu'orh. Of course, she was, kneeling as Reza had, saluting. "Then let it begin."

Reza had not even looked up when the first attack came. He brought his sword up just in time to deflect the whirring shrekka from hitting his face. With sparks trailing after it, the weapon slammed into the stone pillar behind him.

He had one shrekka left, but dared not use it until the right moment. With only one good hand, he would have to leave go his sword to reach the flying weapon, and in that moment he would be terribly vulnerable.

Moving quickly now, the two spiraled in toward one another in a half-walk, half-crouch, weapons held at the ready. Rigah-Lu'orh's cunning was surpassed only by the wiliest genoth, and Reza would not allow himself to underestimate her. Among all those at the kazha, the Challenge had selected her as the best to face him.

Closer they came, until they reached that finite point in time and space where planning gives way to action. In a flash of silver, Rigah-Lu'orh's two short swords slashed at Reza, attacking his upper and lower body at once.

Reza was unable to fend off both weapons, and she scored a flesh wound on his upper thigh. With a roar of anger, he lashed out with the broadsword, cutting a vicious arc through the air where his opponent had just been. Moving in again, she struck quickly at his lower body, slashing his left leg to the bone before darting away again, just ahead of Reza's hissing blade.

The fire in Reza's veins burned so hot that it blinded him. Time and again Rigah-Lu'orh's blades found their mark, his own weapon only occasionally diverting them. Her strategy was one of attrition, not of full commitment. She knew that Reza's sword could cut her in half, armor and all, and so she was careful to stay just out of reach. But she also knew that she was stronger and faster. She had conserved her strength, and knew well how to channel the power of the Bloodsong. Reza possessed the power, but not the knowledge to control it. Now, pouring through his exhausted body and unprepared mind with the fury of lightning, it was quickly – and effectively – killing him.

Reza was staggering backward now, reeling under her assault, his life pouring from his body through a dozen new wounds. Holding the sword up like a shield as she stalked him, he suddenly found himself backed against a stone pillar. There was nowhere left to run.

Dropping the sword from his hand, he reached for the shrekka attached to his shoulder armor. It was his last defense against defeat.

But Rigah-Lu'orh had been waiting. With a fluid motion, she hurled the short sword in her left hand like a dagger.

Reza screamed as the weapon pinned him to the stone like a butterfly on a pin. The blade pierced his right side up to the hilt, the tip burying itself in the ancient stone behind him. His concentration shattered, he dropped the shrekka.

On the dais, the talons of Tesh-Dar's hands cut the stone banister upon which she had been leaning, and her heart leapt to her throat. "No," she whispered to herself.

She did not notice as the Empress glanced her way.

Rigah-Lu'orh regarded Reza as he writhed in pain, twisting around the blade as he reached in vain for the sword on the ground at his feet. Around her, the air was silent except for the thunder of the heartbeats of those gathered to watch. She turned around and saluted the Empress. Receiving a nod in return, the young warrior detached her own remaining shrekka and turned to Reza. He was watching her now, but the look on his face was not one of defeat, but of defiance. With a wail of fury, she cast the shrekka at his heart.

Reza was in a kind of agony he had never experienced before. It was not the agony of physical pain – he could no longer feel the metal burning in his side – but of emotional and psychic overload. The Bloodsong was so strong now, stronger than it had ever been, that he felt about to explode. His eyes were fixed on Rigah-Lu'orh. Even before she reached for the shrekka, he knew what she was about to do.

"It must not end this way," he hissed at himself, his voice lost in the maddening cacophony of fire in his skull and the flames that burned in every cell of his body. "*It cannot...*"

Rigah-Lu'orh watched in amazement as her shrekka struck the stone pillar on which Reza had been impaled. The weapon shattered uselessly against the rock, a prelude to the roar of surprise that rose from the watching multitude.

Reza was gone, vanished.

The Empress leaned forward, eyes wide in amazement and swift acceptance of what She had seen, what She now felt stirring in the fabric of the Way.

Beside Her, Tesh-Dar gasped in surprise as she saw Reza's body vanish, leaving behind only the shimmering air of a desert mirage. As her eyes beheld the spectacle, her blood suddenly burned with a surge of power that struck her like a reflected shock wave. In that instant, she knew. If he demonstrated the will and the wisdom required of what was to come, what must come, the Ancient Ones would protect him, as they would Esah-Zhurah. Both had proved themselves worthy of one another and of the Way, and the Ancient Ones could give them powers that Tesh-Dar had studied her entire life to master. And more. What the peers were witnessing now was only the beginning.

"And so is The Prophecy fulfilled," the Empress murmured wonderingly. She closed Her eyes and listened to the song of Reza's soul as it danced through the darkness beyond time, waiting to return to the bloodied sands before Her and claim his final victory.

Rigah-Lu'orh whirled around in search of her vanished opponent, but he was nowhere to be seen. "Where has he gone?" she cried angrily, feeling cheated of her triumph. "What kind of trick is–"

A brush of air against her back, like the tiniest of zephyrs, was the only warning she had before Reza's armored body slammed into hers, carrying them both to the ground.

As they fell to the sands of the arena, Reza was clamped tightly to her back, trying to reach his arms around her neck for a chokehold. Securing his grip, he applied pressure, but Rigah-Lu'orh made no attempt to resist him.

Then he saw why. The other short sword she had been holding, waiting for his attack, was now protruding from her back, pointing like a bloody finger at the sky above. Totally surprised by Reza's attack, she had fallen on her own weapon. Only by a narrow margin had it missed piercing his own armor over his vulnerable heart.

The arena went silent after a collective gasp of surprise.

Reza lay atop Rigah-Lu'orh's lifeless body for what seemed like a long time, fading in and out of consciousness. Finally, realizing that he still had one last duty to perform before joining her in death, he struggled to his knees. Crawling across the sand like a dying crab, he gathered up the sword that bore his name and began the long trek toward the dais where the Empress and Tesh-Dar awaited him.

He finally brushed against the stone stairs that led up to the dais. With a groan of effort, he got to his knees and peered up with one sparkling green eye, the other now scarlet and blind.

"May this one forever dwell in Thy light, my Empress," he rasped for what seemed like the hundredth time this day, blood from his punctured lung trickling from his lips, "for in Thy name... did she follow the Way."

"And so may it always be," Tesh-Dar finished from the step above, having come down from the dais to meet him. The few warriors within earshot of Reza's weak voice were still muted by shock.

Reza slid forward, his broken hand hanging useless at his side as his good hand held onto the grip of the great and battered sword for support, the point of the weapon's blade buried deep in the sand under his weight.

"My priestess," he whispered, tilting the weapon toward her in invitation as he slumped toward the ground, "let it be finished." Letting go of the weapon, he waited for her to complete the experiment begun so long ago; nicked and scarred as it was, in Tesh-Dar's hands the sword would still make quick work of his neck, and the story would be finished.

But the expected blow never came. Instead, Reza felt hands gently touching his face, and he found himself staring into the eyes of the Empress. It was a privilege very few had been granted over the ages.

"In My name have you fought and suffered," She said, Her words barely audible as his body lapsed into shock, "and in My name shall you live. When you awaken, you shall be as one with My children."

As Reza collapsed into the sovereign's arms, Tesh-Dar heard the eternal whispers of the Ancient Ones stir in her bones. With life granted to Reza and Esah-Zhurah, they had broken the silence of their spiritual vigil.

The blood that would break the curse of their people had at last been found.

* * *

"I would not have believed it, had I not witnessed it with My Own eyes," the Empress said. She watched as the healers hovered over Reza and Esah-Zhurah, anointing their bodies with healing gel. They applied it carefully to the wounds in Reza's chest, and the Empress watched their hands brush the gleaming black metal of the Collar of Honor that now hung around his neck. When he awoke, he would no longer be an Outsider. He was Hers, now. "To vanish before an enemy, and then to reappear as he did is a feat known only to the ancient orders, such as your own. Never has a tresh done such a thing, in all the time since She... Keel-Tath left us. Never."

"He has been given a tremendous gift," Tesh-Dar acknowledged, kneeling beside Her. "Her blood gave voice to the song of his spirit, and the

Ancient Ones have given him the power to use it." She lowered her head. "And I would give him the knowledge, if you would bless it, my Empress."

"You would accept him as your successor, and teach him the ways of the Desh-Ka?" The sovereign considered the thought for a moment before she answered. "Many firsts has this day brought upon us, Tesh-Dar," She said quietly. "I can see no reason to deny yet another. And, should you wish it, I give my blessing to the daughter of My Own blood; she is yours, as well."

Tesh-Dar lowered her head to her chest in gratitude. In all the thousands of generations of warriors who had worn the order's rune upon their necks, never had a priestess been given such an honor as to bring more than a single disciple into the fold of the Desh-Ka as a priestess... or a priest. Had she been capable of tears, she would have wept with love and pride.

"In Thy name," she whispered huskily, "it shall be so."

Sixteen

When Reza awoke from the curing sleep induced by the healers, he was immediately aware of something cool and sleek around his neck. His probing hands found not the rough steel band of a slave that he had worn since childhood, but the Collar of Honor, made of living steel attuned to his body, and half a dozen pendants. Five inscribed his name, with the glittering runes poised relative to each other, as were the Five Stars in the night sky. The last pendant proclaimed him the victor in his final Challenge, an honor made all the greater because it had been fought to the death. It was an honor to which precious few warriors could lay claim.

The week that followed was one of quiet but intense celebration. In pairs and threes, sometimes singly, the tresh made their way to his bedside to pay their respects with a salute on bended knee. There was no mockery here, no false pretenses. Their sincerity was as real as the sound of their fists hammering against their breastplates as they knelt beside him. He was a part of them now, and they felt and accepted the new voice that sang in the choir of their souls as one of their own.

Beside him, Esah-Zhurah recovered quickly, the horrible wounds in her back fading into oblivion under the care of the healers, leaving not even the smallest scar in their wake.

As they both healed, they lay quietly together, saying little except when the priestess paid them a visit to check on their progress. At night, when the healers had retired for the evening, they held each other close, but they did not make love. The spirit was willing, but the flesh was yet weak.

They had time now.

They could wait.

* * *

"The priestess would see you, Reza, Esah-Zhurah," the young tresh announced as she knelt and saluted. The two who stood before her – both Kreelan, now – were no longer tresh. The Seventh Challenge was the demarcation line between the learning cycle begun in the Nurseries and the beginning of one's true service to the Empire. Esah-Zhurah and Reza were now warriors.

"Thank you, Te'ira-Khan," Reza replied. "We shall come at once."

As the young tresh trotted away, Reza appraised Esah-Zhurah with a raised eyebrow. It was a gesture she had once tried to imitate to humor him, but the ridge of solid horn that served as her own eyebrows was entirely immobile. Instead, she had stuck out her tongue.

"An assignment?" he asked.

"Possibly," she replied, walking beside him as they made their way toward the priestess's quarters. She knew how much Reza wanted to begin his service. Night after night, as they lay close to one another in the infirmary, he spoke to her about his hopes and dreams. Of venturing into the wastelands in search of the unknown, of traveling to the stars of the frontier, of spending endless days in the halls that held the Books of Time to learn of his adopted culture and of so many other things.

And each night she was warmed by her dreams and by his gentle touch. She knew that she would take him to see the stars. But her hopes stood on a trembling foundation of fear, for she dreaded the possibility of their separation. At no time since the death of the First Empress had tresh been assured of serving together. Some did by a twist of fate, but most spent their entire lives separated one from the other, to live, serve, and die in Her name without the comfort of the companion with whom they had shared most of their young lives.

She had no way of knowing that the Empress had expressly forbidden their separation in service. It was not an act of charity on Her part; She was simply doing what She could to ensure that The Prophecy would be fulfilled. Neither Esah-Zhurah nor Reza knew of their role in the fate of the Empire, nor would they until the time came that such knowledge was necessary. For now, only Tesh-Dar, the Empress, and a handful of others truly understood. In any case, the Empress was determined that wherever the Way took them, they would go together.

But Esah-Zhurah did not have this knowledge from which to draw reassurance as they entered the priestess's quarters. They could easily be ordered to opposite ends of the galaxy. Esah-Zhurah's heart trembled.

They found Tesh-Dar alone, waiting for them. After paying their respects with a salute, they knelt before her.

"The time has come for you both to make a decision," she told them. "You have completed your obligatory training here, and are within your rights to claim your entry into service of the Empire. But I ask you to consider another option."

"What other is there?" Reza asked, puzzled.

"I wish you both to accept the ways and powers of the Desh-Ka," she told him, "to become members of my order." Reza and Esah-Zhurah both gaped at her in shocked amazement.

"For as long as our people have walked the Way," Tesh-Dar told them, "the ancient orders have preserved and strengthened the Empire with their blood and skills. The priestesses have led their children in battle, and in their twilight years have taught the young ones the fundaments of the Way, as I have taught you.

"And for the service that we render unto Her, we are given one right that no other – even the Empress – is granted: we may choose our own successors, those to whom we would pass the stewardship of the order. It is a thing we may do only once in our lifetime, for when the torch is passed, no longer do the powers we shepherd dwell within us. We are left as we were as young tresh, but older, waiting for Death's embrace. It is the greatest gift we may give, but it is still a gift; no one may force you to take it, and you must be sure in your heart that it is what you desire. It is a responsibility and a burden only for the most worthy and dedicated of warriors.

"Tradition demands that a priestess pass her legacy on to only one other. My order, the most ancient of all, predating even the First Empress, has only one keeper remaining: myself. Of all the young warriors I have seen in my many cycles, you are the most deserving, but not one over the other. Together have you loved and suffered; together may you receive my offering, as the Empress has granted."

Reza and Esah-Zhurah were silent for but a moment. But when they spoke, it was with a single voice. "We accept, my priestess," they said, their lips moving in unison.

Tesh-Dar felt a tiny bit of tension fall from her shoulders. This was the last and, in some ways, the most important of her duties to the Empress. The ways of the Desh-Ka would not die with her, and these children, who had yet to realize their own importance to the Empire's future, would be much better equipped to survive the rigors of the Way. For survive they must, she thought to herself. "It is done, then," she said quietly. "Gather your things and say your farewells, for we shall be leaving on the morrow, and shall not be returning to this place."

* * *

Reza walked slowly, his arm held out in support of the ancient woman who shuffled beside him. Overhead, the Empress Moon glowed warmly, lighting the sky with its emerald light, illuminating the path before them. The kazha was quiet, most of the tresh having retired for the evening after reviewing the day's lessons and having their evening meal. The only sounds came from the stables, where a handful of tresh were preparing several beasts for the long journey that lay ahead for the priestess and her two disciples.

"Proud am I of you, young one," Pan'ne-Sharakh said in her raspy voice. "Far shall you go upon the Way, and well shall it be for those who tread in your footsteps."

"Thank you, mistress," Reza said, humbled by her words. "But I am saddened greatly by leaving you behind. More than any other, you have shown me kindness. You have left me with a debt I can never repay."

Pan'ne-Sharakh patted him on the arm. "You are one with us, child," she said. "That is payment a thousand-fold over anything you received from this living relic. The blood of the chosen flows in your veins, and great glory shall you bring to the Empress, you and your tresh." She leaned a bit closer. "Your mate."

She paused for a moment, thinking. "I only regret that my Way comes to an end, for I would have liked to craft the first set of armor for your children."

Reza stopped in his tracks. "But, mistress... Esah-Zhurah was born of the silver claw," he said quietly. "She is barren."

Pan'ne-Sharakh looked at him blankly with her blind eyes, an unsure look on her face. Then she blinked, and her features turned downward into a frown. "The truth do you speak," she said, as if acknowledging an argument that carried the superior weight of logic. "This, I had forgotten. Such is the trouble with age." She continued to shuffle along, and Reza had to take an extra large stride to regain his place next to her. "But the dream remains. And perhaps..."

"Perhaps what?" Reza chided her gently. "This, even the Empress cannot change."

Pan'ne-Sharakh looked at him sharply. "The powers of the Empress are legion, child," she told him, "and you would do well to never underestimate Her strengths. She presides over the world of the living and the dead, and is forever stronger than all the priestesses who have ever set foot upon the Way. I, an old mistress who long has served Her, know not what will come to pass for you and Esah-Zhurah, for the future and Her desires are far beyond my sight. But Her will is the river that carves the Way from the rock of Time, and it shall not be denied. It shall not."

Reza knew that the old woman spoke the truth, but what Pan'ne-Sharakh had implied was simply too much to hope for. He had lived a life of shattered dreams and hopes, but had at last found a home and a love that could carry his spirit forever, and he dared not ask any more of Fate. He consciously pushed her words from his mind. He was content with what he had.

When they reached the overlook to the valley, Pan'ne-Sharakh sat down on one of the stone benches with a heavy sigh, beckoning Reza to take a seat beside her.

"Tired am I," she said softly as she sat, her head slumped forward as she waited to catch her breath.

After a moment, she looked up at Reza. "Something I have for you." Reaching into her robe, she extracted a leather box that looked about the size and shape to hold a small dinner plate, or perhaps a shallow bowl, about as big across as Reza's hand spread wide. Handing it to Reza, she said, "Long have I worked upon this, in hopes that this day would come. Many hours have I spent in the great halls, poring through the Books of Time. I knew that which I sought existed, but I had to be sure, to find a record of it. And so I did," she finished with the impish smile that he had come to know so well.

"What is it?" Reza held the box carefully in his hands, almost afraid to know what lay within.

"Open it, child, and see."

Reza undid the clasp, which itself was ornately decorated with silver and gold, and slowly lifted the lid. "Oh, mistress..." he breathed.

Inside, surrounded by the softest black felt lining, lay a tiara the likes of which Reza had never seen. Black it was, with mystifying swirls of color that were ever-changing under the light of the moon and stars. Its edges were crowned with gold inlaid into the dark metal, and as Reza held it up, he could just see the tiny runes that made up an ancient prayer to the Empress in the Old Tongue, which he had not yet been taught. And in the crown of the tiara were two sets of the Five Stars displaying the names of Esah-Zhurah and Reza in diamonds against emerald sunbursts. He held it in shaking hands, wondering at the time Pan'ne-Sharakh must have spent in creating it, hunched down over her worktables, her dying eyes lending what aid they could to her nimble fingers. She had known this day might come. Somehow, she had known.

"A custom it was, long ago," Pan'ne-Sharakh explained quietly, her voice barely a whisper, "for the suitor of a warrior priestess to present her such a gift, in the days when suitors were to be found. Thus speak the legends of the time." She placed a gentle hand on his. "When upon your collars is inscribed the rune of the Desh-Ka, then will be the time to give it to her, and she may wear it with the Empress's blessing. It is the last work I shall do in Her name, my child, and in my heart I know it is my best. It is my gift to you and your mate."

She paused, and Reza felt her hand squeeze his tightly. "May thy Way be long and glorious, my child."

He turned just in time to catch her as she slumped forward, a soft sigh escaping from her lips. As he held her he saw that her eyes were closed, her face serene. In his heart, Reza felt a slight change in the spiritual chorus that had become a cherished part of him in these last days: the trembling of a single spirit crossing the threshold from this life into what lay beyond.

Pan'ne-Sharakh was dead.

* * *

"We are nearly there," Tesh-Dar said as she halted, pointing out the overhang that jutted from a peak high above. Atop it was perched a large structure that overlooked all but the snow-capped ridge above.

Thirty-four days had passed since they had laid Pan'ne-Sharakh's body on the funeral pyre and departed the kazha, and their travels had taken them farther than Reza had ever been on this world, or any other. The journey had been a long but uneventful one, the caravan of three warriors and their half dozen animals making its way through the great forests west of the city and into the mountains that lay beyond.

"We shall be there before sunset," the priestess told them before urging her magthep forward along the rough trail. The ancient path was barely visible, so overgrown was it with clinging vines and ferns. It suddenly occurred to Reza as he guided his beast upward that the trail had not been used in a very long time: a young warrior named Tesh-Dar had been the last to go this way before them, nearly two hundred human years before.

At last the magtheps struggled to the top, their chests laboring in grunting heaves as they sought to leach more oxygen from the thin atmosphere.

Reza, too, suddenly felt his breath stolen away, but not from the thin air. As they topped the last rise to the overhanging plateau, the temple – barely visible from the trail up the mountain – suddenly came into full view.

It was an enormous complex of structures, the largest greater in size than even the great amphitheater in the city far behind them. The buildings had been hewn of a hard green stone that had once boasted beautiful ornate carvings of warriors engaged in battle, but now were worn with age, the green faded by countless millennia of sun and storm, the carvings dulled to illegibility. The arenas had not been the simple rings lined with stone pillars that he had come to know so well; they had been elliptical domed structures of various sizes, each apparently tailored to suit a particular function, although he could not imagine what. In its day it must have been a place of indescribable magnificence. But the temple had fallen into ruin with the inexorable march of time and all it entails, and there was no longer a host to maintain it.

"Long has it been since the stone was cut from the mountains," the priestess told them in wonder and awe, "and harsh has Time been upon its ancient skin. But the temple still stands, as I pray it shall for all time. For this is where my ancestors learned the Way, and this is where it is reborn in the spirits of Her children."

With mounting anticipation, Reza and Esah-Zhurah stripped the magtheps of their harnesses and provisions for the return trip to the city, stashing them in a stone cellar that Tesh-Dar somehow opened. Once the priestess closed the enormous doors with little more than a wave of her hand, no animal would ever be able to gain entrance to sample the food they had brought to sustain them.

The priestess led them inside the only building that had been left standing intact, an enormous dome that resembled an enclosed coliseum. They entered through an ancient wooden door, thicker than Reza was tall. Yet it yielded easily to Tesh-Dar's touch, moving aside as if pulled from within.

They entered into a chamber of utter darkness.

"Wait," the priestess ordered. Reza felt more than heard her move off into the blackness. He exchanged a glance with Esah-Zhurah, who only gave the Kreelan equivalent of a shrug, her head tilting just so to one side. They waited silently.

Suddenly, a warm glow arose from ahead of them, and soon they stood bathed in a gentle light that seemed to be coming from the walls themselves.

"Come," commanded the priestess's voice from beyond the end of the corridor in which they stood. They moved forward quietly, their footsteps echoing softly. Their eyes roved the walls and ceiling, taking in the ornate beauty that lay in the carvings there, untouched by the ravages of time. This part of the temple, at least, still lived on.

They found Tesh-Dar standing atop the central dais, although this one was as much a thing of beauty as it was utilitarian, the decay that was so evident outside utterly absent within. The dome crested far above her, seemingly much higher than the building should have allowed, disappearing into darkness as deep as the night sky. Around the great arena lay thin windows that curved gracefully from near the ground toward the apex. Seven doorways, each appearing to have aged not a year since they were made, stood at equal intervals around the arena.

The priestess gestured to one of the semicircular stone pads that encircled the dais and bade them to kneel.

"This place has been the home of the Desh-Ka since before the days of Keel-Tath, before the changes that altered the destiny of our people," the priestess said in a distant voice. Her eyes were on her two acolytes, but her mind lay very far away. "This is one of the five birthplaces of what we know as the Way, built by our hands untold centuries ago, and where the first ritual bonding was performed. The temple lies in ruins, but its spirit lives still.

"I have brought you here to teach you the Old Ways, the ways which were passed on to me by my priestess, many cycles ago. Many have been my disciples since my coming to teach the Way, but I have not found any worthy of this place, save you who now kneel before me." She paused. "In accordance with tradition, I may pass on my knowledge to only one who follows me, but because you are as one in your hearts, both shall learn. So has She willed.

"But I beg that you learn well, my children," she said, her voice a soft, sad command, "for I may not pass this way again." She nodded at the corridor from which they had come. "Once more will I step through those doors into the sunlight beyond, and then will I be forever barred from returning here." She gazed upon them each in turn. "Having accepted the legacy I am about to bestow upon you, you will be the keepers of the keys to the knowledge that was born and lives in this place. Should you survive what is to come, you also shall someday have the honor of passing on what you will learn here to another. Do you have any questions of me?"

Reza and Esah-Zhurah signed no, they did not.

"Then let us begin," Tesh-Dar commanded.

* * *

In his dream – if it indeed was a dream – the three knelt in a tight circle upon the dais. To Reza's right was Tesh-Dar, her eyes closed in meditation. To his left, he found Esah-Zhurah staring at him, wide eyed. When he ran a hand across his cheek, he found not the smooth skin to which he was long accustomed, but a full beard that flowed in a brown and gray cascade to his waist. Looking more closely at his hands, he saw that they were stronger than in his youth, yet weathered and aged.

Esah-Zhurah, too, had changed. Her face and the skin along her body not covered by her armor bore more scars than he remembered. Each of them had come to know the other's body with surgical intimacy, their hands and fingers cataloging the other's skin each night in a ritual of the tresh, coming to know their bodies well since long before they had become lovers.

But the most striking thing was her hair. The braids, coiled neatly at her side, were much longer now than they had been when they had first entered the temple.

For if all was as it seemed, they had been here, in the temple, for at least ten great cycles: twenty-five years or more, as measured by the human calendar.

As he turned to the priestess, to ask her what magic this was, his skin prickled with a knowing sensation that had been cultivated in him for many years, but that suddenly seemed so much more powerful than he had ever known. It was a sense of premonition and understanding that existed independent of its subject, as if he were able to grasp the plot of a book without ever actually having read it. The sensation told him that they were not alone. In the darkness that fell like a velvet curtain just beyond the dais, Reza could see shadows of regular outline. Occasional glimmers of gold and platinum and ruby caught his eye, and he instantly recognized the pendants that hung from around the necks of the phantoms arrayed beyond the glowing amber light thrown down upon the dais from high above. As he became more accustomed to them, they became more real, their existence more of substance than imagination. In only a few moments, he saw them – all of them – clearly in his mind, even while his eyes were still blind in the darkness. Thousands, tens of thousands of them were gathered around, kneeling, waiting. Reza instinctively understood what – whom – he was seeing. These were the spirits of the Ancient Ones who had once bound themselves in blood to this place, those who wore the peculiar rune that adorned Tesh-Dar's collar, and who had died fulfilling Her will on the long journey that was the Way of the Empire.

"It is time, my children," Tesh-Dar whispered.

As if with a will of their own, Reza's hands extended outward, palms up, to Tesh-Dar.

Esah-Zhurah did the same, a look of serene anticipation on her face. Like Reza, she was aware that much time had passed in what seemed like the blink of an eye. But she also knew that she was ready, although for what, she did not quite remember, nor did she care to try. It had been a dream time, when great secrets had been revealed, and many Challenges fought, but which the conscious mind was not yet prepared to recall. It would take time to learn, she knew. Time to understand, to become something new...

Tesh-Dar held aloft a knife whose blade bore the markings of the First Empress in the Old Tongue. Reza's eyes widened at the knowledge that he understood what the symbols meant: during the years they seemed to have lost, he had been taught that arcane but revered language, and could only guess at what other knowledge now lay hidden in his mind.

"In the name of The One Who first blessed us," Tesh-Dar was saying, "and All Who have come after, do we accept Thee," Tesh-Dar intoned in the Old Tongue, its lilt and measure pleasing to Reza's ears. She drew the knife across each of Reza's palms, then Esah-Zhurah's. Finally, she forced the blade into her own palms before placing the knife into a waiting hand that had appeared from the darkness, and that vanished as mysteriously as it had come.

The three of them joined hands, and Reza felt an electric surge flow through him, a fierce tingling sensation – much like what he had experienced with Esah-Zhurah when they had shared blood, but so much stronger – pulsing up his arms in fiery waves.

As he watched Tesh-Dar's face, he felt the dais tremble, and suddenly its center seemed to drop away to infinity, leaving behind a circular abyss that stared at them like a sightless eye. The trembling continued, and suddenly a circular pillar began to rise from the abyss before him, within the triangle formed by their outstretched arms and joined hands. Slowly, as if its weight was an enormous burden for whatever force propelled it, the pillar arose from the pit, stopping as it reached the level of Reza's eyes. Beneath them, the trembling ceased.

The tingling in Reza's arms had become almost painful now, as if jolts of energy were striking his nerves like tiny, ferocious needles. Reza looked at Esah-Zhurah, wondering if it was having the same effect upon her.

But Esah-Zhurah's attention was focused on something far above, and Reza followed her openmouthed stare toward the dome's dark ceiling. A pinpoint of electric blue fire was hurtling down at them like a comet, and Reza knew that it was coming from much farther away than the ancient dome's ceiling could have allowed. He suddenly felt heat upon his face, and knew that the shooting star was about to strike. He tried to cover his face with his hands, but they were beyond his control, locked in a clasp of bonding that was unbreakable by any mere physical force. As the heat became unbearable, and his ears were about to burst from the hellish roaring, Reza opened his mouth to scream–

There it sat, cupped by the precisely made hollow in the top of the extended pillar. Reza stared at the glowing gem, the scream caught in his throat. Slightly larger than his own head, it was shaped roughly like a teardrop, and glowed like a blue flame. Gradually, he became aware of Esah-Zhurah and the priestess. The three of them still held hands. The circle had not been broken.

"In Her light are all things purified, are all things made new," the priestess said, looking first at Reza, then Esah-Zhurah. "And so shall it be this day, my children." She looked upward, and Reza saw that there was now a circular opening in the dome above them, and that streaks of sunlight pierced the darkness of the great arena to form a circle of light just to one side of the dais. "When the light of Her sun strikes the Crystal of Souls, we shall be changed forever. Much pain shall you bear, for what cleanses best of all is fire, and Her fire shall blaze within every cell of your body. Death may come; there is no guarantee of life. But if life finds you afterward, forever changed shall you be in body and soul, crafted to Her will. The strength of ten and talons of ebony did I inherit many cycles ago, when I endured the pain of the crystal. The wonders of The Change are impossible to predict, but I wish no lesser gifts for you, my children. For when you again awaken, you shall be the standard-bearers of the Desh-Ka, and it shall be my honor to teach and serve you for the remainder of my days." She looked at the rapidly advancing pool of light, focused by the great dome as if it was a magnifying glass, now just touching the crystal's sparkling facets. "Soon, now, the Crystal of Souls shall shine. Do not avert your eyes from its fire, do not cry out in pain from the touch of its light, or death will take you swiftly. For in its light lies Her light. In its fire lies Her touch. So has it ever been, so shall it always be. In Her name, let it be so."

The sunlight rapidly swept over the dais toward the crystal. Reza watched, fascinated, as the light seemed to be drawn into the enormous gem; the pool of light that had existed only a moment ago beside the dais had now become a cone focused precisely on the crystal. The hair on the nape of his neck stood to attention, and he felt as if he were standing on a spot about to be struck by lightning. The electric pulses through his joined palms were suddenly overshadowed by a charge that seemed ready to strike his entire body.

And then the crystal exploded with a light that first consumed the pillar on which it stood, a blazing cyan cone that slowly swept upward and outward toward the three joined warriors surrounding it, filling the air with the smell of scorched stone and ozone.

Reza watched as the blue flame crept toward him, eating up the stone floor that separated the light from his knees. The desire to flee was tremendous, but one look into Esah-Zhurah's eyes was all he needed to redouble his courage. She needed him, needed his courage in addition to her own. They needed each other. Forcing himself to be strong, he gripped her hand tighter and held his eyes steadily on the advancing fan of light.

When it touched him, it was all he could do to keep from screaming. Never had he felt such searing agony as when the light crept upon his knees. He felt as if every cell in the flesh touched by it was exploding into flame. Tears flooded from his eyes, but his mouth remained clamped shut, his voice still. Beside him, Esah-Zhurah and Tesh-Dar also fought against writhing in the pain that was enveloping them, and all three of them used all the control they had ever mastered to keep their eyes upon the blazing crystal.

Faster and faster did the light sweep upward over their bodies, consuming them with the agony of burning flesh. Reza felt himself toppling over the edge of sanity, the light having consumed his body below his neck like a ravenous predator. As his bulging eyes fixed one last time upon the crystal, his last conscious effort to follow Tesh-Dar's command, the flame swept over them, and the world disappeared in an explosion of cyan.

* * *

Somewhere, deep in the infinite labyrinth of neurons, an electrochemical impulse burst across the chasm that was the synapse. The command instruction that it evoked followed a journey that would take it far from its birthplace. Slowly, very slowly, more synapses began to fire, discharging their energy in the infinite darkness of the surrounding tissue, carrying their messages into the unknown wilderness.

Far away, after traveling a lifetime, the first impulse was received by a receptor that decoded the messenger's instruction and issued a command of its own. Nearby, a muscle fiber twitched feverishly, contracting as hard as it could, the only way it understood to respond to the nerve's command.

More nerves in the area received the frenzied, sporadic impulses from the Command Center, immediately issuing their own instructions to their subordinate muscle fibers. Hundreds, then thousands, then tens of thousands of the tiny fibers were called to action by the desperate rain of impulses from the Command Center, ordering the muscles around them to contract... *contract...*

A finger twitched. The effort had been Herculean, temporarily exhausting many fibers, damaging a few. But the Command Center was not content with such sacrifices; it demanded more. The darkest recesses of the entity that controlled all within its Universe were slowly alighting. A cascade of impulses exploded along the neural pathways that led away to its lieutenants, associates in life whom it controlled and brought to its will, but who in turn kept it alive in a miraculous symbiosis. Millions upon millions of messages were encoded and dispatched, received and decoded. Slowly did the Command Center come to grips with the status of its domain, and as new information was received, more messengers were sent forth: more commands, more demands for information. The Command Center was not the least bit hesitant to use the authority granted it by nature, and it had an insatiable appetite for information.

Over and over was the cycle repeated, and gradually, within the lifetimes of only a few million of the cells under its unquestioned authority, the Command Center was satisfied that all was prepared for the next step on its programmatic cycle. Under a barrage of impulses, the great gathering of special muscle fibers that was the heart contracted, then released. Another barrage of impulses was rewarded with a second beat, then a third. As the heart warmed to its work, the Command Center allocated the supervision of this most vital of tasks to a subaltern within itself. Thus, it freed the remainder of its resources to concentrate on reviving the many other organs of The Body.

It would be some time yet before the Command Center would begin to apportion effort to analyze the unaccustomed condition from which it had recently emerged. In its haste to make The Body serviceable again, it did not notice, nor pause to contemplate, the changes that had taken place within the living quilt of its domain.

In the meantime, Reza began to breathe.

* * *

"Reza."

He blinked, then opened his eyes fully. Tesh-Dar's face was close to his, her hands on his shoulders.

"Yes, priestess," he murmured. His face tingled, the muscles tight as if he had been forced to hold a smile for several hours on end. The rest of his body was the same, tingling and burning at the same time, his nerves feeling as if someone had tried to electrocute him. And had very nearly succeeded.

Looking up at Tesh-Dar, he saw the traces of a similar level of discomfort. Her eyes, normally clear and sharp as silver-flecked diamonds, wore a glassy cast that made them look almost hazy, slightly opaque.

"Esah-Zhurah?" he asked, allowing Tesh-Dar to help him to his knees. Neither his balance nor hers would allow them to stand up all the way.

"I do not know," she breathed, winded from the effort. Her hands trembled as they touched him. Together, they crawled around the pillar, empty now of the strange blue crystal, to find Esah-Zhurah sprawled upon the far side of the dais.

"Esah-Zhurah?" Reza called her name several times with mounting urgency as he cradled her head in his hands. He felt behind her ear for a pulse, but his own fingers betrayed him: his sense of touch was still virtually useless. He fumbled with her breastplate, trying to get it off so he could listen to her heart. His fingers turned black with the carbon of the scorched metal and burned leatherite, both so resilient that only the heat of white-hot coals could affect them. Out of frustration he simply tore the plate from its weakened bindings, brute strength prevailing where simple procedure had failed. He brushed the remnants of the undergarment – like the armor, burned to ashes – to find her skin unmarred, pristine, without a single scar of the many combats she had fought. Kneeling down, he put his ear to her breast and listened intently. After a terrifying moment of silence, he was granted with a slow *lub-dub*. Then another. And another. "Her heart beats," he whispered. And as he did, her chest rose gently as her lungs pulled in a shallow draught of air. "She is alive."

Only then did he notice what had become of the collar she wore. In its center, over her throat, was affixed one of the sparkling eyestones they had taken from the genoth they had killed. The scale had been meticulously polished and shaped into a precise oval. And on its face was carved the ancient rune of the Desh-Ka. He felt his own throat, and his numbed fingers told him enough to know that he wore the stone's companion.

"Priestess," he murmured, "how is this possible?"

But Tesh-Dar did not hear him. She was holding one of Esah-Zhurah's hands in hers, staring at it with a look of awe.

"What is it?" Reza asked, suddenly worried that something was not right.

"Her talons," Tesh-Dar whispered, turning Esah-Zhurah's hand so that Reza could better see it in the soft light that now permeated the great dome like a gentle mist from the sea. Instead of gleaming silver, her talons now shone a fiery red, a bright crimson the color of oxygenated blood.

"Is there something wrong with them?" he asked worriedly. "Are there not talons only of silver and of black?"

"Now, in these times, this is so," she answered cryptically. "But long ago..."

Tesh-Dar did not have time to finish her answer before Esah-Zhurah's lips moved and she called out in a weak, strangled voice, "Reza."

"I am here," he told her, running his hand over her forehead to comfort her.

Beside him, Tesh-Dar reluctantly released Esah-Zhurah's hand. But the image of the crimson talons stayed in her mind. Only one such aberration had been known throughout the Empire's meticulously recorded history, and the significance of their emergence in Esah-Zhurah from The Change could hardly be coincidence. As she turned her attention to her adopted daughter, her mind was cast into a whirlwind of possibilities.

And then Esah-Zhurah opened her eyes. They wandered aimlessly for a moment before fixing on Reza's shocked face. "What... what is it?" she whispered weakly. "At what are you staring?"

"Your eyes, child," Tesh-Dar answered for him, her voice filled with awed wonder. "They are green, now. Green as your mate's. Another gift of The Change."

Esah-Zhurah brought a hand to her face, as if her fingertips could themselves see color, could take the measure of what the others saw in her eyes. Then she reached out to Reza, who took her hand gently and held it to his lips.

"It is true," he told her, amazed at how brilliant the jade green of her irises was against the cobalt blue of her skin, even as he marveled at the fact that the beard he had grown in his dream – or had it been real? – was now gone.

"And what of me?" Reza asked, curious that there seemed to be no outward differences such as his mate's. "I assume I do not look different, nor do I feel changed in any way."

"The Change is often very subtle," the priestess told him, leaning back against the pillar to rest. The crystal's flame had left her with little strength, and she knew that her days of glory on the field of battle were over. She had given up much of what she was to her inheritors, and would never again tap the Herculean strength and most of her ancient powers that she had accepted from her own priestess; these powers were now in the custody of the two young warriors before her. "The changes in the body are sometimes obvious, sometimes not. Only time will tell of that. But the greatest changes lie within your souls and minds, yet shrouded in unknowing. It will be my duty from this day on to teach you both of your inheritance, to use it wisely and well. This I shall do until the end of my days, in my last service to Her. And someday, you will do the same for another, that the ways of the Desh-Ka may continue unbroken."

* * *

Reza lay awake, thinking. Hours uncounted, unnoticed, had passed since the crystal had worked its strange miracle upon them. Shortly after Esah-Zhurah had revived, the priestess had fallen into a deep, exhausted sleep. Her two adopted children worried over her for some time, concerned that all might not be well. But the priestess breathed steadily, if ever so slowly, and they could sense that her blood still sang, though not as strongly as before. The Change had greatly weakened her, but she had many cycles yet to live.

After making sure she was well, they turned their attention to one another. Quietly, so as not to awaken the priestess, they made love, the lingering numbness in their bodies from the crystal's fire fleeing before the heat of passion that set their flesh aflame yet again. The need to be quiet only served to heighten their passion, and Esah-Zhurah's involuntary cries were spent muffled against Reza's chest.

Some hours later, Reza lay awake as Esah-Zhurah slept with her back cradled against his chest. He pulled her slightly closer to him, and she moaned softly in her sleep. He wondered at all that had transpired since they had entered the dome. He had remembered the image of his great beard and their outgrown hair, signs that many years had passed. He and Esah-Zhurah had discussed this as the priestess slept, but there had only been one way to be sure. The two of them had found the door through which they had entered the temple. It yielded easily to their touch. In the world beyond the doorway they found that only an hour or so had passed from the time of their arrival. The magtheps grazed in the same spot in which they had been left, their grazing trail easily gauged. The sun's glow had given way to a brilliant twilight that colored the great mountains with violet and orange rivers. Above, the Empress Moon had just risen, about to take its rightful place among the Five Stars.

Now, lying next to Esah-Zhurah, he thought again of the Empress Moon as it rose above the mountains and of the priestess's last words before she had fallen silent with sleep.

"Tomorrow," she had said, "we must go before the Empress. You have both come of age as warriors, and accepted the ways of the Desh-Ka. It is now time for you to hear Her will, and to seek the next step of your Way."

Listening in wonder to the vast chorus of voices that now sang within him, voices that he now understood, Reza waited for the dawn.

* * *

The next day passed in a whirlwind of activity. When they made their way out of the temple, a shuttle was already waiting for them, perched precariously on the cliff like a peregrine clutching to a limb. Reza had been frightened at first, for he had not seen such advanced technology since his boyhood, and the memories he had of such things were not pleasant ones. But the comfort of Esah-Zhurah's guiding hand overrode his fears, and in but a few minutes they found themselves within the palace. There they were fed and their scorched armor replaced before they were shown to the Empress.

"The Empress would see you now," a warrior announced to Tesh-Dar, bowing deeply as she did so.

It was time.

The trio followed the warrior to where the Empress waited, standing among the very trees and flowers where she and Tesh-Dar had once discussed Reza's fate. They knelt in greeting and rendered the salute of respect to their sovereign.

Acknowledging their presence with Her gaze, She first spoke to Reza.

"*My son,*" She said softly. "My son. So wondrous a feeling is it to speak those words, for they have not passed the lips of an Empress for many, many thousands of generations. Even though you were born of an alien race, My blood flows in your veins as through those of the children of My body, and I hear your song in My heart.

"And you, child," She said, turning to Esah-Zhurah. "Comely are the changes that have been worked upon you by the first of the Seven Crystals, the most holy relic of the Way. The eyes of your mate are now yours, as are the claws of crimson for which we have waited many, many cycles to see."

"My Empress," Esah-Zhurah said, bowing her head to her chest, "I do not understand. The priestess would not speak of it; I can only wonder at your meaning."

"I believe you are the one to fulfill The Prophecy, My child," the Empress said gently. "I believe that there shall come a day when the collar that I now wear shall be yours. And with your ascent to the throne, so too shall return the spirit and power of the First Empress, so long lost to us. Its fulfillment would end the curse that has befallen us these many cycles and bring back the spiritual power of the First Empress, bring Her back from the darkness to which Her soul fled in anguish and rage so long ago."

"But, my Empress," Esah-Zhurah murmured, "I was not born of the white mane, nor of the ebony claw. How can I ascend to the throne?"

The Empress ran a hand through Esah-Zhurah's hair. "The Change has deceived you, child," She said. "Already can be seen the white of the snows of Te'ar-Shelath in the roots of your hair. And the silver of your claws is gone, replaced by the crimson that belonged to Keel-Tath alone, for as long as the Way has been. Someday, your voice shall ring with Her wisdom and power, and the spirits that now dwell in My soul shall serve you.

"But there are many cycles ahead of you before you set aside your name and don this robe and the collar now about My neck. Your generation is graced with a race of worthy opponents, and combat and conquest are our heritage. To them you shall go to seek your fortune and show your honor, and from the priestess shall you learn the ways of the Desh-Ka, that their way of life and knowledge are preserved."

Reza suddenly had the sensation that the ground beneath his feet had dropped away, leaving him spinning downward into a dark, bottomless chasm.

"My Empress," he said slowly, already knowing from the chorus that was now clamoring in his heart what Her answer must be, "can we not show our love to You among the unknowns of the frontier?"

The Empress looked at him curiously, and a frown of concern suddenly began to etch its way across Her face. "You wear the trappings of warriors, not the robes of the clawless ones who explore the frontiers. To fight is your calling, and fight you will. I cannot allow it to be otherwise." She paused for a moment. "This is My will, warrior priest."

Tesh-Dar and Esah-Zhurah were staring at him, an identical look of confusion on their faces as their own hearts registered this unexpected turn of events.

"Reza," Esah-Zhurah said softly, "what is wrong? I know you dreamt of going to the frontiers, but..." She fell silent at the agonized expression on his face.

To Reza, the world had suddenly changed. Images from the past, pale alien faces whose names he could no longer remember, whose voices he could no longer understand, loomed large in his mind. And then alien words, spoken by his own tongue, echoed not in that forgotten language, but as a pure thought: *I will not fight against my own kind.*

The Empress immediately sensed the cause of his hesitancy. "You must choose, My son," She told him, Her own heart aching at the answer She knew would come from his lips. "To stay with us, with Esah-Zhurah, you must fight. Else you must return to the people from whom you were born. There can be no in-between, no compromise."

"Reza," Esah-Zhurah said, her voice filled with desperation as she put her hand upon his shoulder. From him more than any other could she feel and sense the melody of the Bloodsong. His soul was entwined with hers, now, and the mournful dirge in his heart terrified her. "Do not leave me."

Reza began to shudder. The sudden rage he felt at fate, the anguish of making the decision he knew had to be, the fear of what lay ahead, all collided within his mind. His fists clenched so hard that the talons of his gauntlets cut through to his palms, and blood began to weep onto the floor. With all his heart did he wish to remain here; he loved and honored the Empress and the people to which he now belonged. But to destroy those with whom he shared a common heritage – all of humanity – would be to break the most sacred oath he had ever made, and would taint his honor in the eyes of all who ever looked upon him. There could only be one answer.

"Then I must leave, my Empress," he choked. He wanted to scream. He wanted to die.

Esah-Zhurah and Tesh-Dar were silent, stunned. They could only stare at him, the black trails of mourning marks already making their way down their faces like ashen tears.

"Reza..." Esah-Zhurah whispered, her face contorted with pain and disbelief.

"You choose the course of honor, My son," the Empress said sadly. "Deeply does it grieve Me that this has come to pass. This, I did not foresee. But if you cannot obey My will, it must be so."

"But," Tesh-Dar said, fighting through the pain that was tearing at her heart, "what of The Prophecy? What shall become of us?"

"I know not, priestess," the Empress answered quietly, the ageless spirit that dwelled within Her wracked with confusion and gloom. She looked at Esah-Zhurah. "Perhaps it is only that his role is complete, that he has given us what he had to give. Or perhaps it is not yet time and we were wrong in our judgments of what we have seen. But the Way shall not be denied."

The Empress took a small ebony box from its place on a nearby pedestal. "I was going to give you this parcel of memories from your past as a gift, that you might cherish them before they found their way into the Books of Time. Now I give it to you in hopes that the things within shall ease the burden of your return to the blood of your birth." She handed him the box.

Inside, Reza found a folded sheet of paper: the letter of introduction an old man had once written for Reza to get into the Marine Academy. On top of it lay a blackened crucifix on a chain that had once been bright silver, a token of affection from a girl he had once loved, but whose name and face were long lost among his memories. They were the most precious things he had possessed in his lifetime as a human, and their appearance now brought a sob from his throat as hot tears of bitter anguish fell from his eyes. He closed the box with shaking hands.

"Thank you, my Empress," he whispered.

The Empress regarded him with great sadness in Her eyes, mourning marks touching Her face, casting a shadow upon Her soul. She wished with all the spirits that dwelled within Her that She would not have to banish him from the Empire, but there was no alternative, and it could not wait. With his decision to return from whence he came, so did he lose everything She ever could have offered him. She closed Her eyes, and after a moment visualized a place where he might find his Way among those who were beyond Her light, Her love. Because so now, was he.

"When must I go?" he asked.

"This moment, My son," the Empress replied. "I cannot tolerate division among the spirit of My people, Reza." She held out Her hand to him. In it were two black rings. "These shall you place around the first of your braids, that which is woven as the Covenant of the Afterlife. One ring shall remain with you for as long as you live, to bind your spirit to you. The other shall bind the covenant after your knife does its work. When you are gone, this will be all that shall remain of your body and spirit among us, and shall be Esah-Zhurah's until the day she dies." She looked at Reza with eyes that would have wept had they been able. "If you cannot do My will, My son, I cannot shed My light upon your soul. When the knife makes its cut, no longer will you feel the Bloodsong of the peers. No longer will you feel My love. Your memory shall live on forever in the Books of Time, for you have done no dishonor. But you will be alone from this day forward, and when you die, your spirit will fall into Darkness for all Eternity."

She stood before him for a moment, feeling the pain that welled from his heart like lava flung from a volcano. She loved him so much, but there was nothing She could do. If he could not be obedient to the Way of the Empire, the Empire could not give him its love in return. It was a relationship as simple as it was – in this case – tragic, and She offered him the only comfort She could.

She put Her hands on his shoulders. "I beg that you remember this," She whispered. "You are of My blood, the blood of an Empress. And although you have chosen a Way that will take you to be among our enemies, you do so with honor. And thus shall you forever be remembered in the Books of Time. From this day onward you shall never again feel My love, but know that I do love you, and I pray that glory shall forever follow in your footsteps. Farewell, my son, and may thy Way be long and glorious."

At last turning away, the Empress made her way into the garden, her white hair and robes trailing behind her like wisps of cloud.

The three of them stood as the Empress departed, but remained silent for what seemed an eternity.

"I must go." Reza said finally, looking at Esah-Zhurah, then at Tesh-Dar. Their faces were black in mourning, and he could feel the hot sting of tears on his own face. They seemed to be ghosts from a swiftly fading dream. He felt so empty, so alone.

The priestess stepped forward and grasped him by the forearms, the traditional way of parting among warriors. After a long moment, she let go, then handed him the short sword she had worn at her side since long before he was born. The blade bore the names of all who had carried the weapon, written in the Old Tongue that only now, after The Change, could he understand. There were very few spaces left. His, he saw with a painful surge of pride, was the last inscription.

"I am old and my Way grows short," she told him, her voice sounding fragile, ancient to his ears. "This I would leave to you. It has been among the Desh-Ka for over a thousand generations. Now, it is yours. You wear the rune of our order, now also do you bear a weapon in its name." Her eyes were soft and vulnerable. He had never seen her this way, and he suspected that few others ever had. "Good-bye, my beloved son," she whispered. "Go in Her name. May thy Way be long and glorious."

"Farewell, Mother," he said softly. "I love you." He saluted her, bowing his head to his priestess. She bowed her head in response, as befitted her rank, resisting the impulse to take him in her arms, to hold him as if he were but a young child. Then she stood back, her head bowed, waiting for what must come. She looked and felt old, defeated, and it broke Reza's heart to see her so.

Then he turned his attention to Esah-Zhurah, who stood quietly by his side, as fragile as a mirage. He reached out to touch her, suddenly afraid that she would simply vanish and that he would wake up, his entire life having been spent in a dream. But her flesh was firm under his hand. He dropped his gauntlets onto the ground at his feet, wanting nothing so much as to touch her one last time. She did the same, and he saw her hands: they were black with the mourning marks, so great was her pain.

He could stand it no longer. He began to cry as he pulled her to him, crushing her against his chest. She kissed his neck, her fangs streaking the skin. Her talons dug furrows into the metal of his armor as she clung to him.

"Please stay," she whispered, and he felt the echo of the pain in her heart in his own.

"Do not ask me again," he pleaded. "I beg of you. For we both know that I cannot. I must not."

"How shall I live without you?" she whispered, her arms tight around his neck. "My heart shall die when you are gone."

He pulled her away just far enough to see her face. Her green eyes were so bright they seemed to glow. "You must live," he told her, the desperation plain in his voice. "Live for me. All that sustains me even now is the hope that someday, somehow, I shall see your face again. You must believe that it will be so, that someday our Way shall be one again." She nodded her head, but her eyes and the keening in her blood betrayed the hopelessness that dwelled in her soul. He held her to him again, and kissed her softly, running his hands through her hair one last time.

"I have one last gift for you," he whispered into her ear. Reaching into the satchel at his feet, the leather bag that contained all his worldly possessions, he withdrew the box in which lay the bejeweled tiara. Extracting it carefully with his shaking hands, he held it up for her to see. "This was Pan'ne-Sharakh's last gift to us," he told her, "a token of my faith in courtship of a warrior priestess. I was going to give it to you when we met with the Empress, but..." He could not finish. Instead, he carefully placed it on her head, fitting the crown to the woman he would love unto death.

Even old and blind, Pan'ne-Sharakh had divined in metal and minerals a kind of beauty that was the stuff of dreams, beyond the reach of mortals such as himself. The tiara seemed to become a part of her, and he wanted to weep at how beautiful she looked with it on, but his tears were finished. Only pain and the uncertainty of what the future would bring remained. "Priestess of the Desh-Ka," he whispered, "forever shall my heart be yours."

They embraced a final time. Then she pushed herself away. Her eyes had clouded over, becoming hard as she fought to be strong. But he could see that her resolve was brittle, frail. They gripped each other by the arms as warriors. Then it was time for her to play out the last act of his departure from the Empire. Trembling, she separated out the first braid of his hair. Sliding the two black rings down the braid toward his scalp, she tightened them like a tourniquet only a finger's length from the roots. She took the knife that had once belonged to the reigning Empress and put the blade's edge between the rings. With her own hand trembling, she guided Reza's palm to the knife's bejeweled handle. "This," she said, her voice trembling, "is my gift to you, my love."

Reza took a deep breath. His eyes were closed, and his heart stopped. He did not know what to expect. "It is Her will."

Esah-Zhurah closed her eyes.

Reza gritted his teeth, and with a swift cut, the long braid came away, falling to the ground.

"Reza!" Esah-Zhurah screamed as pain ripped into her heart, the voice of Reza's spirit suddenly having been silenced. "No," she whispered. "It cannot be. It cannot." His Bloodsong was gone. The melody that thrilled her in her dreams and when they touched, that gave her strength when she fought, was no more. She wanted more than anything simply to plunge a knife into her breast. But she could not deny Her will. Even her love for Reza could not prevent her from obeying the call of the Empress.

She felt something being pressed into her trembling hands. "This is yours, my child," Tesh-Dar said shakily, as if from a thousand leagues away.

Esah-Zhurah knew what it was. Tenderly, she took the long braid of Reza's fine brown hair into her hands and pressed it to her face, taking in the scent and touch that she would never again feel. Then she opened her eyes to look upon him once more before he was taken away.

But there was nothing for her to see but the garden and Tesh-Dar's grieving form. Except for the bent blades of grass upon which he had been kneeling, there was no sign of him.

Reza was gone.

IF YOU ENJOYED EMPIRE...

The story of Reza and Esah-Zhurah is continued with *In Her Name: Confederation*, which picks up the story with Reza's return to the Confederation. You also have the option of getting the "omnibus edition," which contains the entire first trilogy (*Empire*, *Confederation*, and *Final Battle*).

To give you a taste of what's to come, here's the first chapter from *Confederation* - enjoy!

* * *

"It's going to be light soon."

The statement was more than simple fact. Coming from the young Marine corporal, whose left leg ended halfway down his thigh, the bloody stump capped with crude bandages that now reeked of gangrene, the words were a prophecy of doom. Like many of the others clustered around him, broken and beaten, he was beyond fear. He had spent most of the previous night taken with fever, whispering or crying for the wife he would never see again, the daughter he had never seen beyond the image of the hologram he held clutched to his lacerated chest. There were dozens more just like him crammed into the stone church, waiting for morning. Waiting to die. "They'll be coming."

"Rest easy, my son," Father Hernandez soothed, kneeling down to give the man a drink of water from the clay pitcher he carried. "Conserve your strength. The Lord shall protect and provide for us. You are safe here."

"Bullshit."

Hernandez turned to find Lieutenant Jodi Ellen Mackenzie, Confederation Navy, glaring at him from where she kneeled next to a fallen Marine officer. Her foul mouth concealed a heart of gold and a mountain of determination, both to survive and to keep the people who depended on her – now including these Marines – alive. Momentarily turning her attention from Hernandez, Mackenzie closed Colonel Moreau's eyes with a gentle brush of her hand.

Another life taken in vain, Hernandez thought sadly. How many horrors had he witnessed these past, what, weeks? Months? And how many were yet to come? But he refused to relent in his undying passion that his way, the way of the Church into which he had been born and raised, and finally had come to lead, was the way of righteousness.

"Please, lieutenant," he asked as one of the parish's monks made his way to the side of the dead Marine colonel to mutter the last rites over her cooling body, "do not blaspheme in my church." He had said the very same thing to her countless times, but each time he convinced himself that it was the first and only transgression, and that she would eventually give in to his gentle reason. He was not, nor had he ever become, angry with her, for he was a man of great if not quite infinite patience and gentleness. He looked upon those two traits and his belief in God as the trinity that defined and guided his life. They had served him and his small rural parish well for many years, through much adversity and hardship. He had no intention of abandoning those tenets now, in the face of this unusual woman or the great Enemy, the demons, that had come from the skies. "Please," he said again.

Mackenzie rolled her eyes tiredly and shrugged. "Sure, Father," she said in a less than respectful tone. "Let's see, what is it you guys say? Forgive me, Father, for I have sinned?" She came to stand next to him, the light from the candle in his hand flickering against her face like a trapped butterfly. "The only sin that I've seen is you and all your people sitting around on your butts while these poor bastards," she jabbed a finger at one of the rows of wounded that now populated the church, "throw their gonads in the grinder for you." She saw him glance at Colonel Moreau's body, now covered with a shroud of rough burlap. "She can't help you anymore, priest," Mackenzie muttered, more to herself than for his benefit. Moreau had been as sympathetic to Hernandez's beliefs as much as Jodi was not. "I guess I'm in charge of this butcher shop now." She closed her eyes and shook her head. "Jesus."

Hernandez regarded her for a moment, taken not so much by the callousness of her words but by her appearance. Even exhausted, coated with grime and smelling of weeks-old sweat (water conservation and Kreelan attacks having rendered bathing an obsolete luxury), she was more than beautiful. Although Father Hernandez and the other dozen monks who tended to the parishioners of Saint Mary's of Rutan had taken the vows of celibacy, he could not deny the effect she had on him and, he suspected, on more than one of the monks under his charge. Even for a man of sixty-five, aged to seventy or eighty by a rough life on a world not known for its kindness, she was a temptation for the imagination, if not for the flesh. Hernandez did not consider himself a scholar, but he had read many of the great literary works of ancient times, some even in the original Latin and

Greek, and he knew that Helen of Troy could have been no more radiant in her appearance. He could hardly intuit the heritage that gave her the black silken hair and coffee skin from which her ice blue eyes blazed. In his mind he saw the bloodlines of a Nubian queen merged with that of a fierce Norseman. Perhaps such was the case, the result of some unlikely but divine rendezvous somewhere on the ancient seas of Terra.

"You're staring, father," she said with a tired sigh. It was always the same, she thought. Ever since she was ten and about to bloom into the woman she someday would become, she had been the object of unwanted interest from men. The boys in her classes, sometimes the teachers; countless smiling faces had flooded by over the years, remaining as leering gargoyles in her memory. The only man she had ever truly loved had been her father, who had been immune to her unintentional power: he was blind from birth, beyond even the hope of reconstructive surgery. Jodi was sure that the fate that had placed this curse on him had been a blessing in disguise for her and for their relationship. He had never seen her beauty beyond what the loving touch of his fingers upon her face could reveal, and so he had never felt the craving or lust that her appearance seemed to inspire in so many others. He had always been wonderful to her, and there were no words to describe her love for him.

Jodi and her mother had been equally close, and with her Jodi had shared her feelings, her apprehensions, as she grew. But while her mother could well understand Jodi's feelings, she had never been able to truly grasp the depth of her daughter's concerns, and in the honesty they had always shared, she had never claimed to. Arlene Mackenzie was a beautiful woman in her own right, but she knew quite well that Jodi was several orders of magnitude higher on whatever primal scale was used to judge subjective beauty. Jodi was only thankful that her mother had never been jealous of the power her daughter could wield over others if she had ever chosen to, which she never had. Jodi had always been very close to her parents, and she reluctantly admitted to herself that right now she, Jodi Mackenzie, veteran fighter pilot of the Black Widow Squadron, missed them terribly. The priest's appraising stare only made her miss them more.

"What's the matter, father?" she said finally, her skin prickling with anger. "Did you get tired of popping your altar boys?"

Red-faced, Hernandez averted his gaze. A nearby monk glanced in their direction, a comic look of shock on his face. The Marines lying on the floor beside them were in no condition to notice their exchange.

"Please," Hernandez said quietly, his voice choked with shame, "forgive my trespass. I cannot deny a certain weakness for your beauty, foolish old man that I am. That is an often unavoidable pitfall of the flesh of which we are all made, and even a hearty pursuit of God's Truth cannot always prevent the serpent from striking. But I assure you," he went on, finally returning her angry gaze, "that the vows I took when a very young man have been faithfully kept, and will remain unbroken for as long as I live." Hernandez offered a tentative smile. "As beautiful as you are, I don't feel in need of a cold shower."

Jodi's anger dissipated at the old joke that sometimes was not so funny for those in Hernandez's position. More important, she appreciated the priest's guts for admitting his weakness with such sincerity. That, she thought, was something rare on the outback colony worlds, where men were still men and women were still cattle.

"Maybe you don't," she told him, her mouth calling forth a tired but sincere smile of forgiveness, simultaneously wrinkling her nose in a mockery of the body odor they all shared, "but I could sure as hell use one."

Visibly relieved and letting her latest blasphemy pass unnoticed, Hernandez took the opportunity to change the subject. "Now that you are in command," he asked seriously, "what do you intend to do?"

"That's a good question," she said quietly, turning the issue over in her mind like a stringy chunk of beef on a spit, a tough morsel to chew on, but all that was available. She looked around, surveying the dark stone cathedral that had been her unexpected garrison and home for nearly three weeks. Shot down by Kreelan ground fire while supporting the Marine combat regiment that had been dispatched to Rutan, she had bailed out of her stricken fighter a few kilometers from the village of the same name, and that was where she had been stranded ever since. She had never worried about being shot at while floating down on the parachute, watching as her fighter obliterated itself against a cliff face five kilometers away, because in all the years of the war, the Kreelans had never attacked anyone who had bailed out. At least, that is, until the unlucky individual reached the ground.

In Jodi's case, friendly troops happened to reach her first, but that was the beginning and the end of her good fortune. As she was drifting toward the black-green forest in which Rutan was nestled, the Hood, her squadron's home carrier, and her escorts were taking a beating at the hands of two Kreelan heavy cruisers that a few days earlier had landed an enemy force to clean out the human settlement. After destroying her tormentors in a running fight that had lasted nearly three days, Hood had informed the regimental commander, Colonel Moreau, that the ship would be unable to resume station over Rutan: her battle damage required immediate withdrawal to the nearest port and a drydock. The captain expressed his sincere regrets to Moreau, but he could not face another engagement with any hope of his ship and her escorts surviving. There were no other Kreelan ships in the area, and Kreelan forces on the planet were judged to be roughly even to what the regiment could field, plus whatever help the Territorial Army could provide. On paper, at least, it looked to be a fair fight.

But neither Hood's captain, nor the Marines who had come to defend the planet had counted on a colony made up entirely of pacifists. Normally, the two thousand-strong Marine regiment would have been able to count on support from the local Territorial Army command that was supposed to be established on every human-settled world in the Confederation. In the case of Rutan, that should have been an additional five to eight thousand able-bodied adults with at least rudimentary weapons, if not proper light infantry combat gear.

Unfortunately, the intelligence files had contained nothing about the colony's disdain of violence. But that was hardly surprising, considering that the information contained in the files was for an entirely different settlement. Only the data on the planet's physical characteristics – weather, gravity, and the like – happened to be correct. Someone had called it an administrative error, but most of the Marines had more colorful names for the mistake that was to cost them their lives. They were bitter indeed when they discovered that what should have been a comparatively swift human victory through sheer weight of numbers rapidly became a struggle for survival against the most tenacious and implacable enemy that humans had ever encountered.

Now, a month after the Marines had leaped from the assault boats under protective fighter cover from Jodi's Black Widows, the proud 373d Marine Assault Regiment (Guards) had been reduced to twenty-two effectives, eighty-six walking wounded, and nearly five-hundred stretcher cases, most of them crammed into St. Mary's. The rest of the original one thousand, nine hundred and thirty-seven members of the original Marine force lay scattered in the forests around the village, dead. Among the casualties were the regiment's surgeon and all thirty-one medics. The survivors now had to rely on the primitive skills of the two local physicians (Jodi preferred to think of them as witch doctors), plus whatever nursing Hernandez and his monks could provide.

The remainder of the population, on order of the Council of Elders and with Hernandez's recommendation, had holed themselves up in their homes to await the outcome of the battle. Jodi had often pondered the blind luck that had led Rutan's founders to build their village in the hollow of a great cliff that towered over the forest, much like an ancient native American civilization had done over a millennia before on Terra: it had been the key to their survival thus far. An ordinary rural settlement, situated in the open, would have forced the defenders to spread themselves impossibly thin to protect their uncooperative civilian hosts.

On the other hand, Jodi thought, depressing herself still further, the human contingent was now completely trapped. While the village's natural defenses helped to keep the enemy out, and the sturdy stone construction made its dwellings almost impervious to the small arms fire the Kreelans occasionally deigned to use, they also left no escape route open to the defenders. There was only one way in, and one way out.

She thought of how close victory could have been, had the villagers cooperated. But Colonel Moreau and her Marines had dished out punishment as well as they had taken it, inflicting at least as many casualties as they had themselves taken. Jodi was convinced that even now a completely untrained and moderately motivated militia, led by the few remaining able-bodied Marines, could take the field. They were the defenders, and in this battle of attrition the humans had at least one advantage: they knew where the Kreelans would attack, and when. The enemy did not apply the principles of Clausewitz or Sun Tzu to their tactics and strategy. In fact, it was not entirely clear at times if they really had either, or cared. This confused the bulk of their human opponents, who were conditioned to deal with "logical" objectives like capturing terrain or severing enemy lines of communication, all of which – hopefully – would help accomplish some particular strategic objective.

More often than not, however, the Kreelans simply preferred a stand-up brawl that was more typical of the knights of Medieval Europe than the technologically advanced race they otherwise were. Rarely did they seek a decisive advantage, mostly preferring to duke it out one-on-one, or even conferring a numerical or qualitative edge to the humans. They used their more advanced weapons to strip the humans of theirs, lowering the level of technology employed on the battlefield to not much more than rifles, knives, fists and claws.

The humiliating – and frightening – thing, Jodi thought, was that they usually won, even when fighting at a disadvantage.

Here, on Rutan, Jodi knew that even now the remaining Kreelans were massing for an attack on the village. The first shots would be fired at dawn, as they had for the last three weeks. She also knew that this would probably be their last fight. There simply were not enough able bodies left to cover all the holes in their flagging defenses. Once the Marine line finally broke, the civilians who cowered in their shuttered homes would be massacred.

"Father," she said, trying to drive away the oppressive desperation of their situation, "I'm going to ask you this one last time: will you please at least let people, anyone who wants to, pick up a weapon and help us. You don't have to ask for volunteers, just let them do whatever–"

"And I have told you, Lieutenant Mackenzie," he replied, gently but firmly cutting her off, "that I shall permit no such thing." Jodi, her cheeks flushed with frustration and rising anger, opened her mouth to say something, but Hernandez waved her into silence. "I grieve terribly for the deaths and suffering of these courageous people," he went on quietly, "but we long ago set aside violence as a part of our lives. Rutan has not had a violent crime committed in nearly a century, and neither I nor the council will condone our people taking up arms for any reason, even our own self-preservation. We did not ask you to intercede on our behalf; you came of your own accord, uninvited. I am truly sorry, but this is how it must be."

Jodi just stared at him for a minute, trying to calm herself down. It made her so mad to know that her demise – as well as that of the Marines around her – could have been so easily prevented. She wanted to scream at the old man, but she was too tired, too worn out. "This is probably going to be it, you know," she told him quietly so the others nearby could not hear. Most of them knew that their number was going to come up this morning, but she did not see any sense in advertising the fact. "They're going to get through us today, and then you're going to have a real bloodbath on your hands, father. All your little sheep, hiding in their comfy houses, are going to get more than fleeced. They'll be slaughtered to the last child."

"I am an old man," he told her solemnly, "but I am still young enough at heart to believe, to have faith in God. I don't believe that divine miracles disappeared with the passage of Jesus our Lord from the earth. God has already granted us one miracle in our time of need: your coming to protect us as the enemy was knocking at our gates. I believe that He has not yet abandoned us."

Jodi regarded him coldly. She liked him, respected him. Deep down, she wanted to believe him. She wanted to throw herself on her knees and beg forgiveness if only things would just be all right, if the enemy would just disappear, if someone would wake her up from this nightmare. But she knew it was an illusion. The enemy was not about to simply be sucked into some miraculous celestial vacuum cleaner. The wounded and dying around her and the bloody carnage outside the village gates was clear evidence that, if there was a God, His benign interests were obviously elsewhere, not worth expending on the inhabitants of this insignificant grain of dust in the cosmos. No, she thought grimly. The Kreelans would not just go away, whisked to some never-never-land by a momentarily preoccupied God. They had to be fought and killed to the last warrior, hacked to pieces, exterminated. Only then would Jodi feel justified in thinking about tomorrow.

"The only miracle," she told him, "would be if you and your people suddenly got some balls." Turning on her heel, Jodi stalked away toward the rear of the church to get her equipment ready for what she already thought of as Mackenzie's Last Stand.

Father Hernandez stared after her, not knowing if he should be angry or ashamed at the woman's words. His leathery face shrouded in a frown, he bent to his work, doing what he could to comfort the wounded.

God has not abandoned us, he told himself fiercely. He has not.

Amid the cries of the wounded and the dying, Father Hernandez prayed.

* * *

Jodi picked up the ancient-looking pitcher and poured some cold water into the hand-made clay basin. After soaking a worn strip of cotton cloth, she wiped her face and neck, scraping off some of the grime and dirt that had accumulated since the last time she had allowed herself such a luxury. She considered undoing her uniform and wiping down the rest of her body, but decided against it; not out of modesty, but because she did not have the time.

Here, alone in Father Hernandez's private quarters submerged beneath and far behind the altar, she could have danced nude had she wished. Hernandez had donated his tiny rectory to the female officers, insisting that they take any necessary moments of privacy there. Jodi had originally resented it as a sexually oriented distinction that she initially found offensive, but Colonel Moreau had accepted, if only to mollify the headstrong priest. But now, Jodi was glad to have this little room to herself, just to be alone for a little while. There were no other occupants. She and Jeannette Moreau had been the last two, and now Moreau was gone. That left Jodi as not just the last surviving female officer, but the last surviving officer, period.

She looked for a moment into the palm-sized oval of polished metal that Father Hernandez used for a mirror, studying the face she saw there. She was not afraid of having to lead the Marines in what was probably going to be their last battle, for she had been doing that since shortly after she had been shot down and Moreau had needed her to fill in for Marine officers she had lost. Jodi had not had the Marines' specialized training, but she was tough and quick, both mentally and physically. It had not taken her long to prove that she was more than just another pretty fighter jock, and the Marines had quickly adopted her as one of their own. The Marine NCOs had given her a crash course in how to fight that made a mockery of the self-defense training she had received as a part of her pilot training. And, fitted with a Marine camouflage uniform and armor, she was indistinguishable on the battlefield from her rival service colleagues, such was her courage and tenacity. She had put their teaching to good use and had somehow survived, keeping as many of her people alive as she could in the process.

She set the mirror down. She could handle the upcoming fight, win or lose. She was ready, except for the one thought that nipped at her heels like a small but vicious dog: she was afraid to die. Unlike many of those in her profession, she was terrified not just of how she died, but of death itself. The courage to face the end of life – or at least to ignore the possibility that death would someday come – was the one thing neither her parents nor the years she had spent fighting the Kreelans had given her. Her only religion was flying, but it was little consolation when faced with the prospect of the end of one's existence. Jodi was and always had been an atheist, despite her parents' best efforts, and it had made her life somewhat more straightforward, if not necessarily easier. It was only when one contemplated the end of the line that things became complicated. Not surprisingly, Father Hernandez had taken up the challenge with his customary gusto, but Jodi had argued him to a standstill, as she had with other would-be converters. A belief in any afterlife required a kind of faith that Jodi just did not have, and their intellectual sparring had left them consistently deadlocked, if for no other reason than Hernandez could not prove to her that there was a God or Devil, Heaven or Hell. Her beliefs, of course, did not require proof of anything except the given facts of human existence and the inevitability of death.

Therefore, she had little trouble defending her own views while easily finding logical faults in his. Faith, virtually by definition, transcended logic and empirical knowledge, which always made it vulnerable to attack. Still, Jodi respected the man's vehemence in his beliefs, and was even a little afraid on a few occasions that maybe – just maybe – he might have something. But then he would go on about his "miracles" or some other patent silliness, blowing away any thoughts Jodi might have had of more closely examining her own beliefs.

Despite his apparent latent lecherous tendencies, for which Jodi easily forgave him, she liked the old man, and knew she was going to miss talking to him about things most of her regular companions took for granted.

But the person she would miss the most was her squadron commander, with whom Jodi had fallen hopelessly in love when they met four years before. Jodi tried desperately to push from her mind any thoughts of the woman she loved for fear that she would break down and cry now, just before her last battle. But the image of the woman's face and the imagined sound of her voice were more powerful than the fear of failure, even the fear of death. Jodi knew that the lover of her dreams would never look upon her as anything more than a close friend, because she had chosen a different way of living, finding whatever solace she required with men. Outside of one very tentative advance that was gently rejected, Jodi had never done anything to change her love's beliefs, and had done everything she could to remain her closest and best friend, no matter the pain it had sometimes caused her.

Jodi knew she would never see her again.

"Come on, Mackenzie," she chided herself as she wiped a threatening tear from her eye. "Get a fucking grip."

Grimacing at the opaque water left in the basin after rinsing out the rag, Jodi forced herself back to the present and bent to the task of putting on her armor, donated by a Marine who no longer needed it.

The candle on the washbasin table suddenly flickered, a tiny wisp of black smoke trailing toward the ceiling as the flame threatened to die. Then it steadied again, continuing to throw its melancholy light into the rectory.

Jodi, concentrating on closing a bent latch on her chest plate, did not need to look up. She had not heard the door open, but had no doubt that the regiment's acting sergeant major had come to fetch her.

"I'll be there in a minute, Braddock," she said, smiling. She liked the crusty NCO, lech or not. "If you want a peek or a piece of ass, you'd better try the monks' quarters." She finished dealing with the recalcitrant latch on her breastplate, then grabbed her helmet and turned toward the door. Braddock had been almost like a big brother to her since she had fallen from the sky, and she was going to give him one last bit of hell before they plunged into the real thing. "This is off limits to enlisted scum–"

There was someone – some thing – in the rectory with her, all right, but it was not Braddock. Looming in the shadows just beyond the candle's reach, she saw that it was neither a Marine nor one of the church's robed inhabitants. In fact, it did not appear to be human at all.

Her hand instinctively went to the pistol at her waist, but she never had a chance. With lightening speed, so quick that it was only a dark blur in the dim candlelight, the thing covered the two or so meters between them. Before Jodi's hand was halfway to the gun she sought, her arms were pinned to her sides in a grip of steel as the Kreelan warrior embraced her. As she opened her mouth to shout a warning to the others, a gauntleted hand clamped down over her lips, sealing her scream in a tomb of silence and rapier-sharp claws that rested precariously against her cheek. She struggled, throwing her weight from side to side and flinging her knees upward in hopes of catching the warrior in the crotch and at least throwing her off balance, but it was to no avail. It was like she was being held by a massive slab of granite. The pressure around her ribs suddenly increased, crushing the air out of her lungs and threatening to break her upper arms. Gasping through her nose, she closed her eyes and relented, helplessly surrendering herself to the inevitable.

But Death did not come. Instead, the pressure eased to a bearable, if not exactly gentle, level. Then she felt the hand over her mouth slowly move away. She wanted to scream, but knew it was probably futile. The warrior now holding her was stronger than anything or anyone she had ever encountered, and she had no doubt that with a single determined twitch the arm still around her chest could crush the life out of her. She bit her lip, stifling a moan that threatened to bubble from her throat. Her eyes were still closed; she had seen enough Kreelans close up to know that there was nothing there that she wanted to see. It was sometimes better not to look Death in the face.

She heard a tiny metallic click in the darkness. So quiet that normally she would never have noticed it, the sound echoed in her skull like a thunderclap. It was a knife, she thought. Or worse. Involuntarily, cursing her body for its weakness in the face – literally – of the enemy, she began to tremble. She didn't want to be afraid, now that her time had really come, but she was, anyway.

Something touched her face. She tried to jerk her head away, but realized that she had nowhere to go. Her breath was coming in shallow pants, like an overweight dog forced to run at his master's side under a hot sun. The dark world behind her closed eyes was beginning to spin, and suddenly the most important thing in that tiny world seemed to be that she was on the verge of losing control of her bladder.

She felt something against her face again, but this time she did not try to draw away. She knew that it must be a knife, drawing a pencil-thin bead of blood down her cheek, painless because it was so sharp. Strange, she thought, that the Kreelans so often used knives and swords when they had such weapons built into their bodies. Of course, she absently reflected, as she imagined the skin of her face being carved away, they used their claws often enough, too.

The knife – What else could it be? she wondered – slowly traced the bones of her cheeks, then moved along her proud and intelligent brow, pausing as if to investigate the anomaly of her eyebrows, of which the Kreelans had nothing but a ridge of horn. Then she felt it spiral around her right ear, then move to her lips.

God, she thought, there won't be anything left of me. She wanted to cry at what must be happening to her once-beautiful face, but she stifled the urge. It would avail her nothing. Surprisingly, she neither felt nor smelled any blood, which should by now be pouring from her wounds and streaming in rivers down her face and neck.

Whatever it was continued to probe at her lips, gently insinuating itself into her mouth to brush against her teeth. Like some absurd dental probe, it dallied at her canines. Then the thing – a finger, she suddenly realized – extracted itself, leaving Jodi to ponder the tracks and swirls upon her skin that were now burned into her memory.

Again, she waited. She wondered how much time had passed, hoping that someone would come looking for her and burn this alien thing into carbon. But a hasty reflection revealed that only a minute or two, if that, could have passed since the thing mysteriously appeared. And how–

Her thought was suddenly interrupted by a sensation she instinctively recognized, and it jolted her with the force of electricity. She had no idea what had run its course over her face only a moment before, but what touched her now was immediately recognizable. A palm, a hand, gently brushing against her face. She could tell even without seeing it that it was rough, callused, but warm and almost timid in its touch.

Unable to control her curiosity at what was happening, and against her better judgment, she forced her eyes open.

What she saw in the dim candlelight stole her breath away: a face that was unmistakably human. The skin, while not exactly any easily catalogued shade, was obviously not the cobalt blue of the enemy. She could see eyebrows where there should be none, and hair that was somehow of the wrong texture – a bit too fine, perhaps – and undeniably not the ubiquitous black found among the Kreelan species. It was instead a dark shade of brown. Even the general shape of the face was different, slightly narrower in a jaw that did not have to accommodate large canines. He even smelled human somehow, if for no other reason than the almost-sweet musky smell of Kreelan skin was absent from the air.

But even with all the other differences immediately noticeable, the most obvious giveaway was the eyes. They were not the silver-flecked luminescent feline eyes of the Kreelans, but displayed dark, round pupils surrounded by irises that were an unusual color and brilliance of green, easily seen even in this murky light and with the pupils dilated fully open. The eyes were not exactly cold, but were nonetheless inscrutable, impenetrable, and she could see that the intelligence that lay behind those eyes was not human, not by any measure.

There was another difference, too. It was more difficult to pin down until she noticed the shape of the chest plate against which she was pinned. The creature – human or otherwise – that now held her captive was male. It was not just the chest plate's lack of the two protrusions that customarily accommodated the females' breasts that grabbed her attention. It was also her instinctive understanding of the signals that defined sexual orientation on a primal level, the way one could tell if an unseen speaker was a man or woman. And the individual now holding her was unmistakably male.

She blinked once, twice, to make sure she was not just seeing things, but the human apparition in Kreelan garb remained. It – he – stared at her, unblinking, as he gently ran his hand over her face, acting as if he had never seen another of his own kind.

It was then that she saw the wet streaks on his face. He was crying. That sight shocked her more than anything else.

"Who..." Jodi whispered, trying not to speak too loudly for fear of frightening her captor into using his powerful grip to silence her, "... who are you?"

His hand stopped its inquisitive caressing, and he cocked his head slightly, his face silently voicing the obvious fact that he did not understand her words.

Jodi slowly repeated the question, for lack of any better ideas at the moment. "Who are you?" she asked him again, slowly.

His lips pursed as if he was about to speak, but then he frowned. He did not understand.

Awkwardly, her movements hampered by his arm around her chest, she began to raise a hand toward him. His grip tightened at her movement, eliciting a grunt of air being pushed out of her lungs, and his eyes flashed an unmistakable warning. But Jodi was unperturbed, and after a moment of indecision, he allowed her to continue.

"I'm not going to hurt you," she said, hoping that she sounded convincing. She did not really know what she should – or could – do in her present situation. On the one hand, she desperately wished that one of the Marines outside would suddenly burst in and free her from this surreal rendezvous. On the other, she found herself oddly captivated by this... man. If he was what he appeared to be, a human somehow converted by the Kreelans, and not one of the Marines playing out a cruel joke at the eleventh hour, his discovery might be terribly important. Assuming, of course, that any of the humans here survived long enough to tell someone about him.

And that he would allow her to live.

Tentatively, she touched the hand that had been exploring her face, feeling a tiny jolt of excitement, almost like an electric shock, as her fingertips touched his skin.

"Please," she said, her trembling fingers exploring his opened palm, "let me go. I'm not going to hurt you. I promise." She almost laughed at the words. Here she was, pinned by a man who had extraordinary strength and whose intentions were entirely unknown, saying that she was not going to hurt him. It was ludicrous.

But, much to her surprise, it worked. Slowly, his other arm fell away from her, and she breathed in a deep sigh of relief. He was holding her hand now, gently, as if he was afraid of damaging it, and his blazing green eyes were locked on her face, waiting. It was her move.

"Thank you," she said, taking a small step backward, giving herself a little breathing room, but not moving so far as to arouse any suspicion that she might be trying to flee. Besides, with him between her and the door, and only a tiny dirty window looking to the outside behind her, there was nowhere for her to escape to.

Taking his hand, she held it to her chest, just above her breasts. "Jodi," she said, hoping to convey the idea of a name to her uninvited guest. She felt slightly foolish, because she had no idea if Kreelans even had names. No one knew the answers to even the most mundane questions about their culture. "Jodi," she repeated. Then she moved his hand to his armored chest, gingerly, shocked at how warm the ebony metal was, and asked, hoping her tone might convey her message better than the words themselves, "Do you have a name?"

He looked at her for a moment, his brow furrowed in concentration. Then his eyes cleared. In a quiet tenor that made Jodi's flesh prickle with excitement, he said, "Reza."

"Reza," Jodi repeated, smiling as she felt a shudder of nervous relief through her body. Perhaps he was not going to kill her after all. At least she had some hope, now. She might yet leave this room alive. Surely he would not bother with this little game if he had come only to kill her. But then again...

"Say my name, Reza," she said, moving his hand back to her chest. "Jodi," she said.

"Jo-dee," he managed. Even that simple utterance was nearly lost to the guttural accent that filtered his speech.

"Good," she said, elated by this tiny success. She edged slightly to one side, trying to move closer to the door without him becoming suspicious of her intentions. "Come on, now. Say it again."

He did, and she nodded, breathing a little easier. As she looked at him, forcing herself to ignore the door that was only a few feet away, but still so far out of reach, she was taken by the moist tracks that ran down his face. With her free hand, she touched them, feeling the wetness against her fingertips. "Why are you crying?" she whispered wonderingly. She did not expect an answer.

Reza worked his mouth, as if he wanted – or was at least trying – to say something more than just repeat her name, but a change flashed across his face, a look of such cunning and knowing in his expression that it frightened Jodi. His eyes narrowed suddenly, and he took hold of her and spun her around in his arms like they were on a dance floor, whirling to some insane waltz. In the blink of an eye, she found herself facing the door to the rectory, staring into Gunnery Sergeant Braddock's surprised and confused face as he opened the door.

"You, ah, all right there, ma'am?" the regiment's acting sergeant major asked quietly, a frown of concern turning down the corners of his mouth as his hand gripped his rifle a little tighter.

Jodi spun back around to where Reza was and found... nothing. She was alone in the rectory.

"There was..." she began, then shook her head. "I... I mean... oh, shit." She looked back at Braddock, her face pale, then reddening from embarrassment. She was shaking. "I think I'm flipping out, gunny," she said with a nervous smile. "I could've sworn I was just talking to a Kreelan that looked like a human, a man."

"That'd be a bit odd for you, wouldn't it?" he joked, poking fun at her sexual preference, but he got only an uneasy grimace in return. Jeez, he thought, she's really spooked. He came up to her and put a hand on her shoulder, offering her a sympathetic smile. "Look," he said quietly, "I know what you mean, lieutenant. I've had some pretty freaky spells myself lately. We're just strung out a bit thin, getting tired and a little jumpy, is all. You'll be okay." He handed her the helmet that had been sitting on the priest's tiny bed. "We've still got a job to do, ma'am. Morning's on the way, and our blue-skinned lady friends will be along any time, now, I imagine. I'll get the troops started along while you get your stuff together. Maybe we can have one last formation before the carny starts."

"Yeah, sure," she said, trying to control the trembling that was shaking her so hard that her teeth threatened to chatter as if she were freezing. "Thanks, Braddock," she told him.

Favoring her with a compassionate smile, he left her in peace. A moment later she could hear him barking orders in the main part of the church, rousing the remainder of the able-bodied Marines to yet another fight, their last. Shaking her head in wonder, Jodi rubbed her eyes, then stopped.

Her fingertips were noticeably moist. With her heart tripping in her chest, she looked at them, saw them glistening wetly in the candlelight. Cautiously, she put a finger to her lips, tasted it with the tip of her tongue. It was not water, nor was it the bitter taste of sweat. She tasted the soft saltiness of human tears.

"Jesus," she whispered to herself. "What the hell is going on?"

* * *

She met Father Hernandez as she was moving toward the front of the church and the roughly aligned ranks of her gathered command.

"I see that, yet again, you refuse to have faith, lieutenant," he said somberly, his eyes dark with concern. He had said the same thing to all of them every morning that they had gone out to fight, hoping that someone would accept his wisdom as the truth and lay down their weapons to let God do the work of feeding them to the Kreelans' claws. "If only you would believe, God would–"

"Please, father," she said, cutting him off more harshly than she meant to. But the incident, hallucination, or whatever the hell it had been back in the rectory had really rattled her, and she did not need his well-intentioned mumbo-jumbo right now. "I don't have time."

She tried to push her way past him, but he held her up, a restraining hand on her arm. "Wait," he said, studying her face closely. "You saw something, didn't you?"

There was no disguising the look of surprise on her face at his question. "What the hell are you talking about?" she blustered, trying to pull away.

"In there, in the rectory," Hernandez persisted, his eyes boring into hers with an intensity she had never seen in him before. He gripped her arm fiercely, and she suddenly did not have the strength to struggle against him.

It reminded her too much of what had happened only a few minutes ago. "I know when people have seen something that has touched them deeply, Jodi, and you have that look. Tell me what you saw."

"I didn't see anything," she lied, looking away toward the crucifix hanging above the altar. The wooden statue of Christ, forever pinned to the cross by its ankles and wrists, wept bloody tears. A shiver went down her spine as she imagined the statue's eyes opening, revealing a pair of unfathomable green eyes. "Please, father, let me go." She looked at him with pleading eyes that were on the verge of tears. "Please."

Sighing in resignation, the old priest released her arm. "You can close your eyes and ears to all that you might see and hear, you can pretend that it never happened, whatever it was, but He is persistent, Jodi," he said. "Even you cannot ignore God's Truth forever." He leaned forward and kissed her lightly on the forehead, surprising her. "Go then, child. I do not believe in what you do, but that will never stop me from praying for your safety and your soul."

Jodi managed a smile that might have been more appropriate on the face of a ten-year old girl who had yet to experience the pain and sufferings of adult life. "Thanks, father. For whatever it's worth–"

"Lieutenant!" Braddock's voice boomed through the church over a sudden hubbub that had broken out near the great wooden doors that led to the outside. "Lieutenant Mackenzie! You better take a look at this!"

"Now what..." Jodi muttered under her breath as she made her way through the rows of invalid Marines, running toward the doorway.

"What is it?" she demanded as she pulled up short next to Braddock.

Her voice was all business now, the acting sergeant major saw. She had it back together. Good, he thought. "Look," he said, pointing through the partially opened doors toward the village gates. "Just who – or what – the hell is that?"

Jodi looked toward where Braddock was pointing. The village gates were at the apex of the semicircular stone wall that formed Rutan's external periphery beyond the cliff into which the settlement was recessed. The church, located under the protective shelter of the cliff itself, was in line with the gates and elevated by nearly fifteen meters, giving anyone at the church's entrance an unobstructed view of the approaches to the village. The only approach of concern to the Marines had been the stone bridge that spanned the swift-flowing Trinity River. It was there, along the deforested stretch from the river to the village gates, that most of the battles for Rutan had been fought. The Kreelans had taken refuge in the thick forest on the far side, unable to find any suitable ground closer or to either side of the village, and it was from across the bridge that they attacked each morning. It had not been so in the first week or two, when they had engaged in fluid battles away from the village. But after the humans' heavy weapons and vehicles had finally been knocked out, the Kreelans had set aside their more powerful war machines and contented themselves with a small war of attrition, virtually forcing the humans into daily fights at close quarters, often hand-to-hand.

"I don't see..."

Then suddenly her voice died. There, facing the bridge and the Kreelans already advancing across it, was the man who had come to her in the rectory, standing like an alien-inspired Horatius.

"Reza," she whispered. She suddenly felt very, very cold.

Braddock was staring at her. "Is... is that him?" he whispered incredulously. "He was real?"

"Looks that way," Jodi replied hoarsely. She did not have enough energy for anything more. "I, ah, think we better get out there and get ready. Don't you?"

"Yeah," Braddock replied absently as he pulled out his field glasses and held them up to his eyes, focusing quickly for a better look.

But neither of them moved. Behind them, the Marines murmured among themselves, unsure and afraid at their leaders' strange behavior. A few of them were standing up on pews to see what was happening, peering out the narrow windows and reporting the action to their fellows. The church grew uncharacteristically silent, even for a holy place filled with the injured and dying.

Nearby, Father Hernandez watched the two figures peering out the door. A curious smile crept onto his face.

Fascinated into inaction by what they saw, Jodi and Braddock watched the Kreelan phalanx converge on the mysterious figure that awaited them.

* * *

La'ana-Ti'er stepped forward from the group of warriors who had come in search of combat. Kneeling, she saluted her superior. Behind her, the other warriors kneeled as one.

"Greetings, Reza of the Desh-Ka," she said humbly. "Honored are we that you are among us, and saddened are we that your song no longer sings in our veins." She bowed her head. "To cross swords with you is an honor of which I am unworthy."

Reza regarded her quietly for a moment. He was chilled by the emptiness he felt at no longer being able to hear in his heart what she and the others could, at being unable to feel the Empress's will as a palpable sensation. Although he had possessed that ability for only a brief period, its absence now was nearly unbearable. The severed braid that had been his spiritual lifeline to the Empress throbbed like a violated nerve.

"Rise, La'ana-Ti'er," he told her. They clasped arms in greeting, as if they had known each other their entire lives, had been comrades, friends, as if they were not about to join in a battle to kill one another. "It is Her will." He was left to interpret Her desires from his own memories of what once was. With his banishment to this place, wherever it was, all he had left were his memories and the single, lonely melody that sang to him in the voice of his own spirit.

La'ana-Ti'er looked upon him with respectful and sympathetic eyes. She did not pity him, for pity was beyond her emotional abilities; she mourned him. "Should you perish on the field of battle this day," she told him, "it will bring me no joy, no glory. I will fight you as I have fought all others, but I pray to Her that mine shall not be the sword to strike you down and cast you into darkness." She dropped her eyes.

"My thanks, warrior," he told her quietly, "and may thy Way be long and glorious." He drew in a breath. "Let it begin."

* * *

Jodi blinked at the sudden violence that erupted on the bridge. One moment, the Kreelans who had come to finish them off were all bowing in front of the strange man who had come to her. In the next there was nothing to see but a whirlwind of clashing swords and armor. A memory came to her from her days as a child on Terra, when a neighbor boy released a single black ant into the midst of a nest of red ones. The savagery and intensity she had seen in that tiny microcosm of violence was an echo of the bloody chaos she was witnessing now. The church reverberated with the crash of steel upon steel, the cries of blood lust and pain raising gooseflesh on her arms.

"What the hell's going on?" Braddock whispered, his eyes glued to the binoculars. "Lord of All, they're fighting each other!"

"Can you see him?" Jodi asked. Her eyesight was phenomenal, but the distance was just too great to make out any details in the raging rabble that had consumed the old stone bridge. All she could see was a swirling humanoid mass, with a body plummeting – hurled might be a better word, she thought – now and again from the bridge like a carelessly tossed stone. She had lost sight of the man after the first second or two as he waded into the Kreelans' midst, his sword cutting a swath of destruction before him.

"Yeah... No... What the hell?" Braddock wiped his eyes with his hands before looking again through the binoculars. "I see him in one place, then he just seems to pop up in another. Damn, but this is weird, lieutenant." He turned to her. "Should we go take a closer look?"

"How much ammo have we got?" she asked.

Braddock gave her a grim smile. "After we redistributed last night, three rounds per rifle and a handful of sidearm ammunition that isn't worth shit. Everybody's got their bayonets fixed for the rest of it."

Jodi sighed, still concentrating on the scene being played out on the bridge. It was no worse than she expected. "Let's do it."

Braddock turned to the Marines now clustered behind them. "ALL RIGHT!" he boomed. "MOVE OUT!"

Twenty-two Marines and one marooned naval flight officer burst from the safety of the church's stone walls and began to move in a snaking skirmish line toward where the unexpected battle still raged at fever pitch.

* * *

Reza paid no attention to his eyes and ears, for he had no real need of them at the moment. His spirit could sense his surroundings, sense his opponents far better. He was living in a state of semi-suspended time as the battle went on, his opponents appearing to move in slow motion, giving him time to analyze and attack with totally inhuman efficiency, his body and mind acting far outside the normal laws that governed physical existence. His fellow warriors knew that they would die at his hand, but none of them would ever have dreamed of turning their backs upon an opportunity to face a Desh-Ka in a battle to the death. It was unspeakably rare to engage in such a contest since the Empire had been born; the Empress had sought external enemies to fight, allowing Her children only to fight for honor among themselves in the Challenge, without intentionally killing one another except in the most extreme of circumstances. To face one so skilled, regardless of whether they lived or died, would bring much honor to the Empress and their Way.

Now their blood keened with the thrill of combat, and as they died, slain upon Reza's sword, their spirits joined the host that awaited them and welcomed them into the Afterlife. By ranks they charged the warrior priest who for the briefest of times had been a part of their people, throwing themselves into his scything blade like berserkers bent upon self-destruction. Time and again they converged upon him in a ring, swords and axes and pikes raised to attack, and time and again he destroyed them. There was no sorrow in his soul for their passing, save that they would no longer know the primal power of battle, and never again could bring glory to Her name through the defeat of an able foe.

At last, it was over. His great sword still held at the ready, Reza surveyed the now-quiet scene of carnage around him. There were no more opponents to fight, no one else to kill. The bridge was slick with the blood that still poured from the dead Kreelans' veins, blood that turned the churning white water of the river below to a ghastly crimson swirl. La'ana-Ti'er's lifeless body lay nearby, her hand pressed to the hole in her breast, just above her heart, where Reza's sword had found its mark.

Replacing his bloodied weapon in the scabbard on his back, he knelt next to her. He saw Esah-Zhurah's face on the woman sprawled beside him, and a terrible realization struck him. He knew that he would see his mate's face upon every warrior he fought, and would feel the pain of loneliness that now tore at his heart, that burned like fire in his blood, for every moment of his life. Worse, he knew that she would be enduring the same pain, and would never again sense his love, or feel his touch.

He had touched her for the last time but a short while ago, and already it seemed like an eternity.

He bowed his head and wept.

* * *

"My God," someone whispered.

Only a few minutes after Jodi, Braddock, and the others had reached the village wall, only a hundred meters or so from the church, the battle was over. The Marines who now overlooked the scene on the bridge were not new to battle and its attendant horrors, but none of them had ever witnessed anything like this. Even Braddock, a veteran of eight years of hard campaigning ashore and on the ships of the fleet, had to look away from what he saw. Fifty warriors, perhaps more, lay dead upon the gore-soaked bridge, or were now floating downstream toward the distant Providence Sea. They had ceased to be a threat to the inhabitants of Rutan, and Braddock seriously doubted that there were any more to contend with, except maybe injured warriors who would only kill themselves to prevent capture.

Braddock turned to Mackenzie. "Looks like Father Hernandez got his bloody miracle, doesn't it?"

"Yeah," she whispered, still not believing the incredible ferocity and power of the man who now knelt quietly among the dead. "I guess so." Somewhere down the line of Marines, huddled against the stone of the chest-high wall, someone vomited, and Jodi fiercely restrained the urge to do the same.

"What do we do now?" Braddock asked, clutching his pulse rifle like a security blanket.

Jodi licked her lips, but there was no moisture in her mouth, her tongue dry as a dead, sun-bleached lizard carcass.

"Oh, shit," she murmured to herself. There was only one thing they could do. She began to undo her helmet and the web gear that held her remaining weapons and ammunition. "I want you to keep everyone down, out of sight, unless I call for help," she told him.

"What are you going to do?" he asked, suddenly afraid that she really had flipped. "You're not going out there by yourself, are you?" he asked, incredulous. "After what we just saw?"

Shrugging out of her armor, glad to be free again from its clinging embrace, Jodi smiled with courage she didn't feel inside and said, "That's the point, Braddock. After what I just saw, I have no intention of giving him the idea that I'm a Bad Guy. I don't know how he's choosing his enemies, since he just waxed a wagon-load of what I suppose are – were – his own people. But walking up to him with a bunch of weapons in hand doesn't seem too bright." Finally free of all the encumbrances demanded by modern warfare, she fixed Braddock with a look of concern that failed to mask her fear. "If he polished off that crowd by himself," she said quietly, "we wouldn't stand a chance against him should he decide to turn on us. I don't know who – or what – he is, but he scares the piss out of me, and I want to do everything I can to try and get us on his good side before he starts looking for some more trouble to get into."

Standing up, she put her hands on top of the wall. She did not have the patience to walk the fifteen yards to the bolted gates. "Give me a boost, will you?"

"You're nuts, el-tee," Braddock grumbled as he made a stirrup with his hands to help lift her over the wall.

"Look at it this way," she told him as she clambered to the top. "At least he's human. Besides," she went on with faked cheerfulness as she dropped to the ground on the far side, "I know his name. Maybe he'll take me out for a beer."

Worried like an older brother whose sister has a date with a known psychopath, Braddock kept an uneasy watch through the sight of his pulse rifle. He kept the cross hairs centered on the strange warrior's head, as Jodi slowly made her way toward the bridge and the silent, alien figure that knelt there.

The closer she got to the bridge, the faster Jodi's forced upbeat attitude evaporated. She was excited, which was good in a way, but she was also terrified after what she had just witnessed. The memory of this man holding her captive only a little while ago, holding her closer than she had ever allowed a man to hold her, overshadowed all her other thoughts. It was also a sliver of hope: he had not harmed her then, and she prayed to whatever deity might listen that he would not harm her now.

As she stepped onto the old stone blocks and saw more closely the destruction that lay just a few meters away, she stopped. The thought that one individual, wielding what she had always considered to be a very primitive weapon, a sword, had shed so much blood in so brief a time, was beyond her understanding.

But looking at Reza now, she saw no trace of the monstrous killing machine that had slain her enemies only minutes before. He appeared bowed under, crushed by some incredible pressure, as if his spirit was that of an old, broken man.

Stepping gingerly around the ravaged Kreelan bodies, Jodi slowly made her way toward him.

"Reza," she said quietly from a meter or so away, trying not to startle him.

After a moment, he slowly lifted his head to look at her, and she cringed at the blood that had spattered onto his armor and his face, coating him like a layer of crimson skin. He stared at her with his unblinking green eyes, and she began to tremble at what she saw there, not out of fear, but with compassion for another human being's pain. Kneeling beside him, she took the sweat-stained bandanna from around her neck and began to gently wipe some of the dark Kreelan blood from his face. "It's okay now," she soothed. "Everything will be all right now."

Reza did not understand her words, but her feelings were as plain to him as if they had been written in stone. He had found a friend.

A Small Favor

For any book you read, and particularly for those you enjoy, please do the author and other readers a very important service and leave a review. It doesn't matter how many (or how few) reviews a book may already have, your voice is important!

Many folks don't leave reviews because they think it has to be a well-crafted synopsis and analysis of the plot. While those are great, it's not necessary at all. Just put down in as many or few words as you like, just a blurb, that you enjoyed the book and recommend it to others. Your comments *do* matter!

And thank you again so much for reading this book!

Discover Other Books By Michael R. Hicks

The *In Her Name* Series

First Contact
Legend Of The Sword
Dead Soul
Empire
Confederation
Final Battle
From Chaos Born

"Boxed Set" Collections

In Her Name (Omnibus)
In Her Name: The Last War

Thrillers

Season Of The Harvest

Visit *AuthorMichaelHicks.com* for the latest updates!

ABOUT THE AUTHOR

Born in 1963, Michael Hicks grew up in the age of the Apollo program and spent his youth glued to the television watching the original Star Trek series and other science fiction movies, which continues to be a source of entertainment and inspiration. Having spent the majority of his life as a voracious reader, he has been heavily influenced by writers ranging from Robert Heinlein to Jerry Pournelle and Larry Niven, and David Weber to S.M. Stirling. Living in Maryland with his beautiful wife, two wonderful stepsons and two mischievous Siberian cats, he's now living his dream of writing novels full-time.

CPSIA information can be obtained at www.ICGtesting.com
Printed in the USA
BVOW07s1707061114

373744BV00001B/133/P